PERCEPTION

Terri Fleming is an experienced senior advertising copywriter. She was born in Hobart, Australia, and lives in the UK. *Perception* is her first novel.

PERCEPTION

Terri Fleming

First published in Great Britain in 2017 by Orion Books,
an imprint of The Orion Publishing Group Ltd
Carmelite House, 50 Victoria Embankment,
London EC4Y 0DZ

An Hachette UK company

1 3 5 7 9 10 8 6 4 2

A CIP catalogue record for this book is
available from the British Library.

ISBN 978 1 4091 7062 4

Typeset by Born Group
Printed in Great Britain by Clays Ltd, St Ives plc

www.orionbooks.co.uk

Acknowledgements

I wrote *Perception* for the sheer joy of the story and in blissful ignorance of how indebted I would come to feel towards so many incredible people. Such a debt is a truth, universally acknowledged by any number of writers, I imagine.

Within one freezing, life-changing March week I met three people to whom thanks doesn't seem an adequate word. The wonderful Andrew Wille, talented Shelley Harris, and my amazing agent, Jo Unwin.

I am grateful to Jemima Forrester for acquiring *Perception* before she left Orion to become an agent herself. Lovely Laura Gerrard picked up the editing baton and along with a team of friendly, helpful professionals, supported this novice and her debut novel through to publication.

My diamond writing pals, Fenella Forster, Joanne Walsh and Sue Mackender have all been generous with advice and huge doses of hilarity. My friend Helen Ott bravely read the first draft.

Becoming a writer starts with an early love of reading. My mother, Janice, ensured I was never without a book. I must not forget those unsung heroes, my English teachers. For my husband, David, there cannot be enough thanks for his star support and delicious dinners.

Finally, a great debt of honour is due to the late, great Jane Austen, for writing a world many of us are reluctant to leave.

It is an opinion widely held, that a young lady lacking prospects must dream of defying expectations. Mary Bennet harboured no such dreams. Indeed, she had very little time for dreams at all.

In the words of her younger sister, Catherine, over-heard complaining bitterly to their mother as she arranged embroidery silks by the fireside, 'Mary thinks herself the most intelligent person in Meryton and allows herself every occasion to mock me.'

Such plaintive wails and a scowl quite obliterated the rosy glow of Catherine's good looks.

'Nonsense, Kitty, your *father* is the most intelligent person in Meryton and very like the entire county. That is well known amongst persons of quality.'

Kitty pouted and kicked an imaginary ball of wool with her Moroccan slipper.

'I have told you before that such fits of the sulks will turn you into an old maid. No gentleman wants a disagreeable woman for his wife.' Mrs Bennet tucked a greying curl beneath the lace of her cap with a satisfied air. 'Your own dear papa was attracted by my charm.'

Kitty regarded her mother sourly. At that moment the object of her ire stepped lightly into the room, as unobjectionable a small personage as one could ever imagine. So blank were her features and so restrained was her toilette and her gown she might have been mistaken for a servant. Kitty glared at her older sister and flounced from the room.

'Mary, a word, if you please.'

'Yes, Mama?'

'Have you been baiting your sister again?'

'Mama?'

Mrs Bennet carried on heedless. 'I do not know what to do with you two girls. You fray my poor nerves to shreds.'

'I beg your pardon, Mama.' Mary lowered her gaze and resigned herself to the words she knew well enough to repeat as a catechism.

'You would do well to take a leaf out of your sisters' book.'

'One of them, or all four books, Mama? I doubt that Kitty or Lydia ever read a book.'

Mrs Bennet threw up her hands in an attitude of exasperation.

'That is what I mean! You think yourself very clever, miss; well I do not. Men do not marry clever women. They especially do not marry clever women who look like dowds. If you have no pride then consider my feelings as a mother. Heaven help me, I have managed to marry off three with great credit. Of Kitty, I may have hopes. But do you make shift to attract a gentleman? No, you do not! I am to be shamed by you, and what will become of you I don't know.'

Mary sighed deeply. 'Must we have this conversation again, Mama? Marriage holds no allure for me. At least one of us will be happy if you accept the situation.

There are no gentleman of interest to me among our acquaintance. Indeed, most are repugnant.' She held up her hand. 'No, stay – allow me to speak. I am aware that gentlemen hold me in disinterest and I care not a whit. The majority I have met are foolish. I should not wish to be the subject of a gentleman's whims; to enslave myself in the running of his house whilst he lives as he chooses and treats me as a breeding machine.'

'Mary, you give me a disgust of you! That such words should soil the lips of a daughter of this house!'

Mary averted her gaze in a gesture she hoped gave the appearance of meekness. 'Forgive me, Mama, but you must see that I am ill-suited to the marriage market.'

'I see no such thing! I suggest you repair to your room and examine your conscience, young lady. It is too much. I must visit my sister for some calm society.'

Such an event was unlikely at the home of the redoubtable Mrs Philips, whose Meryton parlour was ever open to gossips and the more boisterous members of the gentry.

Mary did indeed repair to her room, smarting at the injustice of her lot. Gentlemen! What had they to offer her? Those who were not managed by their wives were often overbearing, lived for hunting and the decanter. The thought of her two brothers-in-law, Mr Bingley and Mr Darcy, surfaced with some guilt to her mind. Those two gentlemen possessed none of the aforementioned traits. Her sisters, Jane and Elizabeth, now married above a few years, were both exceedingly happy. Mary tossed off the thought as she flung on a shawl. Jane and Lizzy each had beauty and intelligence. Fortune had blessed them. As Mary saw it, her sisters' intelligence went to waste, subsumed by children, husbands, society and the ordering of large households. Imagine having the wonderful library at Pemberley at your disposal. One could become really immersed in that magnificent room's treasures. The old Lizzy would have revelled in such a room but the married Lizzy had so many other claims on her time and seemed not to mind at all. Mary resolved anew to ignore her mother's pressing and to abjure any discussion of marriage.

The two sisters, having the freedom of the house, each chose the solace of her room. Locked in their individual ill humours, it was with some irritation that they heard their mother's excited call from the hall before two hours had passed.

'Mary, Kitty, come quick! Why is it that I am ever unattended? Kitty, Mary, come quick, I say!'

The young ladies, well versed in their mother's ill humours, hurried down to the parlour.

'What do you think, girls?' cried Mrs Bennet. 'My sister had such news. Oh my sister begins to look quite old, I fancy. But then I was always the gay one who caught the gentlemen's attentions.' Neither sister responded. Mrs Bennet was given to such excursions in her favour and required no response. 'But I digress. Oh girls, it is so exciting. I am quite reminded of the time Mr Bingley came into our lives and chose our beautiful Jane over all the heiresses in society.'

Kitty darted forward to help her mother settle on the best chair.

'Pray, Mama, tell us the news.'

'Well, Mrs Philips had it from the lady's maid to Lady Sandalford who is the sister-in-law of Mrs Montagu, so it must be so.'

'What must be so?' demanded Kitty.

'Don't interrupt me, Kitty. It is a very unladylike habit in you, which I cannot like. You would do well to learn a little from your married sisters.'

Thus chastened, Kitty seated herself by the fire and poked the flames with unnecessary force. Mary regarded her sister with a mixture of pity and scorn. Kitty was avid for excitement now that Jane, Lizzy, and particularly Lydia, were gone. Nothing else held any consequence with her.

'What is your exact news, Mama? For it will soon be time for dinner and Papa refuses to wait, you know.'

'Yes, yes. Mr Bennet must not await his dinner, however important the news. The matter has tried my poor nerves these many years,' Mrs Bennet snapped. Then she smiled and spread her small hands as though laying out a card trick. 'Well, I will tell you. As I was saying, Mrs Philips has some intelligence of particular import to this house. Lady Sandalford says Mrs Montagu is joyous at the prospect of her only son returning to Cuthbert Park. He is expected any day. I hear the servants are working near to exhaustion to prepare.'

It must be owned that any new arrival in a quiet rural area is a welcome diversion to the tedium of one's ancient acquaintance. But further details were delayed by the dinner bell.

Mr Bennet tucked his spectacles in his jacket's breast pocket – this being specially cut for the purpose. His happiness from a day's fruitful deliberations in the library was evident in a crinkled eye and an apparent playful mood. Such moods were rarer these days, with a smaller family party at table. After several short diversions Mrs Bennet managed to communicate the news of Mr Montagu's imminent arrival.

'Well, my dear,' said Mr Bennet, 'how happy all you ladies will be for fresh blood to sink your teeth into.'

As Mrs Bennet appeared to deliberate if Mr Bennet should be admonished, Mary enquired, 'What I wish to know is why you said this news was of particular import to this house, Mama? What does it signify that a neighbour returns to his home?'

Mary's tone was mocking as she glanced around the table to lend her questions significance. Mrs Bennet answered with asperity.

'Really, Mary. For all your reading, you can be quite stupid sometimes. Are you not twenty-three? Is not Kitty nearly twenty-one? Here we have a young man returning to manage his family estate: a young man I believe to be most comfortable about the pocket. How many such marriageable young men are to be found inside twenty miles, I ask you? Mr Bennet, you will oblige us all by calling on young Mr Montagu promptly. His late father, after all, was your friend.'

'Oh, no, Mrs Bennet, you must not ask me to perform such a service again. Only think what happened when you asked me to call on Mr Bingley. Why before you could say "wedding day" the house was in uproar and two of my dear girls were borne away.'

Kitty choked on her syllabub.

'Mr Bennet! How can you be so cruel? My nerves cannot support it. We live in daily terror of your odious cousin Mr Collins, and his Charlotte, casting us from our beloved Longbourn before you are quite cold in your coffin. Am I alone in trying to secure the future of our daughters?'

6

'I think Mr Montagu is only legally allowed to marry one of them, my dear. But you may rely on my doing all that is possible to escape my coffin in the meantime.'

Kitty's shoulders could be seen shaking as she adopted the ruse of fetching her dropped handkerchief. Mary permitted herself a tight smile at her father's playful baiting.

'Mr Bennet, you cannot allow Lady Lucas to put forward Georgina ahead of our girls. She is out of the schoolroom, you know. Maria Lucas is away visiting Charlotte but she will return soon. She is not nearly so plain as her older sister, though vastly more stupid. It was bad enough that Charlotte Lucas snatched Mr Collins from our prospects. Good heavens, there are several young women who would welcome a beau like Mr Montagu.'

'Our cousin held no attraction for any of us, Mama. He's a fool.'

'Be quiet, Mary! You should have been glad to accept Mr Collins if he had offered; which he did not.' Mrs Bennet uttered the latter words with bitterness.

Kitty giggled. 'But how do you know Mr Montagu will be welcome as a beau, Mama? He might be very ugly or have bad teeth.'

Mrs Bennet resorted to her handkerchief.

'Upon my word it is too much. My efforts are not appreciated.'

'My dear, I can see that you will not be content until you have removed all of our daughters from this house. There is nothing for it but to meet the young Montagu on his return and beg him to take one of them off our hands. Which daughter would you have me petition first?'

'Oh, you are provoking me. Yet I will be content, Mr Bennet, if you will but call upon Mr Montagu without delay.'

2

Easter passed with a slew of murky weather. Very little gossip of Mr Montagu's impending arrival filtered through Meryton. Mr Bennet casually observed that fireside comfort had a remarkably dampening effect upon the news of the day.

To Mrs Bennet's certain disappointment, very little was known about Mr Montagu. He was reckoned to be nine-and-twenty. His countenance was barely known even to his own mother, so long had he been absent from the family estates. Mary noted he was reputedly devoted to scholarly pursuits. How interesting if he should also show a sensible intellect, she mused. Was it possible that someone near her own age could offer interesting conversation?

At last April shuffled forward and the countryside was bathed in sunshine. At the first opportunity Kitty made for the few small shops to be found in Meryton. Mary, who showed a most unmaidenly disinterest in clothing, flung a shawl over her blue cambric gown and selected a volume with the intention of an hour or two's uninterrupted reading at her favourite haunt. She walked purposefully down Honeycombe Lane, slowing only to avoid the last remaining patches of mud or to marvel at clouds of blossom among the hedgerows. She loved this walk for its beauty and quiet. Not another living soul crossed her path. One particular oak tree along the path was the object of her walk. Graceful ancient branches canopied a tufted knoll above a sea of bluebells. A seat perfected by nature for a lady's skirt. Mary quickened her pace and rounded the tree.

'Oh.'

'Good heavens!'

Mary leapt back in alarm and promptly stumbled and fell over a root. The young man, whom Mary had narrowly avoided falling upon, leapt to his feet and offered her his hand.

'Are you hurt?'

'No . . . no, I think not.' Mary struggled to regain her composure.

'One cannot be sure. Pray, take a seat. I shall fetch assistance.'

He was dressed in sober travelling clothes. The quality and cut together with a clean neckcloth indicated he was a gentleman. She noticed a travelling coat flung over a log. Mary felt hot colour creeping above her neck. Her retort was sharp.

'I am not hurt, I tell you. You just surprised me; that is all. I am not used to anyone being here.'

He bent to retrieve her book and smiled. 'It *is* the perfect place for reading. I was just whiling away a few paragraphs myself. Don't tell anyone, for I should be on my way home.' He indicated his fine bay horse munching away at the verges.

'How could I tell anyone, as I do not know you, sir?'

She spoke with cool calmness, but Mary felt the sting of embarrassment at her fall and irritation that her special sanctuary was occupied. She wished he would leave.

'Where are my manners? I do beg your pardon. Allow me to introduce myself, since there is no third party to effect an introduction: Sebastian Montagu.' He extended a hand as brown as a hazelnut.

'You are returned? We had not heard.'

In her surprise, Mary's impassive features were transformed into animation. So this was the noted scholar. How tall he was, perhaps as much as a foot taller than herself.

'That is because I have not quite yet returned, Miss . . .'

Flustered, Mary replied. 'Oh, now I must beg your pardon. I do not see why a lady should not introduce herself. Society's rules can be so insipid.' Mary bowed. 'Miss Mary Bennet of Longbourn.'

'Longbourn. My late father spoke of Mr Bennet and his library at Longbourn in his letters to me.'

'Indeed, sir, we are sorry for your loss. My father and yours were friends, and I think sometimes rivals in their scholarly pursuits.' A small frown creased two vertical lines in the centre of her forehead. 'Not quite returned'. What a curious statement. 'But how is it that you are, as you put it, not quite returned?'

'Well, Miss Bennet, it seems all the town knows that I'm expected at Cuthbert Park. Indeed, I am expected. But the chance to have a quiet half hour before I go to greet my dear mama and the entire household was too tempting. I fear it does me little credit, but the thought of their expectations is more than a little daunting.'

With a warmth that startled her, Mary replied,

'I do understand, sir. The town gossips will be in a flurry at your return. To be the focus of so many is highly undesirable and does not hold a candle to a good book.'

He uttered a light laugh, which made his grave face appear younger.

'Well said, Miss Bennet. I do believe that we shall be friends. May I presume upon our new acquaintance to beg your silence over my prevarication? I fear that Mama will not understand a lack of eagerness to be returned to her bosom.'

Mary felt herself approving of her new neighbour, something she rarely felt on short acquaintance.

'That assurance is easily given, sir.'

Mr Montagu swept her a deep bow before mounting his horse and departing.

The following evening Mary had the private pleasure of confounding her family. Supper's remains had been removed from the dining parlour and the family sat replete by the fire.

'What news,' crowed Mrs Bennet, 'Mr Montagu has returned to Cuthbert Park. His mama is overjoyed. That poor lady has endured much sadness since the death of Montagu senior. I hear that young Montagu behaved very nicely, though he has an unfortunate colour from abroad, I believe. Still, looks are not all where fortune pleases.'

Mary could not resist the lure.

'Mr Montagu is not ill-looking, Mama.'

'What's this? Do you say that you have met Mr Montagu, Mary? Why did you not tell it before, girl? What is he like?'

'My dear,' interpolated Mr Bennet, 'even our dear Mary cannot answer four questions at once.'

'Oh pray, do try,' said Kitty, casting aside her embroidery silks in eager anticipation.

'There is little to tell.'

Mary shifted uncomfortably in her seat as three pairs of eyes focused upon her. She was not certain that her actions of the previous day befitted a lady.

'I was walking down Honeycombe Lane and stumbled. Mr Montagu came to my aid. It is of no consequence.'

'Ha, ha. Clever, sly girl. You show some of my way of doing things.'

Mary blinked hard and could barely conceal her disgust. She spoke repressively but to no avail.

'I did not fall on purpose, Mama.'

'Of *course* you didn't, dear. But it does one no harm to fall into a gentleman's arms *accidentally*.'

Mary's lips set in a grim line and she remained silent. Kitty observed her with interest.

'I am sure it was very gentlemanly of him, Mary. Was he so very dark-skinned?'

'A little.'

'What does he look like?'

'I don't know.' This latter was untrue, for Mary had been afforded leisure to inspect Mr Montagu.

Kitty clattered her embroidery scissors onto a tray.

'That is typical of you, Mary! You spent several minutes at least with our new neighbour and you don't know what he looks like? Ridiculous.'

'Unlike you,' Mary retorted. 'If you had met him, no doubt we would all be here past bedtime hearing every detail down to his last button.'

'Girls,' Mrs Bennet groaned, 'my nerves. Have pity.'

Mary reluctantly offered up the sop of a few words. 'Oh, I suppose he was quite tall and angular. Also rather fair, I believe.'

Kitty pouted. 'He sounds rather disappointing.'

Mr Bennet called an end to the discussion.

'Disappointing or not, we shall soon see our neighbour and judge for ourselves. For his part, I hope he will judge us with kindness.'

3

Mrs Bennet daily cajoled Mr Bennet to visit Cuthbert Park. 'For, Mr Bennet, you can be sure that Sir William Lucas will have been.'

Mr Bennet momentarily lowered his newspaper.

'Sir William is everything gentlemanly, my dear.'

His wife continued speaking to the screen of newsprint blocking her view.

'You are a greater gentleman than Sir William Lucas. But the Lucas family is sensible of the need to establish Maria and Georgina. With all of those children, I shudder to think how they manage.'

Mrs Bennet executed an exaggerated shudder, but the newspaper remained unbending. At length her husband gave her his attention.

'Would you have me form a queue among the fathers of all daughters in the neighbourhood, Mrs Bennet? I imagine our number would reach halfway down the long drive of Cuthbert Park.'

Mrs Bennet was so moved as to bestir herself from her comfortable seat by the window.

'Oh, you are impossible. Why do you goad me so? Have I not been a good wife? Do I not keep an orderly house and a good table?'

'Enough, my dear. I fear you seek such flattery from me that would turn your head. I have promised to call upon Mr Montagu, but you must allow me to choose a suitable time.'

Thus it transpired that Mr Bennet eased his frame into a well-stuffed chair near the library fire at Cuthbert Park before the week ended. Encircled by books almost as familiar as his own, he made polite enquiries of the distracted young man opposite.

'My commiserations on the loss of your excellent father, Mr Montagu. He was a good friend. I shall miss our many verbal duels.'

'Thank you, Mr Bennet. Please do call me Sebastian. My esteemed father mentioned you many times in his letters to me. Long letters are a great comfort when one is abroad. He once sent me a full account of your disagreements over the influence of language on the human psyche.'

'Ha! I'll wager he dispatched my theories with disdain.'

'On the contrary, sir, he suspected that you were right and wanted my own opinion as a humble scholar living among people who speak a different language.'

'May I enquire as to your opinion, Sebastian?'

The young man stretched out his long legs and stared deeply into the flames for some time.

'I do not pretend to have investigated the matter. Nor do I pretend to speak Portuguese well. My purpose there was to oversee family interests at my father's bidding. So on such flimsy foundations do I suggest that in my experience language *is* one of the factors governing the human psyche.' Sebastian became more animated as he warmed to his theme. 'In English we have a wide vocabulary, yet certain words have quite diverse meanings. Other languages, despite having a smaller vocabulary, often pinpoint important meanings with several overarching words or phrases which appear to mean the same thing at the outset yet have specific designations.'

'How do you perceive the effect in your experience?' said Mr Bennet.

'I fear that my being educated as an Englishman did not always help my cause. I am blessed or cursed – one cannot say which – with a strong measure of the reserve for which we are all known. When I became proficient in Portuguese, that easy phraseology assisted me in making my way among the native people. But I am quite like my father in being rather solitary by nature. A little society is a pleasure but I find myself happiest in a measured existence.'

Mr Bennet polished his spectacles.

'Well, sir, I look forward to continuing a lively debate with you in your father's stead. But have I outstayed my welcome? You look quite weary, young man.'

'No, sir, you are the most welcome visitor I have had since my return. It is true that my family acquaintance has appeared in number to welcome me home. I had not realised quite how wide our circle rippled. It is just that – may I count on your discretion, Mr Bennet?'

'But of course. Can I be of some assistance?'

'I would not trouble you, sir, really I would not, but I could use some advice. What with Father's illness and the time it has taken me to arrange good management in Portugal, then travel home, I find that almost a year has passed and matters here have been left to their own devices. My desired life as a gentleman with time for scholarly pursuits seems merely a fond imagining.' He began to enumerate his tasks by counting off his fingers.

'There is much left undone in the park's maintenance. If I am to repair tenants' homes and ensure the land prospers, I shall need to be attentive. Then there is the matter of this library. My books were my solace both at school and abroad. I treasure each and every volume. Soon they will arrive back here and there is no space.'

He looked about at the groaning shelves of spines, which seemed to mock him.

Mr Bennet gazed around the room as though looking at it for the first time.

'I have no head for business and shall not presume to advise you, but the library should surely be catalogued and those books you no longer wish to keep might be dispatched for specialist sale.'

'But there's the rub. You hit the bullseye squarely with your plan, but cataloguing takes a great deal of time, which I lack.'

Both gentlemen subsided in contemplation of the flames.

'I have it!' Mr Bennet began to pace along the shelves, touching a familiar volume here and there. 'My boy, I would do it myself but I fear that my judgement would be clouded by my relationship with your dear father and my intimate knowledge of many of his books. Yet there may be a solution. My daughter Mary is an intelligent girl with a very neat hand. She is quite capable of cataloguing the contents of your library.'

'Mary is the young lady I met on Honeycombe Lane?'

'The very same.'

'But she might not like it, sir. The work would be very dull for a young lady.'

'Mary is unlike other young ladies. I say that as the father of five daughters. A good book is always preferable

17

to bonnet ribbons for Mary. I fear she enjoys solitary pursuits rather too well.' Mr Bennet sighed. He flicked through a military compendium with absent enthusiasm. 'I suppose it comes of being in the middle. The older two, who you may meet in the future, for they both reside in Derbyshire, are great friends. So it also was between the younger pair before the youngest married. Their love of frivolity is at odds with Mary's serious nature. I have no doubt she would relish the task at hand.'

'Mr Bennet, if Miss Mary Bennet would spare me some time, it would be a very great favour indeed.' His face broke into a smile, which flashed white against the deep tan of his skin. 'It is hard to imagine a young lady might be so inclined.'

'Well, that's settled then. I will ask Mary this evening. Now, sir, I must not detain you from your onerous responsibilities any longer.'

The two gentlemen arose, the elder pleased to be of service, the younger happy to have released one of his problems to another.

'Thank you, sir, for hearing out my troubles. I do not feel that it is right to lay my burdens at Mama's feet. She can think of nothing but seeing me married. Can you imagine? I have no time for such things.' His wry smile was accompanied by a firm handshake. 'Oh dear, I almost forgot. Mama asks that your family attend a welcome home party next Friday evening. Nothing too formal.'

Mr Bennet took a last, longing look around the library. 'The ladies will be glad of it, I dare say. There is little of the novel to keep them entertained in Meryton. I shall be chased into seclusion by a flurry of frills and furbelows. Until next Friday then.'

4

Meryton's haberdasher rejoiced at the news of the forthcoming party at Cuthbert Park. As that portly gentleman remarked to his wife,

'I have never known a winter so dull. It is a miracle that we are still in business.'

His good lady clucked her agreement and absently murmured soothing comments as she busied herself about the pantry. Such statements were annual visitors in her household. Dire protestations of financial ruin no longer frightened her as they had when a new bride. Mrs Blain knew only too well that even in the dead of winter, ladies would venture forth for some ribbon to trim an old bonnet or a bolt of cloth to cheer in the New Year. Their shop was often the social hub of Meryton; tinkling with excited voices here, hissing with gossip there. Mrs Blain made it her business to hear it all.

It was true that when young ladies married out of the neighbourhood their custom was much missed. Equally, their gaiety and regular visits enlivened the pace of business. The loss of the three Bennet sisters and Charlotte Lucas in a twelvemonth was cruelly felt. Mr Blain had determined to close his business and move to a larger town. It had taken a great deal of effort to dissuade him from such upheaval. While she braised a rabbit, Mrs Blain mused on the fortunes of the young women and decided life offered up surprises as regular as the mail coach. A body couldn't always rely on it but it came along often as not.

Jane and Elizabeth Bennet had captured the matrimonial prizes. There was the surprise marriage of the youngest Bennet girl, Lydia, to that officer, Mr Wickham. Mrs Blain snorted to herself. Soldier of fortune more like, that one. His credit with the shopkeepers soon ran thin. There had been much entertaining gossip when Charlotte Lucas married Mr Collins. He was expected to offer for one of his Bennet cousins.

She shifted the heavy pan off the heated plate and gave it a liberal seasoning as she contemplated what surprises the two unmarried Bennet girls might deliver. Just this afternoon Kitty and Mary Bennet had come in. Mary was a rare sight in the shop. Such an odd girl. Though any woman, young or old, with no interest in fashion plates was an oddity to Mrs Blain. She decided that Mary could be almost attractive if only she smiled and made more effort with her toilette. Yet one barely heard a word spoken. This afternoon's conversation was typical:

'Do try these red ribbons, Mary,' pleaded Kitty.

'No, the navy will be more serviceable.'

'But, Mary, we're attending a party not a wake. Look, do you think green agrees with my complexion?'

'Kitty, would it make any difference what I thought? You should spend less time thinking about your complexion and apply yourself to something worthy.'

Kitty had given her sister a withering glare, with which Mrs Blain could not find fault.

Two halves of one coin, said Mrs Blain to herself. You could scarce believe they were sisters.

5

Kitty set aside her sewing, smoothing the half-finished trail of new trimming on her old gown and taking up a spool of thread. As she pierced the eye of her needle she mused on the forthcoming party at Cuthbert Park.

Papa had been his usual enigmatic self, giving no clue other than the party was to be informal. Informal was as unhelpful a term as she could imagine. There were occasions when she felt in some sympathy with her mother.

It would not do to be conspicuous, but Mr Montagu was the only eligible gentleman to move into the neighbourhood since her three sisters had married. There was no garrison in Meryton now to provide interesting young men. What would Mr Montagu be like? Mary's description had sounded disappointing. Tall, not ill-looking, angular. Kitty had heard better descriptions of trees. For herself, she preferred an officer with a manly bearing and, ideally, a redcoat. Kitty knotted the thread and gathered up her sewing again. Why was she giving credit to a thin description from Mary? What did Mary know about or even care about eligible gentlemen?

Kitty smiled to herself. She must contrive to look as though she had made no special effort, yet aim to eclipse any rival. Special care would need to be taken with her hair. Perhaps she should make new rosettes for her slippers and wear her locket. The sewing dropped into her lap as she daydreamed. How wonderful if Mr Montagu proved to be handsome after all. To be mistress of Cuthbert Park would be a superior position indeed.

Cuthbert Park fairly effervesced. A bright moon conspired with benign weather to cheer this first occasion of spring. After the dismal Easter everyone was keen to be among company. Mrs Montagu had invited her entire acquaintance, so keen was she to show off her son and heir. The lady bustled hither and thither, greeting her guests in high good humour.

'Mr Bennet, welcome, and Mrs Bennet, how well you look.'

Mrs Bennet preened a little. 'I look forward to meeting your son, Mrs Montagu.'

'You shall meet him soon, my dear. For the moment he's surrounded. But where are my manners? The Misses Bennet, how good to see you both.' The sisters made small, formal bows. 'It has been some time since we have seen you at Cuthbert Park. I dare say your elder sisters played with my Sebastian before he was sent away to school.'

Kitty, a more confident speaker than Mary despite her deficit in years, stepped forward.

'Thank you for your kind invitation, ma'am. I shall ask Jane and Elizabeth if they recollect those days.'

Mary shrank back a little even as Kitty stepped forward. This latter action had become her habit – the better to disappear into the background. To this end, her apparel was her aid. A plain woollen gown of dark blue washed any colour from her cheeks. She wore her hair with her traditional severe centre parting, adding a royal blue ribbon to the bun at the nape of her neck. Were it not for a simple gold locket, Mary would appear unadorned. The party drifted away as Mrs Montagu hurried forward to meet new arrivals. Kitty received many compliments as the family progressed through the crowded room. Among her sisters it was generally agreed that Kitty proved the most adept with a needle. For this evening she had transformed her simple sarsenet gown with ribbon-threaded lace around the neckline and sleeves. Matching ribbon wove through the curls piled at random about her crown to great effect. Colonel Johnson was moved to remark that he hadn't seen such a vision of loveliness since her sister Jane departed for the north. Kitty received all of this attention with good humour.

From her humble position on the fringe of each group, Mary credited her younger sister with some small improvement. At least a modicum of good had come from Lydia's imprudent union. Kitty giggled and flirted and was often too easily flattered. But the hoydenish excesses had faded without Lydia's influence and she readily admitted how easily dear, foolish Lydia had been led astray by Mr Wickham. Their mother may still be beguiled by that gentleman, but the girls knew well that their father had aged greatly in the pursuit of the eloped couple. Mary strongly suspected that it had cost him dear to persuade Wickham to marry Lydia. She did not know how close the family's reputation had come to ruin, but did not doubt that such ruin had been in the air. Now Lydia and Wickham had departed to make their fortune on the faraway shores of America. While Kitty sorely missed Lydia's gaiety, the incident had made her grow up a little. Mary now wondered if Kitty and Lydia would have so much in common. She hoped her sister had resolved to never marry a man of Wickham's easy charm and loose character, without any great reliance on Kitty being so prudent. Since Kitty also had little appetite for dullness or the practice of serious economy, Mary wondered if she would find anyone to marry at all. The thought of sharing spinsterhood with her sister, locked in battle as they watched their parents ageing, filled her with silent despair. Kitty had no interest in serious matters. They had nothing beyond family in common. To be forced together by circumstance was loathsome. Yet such a fate must be preferable to the misery of a poorly made marriage.

The sisters drifted around the room attending the various excited conversations and admiring the large salon. Unaware that Kitty had walked away, Mary thought out loud.

'I remembered an imposing room but that seems a trifle fanciful in the present.'

She looked above her head. The ceiling was quite low with enormous ships beams breaking up the width. A few family portraits dotted the walls. Vases of spring blooms wept over the tables. Well-polished sconces glowed bright with fresh tapers. Combined with cheery rose-coloured drapes and comfortable chairs, the salon appeared quite cosy for such a large room. Mary's eyes strayed toward the various doors.

'Miss Bennet, I do believe that you are imagining my library.'

Startled, Mary turned to find Mr Montagu behind her. In his close-fitting evening dress he appeared even taller than she remembered. He stood out all the more for the contrast of fair hair and white cravat against skin the colour of a tanned driving glove. She blushed and was betrayed into a small smile. Mr Montagu folded his arms and surveyed her.

'I see that I am right. Are you sure that you would like to help catalogue my books? 'Tis dull work for a young lady. Believe me, I should not be offended if you say no.'

'Oh, not at all, Mr Montagu. The pleasure would be all mine, I assure you. To be surrounded by books will be quite the happiest diversion.'

Mr Montagu smiled. His eyes crinkled and his angular joints appeared to relax as he spoke.

'Nothing would give me greater pleasure than to show it to you this minute, but for my duties as host. Do you think you could come next week?'

He was answered with a smile, which seemed to light Mary's face from within.

'Sebastian, there you are. I see that you are acquainted with Miss Mary Bennet. You must come and make your bow to some late arrivals.'

Mrs Montagu laid her arm on her son's jacket and ushered him away. He glanced apologetically over his shoulder. Mary stood momentarily nonplussed before spying her family speaking to the Lucases. She crossed to the familiar group and remained on the fringes until suppertime, rarely spoken to and rarely speaking. Scarcely bothering to attend the easy chatter, Mary anticipated the pleasure of having Cuthbert Park's library all to herself. She savoured the recollection of her father bringing her the news.

*

He had called her into his own library that damp afternoon. Such a circumstance was often a cause of dismay. A reprimand given with much throat-clearing ambiguity or an unwelcome request, which would be impossible to refuse; such were interviews with papa. Mr Bennet's contribution to household matters constituted a sacrifice of time wanted for other pursuits. Mary smiled as she remembered seating herself at his desk with eyes downcast.

'Mary, raise your eyes, child.' As she had looked up, a smile played about her father's lips. 'This is an interview we might both enjoy.' As she began to frame a question, he continued. 'I have found you gainful employment. What do you say to that?'

She felt a thud somewhere in her stomach. Was he really sending her away and with such cheer?

'I . . . Employment? Father?'

Mr Bennet's benign smile continued to play about his features. He removed his spectacles and gave them a careful clean with a monogrammed handkerchief.

'Really, Mary. I may not have educated you as well as I would have liked, but a little more erudition might be expected.'

Mary fought to wrap her tongue around a reply. Her mouth was dry.

'Yes, Papa. If that is what you wish for me.'

'Ah, but the choice is yours, dear child. You can remain here at your mother's side or you can be of assistance in cataloguing the library at Cuthbert Park. Young Montagu assures me he would be very grateful indeed.'

The chair rocked as Mary pushed out of it. 'Oh, Papa.' She steadied the chair, while being seized by a rush of emotions. Papa wasn't sending her away. Instead, she was being presented with some worthy occupation for once. At last, something she would enjoy that allowed her to spend her days away from the boredom of Longbourn.

'I told him you might like to help. I hope I was not wrong to do so?'

Mary's answering smile came with the reply,

'You know very well I should like nothing more. I shall not disappoint you, Papa. Now, please tell me everything.'

Kitty recalled her to the present by catching her sleeve. She took her aside.

'Mary, you seem so awkward on these occasions. You do not speak up, yet when your hands are at the pianoforte, you know just what to do. We must hope that someone asks you to play, though it would not do for you to sing, as people are apt to shuffle and cough.'

'How you flatter me,' Mary mocked. 'If opinion matters so much to you, perhaps you should behave with more propriety. For myself, I set no great store by courting society.'

They were interrupted by the supper bell.

Mrs Montagu's excellent supper delighted the entire company. There were exceptional game pies along with a large cold collation. Exotic early asparagus from the park's greenhouses, rhubarb syllabub, and Charlotte tortes drew impressed comments from the assembled company.

Sandwiched between Kitty and Georgina Lucas, Mary could be overheard by the attentive listener, admonishing the pair to hush. For a young lady fresh from the schoolroom, Georgina was rather forward. She and Kitty were competing to speak in caricatures of old friends.

Each proved an excellent mimic. Having exhausted the most entertaining characters, Georgina turned to gossip.

'Who is that lady across the room speaking to Mr Montagu? Her gown is beautiful.'

Kitty followed the direction of Georgina's painted fan. A tall, handsome lady was nodding her head in response to something Mr Montagu had said. She was dressed in the height of fashion in a moire silk with a large amethyst necklace, which she carried off with aplomb.

'I overheard Colonel Johnson say that she is Mr Montagu's aunt, Lady Sandalford,' said Kitty.

Curiosity sated, Georgina's notice shifted to their host.

'Do you think Mr Montagu handsome, Mary?'

'He is neither handsome nor ugly. His character is more important, I think, and we do not know him well enough to judge. You, miss, have no business judging your elders.'

Kitty disagreed. 'Pish! You can tell well enough that he is friendly, but I do not accord him to be handsome.'

'He is quite tall,' ventured Georgina.

'I am not sure that tall is a qualification for a beau,' replied Kitty.

Guests began to drift away from the tables. The girls were preparing to depart when Mrs Bennet flopped down beside them, flapping her handkerchief.

'Such a crush of people! I expect that you are discussing our host,' she added in arch tones. 'Such a handsome young man with such a wonderful home. I don't doubt your hearts are all aflutter.'

Mary scowled. 'Really, Mama, can you talk of nothing else but gentlemen? Some ladies turn their minds to more serious matters.'

The imposing lady reckoned to be Mr Montagu's aunt, appeared at Mrs Bennet's side.

'These young ladies should not trouble their hearts too seriously, Mrs Bennet. I fear that my sister-in-law has her sights set on an heiress or a title for my nephew.'

'Lady Sandalford, you must know that I meant only to tease the girls.'

'I'm sure you did, my dear Mrs Bennet. But it would not do for my sister-in-law to hear you. After all, your accomplishment in marrying three daughters in one year cannot be overlooked. I dare say the mothers of sons tremble when you approach.'

'My dear Lady Sandalford, I am shocked.'

'Do not be, Mrs Bennet, for I am funning you – but hark, there is a grain of truth in what I say.'

Lady Sandalford resembled her late brother for height and slenderness. Where she might have looked severe, her demeanour was softened by a bright eye and a ready wit. Mrs Bennet regarded her with a degree of awe, such was the lady's wealth and bearing.

'Well, I wish Mrs Montagu well with her plans, I really do. But might not your nephew have his own ideas about matrimony?'

'I sincerely hope he does, Mrs Bennet. A man should know his own mind. It is many years since I have spent any appreciable time with Sebastian, but the little I have seen these past weeks fosters encouragement. It may sadden all the young ladies to learn that he shows no inclination to marry at all.'

6

Immediately after lunch on Monday, Mary set out for Cuthbert Park. Bluebells peeped beneath low branches, tipped with tender pale green leaves. Lambs frolicked in their creamy coats against a backdrop of grass, seeming to have grown overnight into fat, lush tufts. The sound of axe and saw rhythmically sighed as every spare man attended to the land. Cuthbert Park nestled low into the surrounding parkland like a wide smile. Honest hewn stone, owing nothing to artifice, bounced hundreds of playful shadows onto shrubs under the windows. The simple beauty of the house from the lime walk so diverted Mary that she failed to hear a horse approaching until the steady snort of its nostrils were within earshot.

'Ha, you are come. I feared you had changed your mind.' Mr Montagu leapt from his bay, his long legs seeming to make it but a step. He looked suddenly stricken. 'You haven't, I hope, changed your mind?'

Mary bowed her head demurely.

'No, sir. I am not in the habit of changing my mind.'

'Of course, your father said that you were unlike other females. Excellent.'

They continued to the house in silence. Mr Montagu's

bay was handed to a groom and he extended his own brown hand to Mary's elbow as they mounted the sandstone stairs to the portico, causing Mary to blush. She searched for something to say.

'Cuthbert Park is very beautiful, sir. You must be delighted to be at home.'

He paused, his hand still on her arm. 'Somewhat, Miss Bennet. There is so much to do that I find little time to take in the pleasures.'

Mary found her eyes to be transfixed on the fingers resting on her arm. She gently detached herself.

'That is a great pity, for all about us today is alive with beauty. But you have the future in which to savour such delights.'

'Your thoughts will serve as a reminder to me. It takes but a moment to observe one's surroundings. Such a moment can be of no detriment to urgent purpose.'

By now they had progressed to the salon, calm after the party and to Mary's eye, more beautiful. Mr Montagu rang the bell. A maid appeared in an instant.

'Please tell Mama that Miss Mary Bennet is with us. We shall take tea with her later. Then ask Peters to join us.'

The large, heavily glazed room where supper had been served lay at the far end of the salon. Mr Montagu headed to the rear corner of the salon, opening a door into a small octagonal anteroom containing a chaise and a screen. From there a further door led into the library. Tall windows cast light onto the Indian rug. The afternoon sun slanted towards two easy chairs by the fire. A gallery ran from the windows around the remaining walls of the room to a spiral staircase. Books in glazed cabinets crammed every available space. Even the desk between the door and the armchairs provided a surface on which to stack tomes. Mary paused on the threshold. She had seen rooms in great houses with more grandeur, but to her mind, this room was the loveliest she had seen. She stepped into the room allowing her eyes to rove.

'This is my favourite room in the house. As a young boy my visits here were strictly supervised. I cannot quite believe that it is now all mine.'

They stood as though in silent homage. He gave a deprecating shrug.

'It's actually quite a small room, although the gallery certainly helps.'

'I think that it could not be bettered.'

Mary spoke with determination as she looked up at his pleased countenance. He smiled down at her.

'My father thought so too. He loved this room. It is a shame to have to remove some of his books to make way for my own.'

'I imagine so. Yet perhaps some of the subjects, though not of interest to you, will be prized by others. So it is less a loss than a service.'

He ushered her to a fireside chair, which rather dwarfed someone of her small stature. 'Miss Bennet, you talk much good sense. Remind me to ask for your advice in future.'

Mary blushed. She wondered if she might be contracting a fever for she rarely blushed. Twice in several minutes must be cause for mild concern. On reflection, she decided she was unused to such approbation.

'You rang, sir?'

'Peters, I expect you know Miss Mary Bennet.' The butler bowed. 'Good. Miss Bennet is doing me the honour of cataloguing all of Father's books. She will be here often. Please see that she has everything she requires. Have you any special requests, Miss Bennet?'

'Nothing particular. But I may need a stool to reach some shelves, and a ledger, of course.'

'It shall be done. We must not forget to bring her sustenance as well, Peters.'

'Very good, sir.'

'You must not carry heavy books.' Mr Montagu gave her one of his direct looks. 'Peters will arrange for someone to do any heavy lifting. Now, down to business. Let me give you an idea of those subjects I particularly like or dislike so that you can mark them accordingly in the ledger.'

Mary rose and directed a meaningful glance towards Peters.

'Perhaps it would be as well for Peters to hear the details as well. For myself I see no need, but Mama will insist of preserving the proprieties.'

'Oh, I see, we should be chaperoned. My pardon, Miss Bennet. I have lived abroad too long. No matter, if Peters doesn't mind us detaining him, let us begin.'

In no time at all it seemed the bell for tea pealed. In fact, they had been engrossed in discussion for fully an hour. Peters led the way back to Mrs Montagu in the salon where tea was laid out on a Sèvres service. Mary wondered if important company was expected. Her mother's friend was attired in a formal grey silk, tight to the frilled neck and cuffs. She wore pearls and a large brooch. Mrs Montagu rose stiffly and indicated that Mary should sit opposite. Her tone was as crisp as her silk ruffles.

'Miss Bennet, my son tells me that you are kindly cataloguing my late husband's library. We are most grateful. Sebastian has much on his mind at present.'

'It is a pleasure to assist, ma'am. Your library is a jewel.'

The lady touched her hand to her frilled cap as though wearing a jewelled headdress. 'As to that, I can only say that my favoured jewels lie under lock and key upstairs. I do not quite understand what you all see in these books.'

Mr Montagu bent to touch his mother's shoulder, his voice gently teasing.

'Would you have us all be the same, Mama? Without books we would not have a civilised society.'

'That's as may be, Sebastian. But I don't thank you for it. Your father spent half his life cooped up in the library and I do not see that his health fared any better for it.'

Mr Montagu's response was quiet.

'But he was happy.'

'It will not do for you to follow him.'

'You must allow me to make my own choices, Mama. Now, we are neglecting Miss Bennet.' As his mama hastened to pour the tea, Mr Montagu proffered a plate of the most tempting cake. 'Can I persuade you to try some of this excellent cake? Cook has taken it upon herself to fatten me up.'

Mrs Montagu scrutinised her guest with severity.

'Yes, do help yourself, Miss Bennet; you are too pale and thin. We must attempt to feed you up.'

'I fear you will fail, Mrs Montagu. My own mama despairs of me.'

Mary bit her lip in discomfort. Until teatime the afternoon had passed happily.

'I daresay you care more for your dusty books.' Mrs Montagu passed Mary her tea. 'One oddity among five daughters must be acceptable odds, I suppose.'

7

Mrs Bennet could scarce contain her enthusiasm for Mary's new enterprise. When Mr Bennet removed himself from the parlour after dinner, she motioned Mary and Kitty to sit beside her and began to question Mary with eagerness.

'Tell us all about your afternoon, dear, and please, spare no detail.'

Mary sighed. She ought to have realised that she would be subject to interrogation upon her return.

'It was most interesting. Mr Montagu's library is the most pleasant room I can imagine. There's a gallery and so much light from the tall windows . . .'

'Yes, yes, I'm sure. But what of the rest of the house?'

'I saw only the salon we visited last week and a small anteroom.'

'Did you take tea?' Mrs Bennet's hand delicately fingered the stem of her glass. 'I must admit to approval of Prunella Montagu's accommodations.'

'Yes, Mama. I believe you would have admired the Sèvres service. Mrs Montagu was most generous in her insistence that I eat more cake.'

'What was Mrs Montagu wearing?' Kitty asked.

Her mother threw her an approving glance.

'Something grey, I think.'

Mrs Bennet banged down her glass with impatience. 'Well, of course she wore grey or black; she is not a year past mourning. Really, Mary, is that all the detail you can manage?'

'I believe she had a ruffled collar and cuffs,' Mary muttered.

Mrs Bennet tutted. 'You must be more attentive, Mary. The Montagus will think you a provincial.'

'But I *am* a provincial, Mama. I do not believe that I have been above thirty miles from Meryton in my whole life, excepting a single visit to Derbyshire.'

Kitty fell into a fit of the whoops. 'She's right, Mama,' she gasped through her laughter, 'we *are* provincial.'

'Well, there's no need to act like it,' snapped Mrs Bennet. She stood and turned to face them in some agitation. 'You have the accomplishments of young ladies of fashion equal to anywhere in England and your father is a gentleman. That is all that is required to meet a suitable gentleman to marry.'

'Lest we forget our enormous dowries,' snorted Kitty. She sighed. 'Without a fortune or title or superior claims we cannot pretend to offer any great inducement to marriage.'

'Really, Kitty, do you not see my own fine example? I wed your father without superior birth or fortune.' Mrs Bennet turned to adjust her necklace before the overmantel mirror and appeared momentarily lost in contemplation of a more youthful likeness. The sight of Mary moving behind, brought her back to the present. 'Of course, I was acknowledged to be exceptionally fair of face. But notwithstanding, look at the example of your older sisters. Have they not both made excellent matches?'

'Jane and Lizzy were most fortunate, Mama. Perhaps we have used up our family luck,' ventured Mary.

'I will not hear of it! Mary, if you show yourself friendly to the Montagus, who knows what may come of it? While you're about it, pay some attention to your looks. Those plaits are too severe and you might pinch your cheeks to show a little colour.' Two red spots of colour dotted Mrs Bennet's cheeks. 'And you, Kitty. More effort could secure you a fine match.'

Mrs Bennet plopped back in her chair as though spent with the effort required to guide two such daughters. The sisters exchanged significant glances. With each passing birthday such maternal lectures increased in frequency. Mr Bennet's arrival back in the room was a great relief to both young ladies. Silence reigned for a few minutes before Mrs Bennet began to wave her lace handkerchief. Her expression alight, she said,

'Why did I not think of it before? Nothing could be better. We must find a reason for Kitty to accompany you to Cuthbert Park, Mary. That is how we may put her in the way of meeting Mr Montagu more often.'

Mary turned away, aghast at the prospect of having her solitude invaded by Kitty. She did not see Kitty's equally dismayed expression. Kitty recovered first.

'I do not think Mr Montagu and I would suit, Mama. Besides, I could not bear to spend hours among all those books,'

'Not suit? You have met him once. What is that? One cannot expect to know someone in a single meeting. He would do very well for you. Such wealth.'

'Mr Montagu is almost never there, Mama. He has a great deal to do improving the estate.'

Mary seized her opportunity to quash the notion.

8

Mrs Bennet returned from her morning calls in good humour. She had news. Among the family there was only Mr Bennet to be found in the house. A maid pointed her in the direction of the walled garden, where Mary sat with her feet drawn up on a bench and a book perched against her knees. Kitty stood several yards away amongst the herbs, tying off bunches of rosemary for drying.

'Girls, such a diverting morning. You will want to hear all about it.'

Kitty put down her twine, while Mary lolled her head in her mother's direction.

'Maria Lucas has returned home. I have just been there. Mr Collins brought her back. Charlotte did not make the journey.'

'Good for Charlotte,' Kitty smirked.

Mrs Bennet carried on. 'I must say Maria's visit to Kent hasn't served her well. I fancy her bloom is fading. Poor Lady Lucas. Maria was the fairest of her girls. She will have no chance with Mr Montagu now.'

'Maria will be in spirits the moment Mr Collins' carriage turns out of the drive.' Mary turned back to her book.

'I should like to visit Maria, Mama, but not if our cousin is there.'

Kitty gathered up her things and gave the rosemary an appreciative sniff.

'Mr Collins leaves tomorrow and good riddance to him, I say,' Mrs Bennet announced. 'No doubt he will call on us this afternoon to check that his inheritance still stands. It is more than I can bear.'

Mary snapped her book shut. 'I think I am required at Cuthbert Park.'

'And I shall walk with you part of the way,' said Kitty. 'It would be uncivil if one of us did not welcome poor Maria back home.'

Kitty found Maria in high spirits, chattering with two of her brothers and Georgina. Maria's best feature was a cloud of dark hair. She had the misfortune to possess a smattering of freckles across her nose, which no amount of strawberry water managed to cure. A placid nature and an empty head meant that she lacked the animation of her younger sister. Kitty preferred their easy company to her own sister's waspish asides. Maria and Georgina could be relied upon for a discussion of fashions and a little gossip. The brothers tired of such talk and went off to the gunroom.

'Tell me about Mr Montagu,' said Maria, 'Georgina will only say that he is very tall and too old for her interest. Will I be charmed by him?'

Kitty pretended to give the matter some thought. In truth, this was unnecessary, as she could not see Maria and Mr Montagu as a match.

'He is quite a pleasant gentleman, though somewhat reserved for my taste. Papa says he is quite the scholar.'

'Stop!' Maria gurgled with laughter. 'You have quite put me off. I could not abide a scholar, however wealthy. What would we talk about?'

'You will break Mama's heart.' Georgina teased.

'But please my mama,' said Kitty. 'Mary is cataloguing books at Cuthbert Park and Mama is seeking excuses for me to go with her.'

Georgina gave out a little squeak. 'Is Mary interested in Mr Montagu?'

'Mary? Can you imagine Mary flirting with *any* gentleman?' They all giggled. 'Mind you, if she were ever to marry anyone, he would have to like books and music.'

9

When next she exited the lime walk approaching Cuthbert Park, Mary pinched her cheeks, then grimaced at her own absurdity. She wondered what she hoped to achieve by such a measure. Was she not marked among her sisters as quiet, intelligent, plain and uncomfortable among strangers? Living in a small society such as Meryton, one saw expectations and hopes with clarity. Therefore, Mary expected to remain a spinster and hoped for life to afford her some measure of comfort and leisure to pursue her quiet interests.

She had long deduced that Kitty, while expecting to join her in caring for their ageing parents, hoped instead to form a happy married alliance. It is a great pity we are not close in our pastimes, thought Mary, for we may be yoked together in our futures.

This gloomy turn of thought was soon cast aside as Mary set about her ledger, working her way along the library's upper gallery. The task was proving as absorbing as she had hoped when her father had first mentioned the notion. It was her habit to give any new idea full consideration, but she had leapt at this opportunity. How fortunate I am, she thought as she leafed through a thick volume on the ancient Greeks. The illustrations of classical architecture were exquisitely drawn. She noted the details and moved on to the next volume. A movement below caught her eye.

Mr Montagu stood below at the desk, his fair head bent over an illustrated botanic. One large brown hand turned the pages. Mary held her breath. She was unsure if she should announce her presence or wait to see if he departed. The longer she stood there, the more foolish it seemed to speak up. Once again she felt the telltale flush rise up from her collar. In panic, she spoke.

'Good afternoon, Mr Montagu.'

He looked up to the gallery and, on finding her petite frame, his eyes led his features into a smile.

'Miss Bennet, you are perfectly concealed up there.'

'I hope I did not startle you, sir?'

'A little perhaps, but I am glad to see you. How are you finding your task; odious or enervating?'

Mary moved over to the painted iron railing and spread her fingers on the smooth gallery banister, as though addressing a crowd.

'Illuminating for the major part. Your late father had wide-ranging interests.'

'He most certainly had. Even more than I had credited until I read some of your most excellent and detailed ledger.'

'The variety makes the work absorbing. I confess that I am learning a good deal as I go along, which no doubt impedes the pace of my progress.'

''Tis small reward for the service you provide, Miss Bennet. I urge you to linger at will.' He shrugged his shoulders and pointed down to his well-worn hessian boots. 'Would that I could spare more time to do so myself.'

Mary picked her way down the spiral staircase with care. Her lilac skirts fanned through the railings.

'Yet I see that you are reading.'

'Researching rather. My memory of English plant life diminished the more I sought to study local Portuguese flora and fauna.'

She halted on the second last stair and smiled to herself as she realised they were matched for height at this moment.

'Were you there a long time, sir?'

'Above six years. Before that I was at Oxford and before that, boarding school in the north. So you see I have passed but little time at my own home. I envy you the pleasure of studying at home.'

Mary regarded him with incredulity.

'Yet I envy you the excitement of Oxford. To be surrounded by theatre, music and so many brilliant minds. All women seem to care about is finding husbands.'

She did not trouble to keep the scorn from her final words.

He walked across to her; his frank, open eyes never leaving her own.

'As always, you are right. Though,' he laughed, 'many minds were far from brilliant and society could be quite shockingly dissolute. But I confess I would rather have stayed on at Oxford than go to Portugal. The choice was not my own.'

'But surely it was an exciting adventure?' Mary's eyes were alight with the promise of the unknown.

He returned to his large desk and perched on the edge, crossing his long legs at the ankles.

'Less than you might imagine. For a young man of two-and-twenty there was much to fear. Unknown people and a foreign language were just the beginning of the obstacles to face.'

'Were there wild animals?' Mary was unsure if she were fearful or hopeful.

A wide smile lit his features.

'Yes, though not too ferocious. One travels up the Douro river from Oporto for many miles. The land on either side seems to bank up to the sky. Vines climb the slope first this way, then that and in the gaps there are pine forests full of wild native boar.' He sighted an imaginary rifle. 'The Portuguese are very fond of eating boar. You cannot imagine the many ways our cook found to fashion it. Every kind of sausage, stew and roast, each as well liked as the last.'

'It all sounds so exciting and so different to Meryton.'

'I shall take that as permission to tell you more over tea. Mama also likes to hear my tales, though I often manage to confuse her.'

Thus a new ritual ensued. On alternate weekdays Mary's ledger grew as she inched her way shelf by shelf through the library. Over tea Mr Montagu would tell his mama and Mary stories about his life in Portugal. Mary asked most of the questions, which relieved the older lady of troubling to think. In all, the arrangement worked perfectly. Mary was spared awkward conversations with her hostess and absorbed the armchair travel with near breathless curiosity. Mr Montagu proved a fine raconteur, always taking care to carry his small audience with him on the journey. Mary found herself admiring him more each day.

10

Mrs Montagu arrayed herself with a grand manner in a central position on the sofa, forcing the ladies who were her morning guests to sit in pairs around their hostess.

'I have in mind a picnic,' she announced to general approbation.

'It is wonderful to see Cuthbert Park come alive again,' said Major Luckington's wife. Although unexceptionable in face, figure and fortune, the matronly Mrs Luckington was sure of an invitation to every gathering by virtue of her knack for saying just the right thing at all times.

'Now that Sebastian has taken his rightful place, it is time he thought about the future.' Mrs Montagu paused and swept a glance around her eager guests. 'Of course, he is very busy organising the park, so it falls to me to bring suitable young ladies to his attention.'

'Well, I think Meryton can provide several young ladies of good breeding,' offered Mrs Bennet.

Several other mothers with marriageable daughters nodded agreement.

'That may be so,' rejoined her hostess, 'but my son can afford to be selective. Our local acquaintance is most welcome, but I shall also invite Lord Drummond with his Honourable daughters, Sylvia and Imogen. Countess Glendinning and her daughter, Lady Sarah, also live near enough to attend.'

The guests exchanged nervous glances. It was clear that Mrs Montagu desired a very superior young lady indeed for her son. As Mr Montagu possessed no title, such a plan was ambitious. Mrs Bennet and Lady Lucas in particular struggled to hide their disappointment. The Lucas title was not hereditary to the great regret of Lady Lucas. Feigning not to notice the dampening effect her statements had made upon her friends, Mrs Montagu continued:

'Of course I have enjoyed only a small acquaintance with Lord Drummond and the countess. But that shall change now I have Sebastian to entertain the young ladies. I have invited them all to dine this Saturday so that the young people can get to know one another before the picnic. It is high time we Montagus began to take our rightful place in distinguished circles.'

The remainder of the morning call was an unusually subdued affair. Once outdoors though, the ladies made their way home in chattering pairs. Mrs Bennet seated beside Lady Lucas in her gig, burst forth as soon as they had departed the park gates.

'Well, what think you of this morning's news?'

Lady Lucas, though appearing much agitated herself, teased her friend. 'A picnic is just the thing. I do hope that the weather holds.'

Mrs Bennet tugged at her gloves. 'Fie on the weather! You know perfectly well that I'm referring to Mrs Montagu title hunting. I could not believe Lady Sandalford when she spoke of it at the party, but she spoke with sincerity.'

Her friend turned to her in consternation.

'In truth, I am sorely exercised. It's a pity for my two girls and your Kitty. Three prettier girls you will not find in the county. Georgina promises fair to follow Maria in looks, if I do speak with excess pride.'

Mrs Bennet's aggrieved tones rang through the mighty oaks lining the roadside. 'I agree with you, my dear. With Jane and Lizzy married, Kitty is the prettiest girl in the district. Indeed, your own girls look well too and what is to become of them all, when the first new young man in our midst is flung at the head of every insipid spinster with a title?'

They journeyed in a rare, tense quiet for some minutes. At length Lady Lucas' old high-crowned bonnet turned toward Mrs Bennet's fetching straw concoction.

'Mrs Montagu is perhaps mistaken in her plan. It is my belief that the families of these young ladies will wish to improve their aristocratic connection. However well-breeched the Montagus, there is no title and some connection to trade, you know.'

Mrs Bennet raised her hands to the sky. 'But of course! Now I see it clear. Mrs Montagu wishes to banish her connection to trade. 'Tis my opinion that she is jealous of her sister-in-law's title.'

Lady Lucas considered. 'There may well be something in that. Lady Sandalford is a naturally superior female and I suspect Mrs Montagu frequently finds herself overcome by both consequence and wit. It would be unwise of us to speak of it, my dear friend, but we can cherish the happy thought that her plan is likely to come to naught.'

*

Mr Bennet peered over his pince-nez as Mary delivered the post to his desk.

'My dear Mary, I am not in general an observant or doting papa, I will admit, yet I see that you appear very happy these days.'

'Indeed, Papa, I have you to thank.' Mary stood before him, hands folded.

Mr Bennet's eyes twinkled. 'Me? Can it be that I have done something right for a change?'

'You know it is true. It was you who suggested that I catalogue the library at Cuthbert Park.'

Mary began to tidy his desk. How *does* he keep track of his correspondence and papers, she thought.

'I'm glad that you are enjoying yourself, my dear. It is a splendid library, is it not?'

'Quite, quite wonderful, Papa. The books, the aspect – really, everything.'

'I see that you have found your true passion, Mary. Would that I could find endless libraries to occupy you.'

He clasped her small hand and stilled her efforts.

'This one is sufficient, Father.'

'Ah, that is my Mary. Always so contained and sure. But mind you, your work must come to an end sometime.'

In that single sentence Mary's happy face, like a rare flower unfolding, closed tight as a bud. Pulling her hand away, she turned to the window just as a cloud shadowed the sun. Dear God, she prayed, do not take away my happiness. Her father's voice interrupted her thoughts, kind and rallying in equal measure.

'Come, that is some way off, I suspect, and I'm sure Mr Montagu will be happy to give you access in the future. Now, be off with you.'

'Yes, Papa. One more thing. Mrs Montagu invites us to a picnic in the park. Should it rain we will be reaccommodated.'

He winked. 'I daresay the weather would not dare incommode Mrs Montagu. I have no doubt that your mother will insist we attend.'

11

A frown played upon Mrs Blain's broad brow. Her husband, by habit a worrier, sought the nature of the problem and the likelihood of his playing a guilty role.

'Was the butcher's delivery not up to scratch again, my dear? They never upset the gentry, but it is us what pays regular.'

He unhooked a tape measure hanging around his bulging raised collar and automatically passed it to his wife.

'Do not trouble yourself, Blain. The butcher would not dare cross me again.'

'Then what troubles you, my love?'

Mrs Blain began to wind the tape with practised precision around her chubby fingers. 'I am not troubled. But something curious did happen in the shop today.'

The haberdasher fixed his attentions upon his good lady. They occupied the same space all day long, yet Mrs Blain always learned so much more from the customers.

'The Bennet sisters were seeking to make new summer dresses; for Mrs Montagu's picnic, I shouldn't wonder.'

'Thank the good Lord for Kitty Bennet.'

Mrs Blain snapped the tape into its case and turned with a speed that belied her bulk.

'But that's just it, Blain! It was Mary Bennet who called the tune.'

'Eh?' Mr Blain turned to his wife with raised eyebrows.

'Mary Bennet, I tell you, or my eyes deceived me. I can scarce believe it now. She had me pull down every sprig muslin from the shelves.'

'"Which do you think, Kitty?" she says. She, who a few weeks ago wouldn't pass word on a ribbon. I can tell you now, Blain, I was fair put to the sweats. Well Kitty Bennet, of course, was in her element. "Take the yellow buds," says she, "they will suit you well." So Mary did. But then, you could have knocked me down with a feather. She asks us both if she should buy yellow ribbon as well. I can tell you, I had that reel of ribbon out on the counter quick as you can say tankard of ale.' Mr Blain chuckled as his wife's story gained momentum. 'What do you think, but she asks her sister again about the trimmin' and if it's too much to put in her hair. That floored me, it did. But Miss Kitty saw her right enough. She persuaded her to take a straw band and a rosette for her bonnet.'

'Well, my dear, perhaps we have made a proper customer of Miss Mary Bennet at last.'

Blain carefully closed the large bolts at the top and bottom of his shop door. The lady harrumphed as she removed her cap to replace it with a more serviceable mob cap.

'As to that, I cannot say. But what I can say is this: there's a gentleman behind these events as sure as eggs is eggs!'

12

With the picnic but a short time away, every spare moment was devoted to the stitching of new summer gowns or the trimming of bonnets. Upon learning that Mary and Kitty were to have new clothes, Lady Lucas had lost no time in leading Maria and Georgina to the Blain's emporium for new muslins of their own. Four young ladies shared the morning room at Longbourn or the sitting room at Lucas Lodge as they stitched in anything but companionable silence. As a regular visitor to Cuthbert Park, Mary found herself plied with questions instead of maintaining her usual quiet disposition. Maria was quite pointed.

'Has Mr Montagu invited any of his gentlemen friends to the picnic, Mary?'

'I am not aware of any. I believe he went to Portugal soon after Oxford, so he may have lost touch with his English friends.'

Georgina puffed out her cheeks.

'I wonder why we are all bothering to make new gowns if the same old neighbours are going to see them.'

Kitty soothed, 'There are bound to be some strangers, aren't there, Mary?'

'I am sure of it. Mrs Montagu keeps mentioning names over teatime and it is very hard for me to behave as though I am impressed.'

The other three chuckled.

'Mrs Montagu has chosen the wrong person if she wants to impress,' said Kitty.

Mary dropped her stitching onto her knees.

'Oh, it is the worst thing. I try, honestly, but how many expressions of interest can one have?'

At this her companions collapsed with laughter.

'Oh, Mary,' Maria fanned herself with her unmade sleeve, 'I wish I could have been there.'

Mary snapped, 'It isn't funny. One has no idea what to say to her and then Mama and all of you will keep asking who is coming, as if it matters at all.'

Her annoyance was met with another bout of laughter. Kitty wondered quite how Mary had managed to grow up in a house full of women and have no interest in the small joys all ladies found in their lives. She watched as Mary bent her head back to her yellow sprigged muslin. At least her sister had shown interest in the choice of fabric and style of this gown. Perhaps she might be improving on that score. Kitty sighed. How welcome it would be if Mary could become more like a normal sister with whom one could discuss fashion plates or parties and confide thoughts. She thought of all the girlish confidences she and Lydia had shared. They were, she admitted to herself now, foolish, but they had seemed so vital at the time. She knew Lydia always went too far in her behaviour, but despite being the elder, Kitty had always felt drawn to follow her.

Her companions of the moment were congenial, but Kitty felt a moment's tearfulness. Lydia was now in America. She was the most terrible correspondent and Kitty was lucky if she wrote once a year. Lydia and Mr Wickham seemed to move house or town almost at will. Lydia boasted of people they had met and of how the more relaxed code of conduct suited them both. In her heart, Kitty knew that neither success nor failure would bring them back from that vast continent.

As though to pass comment on the vanity of hosting picnics, the fine weather broke. Screens of rain obliterated all but the near terraces of the garden from view. The few remaining camellias hung brown and limp on the stem. Twill gowns re-emerged from trunks and were shaken out of their folds.

The Bennet ladies bent their heads to the needle over summer gowns and wondered that they might ever need them, so complete was the change in the weather. No social calls were made or received for more than a week, so the sewing progressed at a lively pace. Kitty's nimble fingers had moved on to fashioning a jacket to complement her gown. Both sisters wearied of Mrs Bennet's nervous headaches, which were apt to turn a cosy afternoon sour. Thus it was unanimous delight that greeted the sound of approaching carriage wheels. Mrs Bennet motioned to her daughters with eagerness. 'Bid a servant to answer the door with haste. Whoever it is will be soaked.'

Presently Mr Montagu was announced. Mrs Bennet proved a little unequal to her surprise visitor, whose height seemed like to top the door frame.

'Mr Montagu, such a surprise. You are very welcome here, I am sure. We shall send for Mr Bennet at once.'

She ushered the young gentleman further into the parlour with inadequate motions more suited to shooing a chicken.

'Your pardon, madam, please do not disturb Mr Bennet on my account.'

Mr Montagu stood in the centre of the room, dominating his surroundings and seeming marooned on the Aubusson rug.

'It is no trouble, sir. He will be glad of the company. We are all plagued by poor spirits in this dreadful weather. Do sit down over here next to Kitty. We shall have tea presently.'

'I should not like to impose.'

'Nonsense. We must take tea in any event.'

Mrs Bennet rang the servants' bell. Mr Montagu sat somewhat awkwardly, his long limbs appearing not to know how to arrange themselves for comfort. He glanced at Mary who smiled politely. He cleared his throat.

'The weather is indeed a nuisance, Mrs Bennet. I find myself thwarted in many endeavours. Even the accounts are as nearly up-to-date as my attention can bear. Of course the library is lacking the admirable attentions of Miss Bennet.'

Mary met his direct gaze. 'And I miss the library. The upper level is finished and I'm looking forward to commencing the lower bookcases.'

'Might it be possible to progress if I conveyed Miss Bennet to Cuthbert Park on inclement days?'

His question, directed to Mrs Bennet, hung in the air as that good lady appeared to be rendered dumb by the number of her thoughts.

'That sounds like a sensible plan, if Mary is agreeable.' Mr Bennet had entered the room unseen. Mary looked up at her father with a rush of gratitude. 'Mary, when would you like to begin?'

'Tomorrow, Father, if it continues wet and that is agreeable to Mr Montagu.'

Mary cast a look of appeal to Mr Montagu, who nodded and agreed without delay.

Kitty, who had been covertly studying her sister and Mr Montagu through the visit, formed a suspicion, with not a little wonder, that the pair were far from indifferent to one another.

Late that evening Kitty knocked and entered Mary's room. By candlelight, the room had changed little from the days when Jane and Lizzy had resided here. The floral drapes were the worse for wear, but the large four-poster bed bore fresh white linen and a colourful quilt, and Mary's most treasured books were lined up along the mantelpiece. Kitty had never entered the room without seeing a book on the chair and another on the bedside table. Mary sat before the fire in her nightgown, unbraiding her chestnut hair.

'Mary, I came to ask if you had trimmed your bonnet for the picnic.'

'No, I am still working on my gown. I have neither your speed nor skill with the needle.'

'I thought I might be able to help you with it, if you like.'

Mary raised an eyebrow. 'Thank you. I might need the help. Though if this weather continues, Mrs Montagu will have to cancel.'

As though to underscore Mary's words, the wind drove the rain to rattle against the windows.

'I'm sure it will change again soon.' Kitty deposited herself on the bed. 'What do you think of Mr Montagu?'

'I don't know him that well, really. I generally work alone in the library.'

'But you take tea together,' Kitty persisted.

'Oh yes, though always with Mrs Montagu. She makes me feel uncomfortable, but fortunately I don't have to converse with her very much.' Mary began to brush out her tresses. 'Mr Montagu tells us stories about his time in Portugal. I wish you could hear them, Kitty. We are so dull here in Meryton.'

Kitty sighed. 'We certainly are. You will be glad to return to Cuthbert Park.'

'Oh, yes, indeed.'

Mary stopped brushing and stretched out her hands and toes to the luxurious glow of the fire.

'Mr Montagu is eager to have you there.' Kitty joined her, sitting on the hearthrug.

'Do you think so?'

Mary curled back in her chair, eyes searching her sister's face.

'There is no doubt about it. I think he may like you very well, Mary.'

Mary gave a short, nervous laugh. Kitty cursed herself for having put down her candle, so that she was unable to see Mary's face clearly.

'I am being of service to him, I am sure that you read his gratitude as something more important.' She paused. 'Not that I mind of course.'

Kitty was now sure her sister was far from indifferent to Mr Montagu. Mary always spoke with decision, but tonight her speech was far from certain.

'I would not be so sure, Mary. Are you certain that you do not harbour feelings for him?'

'Of course not,' Mary cried. 'As usual you invest everything with your romantic notions, Kitty. What would be Mr Montagu see in me; a plain woman without fortune? I know my fate and I am resigned to it. If either of us is to marry, it will be you.'

Kitty padded to the door and paused.

'Then I fear we are neither of us are destined to know the happiness of our sisters.'

Mary did not sleep well. She lay awake for some time going over the conversation with Kitty. Kitty's suggestions had been typical of her and ridiculous. Yet there was a strange feeling coursing through Mary's veins that she could not name. Fear, excitement, energised spirits – she simply could not define her emotions. She turned her pillow several times, but could not settle. For some reason she recalled Lady Sandalford saying at the party,

'My nephew shows no inclination to marry.'

Then, over and over, Mary heard Kitty ask,

'Are you certain that you do not harbour feelings for him?'

13

Despite her protestations to Kitty, Mary's nerves held her tongue captive while seated beside Mr Montagu in his curricle. She knew her face to be white and strained. Where to put one's hands – should they be in her lap or holding the side rail? She felt cross with herself for worrying about such trivial matters. Luckily, Mr Montagu was too much occupied with avoiding large puddles to observe her face. He handled his horses very well. His touch was light but assured on the reins. Before setting off from Longbourn, Mary's skirts had been skilfully tucked inside a large blanket. A steady clop of hooves and the occasional caw of birds riding the wind provided the only sounds. Mary wondered if she should be making conversation but felt unequal to the task.

'I must apologise to you, Mr Montagu. I have no talent for general social discourse.'

He glanced down at her. 'That is a rare virtue in my eyes, Miss Bennet. I see no need for the constant idle observation so popular among society.'

An observer would have noted both parties visibly relax. Not another word was uttered until they reached Cuthbert Park. Mr Montagu's hands spanned Mary's waist as he helped her down from the carriage. 'Why, you're as light as a child.'

Mary felt as light as air, but muttered, 'I am sure that you are mistaken, sir.'

'I am rarely mistaken, Miss Bennet.' He strode off at a brisk pace. 'Now, shall we go in and discuss our findings of the upper level? Peters shall supply a footman to remove those volumes we agree for sale.'

So engrossed were they in their task that they failed to hear the bell for tea.

'Really, Sebastian, what are you about in here? Your aunt has come to tea. What will she think of your behaviour?'

Mrs Montagu burst into the library with considerable momentum. Lengths of lace rippled from every edge of her cap and gown. Mary noticed that her cheeks formed two round, red stains when she was cross.

Sebastian placed a pile of books carefully on the table.

'Has the tea bell rung? My apologies, Mama, we did not hear it. We will come immediately.'

'Do not hurry on my account, dear boy.' Lady Sandalford swept into the library, elegant in blue grosgrain relieved by a quantity of pearl buttons along the tight sleeves.

'Miss Bennet, how do you do? It has been some time since our paths crossed.'

Mary, who was on her knees sorting books, rose in an awkward manner to make a hasty bob.

'Lady Sandalford, I beg your pardon, and Mrs Montagu. I'm afraid we lost all track of time.'

Mary looked from one to the other and restrained the childish impulse to bite her lip in contrition.

'Ah, the famous cataloguing of my late brother's library.' Lady Sandalford waved away the apology.

'Yes, your ladyship, the upper level is finished and we are now sorting the volumes.'

'Bring your ledger into tea if you will be so kind.' Her ladyship scanned the room and nodded to herself. 'I should like to reacquaint myself with some familiar names.'

The older ladies returned to the salon.

Mary looked down at her muslin gown with some distress.

'Oh dear, I am quite dusty. Do you think I have time to make myself tidy?'

'Dust suits you. Your hair has come a little loose.' He reached a hand towards her hair. 'Go ahead, I shall face the dragons alone.'

Mary hurried away, her face burning. She washed her hands and pressed them to her face, then stared at her reflection in the polished steel mirror, before quickly tucking the loose lock of hair and hurrying back to the salon.

Lady Sandalford looked up from the ledger.

'Well, Miss Bennet, you are an accomplished secretary, are you not? Where did you learn to create such a fine catalogue?'

Mary looked from Lady Sandalford to Mr Montagu in confusion.

'I have no formal training, my lady. Surely it is only common sense?'

'Perhaps you are right. But then, common sense is surely in short supply.' Lady Sandalford's smile transformed her long face. 'I hope that you will pay me a visit when you have finished here. I could do with your advice in my own sadly neglected library.'

Mary wondered if the lady, famous for her wit, was quizzing her.

'It would be an honour to visit your Ladyship's library, though I cannot think that my advice could possibly be of benefit.'

'We shall see, Miss Bennet. In any event, I hope you will accept my invitation.'

'With pleasure, your Ladyship.'

Mary smiled with happiness. She glanced at Mr Montagu and received an encouraging smile.

Mrs Montagu broke into this polite exchange with a show of impatience.

'Speaking of invitations,' she said, 'Lord Drummond and his daughters, as well as Countess Glendinning and Lady Sarah, have all accepted invitations to the picnic next week. I believe that there is a cousin who may join them.'

Lady Sandalford turned a baleful eye upon her sister-in-law.

'Countess Glendinning is the silliest woman in England and her daughter is hoity-toity. What possessed you to invite them, dear?'

Mrs Montagu snatched up the teapot as though in defence.

'Sebastian must have some young people to call friends, Arabella. They all came to dine recently and we enjoyed a jolly afternoon.'

Lady Sandalford regarded her nephew and her hostess with cool composure. Mary's eyes darted to Sebastian before dropping her gaze. She bit her lip, mortified that Mrs Montagu had not even tried to hide the fact that she considered her too inferior to be a friend of her son.

'I would not describe the occasion as jolly, Mama, though Lord Drummond's conversation was interesting.' Mr Montagu, as ever, addressed his mother in light tones.

'Lord Drummond indeed,' she scoffed. 'He is most certainly distinguished, but what of the young ladies? They were quite taken with you.'

Mrs Montagu shot her sister-in-law a triumphant glance.

Mr Montagu shook his head. Embarrassed, Mary concentrated on the contents of her teacup and failed to notice.

'I shall be pleased to see Lord Drummond and the fair Sylvia again. I should think the other girl is a chit barely out of the schoolroom. As for the dreaded Countess Glendinning and haughty Lady Sarah . . . Well, one can only hope that the cousin is neither dull nor a turnip top!' Lady Sandalford laughed at her own joke. 'Miss Bennet and Sebastian, you must save me if I am in danger of infection from the terminally stupid.'

Lady Sandalford kindly offered to convey Mary home in her handsomely appointed carriage – an offer Mary was glad to accept. She realised that Lady Sandalford was an intriguing person, once one ceased to be intimidated.

'You are not at all like your mother, my dear.'

Mary watched the men toiling in the fields from her seat by the carriage window.

'No, I fear that I am a great disappointment to Mama.' She turned to Lady Sandalford, 'I am a little more like my father, but mostly I think I am like no one else.'

'You are like yourself and let nobody tell you that is a bad thing. I have never allowed being different to alter my behaviour. Neither should you.'

The remainder of the short journey was devoted to a discussion of various volumes in the library at Cuthbert Park.

Mrs Bennet gushed and exclaimed over the kindness of her ladyship in driving Mary home. As soon as she could dart away, Mary sought the sanctuary of her room. Privately, she considered that Lady Sandalford with her title and fortune could afford to celebrate being different. Not so, someone as undistinguished as herself.

14

Mr Montagu was required to drive Mary to Cuthbert Park once more before the weather improved. On this occasion the silence was a little less companionable. Mary could not forget Mrs Montagu's inference that she was too inferior to be a friend to her son. He had not spoken out in contradiction. A frisson of tension hovered under the curricle's oiled canopy, which served to protect the pair from a light shower of rain.

'Are you looking forward to the picnic, Miss Bennet?'

Mary sat a little hunched and spoke to him in the prim voice that she reserved for anyone with whom she disagreed.

'It is kind of you to invite us humble locals.'

'Pray, who else would be invited?' he said, sounding both surprised and wounded.

'Lord Drummond and Countess Glendinning perhaps?'

'Ah, I see. My mother's want of tact the other afternoon. These people are her choice. You must not mind her ways. She means well by her actions. For my part I prefer people with whom I can be comfortable.'

'Oh.' Mary ventured a glance from under the protection of her velvet bonnet. Mr Montagu's features were set in grim focus on the puddle-strewn road. Guilt settled about her shoulders and she sought to repair her rudeness.

'Your aunt, Lady Sandalford, is very kind. At first I thought her very grand.'

She had the satisfaction of seeing Mr Montagu turn to her and smile.

'My aunt is quite wonderful. She terrifies many people, but she has always been my champion. She liked you.'

'She was most gracious, and I cannot think why.' Her words formed a question. She looked up at his open features.

'Anyone with a good mind gains my aunt's approval. It was clear from your interest in the library and from your ledger that you are intelligent. You must not be too self-effacing, you know.'

'I am not as a rule. In fact, I am apt to believe myself intellectually superior to most of my acquaintance. Does that shock you?'

He laughed. 'No, I admire your honesty. Am I included in the number?'

A small smile played around Mary's lips.

'I have yet to decide, for I do not know you well enough.'

'Then I shall have to look to my laurels! But perhaps I will rise in your estimation if I tell you this: I have been thinking about the situation of women in your position in life. It had not occurred to me to do so before our conversation about Oxford. There is unfairness at work in the world, Miss Bennet.' He glanced at her. Mary was all attention. 'Take a young woman such as yourself, interested in books and knowledge. Why should you not have the same chance to go to Oxford or Cambridge as any young gentleman?'

Mary looked at him, quite lost in wonder. The carriage hit a ditch. Steadying her bonnet, she replied,

'You do rise in my esteem, sir. No other gentleman, to my knowledge, voices such sentiments; not even my father. A woman may be without superior physical strength, but is that not all the more reason why she has the leisure to invest in her mind? Society demands that we are confined to the home while gentlemen have the freedom to roam the world at will. I admit I do resent the inequality!'

Mr Montagu burst out laughing. She noticed how his eyes crinkled and his head was flung back in abandon. How she would love to possess such a free attitude.

'What would you choose to do if you might do anything, Miss Bennet?'

Mr Montagu gave her his full attention for a few moments after they had swung through the gates of Cuthbert Park. Mary hardly knew where to begin answering such a bold question, made, she knew, with sincerity. She hesitated, her voice soft against the sound of the wheels, but growing in force as her thoughts took over.

'I would study music – more for my own pleasure than to perform. Then, I would learn about matters of business and law, because such things are held apart as too complicated for ladies.' She took a deep breath and her voice throbbed as he turned to face her. 'After that, I should make it my cause to help other women with limited choices.'

'Why, Miss Bennet, hiding behind that blue serge gown is a revolutionary. Who would have thought it?'

As they alighted the carriage their laughter rang across the courtyard.

15

On the morning of the picnic, Mr Bennet set his party in good spirits by suggesting that he was a thistle among roses. They alighted the carriage in merriment.

'Mr Bennet, I fear the entire neighbourhood has arrived before us. We shall have difficulty finding a seat.' Mrs Bennet sallied forth to greet one and all, tossing an order to Kitty over her shoulder to keep a lookout for their host.

Kitty, who had not been to the gardens of Cuthbert Park since she was a young girl, gazed about her in awe.

'Why, Mary, you did not do the park justice in your descriptions. It is quite beautiful.'

'I do believe that you haven't properly attended me. It is wonderful, I agree. You can see the second lake here on our right from the library and the first from the salon, along with the ha-ha. They make a fine prospect in any weather.'

The two connecting lakes were divided by a wide walk ending in an ornamental Japanese bridge. Beyond lay a rhododendron walk, parallel to both lakes. Mrs Montagu had set up her tables to maximum effect on the wide walk between the lakes. Commodious chairs, stools and rugs were arranged in small groups under trees on the nearside of the lake. People drifted between friends on the lawns leading down from the house. Servants ran to and fro, depositing large silver platters of cold meats, pies and all manner of delectable dishes on the long buffet. Nothing had been left to chance. Even the sun had conspired to make the setting quite perfect. Mary knew that she would carry the sight in her memory for ever.

Mr Montagu joined them. His blue superfine coat moulded his slender form to perfection. Mary thought how fitting he looked as host in these beautiful surroundings.

'The Misses Bennet and Mr Bennet, you are a most welcome addition to the party.'

Mr Bennet stepped forward and shook his host's hand with genuine warmth. 'Mr Montagu, how well you look. Cuthbert Park is showing to great advantage today.'

'Thank you, sir. To the first, Miss Mary Bennet deserves some of the thanks for relieving me of a burden. As for the second, I do believe that all the ladies in their various gowns and parasols, create a veritable garden of colour. Perhaps I should plant roses to remind me of the spectacle.'

Kitty appeared struck by the notion.

'Why, sir, what a lovely idea. Which colours will you plant?'

'Well, I could start with the colours in your two gowns. A yellow and red. I think they will look well together.'

Mrs Bennet approached, her bonnet strings whipping from left to right with the swivel of her neck as each fresh group of guests came into her sights. Her eyes sparkled at the sight of her host.

'Sir, you have done us proud. Such inviting delicacies and so many friends among the company. I recognise

Lord Drummond, but do tell me, is the lady over there wearing puce, Countess Glendinning?'

'They are one and the same, madam. Allow me to introduce you.' Mr Montagu stepped briskly across the lawn with Mrs Bennet in eager attendance, trotting behind at a less than dignified pace. Mr Bennet linked arms with his daughters and followed at a more sedate gait. Introductions were first made to the great lady herself, whose puce gown and cap were made of the finest silk. She possessed a quantity of jerky mannerisms and odd facial manoeuvres through which she introduced her daughter, Lady Sarah. A simple 'how do you do' from Lady Sarah's thin lips managed to be both cold and bored all at once. Such hauteur was a sure sign of nobility, according to some. Even seated, Lady Sarah showed taller than her mother. She too wore a gown of finest striped silk satin, in pale pink with crisp pintucks down the bodice and short sleeves. Save for rather dull and badly dressed brown locks, she could have been very handsome, if it were not for her coldness. Countess Glendinning turned to the other member of the party, who stood behind Lady Sarah's chair.

'This is our cousin, Mr Dalrymple, who visits us from London.'

The gentleman, dressed with great delicacy of fashion, contrasted as day to night with his countrymen. A very high collar served to highlight his fashionable Brutus hairstyle. A red cravat and pink waistcoat reflected in the looking-glass perfection of his shoe buckles.

'Charmed to make your acquaintance. How gaily you all live here in the country. Upon my soul, now I know how many elegant ladies live here, I will visit my aunt at every opportunity.'

As he made this pretty speech he raised his quizzing glass and directed his gaze to Kitty. There was a becoming flush to her cheeks. She bowed her head demurely. Mary instantly felt Mr Dalrymple was exactly the sort of shallow fellow to be avoided. Lady Sarah shot Kitty a look of irritation, while Lady Glendinning tittered.

'My nephew has the most charming manner of speech; no doubt it will serve his future career brilliantly. Although I must own, it will sore disappoint me to lose him.'

'My sweet lady aunt, it will sore disappoint me to leave you . . . and my dear cousin of course.' He made his two lady relatives an extravagant bow.

As the Bennet party moved on, Lady Sarah's sulky voice carried on the gentle breeze:

'Are we to be paraded to all of Mrs Montagu's friends? It is not to be borne.'

'Hush, dear, you will be overheard,' Lady Glendinning admonished her daughter with no great conviction.

Mr Montagu begged to be excused to greet other guests, while the Bennets continued to meet old friends.

The picnic lunch was a cheerful affair. Lord Drummond was soon reckoned to be an excellent gentleman of superior manners by anyone who had not previously made his acquaintance. He paid flattering attention to his hostess and made an effort to converse with everyone. His bearing displayed all the confidence of a wealthy man in his prime. Straining waistcoat buttons declared him to be a gentleman who enjoyed a well-stocked table and he did not disappoint the notion, consuming two helpings of apple charlotte and a fruit jelly after several savoury dishes. He approached the Bennets with bonhomie.

'Mr and Mrs Bennet, it has been too long since we met. Now, where was it?'

Mrs Bennet came to his aid. 'I believe that it was Mr Bingley's ball, these five years gone. He is married to our daughter Jane, you know.'

'Lucky fellow. What happened to that friend of his, Darcy was it? The women were in a flap about his fortune for miles around.'

Mr Bennet coughed. 'Our second daughter, Elizabeth, put them all out of their misery by marrying him.'

Lord Drummond laughed heartily. He clapped Mr Bennet on the shoulder.

'Ha, capital! Well done, Mrs Bennet, for I will wager that you had a hand in proceedings.'

Mrs Bennet simpered with a girlish display of modesty involving the lowering of her head and an upward motion of her eyes.

'We are very lucky, sir. Our girls are possessed of both beauty and pleasing ways. A young man will fall in love with a beautiful girl easily, but a gentle hand may guide the lovebirds.'

Mr Bennet collected his manners.

'You may not know of all my daughters, sir. These are numbers three and four, Mary and Catherine.'

'How d'ye do, young ladies? And these are my two daughters, Sylvia and Imogen.' Sylvia held out her hand to Mr Bennet, hastily followed by Imogen.

'Imogen has only recently left the schoolroom, haven't you, miss?' Lord Drummond gave his youngest daughter an indulgent nod.

'Yes, Papa.'

The two girls painted a startling contrast. Imogen, the younger, favoured her father. Her hair was a tumbling morass of dark curls above rosy cheeks and dancing eyes. Judged to be around seventeen like Georgina, she had yet to acquire any of her older sister's poise. Mary reckoned the elder girl to be around her own age. Sylvia presented a vision of silvery loveliness to match her name. Slender, graceful and immaculate, she nevertheless revealed a fine smile and a hint of character in her hazel eyes. She turned to Mary. 'Are you the Miss Bennet who is helping Mr Montagu catalogue his library?' Mary nodded. 'He speaks most highly of you. Although our acquaintance is quite new, I place value upon his opinions. I am very fond of reading.' She lowered her voice, 'Would it be an impertinence to ask you to recommend some books for me?'

'That would depend entirely on your interests.'

Mary wondered what this poised beauty might want with her. Did she perhaps wish to impress Mr Montagu? If so, she had no desire to indulge such artifice.

A few short words from Sylvia made clear her love of reading. They launched into a satisfying discussion of novels, while Kitty cheerfully answered Imogen's questions about passing guests.

As the afternoon wore on, groups settled in the shade of ancient trees. Younger folk were more inclined to perambulate, pausing here and there in the shade to converse. Mary decided to investigate the rhododendron walk. There were very few people meandering down the silent avenue. Many of the blooms had dispersed, leaving a carpet of pink, violet and red on the path. She approached a folly at the lower end, sited to look out onto the lake.

Mr Montagu was seated on the balustrade with a brooding expression on his face. At once she felt she was trespassing on his privacy. Before she could slip away unnoticed, he sensed her presence. Mary halted in her tracks.

'I beg your pardon, I did not know you would be here.'

'Why would you? I expect that you are also escaping to find a little solitude. Come and rest a moment. There's a fine view of the house across the lake from here.'

Mary took her seat and was indeed rewarded by a view of the shadowed west wing, receding beyond the sparkling waters of the lake.

'If I lived here I should visit this view every day in fine weather.'

'Nobody ever walks this far for some reason. I have always had the folly to myself, but I'm glad to share it with you.'

His gaze lingered on her face until she felt impelled by embarrassment to move across to the balustrade. He cleared his throat.

'I often come here to think things through. Do you have a special place?'

'The ancient oak on the path where we first met.' She turned back to face him. 'The path is usually deserted.'

He laughed. 'No wonder you nearly fell over me. You weren't expecting someone to be there. What is to be done with us, Miss Bennet? We are each sorely lacking in the social graces.'

'Perhaps. I prefer to think that we do not care for the sort of conversation which requires one to dissemble. For here we are speaking plainly to one another.'

'I give you good warning, Miss Bennet. If you continue to keep speaking such good common sense to me, my poor male pride will take a beating. Knowing all the answers is meant to be the gentleman's part, you know.'

Mary leaned back against the stone balustrade and smiled.

'Then I give you leave to advise me, sir, on any defect in my character of your own choosing.'

'Stay, I can think of none. But wait – yes. You hide your light under a bushel. You prefer to hover in the shadows. I would see you as you are now in your cheerful gown with the yellow rosette on your bonnet, commanding my attention with your intelligent face.'

The telltale blush arose from her bosom through to her hairline. Mary looked away. Why, oh why did she feel confused at times when she was alone with him? He was, after all, friendly and open. She decided the problem rested with herself.

'I have not been hiding this afternoon. I have been giving a bit of bold advice.'

'Have you indeed? Who is the lucky recipient?

'The Honourable Miss Sylvia Drummond.'

'Then I will wager you have been discussing books.'

'We have. Though your opinion weighs with her so well that I doubt my own effort.'

He raised an eyebrow. 'I was not aware of such an impression, though I must say she is a delightful conversationalist, which is an excellent attribute in a friend.' His eyes held a hint of mischief. 'Lady Sarah on the other hand . . .'

Do I possess the attributes of a friend? I am no great conversationalist. Mary realised his admiring friendship was her fervent wish, and just for a few moments also wished she were Sylvia. The thoughts startled her enough to make her want to examine them in private.

'I ought to be getting back. They will wonder where I am.'

She alighted the steps. He stood up and stepped forward. 'Allow me to escort you.'

She turned to look over her shoulder.

'No need, I will leave you to your problem-solving.'

She hurried down the path, conscious of his eyes following her.

Mr Dalrymple leaned insouciantly against a tree trunk chatting easily to Mrs Bennet while his eyes rested on Kitty. Kitty gazed up at him with rapt fascination. Mr Bennet had nodded off in his chair. As she approached, Mary felt a strong sense of foreboding. She had seen Kitty looking dazzled like this around officers when the regiment were quartered at Meryton. Her mother clearly felt no such apprehension.

'Well, sir, if you have a yearning to discover Meryton, you must come and dine with us. Longbourn is always open to friends and I flatter myself that our table is the equal of any in the county. Is that not so, Kitty?'

'Mama is a committed hostess, Mr Dalrymple.' Kitty favoured him with a winning smile. 'Please do join us.'

'Then I shall make it my business to call just as soon as my aunt can dispense with me. I must hurry back to her now, but I can think of nothing I would enjoy more. Your servant, Mrs Bennet, young ladies.' With another of his flourishing bows, he was gone.

16

'Who would have thought it, Kitty? Two eligible young gentlemen at the picnic. We must make plans.'

Mrs Bennet dawdled along the path to Meryton, forcing Kitty to slow her pace. It was rare for Mrs Bennet to walk so far, but the gig having been pressed into service on the home farm and the coach too grand an equipage for a simple shopping foray, saw the pair on their way together.

'I should like to become better acquainted with Mr Dalrymple, Mama. He is quite different to the young men we know.'

Mrs Bennet halted and fished for her fan, which she proceeded to ply with rapidity.

'Slow down, Kitty. You girls gallop around the countryside like horses. It is most unladylike. The wonder is that Jane and Lizzy managed to find husbands at all, wandering about as they did. If it weren't for me . . .'

'I am walking as slow as I can, Mama.'

'Well, as I said, we must make plans. You have not found reasons to visit Cuthbert Park. Mr Montagu is not beyond the reach of other young ladies, however tall he is.' She stopped to laugh at her own joke. Kitty contributed a weak smile.

'Mr Montagu is very nice, Mama, but you must admit he does not possess Mr Dalrymple's air.'

'True, my dear, but he is wealthy and wealth, you know, is a very attractive quality in a man.'

Kitty decided to change the course of the conversation.

'I thought Mr Dalrymple showed to advantage next to the other gentlemen at the picnic. Did you see how his high-point collar was tied to perfection? Indeed, his every garment was fitted to a nicety. Nothing at all like the creased jackets and dusty shoes of the others. Altogether superior.'

Mrs Bennet favoured her daughter with a shrewd look.

'He was very modern and his manners were just as they ought to be. You are like me in noticing the finer touches in a person. We must make shift to know him better. I saw him looking at Maria Lucas when we were dining.'

Kitty turned to her mother with a frown.

'Maria, surely not?'

'I have to admit, Kitty, Maria's hair does attract attention. Not that she is as pretty as you, my love. Those freckles make one shudder.'

'Maria is a good companion, Mama, but I cannot think she would entertain someone like Mr Dalrymple for long. He has studied the law. I wonder if I am clever enough for him?'

'Clever! What has clever to do with anything, pray? Have I taught you nothing? Why do none of my daughters attend me? Men don't care for clever women, I tell you.' Mrs Bennet stopped again and fanned herself in agitation. 'Never mind Lizzy's fine looks; do you think she would have been so easily married with her clever tongue if Darcy hadn't been such a queer bird and actually liked such behaviour? Look at Mary with her dull books and sharp tongue. What do you suppose will become of her?' She snapped her fan shut and marched forward. 'Do not trouble me with your "clever", Kitty Bennet. I know better.'

Meryton was now in sight. Kitty now trailed her mother, tossing the homily in her thoughts. Of the two gentlemen, Mr Dalrymple was more to her taste. He seemed inclined to flirt and his manners were easy. Perhaps gentlemen wanted soothing or amusing wives because they were busy being clever during the day. She was sure that Lizzy and Mary would think that gentlemen valued cleverness but Jane would say thoughtfulness and good manners mattered most. Kitty smiled to herself. Lydia would say nothing mattered beyond larks. Mr Montagu was a scholar and therefore clever, but he was also wealthy and pleasant enough, if not dashing. Could she come to love such a man?

17

'Mrs Montagu, my mother asked me to bring you a gift from the home farm and also this note.'

'Thank you, Mary dear. Did you enjoy our little picnic?'

'I think I shall remember the day all my life.' Mary replied with sincerity.

Mrs Montagu beamed her gratification. 'It was most special. The countess and her party lent an added air of gentility, I think.'

Mary's face clouded.

'The countess was most civil. I cannot say the same for her daughter. Her behaviour was quite uncivil.'

Mrs Montagu frowned. She bent her head over her tapestry work, signalling that the conversation was at an end.

Mary slipped into the library, uncomfortably aware that she had annoyed Mrs Montagu. Why must her tongue always cause offence? Did people prefer lies to the truth? Did they desire obfuscation over clarity? She would not be so compromised. Let the rest of society dissemble, she would continue to point out the truth. A small voice crept insistently into her thoughts. *Mr Montagu speaks the truth but causes no offence. Why cannot you follow his example?* Worse followed. *Mr Montagu would never marry a woman who offended his mother.* Mary groaned and sank her head upon the desk, forced to acknowledge that her feelings for Mr Montagu had developed beyond friendship.

It was in this state that he found her several minutes later. Concerned, he knelt by her side. 'Miss Bennet, Mary, are you unwell? Shall I fetch someone?'

'No, no, please do not trouble yourself. It is just . . . oh dear, I am afraid that I have offended your mama.'

Mary raised her head from the desk with reluctance.

'But I have just seen her. She is quite unperturbed and rattled on about the picnic in a very happy state. What makes you think you have upset her?'

'It is my tongue. I cannot but tell the truth and then people become upset. I'm afraid I felt the need to point out Lady Sarah's rudeness. Your mother was clearly annoyed.'

Mr Montagu chuckled. 'It will take more than that to truly upset Mama. To tell the truth, I have seen her wince when Lady Sarah gives one of her set-downs. Between you and me, I am in agreement with my Aunt Sandalford about the Glendinnings.'

Mary regarded him with surprise.

'But she was annoyed. I am not imagining it.'

'Lady Sarah was her guest. By criticising her guest so directly, you are criticising her choice as a hostess. My mother likes nothing more at present than to hear praise of her party and by implication, of herself.'

Mary turned her head, for once looking him directly in the eye as he had remained on bent knee just inches away from her; so close that she could see his necktie was not entirely level. She felt an absurd urge to straighten it.

'I had not thought of it like that. Poor Mrs Montagu. I shall beg her pardon.'

'That is not necessary and might well cause you both embarrassment. Better by far to praise some aspect of the party or a guest – the Honourable Sylvia Drummond for example, everyone likes her. Then it is a simple matter to allow her to enjoy the compliment and chatter about the happy moment.'

Her eyes flew wide open.

'Oh, that is clever. It will not be difficult. My own mama is never happier than when commanding company. Indeed, both Kitty and I struggle to bear the load.'

'Miss Bennet, when I am in your company I find myself smiling and laughing for the strangest of reasons. How is it that a serious young lady causes such a reaction? Come, show me your progress along the bookcases.'

They worked away in avid discussion together until teatime. Glancing frequently over the tea and cake to Mr Montagu for reassurance, Mary took care to follow his advice with happy results. No stories of Portuguese valleys or sea crossings sallied forth today. Mrs Montagu delighted in her small audience and withheld no small detail of the picnic or her part in the success of the venture. Several times Mary was perforce to smother laughter as she caught Mr Montagu's twinkling eye.

The afternoon's events played in Mary's thoughts as she walked home. Spring had almost given way to summer now and the world around was lush in every particular. Even at this late afternoon hour the sun warmed her skin through her thin muslin gown, making Mary feel as joyously alive as the lambs gambolling in the pasture leading to Meryton's stream.

In the hour before dinner, while Mrs Bennet took her daily rest to soothe ruffled nerves, Mary knocked on Kitty's door. She lingered on the threshold a moment. 'I wanted to thank you for helping me with my new gown and bonnet. In return I have searched for a novel you might enjoy. It is quite light.'

Kitty scooped up a handful of ribbons from her small beauty table and fluttered them through her fingers.

'Thank you, but in truth, it was lovely to discuss gowns and ribbons and such again. 'Tis one of the things I sorely miss about Lydia.'

Mary seated herself in the nursing chair, which sufficed as Kitty's easy chair. She drew her knees up under her chin. 'I imagine it is difficult for you. Perhaps I should take a greater interest in my apparel.'

'Yes, you should. A little attention would make a difference, Mary. Look at Lydia. She had not Jane or Lizzy's beauty, but she was noticed. Perhaps too well noticed.'

The sisters acknowledged *that* part of family history best forgotten with a meaningful look.

'Did Lydia ever confide in you about Wickham? What I mean to say is, how did she know that she was in love with him in particular?'

'Well, you know Lydia; she rattles on with a dozen thoughts at great pace. But I believe that he did truly capture her heart. When you saw her look at him, especially if he wasn't looking, she would go unusually quiet. She simply stared at him with rapt attention.' Kitty laughed. 'Anything that could stop Lydia in her tracks must surely be unusual.'

Mary didn't return the laugh. Her expression was sober.

'Marriage appears to be a game of chance. Jane and Lizzy have won their hands but Lydia played her cards badly. Wickham's charm covers an unscrupulous character. I am sure there have been further appeals for money.'

'Well, I expect America is expensive. Lydia can't help that.' The sisters lapsed into silence. Kitty tucked the last pin in her hair and announced, 'I have been thinking. Who we love is perhaps pure chance and beyond our control. But maybe we can choose *why* we love someone.'

Mary's puzzled features puckered in a tiny frown. 'How so?'

'It seems to me that love matches are only happy if the parties are suited in character and temperament. In that sense, all of our sisters are happy. Yet if you look at our dear parents, the results are not so harmonious.' She paused. 'I had not voiced this even to myself before, but I think one should not marry for love alone if one is lucky enough to meet with love.'

Mary jerked fully upright in her chair. Her voice emitted in low wonder, 'Do you know, Kitty, it has been the strangest day. It is as though my thoughts keep turning upside down.'

'Take care to keep that from Papa. He will accuse you of turning out like Mama.'

The image of such an occurrence left both sisters laughing, which only abated when their mama arrived to complain at the monstrous disturbance to her peace.

18

The following day Mr Dalrymple came to luncheon, sending the household into a flurry of preparation as luncheons were rarely taken. The housekeeper, Hill, grumbled about the ways of the gentry. Mrs Bennet instructed Kitty to change her gown twice until she was satisfied.

Mr Dalrymple showed promise in repaying such endeavours. He was fulsome in his attentions to his hostess, listening with every appearance of interest to her vanities and opinions in equal measure before Mr Bennet joined them in the dining room. He swiftly turned his attention to his host. 'I understand that you are something of a scholar, sir?' Mr Bennet inclined his head. Dalrymple continued, 'I do not pretend to such lofty abilities, yet I have made some progress with the dusty tomes of the law. My tutors at Cambridge were kind enough to pass my efforts.'

Mr Bennet peered at the level of the wine decanter, then turned to his guest. 'Then you are fortunate, Mr Dalrymple, for nobody passes my efforts at all. Yet I derive satisfaction nonetheless. Have you ambitions in the law, sir?'

'As a means to an end, Mr Bennet. The law, as a useful guide to how a man may conduct himself and profit by it, is the extent of my true interest. As a means to the future, the law holds much promise.'

Mr Bennet flipped open his napkin and enquired, 'You intrigue me, Mr Dalrymple. Pray continue.'

'For a man such as myself, with neither title nor great fortune, the law is the simplest route to a political future. Politics is where the real power and wealth are distributed to those who have not the good fortune to inherit.' Mr Dalrymple addressed his remarks to the whole table with a self-satisfied air that foretold his expectation of their being impressed. Mrs Bennet appeared much struck by these thoughts, while Mr Bennet displayed a glimmer of a smile as he said, 'I deduce that you are a man with a mission. It is a wonder that you elect to rusticate with us in the country.'

Emboldened, Mr Dalrymple spoke up. 'Ah, sir, even in this charming setting I work at my future.' His eyes drifted across the table to Kitty. 'Though I am surrounded by such beauty and good company that I scarce notice any effort.'

Mrs Bennet, having particularly noted Mr Dalrymple's allusion to a lack of fortune, pursued the matter with determination. 'Why, sir, your ambition sounds all that is proper to me. But have you some assistance?'

Losing none of his brio, Mr Dalrymple replied, 'There, madam, I must confess that I am at the mercy of others. Luckily for me, my dear aunt, the countess, has been kind enough to show me favour. Of course, in return I render such small deeds as are within my power to make myself indispensable to her.'

Mr Bennet coughed and raised his napkin. Mary caught his eye and turned her head to smother a laugh.

Mr Dalrymple continued to enumerate some of the ways in which his aunt was becoming inexorably indebted to him. Mary, who had largely escaped their guest's notice, could not resist a question.

'Are you equally indispensable to your cousin, Lady Sarah, Mr Dalrymple?'

The gentleman appeared startled. He sat back in his chair quite suddenly and his brightness of tone abated. Indeed, he sounded rather saddened. 'My cousin is quite an independent young woman, Miss Bennet. I confess that my usefulness to her is rather limited.'

Mary could not help but feel his sadness was rooted in a base desire to help himself, rather than any inadequacy he felt on behalf of his cousin.

After luncheon Dalrymple requested a tour of the garden. Kitty gladly complied while Mary begged to be excused. She wanted nothing more than time alone with her thoughts and a good book. The family were gathered before the long windows in the drawing room, which looked over the major part of the garden. The exploring couple had barely ventured twenty yards into the garden before Mrs Bennet exclaimed. 'My, what a charming man. Mr Dalrymple is a great addition to our circle. There are too few young men. How I miss the regiment. Meryton is far too quiet without the militia.'

'Mrs Bennet, I would remind you that the regiment caused us a good deal of heartache. I, for one, am delighted they have pulled out.'

'How can you say so, Mr Bennet? Why dear Wickham would never have married Lydia if the regiment had not come to Meryton.'

Her husband passed a hand across his brow. 'Just so. You hit the bullseye squarely, my dear.'

'I see a little of Wickham in Mr Dalrymple's mode of address. No regimentals, but he presents very smart indeed.'

'Lord save us, another Wickham will finish me off. I am not by disposition nervous, Mrs Bennet, but I beseech you to desist with talk of our son-in-law and the regiment.'

Mary had been searching for her novel throughout her parents' exchange and triumphantly produced the volume from behind a cushion. 'That Mr Dalrymple puts one in mind of Wickham is bad enough. But at times during lunch it was as though we were listening to Mr Collins. Substitute Countess Glendinning for Lady Catherine de Burgh and the picture is complete.' She saw a look of amused recognition on her father's face and smiled with pleasure that she had entertained him.

Her mother was hot in their guest's defence. 'How can you say so, Mary? Mr Collins, name is a tinder to my nerves. Mr Dalrymple is everything amiable. Kitty has certainly attracted his attention. She could do much worse than marry a man with connexions and ambition.'

Mr Bennet sighed heavily. 'My dear, let us speak no more of marriage. Mr Dalrymple is barely known to us. We know nothing of his background and little of his character.'

Mrs Bennet turned her attention to Mary.

'Your father may not wish to speak of marriage, but he cannot deny that there are two eligible gentlemen nearby and our Kitty is certain to choose one of them.' Her eyes travelled the length of Mary's old muslin gown. 'I've a mind to get you something new, Mary. Ha, what a triumph over Lady Lucas if you were to carry off the suitor Kitty rejects.'

Mary clasped her novel to her bosom and hurried from the room.

Kitty's conversation over the following few days bore several references to Mr Dalrymple. She looked happier than she had been since her last visit to her elder sisters in Derbyshire, many months prior. Unhappily, she was encouraged by her mother to think of Mr Dalrymple as an eligible marriage prospect. His manners, address, raiment and prospects – though the latter were largely unknown – were eagerly dissected by the lady and held up for inspection. Aunt Philips constituted an audience on one such occasion and lost no time conveying every detail to Meryton. As was her habit, some exaggeration of the gentleman's interest in Kitty ensured that their names were linked in drawing-room conversations in very short order.

19

A week later, as Mary walked through the anteroom between Cuthbert Park's salon and library, she heard the unmistakably vibrant tones of Lady Sandalford.

'I simply bid you to beware, Sebastian. I believe you to be sensible, but I beg that you follow pure good sense in your instinct and heart. Your mother's plans give only the appearance of sense, but are sure to end in tears.'

Sebastian's reply was inaudible. Mary held her breath; panicked that one of them might cross the threshold and discover her apparently eavesdropping. As soon as the low rumble of Mr Montagu's voice ceased, she rapped sharply on the door and entered.

Lady Sandalford turned to greet Mary with no trace of the seriousness her words had suggested just moments before. 'Miss Bennet. Now this is a pleasant surprise! How fare you, my dear?'

'Very well, thank you, Lady Sandalford. I hope I find you similarly well?'

'My dear, I am never ill. I know that is quite unladylike in me but there it is and I cannot help it!'

Mary smiled. 'I'm very glad to hear you say so. My mother suffers dreadfully from her nerves, but my sisters and I find ourselves plagued with good health in general.'

Mr Montagu was perched against the desk with folded arms, smiling with delight.

'Ladies, I am humbled to be amongst Amazons. I fear the attractions of our library can be as nothing to two such Dianas. Would you rather be hunting or some such athletic pursuit?'

'Foolish boy,' Lady Sandalford admonished, 'a lady cannot present the truth to society. No, we must be perceived as gentle weaklings with no thought greater than our drawing or stitchery.'

Mr Montagu crowed. 'My dear aunt, no one who met you would believe such nonsense. Now Miss Bennet here is a trifle more successful, by dint of retreating into the background whenever possible, but she also fails at the first inspection. Just look at the wonders she has achieved here.' He swung an arm to indicate the piles of books stacked in every free space in the library. 'I shall have plenty of space for my books, which must surely arrive soon, and realise a tidy sum for all of these.'

Lady Sandalford seated herself behind the wide, old desk, looking very regal. 'You are both to be congratulated. Now, will you press me into service? For if you do not, I shall be forced to endure another round of Prunella's picnic tales.'

The three worked together in harmony. Initially Mary felt intimidated in directing Lady Sandalford, but was soon put at her ease. The work in the library was coming to a swift end. Mary had decided to push the fact to the back of her mind. Having taken Mr Montagu's advice to heart, she now took great care in her conversations with Mrs Montagu and was rewarded with more comfortable relations, though genuine warmth felt a distance yet to be travelled.

Tea in Lady Sandalford's company gained an air of festivity. Her fondness for her nephew was transparent. She both teased him and listened carefully to him. Relations with her sister-in-law were cordial. The lady also enjoyed teasing Mrs Montagu by leading her through a verbal maze; though her object did not always notice the fact. Mary noted an underlying tension between the two ladies at times. A sharp word here or a hard stare there, particularly from Mrs Montagu, occasionally interrupted the gentle flow of conversation.

At length Lady Sandalford clapped her hands: 'I have decided to throw a little party. Nothing too grand, though we might manage some dances.'

'Splendid,' approved Mrs Montagu, 'whom shall you invite?' She wriggled forward in her chair with eager anticipation.

'The neighbouring estate owners, of course, and the usual families. I must ask that nice Major Luckington and his wife, and Lord Drummond with his daughters.'

'Countess Glendinning?' enquired Mrs Montagu.

The corners of Lady Sandalford's mouth turned down. 'I'd rather not, but she does have that young relation staying and we are always short of gentlemen.'

Mr Montagu enquired. 'Are you fond of dancing, Miss Bennet?'

Mary jumped slightly at his address. 'I do enjoy it, though I rarely have the opportunity for many partners.' She looked away, wishing she had not divulged her lack of popularity.

'Then you must promise to save me a dance,' he indicated his boots, 'though I give you fair warning that I am a clumsy oaf.'

Mary flushed. 'I am sure that you are not, sir. I shall try not to step in your way.'

Lady Sandalford rose, stating her need to depart. She offered Mary a lift home in her carriage, which was taken up with pleasure as a shower threatened the previously bright day.

When they reached Longbourn, Lady Sandalford stepped down to invite the Bennets to her party in person. Mrs Bennet lost no time in accepting. Mary escorted Lady Sandalford out to her carriage, thanking her for her kindnesses.

'Think nothing of it, my dear. I hope to see a good deal more of you in future.'

In the parlour, Mrs Bennet's spirits were high. She was so much moved as to place her hands on her daughter's shoulders. 'I am very pleased with you, Mary. Lady Sandalford would like as not have invited us, but to honour us with a personal invitation can only be attributed to her liking you.'

Mary glowed with pride. It was rare to be in her mother's good books. Kitty enquired if Mr Dalrymple would attend the dance. Still smiling, Mary assured her. 'Lady Glendinning's party are to be invited.'

Kitty's eyes shone. 'Tomorrow we must see what can be done about gowns. Everything will need a good shake out.'

20

M r Blain closed the door between his shop and his home, then craned his neck to see what his wife might have in mind for his dinner. A small sigh of satisfaction escaped his moistened lips as he saw her expert fingers crimping the edge of a pie.

'A good day's business, my dear. Most satisfactional.'

Mrs Blain dusted her hands on her large apron and delivered the pie to the black oven in the wall.

'It was indeed, Mr Blain. An' no prizes for guessin' as to the means of it.'

'You are right there. Lady Sandalford's party. Pity she lives too far away for regular trade.'

'Well, yes, Lady Sandalford in a manner of speakin'. But I meant young Mr Montagu. Without him, his aunt wouldn't be inviting Meryton folk to her party.'

Mr Blain settled himself into his old chair, which bore the indents of his plump body. The worn covering was an embarrassment to Mrs Blain, given their profession in the drapery and haberdashery business, but Mr Blain was firm on this one matter and would brook no change.

'I imagine all the mothers and daughters are setting their sights on the young gentleman?' He settled back with his hands folded over his belly in anticipation of a tale.

'You never saw the like of it since Mr Bingley came.' Mrs Blain tapped her forehead. 'No, come to think of it, they're in more of a taking this time. Lady Lucas has Maria and now Georgina to marry off and you can see she's determined to best Mrs Bennet this time.'

'That Maria's a pretty one. I'll wager she's a fair match for Kitty Bennet. They must be of an age.'

'Save your money, Blain.' His wife clattered cutlery onto the scrubbed pine table and eased onto a chair to arrange the pieces. 'Mrs Bennet's been boasting of Kitty's attractions all over the street and her sister, Mrs Philips, if you please, has been saying Countess Glendinning's nephew is dangling after the girl.' She turned and pointed a spoon at her husband with a sly smile. 'Say what you like about her, but Mrs Bennet has married off three. I'd not put it past her to marry off Kitty to young Montagu.'

The pleasant aroma of baking pigeon wafted past Mr Blain's nose. He sighed with pleasure.

'Well, and happy I'd be for them. She's a nice girl is young Catherine Bennet, now she's growed up some.'

Mrs Blain checked on her pie and turned back to her husband.

'Don't spring the horses yet, my dear. Mrs Montagu has come over all hoity-toity since her son came back. She came in for some lace gloves today. "Mrs Blain," she says to me, "if I am to continue to patronise your establishment, there will need to be greater quantities of silk and satin. We're moving in high circles" – she said it overloud so anyone could hear – "and I simply must have the very best."' Mrs Blain banged the pickles on the table. 'Could have swiped her, I could.'

'Now, dearest,' Mr Blain leaned forward giving a little sideways wave of his hand. 'Don't be taking on so. We shall rearrange the stock and she won't know the difference. We will get rid of some old stock and I'll charge her two shillings extra for each yard too.'

Mrs Blain whooped and bent over laughing.

'Was there ever a man like you? You never would.'

'I would and I will. If she wants to be like that, my dear, so we shall serve. Now what else did we sell today that I didn't see?'

'Really, Blain, how would I know what you didn't see? I shall only tell you the gentry fripperies else the pie will burn.' Mrs Blain proceeded to count off the various items on her still floury fingers. 'Maria Lucas – a green brocade shawl and matching hair ribbons. Georgina Lucas – shoe rosettes and some picot lace to change the neck of her gown. Mrs Lucas – purple silk for a turban. Suited her. Mrs Bennet – new long white gloves.'

She stood up to retrieve the pie, which had turned the perfect golden tan.

'Lovely, my dear,' said Mr Blain as he took his seat at the head of the table.

Mrs Blain stabbed her large kitchen knife into the piecrust, allowing some of the steam to escape. She stood there with her hand balanced on the knife.

'Now where was I? Oh yes. Kitty Bennet, she was another one for rosette ribbon and a fancy hair comb to go with that pale pink she ordered earlier in the year. Who else? Ah, Mary Bennet. She had new gloves too and some expensive gauze ribbon. Her mother said no, but Mary reminded her that she hadn't had a new assembly dress this year. More's the pity for us.' She plunged her knife into the pie. 'She'll be a spinster, no doubt. Shame that girl hasn't troubled with her looks. She's the one who's got a foot in the door at Cuthbert Park.'

21

Mary found herself looking forward to Lady Sandalford's party with greater regularity and enthusiasm than she normally felt for such events. The prospect of dancing with Mr Montagu, she told herself, was pleasant, but by no means her chief reason for anticipation. She reasoned that the opportunity to see Lady Sandalford in her home would be most interesting.

Kitty entertained no such illusions. As the sisters sat in an arbour in the garden embroidering new reticules, she said, 'I do hope that Mr Dalrymple will ask me to dance more than once, Mary, for that will mean he has singled me out for his favour.'

Mary's face showed some alarm. All the talk of Mr Dalrymple had whipped up high expectations based on a single visit.

'Kitty, I would hope that Mr Dalrymple would consider it improper to subject you to such notice as would cause tongues to wag. He is very nearly a stranger to us all.'

Kitty scowled. 'We have met him twice, Mary. Surely he may be considered known to us? You are always so reproving.'

Mary grimaced. 'You forget that Lydia's hoydenish ways and her foolish elopement brought us to uncomfortable notice. I hope that you know better.'

'Would you stand up for two dances with Mr Montagu?' Kitty returned with a peevish edge.

'I do not suppose that is very likely. He was kind enough to engage a dance from me, but then he's all gratitude and politeness.' Mary's face, so often passive, if not severe, had gained a softness of expression.

'But if he asked you, would you say yes?'

'I don't know. I suppose so, but it is all fruitless conjecture.' Mary flung down her work. Really, her sister was always so provoking with her constant questions.

'Perhaps.' Kitty picked up her sister's work to examine it. 'Well then, we both have something to look forward to between now and the dance. Shall we practise our steps in the hall? There were so few assemblies during the dreadful winter weather that I feel we have forgotten all but the country dances.'

They hurried to put away their sewing and entered the house to practise, taking turns for the gentleman's part and with no small degree of laughter, until Mrs Bennet complained bitterly of the headache.

The late Lord Sandalford's fondness for all forms of gaming meant that he had devoted little time to his estates. His nickname, Lucky, was complete to a shade; so though rarely present, he lavished the best upon his home and land, appointing a fine agent. The couple had spent so much time in London that very few people were acquainted with the sprawling Palladian building at Clovisford. Being some fifteen miles from Meryton and with only a village nearby, neighbours were scarce.

The park was unusually flat, allowing a vista of the house from afar. The Bennets' carriage awaited those ahead, disgorging their passengers under the wide porte cochére. The family saw a pedimented central entrance flanked by two broad wings with deep windows glowing golden in the setting sun. A pair of footmen bearing flaming torches taller than a man flanked the grand entrance, which was wide enough for four ladies' skirts to pass through without touching. A majordomo announced the guests.

'This is more like a grand ball than a small party,' whispered Kitty.

Lady Sandalford received her guests in the assured manner of a well-versed London hostess. 'Good evening, Mr and Mrs Bennet. I am delighted to see you here.'

Mr Bennet bowed over her hand. 'We are delighted to be here, Lady Sandalford.'

Her ladyship turned to the sisters. 'Now, Mary and Catherine, I trust you will be dancing this evening?'

Both young ladies nodded. Kitty added. 'We have been practising.'

Lady Sandalford gave an amused look as Mary directed a fierce frown toward her sister. 'Then we shall make sure we find you plenty of young gentlemen to put through their paces.'

To the left of the impressive hallway a card room led to the supper room. To the right, a richly carpeted with-drawing room was abuzz with arriving guests mingling in small groups between several seating arrangements. Further on lay the ballroom. In the fading light, the soft glow of fresh-lit candle sconces shimmered in a phalanx of mirrors around the eau de nil walls. At the far end, a quartet busily arranged their music sheets. Beyond the tall windows night began to steadily claim the multiple colours of sunset. Guests filtered into the room, the grandeur causing them to speak softly at first, as though in a place of worship, before the claims of an old acquaintance espied across the room resulted in cries of greeting.

The musicians commenced with a gentle air. Georgina Lucas bounced ahead of her parents to greet Kitty, her excitement threatening to topple her curls.

'Isn't it vast? Look at those mirrors; there must be dozens. Lord, I can't wait for the dancing to start. Mama made me wear Charlotte's old slippers, which are far too large, but I don't care a fig!'

'Well, you look very well in them, dear,' Mrs Bennet offered kindly.

Lord Drummond approached with the Honourable Sylvia and Imogen, the former in palest blue satin and the latter in modest cream. Heads turned in Sylvia's direction, yet she appeared not to notice in the least that she was the most beautiful young lady in the room. She linked her arm through Mary's and drew her aside to impart her confidences. 'How glad I am to see you again, Miss Bennet. Of the three volumes you recommended to me I have already read two. They are so superior to the works I have been reading lately. Tell me, what are you reading now?'

Mary stammered her reply, unused as she was to being the target of unaffected friendship by beautiful heiresses. 'I am reading Lord Byron. Please do call me Mary.'

'Only if you will call me Sylvia.'

The bargain sealed, they launched into a discussion of books. Georgina Lucas and the Honourable Imogen, both new to society, recognised a friend in each other instantly. They stood near the curtains vying to exclaim the wonders of their surroundings, with no detail escaping their eagle-eyed notice.

The older gentlemen decided that their duties were sufficiently discharged to adjourn to the card room, Lord Drummond pausing just long enough to make a short plea to Mrs Bennet and Lady Lucas to keep a weather eye on his daughters. A more thoughtful father might have searched a little wider to select his chaperone, but Lord Drummond was a man without fear and in favour of a good hand.

Kitty drifted further into the room, ostensibly in search of company, but in truth hoping to catch a glimpse of Mr Dalrymple. The wish was soon granted. Mr Dalrymple could be seen ushering his aunt and bored cousin to seats in the withdrawing room. They made a distinguished group. Presently he left them and came upon Kitty.

'Miss Bennet.' He directed a brief look over his shoulder in the direction from which he had come. 'I am delighted to see you. I am just on my way to procure refreshment for my aunt.' Then *sotto voce*: 'I hope that I may depend on you for a dance later.'

Kitty dimpled. 'I may always be depended on to dance, Mr Dalrymple, for it is one of my chief pleasures.'

'How I should like to know the others,' he responded in a low voice.

Kitty laughed, which attracted the notice of Lady Sarah. Shock registered briefly upon her cold features, followed by a venomous looked aimed at Kitty. Before she could be sure of the look, Lady Sarah's face returned to its usual cold mask. Kitty instinctively turned back to Mr Dalrymple but he had disappeared, no doubt in search of his aunt's refreshment.

Drawn by the music, the Montagus made their way toward the Bennet and Lucas group. The ladies quickly engaged in a discussion of friends who had the misfortune to be absent. Mr Montagu gravitated towards Mary and Sylvia. Mary felt unaccountably shy and in consequence, mute, beyond a commonplace greeting. Sylvia conversed with innate ease as though she had known them both all her life. Mary found her so sympathetic and likeable a character that she could not envy Sylvia her beauty, social style or fortune. However, she felt an unfamiliar pang of jealousy when Mr Montagu engaged Sylvia to dance later in the evening. She stared down at her slippers, feeling superfluous but unable to walk away without explanation. Mr Montagu bent down to engage her eye from his lofty height. 'I have not forgotten your promise to dance, Miss Bennet. Do not think I shall release you from it.'

Mary could not help a small smile.

In his satin knee breeches, buckled shoes and silk waistcoat, she saw him anew. No longer the scholarly landowner, but a gentleman in a ballroom. She could not but approve his refined taste in eschewing the absurdities and affectations of male attire. 'Indeed, sir, I have taken care to pad my slippers, following your warning.'

He threw back his head and laughed. 'I suppose I brought that upon myself. I shall mince about as daintily as possible, ladies.'

'Oh, pray, sir, do not. We young ladies wear our bruised feet as badges of honour. We have little else to complain about,' Sylvia said with mock solemnity.

At a stroke Mary felt once more among friends.

'I see that one way or another, you two ladies will have me in the wrong. I beg you will both be merciful.'

Mary considered. 'I do believe that Lady Sarah would be disinterested to perfection. You must press your case with her.'

Sylvia chimed in. 'Oh, you must, for I believe she is too high in the instep for above half the company here and must therefore have a dearth of partners.'

Lady Sandalford stood near the double doors surveying her ballroom. Everywhere, guests were enjoying themselves. The musicians played well and the house, glowing in the light of one hundred candles, showed to great advantage. Major and Mrs Luckington paused to congratulate her Ladyship on the success of the party.

She replied with a trace of sadness.

'It is overdue. My late husband was very fond of London's amusements and saw society too infrequently in the country. I am conscious that the lack of engagement may have been taken for rudeness.'

'Not on our part, we assure you. It is a pleasure to see the young people enjoying themselves,' said Mrs Luckington.

Lady Sandalford turned to regard the throng. 'Dear Sebastian is making an effort to speak to as many guests as possible, though he only looks truly relaxed when talking to Sylvia Drummond and Mary Bennet. The three are clearly becoming friends. I wonder what his mother will make of that.'

'Might we see a budding romance?' Mrs Luckington wondered aloud.

Her ladyship's reply was thoughtful. 'For my own part, I consider that love which begins in friendship exceeds all of the choices. That said, I see only friendship in Sylvia's manner. Sylvia Drummond needs but a season in London to have her choice of titled gentlemen. Lord Drummond has let the matter lay for too long without a wife to promote the cause. I must find a moment to speak with him about it in the near future, lest Sylvia strays too near the age where her single state invites speculation.'

Mr Montagu claimed his dance. Mary took his hand nervously. He smiled down at her. 'Shall we? I thought a country dance would allow me a margin of error.'

She saw Kitty in her pretty pink gown at the end of the line with Mr Dalrymple, her face glowing with animation. Then there was no time for distraction as the music commenced. How glad she was of the practice with Kitty. Mr Montagu moved surprisingly well for a tall man, even if a few of his steps were a trifle errant. As he returned down the line to her he said:

'I do believe I trod on Mrs Luckington's toes, but she was too kind to notice.'

'Mrs Luckington is the kindest of women. You were fortunate that it wasn't Mrs Gray. Her severity is well known.'

'Then I'm glad to have escaped. I believe that your censure would wound me most.'

'I, sir?' Mary looked into his eyes in surprise. It was all she could manage to complete the simple manoeuvre of the dance.

'Yes. Your good opinion, I suspect, is not easily won. As such, it is a greater prize. I would not care to lose such a prize.'

Mary decided he was teasing her and replied in kindred spirit, though spoke in truth. 'That is most flattering, sir. But you should rest easy. You do have my humble good opinion and I believe I have already told you that I am not in the habit of changing my mind.'

'Constancy in a female is a rare quality, Miss Bennet. Perhaps that is one of the reasons I find conversation so easy with you.'

Mary blushed deeply. She was spared an answer by a change of partner. Yet her eyes strayed down the line to Mr Montagu several times. As he danced with Sylvia later, she found herself stealing glances towards them. Sylvia's height paired comfortably with that of her partner. With her undeniable beauty and grace, the picture before Mary was striking in its perfection. She looked down at her old white gown, unremarkable in style and looking tired against her new gloves. How she wished she had taken up Mama's offer of a new gown this year. A pang of something deeper than regret caught in her throat. She turned away from the scene, feeling once more a distant third.

'They make an attractive pair, do they not?' said Mrs Montagu.

Mary felt a small barb in her bosom.

'I . . . I am no judge, ma'am.'

'I am excessively fond of Sylvia. She possesses all of the refinements one could hope for in a young lady.'

Mrs Montagu directed a triumphant look at Mary.

Mary levelled her chin and returned the look with a cool composure she could not feel.

'Indeed, she is a most worthy companion.'

'Your sister danced most enthusiastically with Mr Dalrymple.'

Mary snapped, 'My sister has great enthusiasm for dancing. She is happy with all of her partners.'

'Just so. *She* is in great demand. Have *you* engaged many partners?'

'I doubt that I shall dance as often as my sister, Mrs Montagu.'

At that moment Mr Dalrymple bowed before her.

'Miss Bennet, may I have the honour?'

'With pleasure, sir.' Mary regarded her tormentor with exaggerated politeness.

'Pray excuse me, Mrs Montagu, I do so enjoy the dance.'

He led her away. 'Forgive me, Miss Bennet, but I overheard Mrs Montagu speaking.'

Mary bowed her head as tears threatened.

'Then I must thank you for rescuing me, but please do not feel that you must dance with me.'

For the first time, Mary heard a trace of sincerity in his response.

'Come, Miss Bennet, why would I not wish to dance with you?'

'I am not gay like my sister, sir.'

'One must sample more than one dish to enjoy the buffet, Miss Bennet. Let us have no more of this moping talk and enjoy ourselves.'

To her surprise, Mary did enjoy herself. Mr Dalrymple proved an excellent partner. By suppertime she had been engaged to dance twice more and had danced almost as often as Kitty.

*

'Mr Bennet, come quick.'

As Mr Bennet emerged from the card room his wife beckoned to him energetically. Her voice, elevated as always when excited, punctured the conversations of those standing nearby.

'You will not credit it, my dear. Mary has stood up four times! Why, she has almost equalled Kitty.'

'Well, that is splendid, Mary, I would stand up with you myself if I were a young man. Now shall we partake of supper?'

He led his wife forcibly away before she could do further damage.

Kitty shot her sister a look of sympathy and linked arms.

'Pay Mama no attention. She is fond of talking nonsense.'

Mary's reply was laced with heartfelt misery.

'I wish it did not matter what she thought. Yet she so often reminds me by one means or another that my sisters are more beautiful, that I find the wound is open.'

'Beauty is in the eye of the beholder and you have attracted several partners this evening.'

'Mr Dalrymple danced with me to spite Mrs Montagu's unkind words.'

'Did he? Then I esteem him even more highly.' Kitty's eyes glowed.

'I must admit that he is an excellent partner and I was grateful for his intervention. Perhaps I have misjudged him.'

'I feel sure you must have. For my part, I cannot fault him.'

Discussion ceased as Georgina and Imogen, rendered to foolish giggles by an excess of sugary negus, halted in their perambulations. Kitty enquired, 'Have you both enjoyed yourselves?'

'Oh yes,' they chorused. 'We have been dancing—' began Imogen.

'Though mostly with each other,' finished Georgina.

'Never mind, you will soon become better known and there will be plenty of assemblies to come,' Kitty said.

Georgina laughed. 'Oh we don't mind. Some of them are frightfully old. I had hoped that Mr Dalrymple would partner me but he was positively rude.'

'Surely not,' Mary rejoined.

'Oh, yes,' said Imogen. 'When we hinted, he said that he didn't dance with schoolroom chits. Luckily for us, Mr Montagu took pity on us both.'

After supper, Mr Dalrymple led Sylvia in the Boulanger. His cousin had yet to dance with any gentleman. So cool was her demeanour that a gentleman could be set down with a single look. At last she offered her hand to her cousin for a Minuet. They conversed with some concentration during the dance and the lady was seen to look quite animated.

Mr Montagu approached Mary and bowed.

'Would you consider it improper to dance with me a second time, Miss Bennet?'

She flushed, but the corners of her mouth began to turn upward.

'Not improper, no. But the gossips do pray on such actions.'

'I am prepared to risk it. It is just a dance, but I would not wish to embarrass you.' His face was grave. She smiled fully now and bestowed her hand in his.

'I believe that I care to dance more than I care for the tattle of gossips.'

From opposite sides of the ballroom, two mothers looked on in disbelief. Their expressions, however, differed. Mrs Bennet, at first seeming to scarce credit the evidence of her own eyes, broke into the most comical expression. Her lips formed a circle fit for a decanter stopper and her eyes popped. She recovered sufficiently to crow her delight to Lady Lucas. Mrs Montagu stalked out of the room, her face pinched with anger. Lady Sandalford observed her sister-in-law and the cause of her anger. Under her breath she said,

'And so be it. The die is cast.'

22

Unable to bear her mother's questions and comments regarding Mr Montagu with equanimity, Mary escaped for a walk along Honeycombe Lane. Her mother's frequent references over the past two days had interfered with her own pleasurable recollections, which she now indulged with satisfaction. On returning to Longbourn, Mary found Mr Dalrymple taking his leave.

Kitty whispered to her, 'I must speak with you.'

A swift glance at Kitty's face suggested that this would not be a good occasion to excite their mother's attention. Mary suggested,

'The garden is looking lovely. Shall we pick some blooms, Kitty?'

With a few roses and some greenery hastily placed in their baskets, the pair slipped to a quiet corner of the garden.

'Now, tell me, Kitty, what is so urgent?'

'Nothing is urgent. But I simply must speak to someone or I shall burst. I know that we are different, Mary, but we only have each other at home. It is not the same to write to Jane or Elizabeth. Letters take too long and are not the same as a conversation at all.'

'I cannot promise to be as useful as our older sisters, but of course you can confide in me.'

'It is Mr Dalrymple. He is the most exciting gentleman to come into our lives since Bingley came to Netherfield.' Mary felt that there was a world of difference between Mr Dalrymple and Bingley, but kept her feelings contained. Kitty continued. 'I was disappointed that he spoke so little to me at Lady Sandalford's dance. But when he called this afternoon he told me how much he had wanted to dance with me again, but wished to save me from gossip. Oh, Mary, I do believe that he is a good man.'

'I must admit that he was kind to me, Kitty, but we do not know him well. His background is little known to us or his true circumstances. Please do not think me unfeeling or harsh. I know you think me a scold, but I believe that some caution is required.'

'But, Mary, what if his feelings are strong? We do not know how long he may be visiting his aunt. It cannot be an enjoyable visit with his cousin being so unpleasant.'

Kitty shredded a rose in her agitation. Mary's consternation grew. Kitty's romantic nature had led to rash behaviour in the past, when the garrison were quartered at Meryton. She spoke with a calmness that belied her growing disquiet.

'I agree, Lady Sarah would make anyone wish to be at a distance. But if indeed he should develop feelings for you, Kitty dear, then he will show patience if he is truly a good man. A gentleman who is constant in his feelings proves his real worth.'

Kitty sighed. 'You are right. My feelings are so muddled with excitement that I cannot think straight.'

'Time is on your side, Kitty. You are not past redemption like me. Take the time to make sure Mr Dalrymple is worthy.'

'Dear, dear Mary, you have been so helpful. I do not think Jane would have counselled any better. How wonderful it would be to be married and no longer at the mercy of Mama's caprice.' Kitty broke off. Mary's face was filled with dismay. 'No, surely, Mary, you do not believe that you must remain alone at Longbourn? You cannot really think as you say, that you are past marriageable age?'

'But it is true, Kitty. I may still be within the respectable limits of age, but look at me. I am plain and I do not possess your gaiety or Jane's amenable nature or Lizzy's wit.' Her voice trailed off in misery for a moment, but then she spoke up with determination. 'I enjoy books and I have no time for fools. There could be few lesser recommendations in a wife for a gentleman.'

'This is so much nonsense. Come, you have a taste for the negative; that is your problem. Of late you have improved in looks when you have made some effort. As to the penchant for books, surely you can hide this side to your nature?'

'That's just the problem!' Mary cried. 'I cannot; nay, I will not give a false perception.'

The sisters sat in silence. At length Kitty spoke.

'I believe that there is one gentleman who would not care a fig about your bookish ways. It seems to me that he likes you for yourself.'

Mary put her flower basket at her feet and began to pleat her gown with her fingertips. 'You speak of Mr Montagu.'

'I do. The same Mr Montagu who singled out you alone for two dances at Lady Sandalford's home.'

'It would not do to place too much dependence upon it. He might well have asked Sylvia and she would have been perfectly correct to refuse.' Mary's sigh rippled through her slight body. 'Mr Montagu is handsome and wealthy. He can marry as he pleases. Besides, his mother disapproves of me.'

'Mr Montagu may be handsome in your eyes, Mary, but perhaps not to everyone. He is quite angular, you know, and a little awkward. He converses easily with you, but one can tell he is rather shy.' Kitty plucked at a geranium. 'As to his mother, what does she signify if he cares for you?'

Mary regarded her sister with some incredulity.

'Mrs Montagu lives with her son. When he marries she will be present in a house where she has held charge all of her adult life. Pray, imagine the impossibility of such a life for a bride held in contempt.' Mary gathered up her basket, making an angry snatch at a rose, pricking herself in the act. 'Oh, hateful thing.' Tears sprang to her eyes. She felt Kitty's eyes upon her and felt the sting of her words, which followed.

'So you have given the matter considerable thought, I see.'

23

Mary and Catherine were a posy of contrasts. Had two sisters more similar in nature remained at Longbourn they may have provided one another with greater understanding and solace. The sisters enjoyed familial fondness and a tolerance born of knowing one another all their lives, yet each felt some disappointment that they struggled to bridge the gap in understanding. Of late, both had felt gratitude for a well-placed word from the other and each felt that she must hold some responsibility for failing to fully comprehend her sister's nature.

For her part, Mary wished that she had been able to unburden her feelings about Mr Montagu to Kitty. How dearly she desired to relieve herself of her emotions as Kitty had done. Yet her habitual reticence ruled. She had masked her hopes with contrary comments to her sister, but Mary's heart raced when she thought of the bliss to be had in a marriage to Mr Montagu. When he spoke to her she felt a lightness through her whole being and a smile hovering at the corners of her lips. To discuss books and ideas with him was a joy she had never anticipated in any person other than her father. Mr Montagu's wealth and prospects put him beyond her reach. Mary found that he occupied her mind even as she determined to think of something else. Anticipation of a visit to Cuthbert Park was all pleasure: thoughts of the end of her task there, pure torment.

Painful as the end might be, Mary refused to alter the rhythm of her visits to prolong the task. Thus she arrived at her normal time a few days after the events at Lady Sandalford's party. She loitered a while in the park, feeling the sunshine on her face and anticipating the prospect of her diminishing task as much as she contemplated the lake shimmering before her eyes. Reluctantly Mary turned to the house. As spring had given way to summer, her appreciation of the house and the park had grown. The library remained her favourite room, but now it felt like a special part of the whole, rather than a world unique in itself. Preoccupied with her thoughts, Mary greeted Peters and began her work in an abstracted manner. She barely noticed Mr Montagu entering the library.

'You are as dependable as any timepiece, Miss Bennet. It is a comfort to know that I may find you here.'

Startled by the object of her thoughts, Mary answered in a crisp, defensive manner. 'Comfort is an odd choice of word, Mr Montagu. I wonder at your meaning.'

'Forgive me, I am a curs'd fool with words. I meant only to let you know how glad I always am to see you here.'

She softened in an instant.

'Then that is a fine compliment, and I thank you.'

Mr Montagu made a business of shuffling a few papers on the desk, then paced restlessly before the window. Mary's eyes followed his movements.

'Does something trouble you, sir?'

'No. Oh, bother it, yes. I cannot be other than transparent with you, Miss Bennet. Otherwise does not feel at all right.' He halted and gave her a piercing look. 'But pay me no heed. Those matters which weigh on my mind are of no true consequence and show ill upon my character, for they have their roots in vanity.'

Mary could not prevent a burst of laughter.

'Mr Montagu, I know of many gentlemen who may be subject to the caprice of vanity, but let me assure you that you are not among their number.'

He smiled, melting the severity of his expression.

'But you are wrong. I am a sad fraud.'

'I do not believe you.'

'Then come sit with me, and I will confess all.'

They sat opposite one another in the fireside chairs. Mr Montagu proceeded to tell a tale bereft of guilt. He had slowly begun to take a grasp of the estate. He knew each tenant and had familiarised himself with the problems and potential of each farm in turn. He had formed a schedule of repairs, sacked the lazy former agent and was engaged in interviews for a new one. The accounts were nearly up-to-date. Mary began to wonder how she might possibly help. Eyes raised to his own, she said,

'Mr Montagu, your distress is clear, yet you set before me a charter of success. Do you perhaps set your expectations too high?'

He looked at her as sheepish as a lad caught chasing a cat, and her heart seemed to turn in her breast.

'Perhaps you are right when you set it out so. But I feel like my father's son amongst men and not like the master.'

'Please, tell me more.' She leaned forward, all eagerness to help.

'Do I sound foolish? I know that you will tell me truly.' His look was direct. 'Everyone I speak with here knows their path. They have all grown up on the estate and often their forebears before them. I am always at a disadvantage because they know how things go on, while I am merely learning. It is very difficult to behave as the master when you are the pupil.'

That disconcerting, direct look again. He seemed to look into her soul. Mary struggled to remain impassive.

'Do I behave like a child, Miss Bennet, or is there a means to correct my concerns? I beg you to answer me in your own sensible, considered way.'

Mary frowned. 'I believe that your concerns are only natural and must occur in varying degrees to all gentlemen who inherit land or property.'

'Then I am not being childish?'

'No.' Her lips twitched up at the corners as he sagged a little in relief.

'Then I am in need of a plan to right the matter.'

Mary issued a gentle laugh.

'You are impatient, sir. I feel sure that in time the matter will right itself.'

'If I am impatient, Miss Bennet, it is with some cause. I desire to order my present, the better to construct my future.'

His determination was evident in the tightening of arm muscles visible through his well-fitted coat.

The answer came to Mary as surely as if it had been delivered in a note.

'Then, that is where you must begin.'

'With the future?' His face registered both interest and confusion.

'Decidedly yes. In my opinion, only time and fair management will bring you the respect of those who work in your employ. You cannot be your father, therefore you must be yourself. Create the Cuthbert Park of Sebastian Montagu.'

'Miss Bennet, you are a wonder among women.' He leaned forward, all attention. 'Have you any thoughts on how I might create this vision?'

Mary bowed her head demurely.

'It is not for me to tell you your heart's desire or how to go on. But I do believe that you will identify a new interest that will also benefit the estate.'

Mr Montagu rose from his chair and grasped Mary's delicate fingers, pulling her to her feet. He remained possessed of them, forcing her to look up at his intent blue eyes.

'Have no doubt that I shall create the Cuthbert Park of my wishes, Miss Bennet. As to my heart's desire, I trust that shall be revealed soon enough.'

A polite cough interrupted the silence of the room. Peters announced that tea awaited in the salon. As she passed him, Mary thought she detected a twinkle in Peters' eye. Her confusion mounted. Could Mr Montagu possibly be referring to her? She had no experience of matters of the heart and wished she had conversed with her sisters upon the subject in the past.

Throughout the considerable time allotted to tea at Cuthbert Park, Mrs Montagu spoke almost non-stop about Lady Sandalford's dance. Supper was compared to others she had enjoyed. Music selection gained her approval. Her eagle eye had noted a new Wedgewood epergne and a Chinese rug. Mary sat quietly, outwardly attending whilst fighting a tumult of emotions. Mr Montagu spoke but little. His gaze strayed to Mary several times but revealed nothing. At length he arose and excused himself to speak to his groom.

Mary walked home deep in thought. She almost stepped into the path of a passing dray but was saved by the driver's loud, 'Hoi!' Detouring to the grassy knoll beneath her favourite oak, she sat with her arms wrapped around her knees and lost herself in reverie. When she looked up after what seemed to be a very short time, she was startled to find that the sun had begun to drop in the sky. Arriving home in haste she was halted by the querulous tones of her mother, issued from her dressing room.

'Mary, where have you been? Here I am, meant to be at rest before dinner, but my nerves are frayed. You have no consideration. I lie here worrying every time you go out.'

'I am sorry, Mama. I have been collecting my thoughts and if you knew where my thoughts had been, we would neither of us enjoy any peace.'

Mary hurried on before her mother could scold further. Passing Kitty's room she hesitated, then knocked and entered.

'Mary, I'm glad you are here. Pray, hold this lock of my hair while I pin the other. I am experimenting with a new style. Did you want to borrow something?'

Mary held Kitty's hair aloft in a perfunctory gesture; glad of the opportunity to make herself useful and not look Kitty in the eye.

'I have come to ask your advice, Kitty.'

'My advice? Heavens, there's a first.' Kitty dropped her comb and turned to her sister. 'I see from your face that this is serious. Tell me all.'

Mary instantly began to regret her spontaneous action.

'You must promise me not to breathe a word of what I say to another living soul.'

'I promise.'

'Swear it.'

'I swear. This is exciting. You never have secrets, Mary.'

As Mary recounted the afternoon's events, she found herself making excuses as to how she may have been mistaken, causing Kitty to demand with asperity that she repeat Mr Montagu's exact words. Excited now, Mary complied.

Kitty leapt to her feet and threw her arms around her sister.

'He can only mean one thing, I am sure of it. Mr Montagu means to marry you, Mary. But this is wonderful news, and you know,' she added with generosity, 'it is only right that you should marry first.'

Mary sat down with a bump, the shock writ clear over her features. She went alternatively hot and cold.

'I cannot believe it – though I admit I have wished . . . Do you really think that Mr Montagu cares for me?'

'I do, I do.' Kitty made a mock swoon and laughed. 'I have thought so since the first moment I saw you together.'

Mary groaned. 'But Mrs Montagu will be against our marrying. She does not even regard me as a suitable friend for him.'

'She will become accustomed to you, Mary. You do take a little longer than most people to be understood. Now, never mind Mrs Montagu. Oh, let us dance.'

Kitty tugged Mary's hand and tried to dance her around the room until Mary could not help laughing. As she prepared to hurry away to tidy before dinner, Mary paused at the door.

'Please remember, Kitty, do not breathe a word to anyone; most especially give Mama no cause for suspicion, I beg you.'

Kitty delivered her an impish wink.

24

Mary set the last volume back on the shelf with loving care. Behind her on the desk lay a pile of books for Mr Montagu to consider for sale. Most of the selected books had already been crated in preparation for transport to London dealers. She paused for a while to look through her completed catalogue. So many wonderful volumes. She stood in the centre of the room hugging herself and turning slowly as her eyes swept over every dear bookcase in the library. To think that all of this might be at her disposal. Could such dreams come true? A momentary frown clouded Mary's bare brow as she thought of Mrs Montagu's likely reaction if her son were to marry her. Then she recalled Lady Sandalford, whom she had seen arriving earlier. She was sure of a warm greeting from her Ladyship. That Lady Sandalford could be relied upon to be her ally gave Mary pause for thought. Tea must be served soon. She decided to go to the salon early. It would be easier to converse with Mrs Montagu in the happy company of Lady Sandalford. As she passed into the anteroom, Mary was arrested by a raised voice audible through the closed salon door.

'Nonsense, Arabella. You have it all wrong.'

Mary sat down on the chaise to wait. She had no desire to interrupt a disagreement.

'I may of course be wrong, Prunella dear, but I do not think so. I believe Sebastian's feelings to be engaged and I have little doubt of Miss Bennet returning them.'

'Ha, as to that, I am his mother and a mother knows her child. I have placed Sebastian in the way of superior females of rank and fortune. I grant you, Lady Sarah Glendinning is too high in the instep to suit any man, but the Honourable Sylvia Drummond – now there is a fine young woman. Do you suppose the Bennet chit is anything to compare? Now, I can understand a young man having eyes for the sister. She is a taking little thing, but our Miss Bennet of the library, no. She is bereft of looks or charm. She dresses her hair severe, wears the dullest of gowns and her social discourse is a poor creature. You must know that she offers little conversation beyond books and has the most uncomfortable way of looking at one as she speaks some uncompromising truth.' Mrs Montagu's high-pitched laugh had an hysterical edge. 'Oh, no, I would never countenance such a paltry addition to our family. My Sebastian is no fool. You quite mistake the matter, Arabella, I assure you.'

Mary clasped her hand to her mouth. Her eyes searched wildly for another door, though she knew the only exits were through the servants' passage or the salon. She sat frozen in mute horror as Lady Sandalford responded.

'You are extremely harsh on Mary Bennet, Prunella. I cannot imagine what the girl has done to offend you. It seems to me that you owe her thanks. For my part, I like her. She is refreshing in her lack of artifice. An attractive quality to Sebastian, I imagine.'

Mrs Montagu snapped back. 'How very contrary of you, Arabella. I declare you are quite wrong, but if it were so, I would introduce Sebastian to more females of rank and fortune. I am determined he will make a notable match!'

Lady Sandalford continued in serene tones. 'I would further counsel you to bear in mind that Sylvia Drummond has every attraction to *any* gentleman of great wealth or title.'

'I have seen Sebastian in Sylvia's company and they are always happy together. Their partiality for one another cannot be mistaken. I anticipate an announcement very soon.' Mrs Montagu's shrill voice overflowed with displeasure.

There was some asperity in Lady Sandalford's response.

'They do indeed appear to be friends, but Sylvia can, and I believe will, make a more brilliant match.'

Mrs Montagu spoke with venom,

'I repeat, a mother knows her child. He will marry the Honorable Sylvia Drummond.'

Any remaining conversation was lost to Mary as the sound of footsteps issued from the flagstones in the servants' passageway. Mary leapt up and slid behind the huge antique screen. Peters passed into the library to announce tea and finding her not there, retraced his steps past the screen and into the salon. She simply could not contemplate entering the salon. Rushing into the passage, she passed the kitchen where a footman was collecting the tea tray. Mary hurried on and at last found a door to the courtyard. Wrenching it open, she stumbled into the light and leaned heavily against the rough stone wall, gulping in great draughts of air, then bending forward, feared she might be physically sick. In this attitude she was startled by a voice beside her.

'Are you ill, miss?'

A maid carrying a bunch of fragrant wallflowers appeared before her.

Mary straightened her back with no little effort and drawing a shaky breath, managed to speak with some authority.

'Yes, a little. Pray inform Peters that I am indisposed and have returned home. He may pass on my apologies to Mrs Montagu and her Ladyship.'

'Very well, miss. But should we fetch you a carriage?'

'No, thank you, the walk will do me good.'

With that Mary turned and walked as fast as she could out of the courtyard. When she gained the fields out of sight of the house, she ran. She did not stop running until she reached the oak tree in Honeycombe Lane, whereupon she flung herself on the knoll and sobbed with all the bitterness in her heart, until her eyes were glazed red and her gown damp from the grass.

How cruel life could be, her mind raged. She had opened her heart in a way she had not thought possible, only to hear the mother of the man she had grown to love assassinate both her character and her person. How could someone detest her so thoroughly when she had tried to show a willing nature? It was certain that she could never marry Mr Montagu now, even if he should wish it so. But he could not wish it. She had been a fool and mistaken his kind manner for something of deeper substance. Mrs Montagu had said that Sebastian and Sylvia were happy together and that she expected their engagement to be announced.

She could not bear to dwell on how she might feel if her two friends were to marry. At length she sat and brushed down her gown. Tears sprang afresh as she thought of the empty months and years ahead. She did not think that she could bear the pain. Even now, she contemplated returning to Longbourn with dread. Her misery would certainly become known to Kitty. There was no possibility of hiding her feelings from her sister after confessing her heart's desire. Everything must be done to prevent her parents knowing anything at all about her plight.

Luck was on her side when she slipped through the shrubbery behind the house into the hall. The family were not in evidence. Only Hill was to be found, folding linen pudding cloths. Mary hesitated in the doorway.

'Hill, I am indisposed and will go to my bed. Pray do not expect me to dinner.'

With the familiarity of a servant who had known all the girls in leading strings, Hill replied with a tart tongue. 'I am not surprised you are ill. Your gown is wet through and shocking dirty. What have you been doing?'

'I'm sorry, I tripped and fell quite badly.'

'Head in the clouds as usual, I'll warrant.' The housekeeper peered at Mary closely. She presented an exhausted sight and her complexion looked most peculiar. 'Never mind. Go and strip off that wet gown. I'll be up with a light supper.'

'Oh, thank you, Hill, but I don't want any food.'

'What you want and what you get is two different things.' Her tone became kinder. 'Now you go and get under the covers. A light supper will do you wonders. We'll soon have you right and tight.'

Mary did as she was bid, grateful to have escaped her mother's tongue and the notice of her father or Kitty. Her supper remained untouched save a small dish of tea. Even as she imagined sleep would elude her for ever, Mary fell into the heavy slumber of the exhausted. Kitty looked in after dinner and finding her sister sound asleep, crept away.

25

Waking to the slow fog produced by deep sleep, Mary recalled yesterday's events in a slow agony of humiliation. Each separate insult cut her afresh until she once again felt violently ill. Hill found her, white as her bed linen, wild eyed and with small beads of perspiration on her brow. Hill tutted as she pulled aside the heavy, worn drapes.

'Just as I suspected. It's a chill you have upon you, to be sure. Gallivanting about the countryside without so much as a groom. It's small wonder, I say, and not at all becoming behaviour of a young lady. What will your mother say, that's what I would like to know.'

At the mention of her mother, tears began to slide silently down Mary's cheeks.

'There, there. T'was only a scold. What you need is rest.'

Hill plumped the pillows and exited saying she was returning with an egg and would stay until it was eaten.

Mary sank back against the pillows staring out blankly at the clouds scudding past the window and ignoring the insistent tap of a blue tit attacking its own reflection against the glass. She grew hot with embarrassment thinking again about all that had happened. Her mind was so muddled. What had become of her certainty?

Certainty of mind and purpose had been her ally these many years. Now, when she was most in need, certainty had deserted.

Within ten minutes, Hill returned with the promised egg and a dish of tea. She squawked with alarm when she saw Mary's heightened colour.

'Lord, now you have a fever. I'll speak to your mother about the doctor.'

'Oh no, Hill! I am not so ill. I am a little hot because I tangled myself in the covers. Truly, I only require rest. Please do not trouble any more. I promise to eat my egg.'

Hill regarded her with uncertainty. 'Do you promise to ring the bell if you need something?'

'I promise.'

Hill paused at the door. 'Then I will go for now as the butcher's order is due. I expect the others will visit soon.'

Mary shuddered slightly. She must maintain her equilibrium at all costs before her mother. She prayed that Kitty would visit first. Presently Kitty peeped around the door with a worried look.

'How are you feeling?'

'I am not really ill.'

'But Hill said—'

'Hill has reason to think me unwell. In truth, I am exhausted.' Kitty gave Mary a puzzled look. 'It is convenient to let Hill believe in her mistake for the moment,' Mary continued, 'though I do not mean to be unkind. And, please, Kitty, it would be helpful if Mama and Papa thought the same. I need time to think.'

Kitty perched on the bed, a picture of concern. 'Dearest Mary, you are talking in riddles. What is the cause of all this mystery?'

Mary related the events at Cuthbert Park and the reason Hill had mistakenly thought she had a chill. She spoke with an urgency that precluded tears, only too aware that her mother might enter at any moment.

'But this is monstrous!' Kitty raged. 'How *dare* Mrs Montagu speak so unkindly about you. Our families are meant to be friends. What can she be about?'

'Remember, she did not know that I overheard her conversation with Lady Sandalford. Indeed, I wish I had not overheard.' Mary pulled the crisp, white sheet to dab at her eyes.

'Well, I think this is outrageous. No lady should be so cruel. You have done nothing save provide valuable assistance to their household.'

'It does not matter,' Mary concluded miserably, 'she detests me. In her eyes I am everything poor in a female.' Her tears sprang afresh.

Kitty rushed to embrace her. 'You are none of her vile accusations. Mrs Montagu is a foolish woman. You have heard Papa say so. Mr Montagu cares for you, I am certain. You must not let his mother ruin your chance at happiness.'

Mary's tears now ran freely onto Kitty's fichu. 'But she has. I can never marry him now. Besides, he is going to marry Sylvia.'

'I do not believe her. Mrs Montagu fondly imagines her son will do as she wishes,' said Kitty.

'Even if you are right, Kitty, I could not live at Cuthbert Park knowing she holds me in thorough contempt. Mrs Montagu has made it clear that she will stop at nothing to find him an heiress or a lady with a title.'

'My dear sister, Mr Montagu must know his own mind. He seems to be a very thoughtful sort of gentleman.'

Mary dried her eyes and exhaled. 'His wishes are uncertain to me. He has not declared himself. But why would he, Kitty? I do not flatter myself that I am any man's prize. Sylvia is everything I am not. I cannot bear to face either of them as I must when it is clear that I am well.'

Mrs Bennet bustled into the room. 'What has happened to you, Mary? Hill says you have a fever. This is what comes of jaunting about the countryside undertaking manual labour like a servant.'

'I do not have a fever, Mama. I am merely a trifle under the weather and somewhat fatigued.'

'You have no consideration, Mary. Your sister sits with me and attends the worst of my heads with lavender water while you endanger your reputation walking to Cuthbert Park near as often as you ride there with the groom.'

'You need not fear any more, Mama.' Mary regarded her mother with distaste. 'I have completed my task in the library and have no further need to walk, ride or drive to Cuthbert Park. I have no intention of setting foot in that house again.'

'That is all very well, miss, when the damage is done.'

'I believe that my reputation is intact. My walking was nothing remarkable and a servant was present at all times in the library.'

Mrs Bennet shook her head in a sorrowful gesture.

'Well, I am glad it is finished, even if it was not in time to save your health. Prunella Montagu should have taken better care of a daughter of mine.'

The sisters exchanged meaningful looks.

'I believe I will be well soon if I can just rest, Mama. I have the headache.'

'In that at least you take after me. Kitty, fetch your sister some lavender water for her brow. I will leave you to rest, my dear girl. If you should have a fever, it will not bode well for someone of my delicate health to be near you.'

Having dispensed of her motherly concerns, Mrs Bennet made her exit, closely followed by Kitty. Returning a few minutes later with the lavender water, Kitty sat on the bed and tenderly ministered to her sister's brow before leaving her to sleep.

26

By mid-morning the following day, Mr Montagu called and was received in the sunny confines of the dining room.

'I bid you good morning, Mrs Bennet, Miss Catherine.' He paused. Shyness and indecision seemed to lead to his halting speech,

'Miss Bennet departed in haste from the park yesterday. I have come to enquire as to her health.'

Mrs Bennet regarded him as a cat within pouncing range of an injured bird.

'Why, that is handsome in you, to call so soon, Mr Montagu,' she cooed, 'my poor girl is quite unwell at present and we must hope that she recovers.'

Mr Montagu dropped his hat. It lay rolling at his feet as he stood frozen with shock. Then, he barked out,

'Good God! Is the doctor with her?'

Kitty hastened to correct her mother's fanciful expression.

'It is not so dreadful, sir. I think my sister is severely fatigued, perhaps a little fevered, and she is beset with the headache.'

Mr Montagu closed his eyes for a moment.

'Then I blame myself.' He bent to retrieve his hat and

twisted it in his hands. 'I have allowed her to undertake too much in a short time.'

Mrs Bennet flapped a hand and offered nothing but an, 'Ah'.

Kitty took pity on the anguished gentleman before her. 'I believe that my sister has enjoyed being useful to you, sir. She talks of little else save your library.'

His expression brightened somewhat.

'Then I hope she can return soon to show Mr Bennet her successes when she is well again. I should like the opportunity to show her my deep gratitude for all the care she has put into the catalogue.'

Before leaving, Mr Montagu spent an hour in Mr Bennet's own humble library. Though it must be said that no gentleman of scholarly pursuit could find himself in discomfort in that room, which combined an outward vista of the garden, with a snug interior designed to appeal to a gentleman of knowledge. Once Mr Bennet had waved away the younger gentleman's abject apologies, they discussed a wide range of affairs of the day.

When Mr Montagu had quit the house entirely, Mrs Bennet let out sigh of satisfaction.

'I cannot credit it, Kitty, but I declare Mr Montagu has formed an attachment to Mary. When he danced with her twice at Clovisford, I was glad of it, but wondered if he had contracted some foreign ways and was not aware of the consequence of his actions. But now I see he is a man in love.' She clapped her hands. 'Who would have thought our Mary could attract a gentleman of his standing? Why he must be worth several thousand pounds a year. Perhaps more than Bingley! Ha, ha! We must begin thinking about bride clothes.'

With that, the good lady lapsed into a happy daydream, barely attending Kitty's anxious words.

'We cannot be sure, Mama. Mr Montagu has not declared himself.'

'But he will!'

Mrs Bennet's daydreams were punctuated by short exclamations such as 'a list of prominent families' and 'I believe I would show to advantage in cornflower blue'. Kitty paid perfunctory attention to these asides. Her thoughts were in turmoil. She was as sure as she could be in the absence of a proposal that Mr Montagu cared for Mary. But what if Mary were right? What if Mr Montagu did intend to marry Sylvia? Most gentlemen would fall at her feet even without her reported fortune. Kitty felt guilty for thinking so, but when she compared her awkward sister with Sylvia, Mary came a poor second.

She slumped with her elbows on her knees and her chin in her hands, staring moodily into space. Poor Mary. Mr Montagu had wrought a welcome change in her and her sister was more likeable for her new softness and femininity. Kitty had begun to consider that she and Mary might become better friends after a lifetime of bickering. She doubted Mary could bear seeing her love married to another and who could blame her?

Kitty sighed and cast a cushion onto the chaise with frustration. Now she had two problems. Should she tell Mary what had occurred in the morning room earlier? Telling her might raise false hopes regarding Mr Montagu. Worse still, their mother's assertion that Mr Montagu was in love with Mary would cause her real agitation in the circumstances. No, she must try to keep Mary in ignorance, even if she thought Mr Montagu did not care. Mama was the greater problem. Now she had it in her head that Mr Montagu loved Mary there would be no constraining her chatter abroad. How Kitty wished that Jane and Lizzy were here to give her counsel. They would know what to do. She tried to imagine what each of them would say and found some comfort in believing she could hear them speak. She cleared her throat.

'Mama, I have been thinking.'

'Of course you have, dear. You will want a new gown for the nuptials and I am sure Papa will oblige.'

'Thank you, Mama, but there is something else.'

'What is it?'

'I have been thinking about Mary and Mr Montagu. They are both such private, quiet people. It would not do to discuss them openly until Mr Montagu has declared himself. I am very sure he would be easily put off.'

Mrs Bennet pouted. 'But where is the amusement in that approach?' She frowned. 'Though we must not put him off at any cost.'

'Then we cannot speak of it among our friends, even Aunt Philips – especially Aunt Philips.' Kitty pressed her advantage now that she had her mother's attention. 'It would be a terrible fate if Mr Montagu were to turn his attentions elsewhere due to gossip – Maria Lucas for example.'

Her mother started. 'Maria Lucas!'

Kitty relaxed a little, knowing her arguments to have found their mark.

'Indeed, Mama. But I am sure all will be well if we are very discreet. The surprise will be much more exciting if we keep the news to ourselves for now, until we have something certain to tell.'

'Ho, won't they all be surprised!'

27

My dear Jane,

I trust that you are well as the interesting event draws near. Bingley and the dear children must be excited.

Papa, Mama and Kitty are all well, as are those among our acquaintance whom you know and love.

I am writing most particularly to ask you a special favour. Recent events have unfolded that make me wish to be away from Meryton with some urgency. There is no cause for alarm, dear sister, but I do most desperately wish to put some distance between myself and our small community.

To that end, I am imploring you to invite me to stay. In return, I hope to be able to assist you with the children.

I have a second request, which is that you do not allude to my asking for an invitation. While Kitty is aware of my reasons for wishing to leave, neither Papa nor Mama have been taken into my confidence.

Never before have I felt in such great need of my eldest sister. I throw myself upon your mercy, Jane, and beg you to write soon.

Your loving sister,
Mary.

Jane read the letter twice with growing disbelief. Mary, of all people, to send such a letter, was beyond her imagining. Yet, her sister's words rang with sincerity. That she was troubled, there could be no doubt. During the second reading, she paced her pretty morning room. At length, she tucked the letter into her sleeve and made her way to luncheon, while taking the firm decision to omit any mention of the nature of the letter to Bingley. She felt considerable distress at the use of subterfuge, but her beloved was not a man who enjoyed mystery or any form of intrigue.

As Bingley sighed with satisfaction over his favourite jellied fowl, Jane said, 'My dear, I have been thinking that it would be useful to have my sister to stay. She could assist me with the children.'

Mr Bingley was ever joyful of any scheme that would bring pleasure to his wife.

'Why, of course. I should have thought of it myself. By all means write to Kitty today.'

'I was thinking of asking Mary, dearest.' Jane knew herself to be quaking a little.

'Mary?' He frowned.

'I had a letter from her today, and it reminded me that we have entertained Kitty a good deal, but we have not been so generous to Mary. Her sensible nature would be a good influence for the children.'

'You are as ever, kind and even-handed, my dear. Our children and I are the beneficiaries of a jewel.'

Jane blushed. 'Then it is settled. I shall write to Longbourn directly.'

In fact, Jane took a good deal of time and trouble writing to Mary and to her father. The latter proved difficult as she was at pains to express her request while not revealing Mary's entreaty. Jane made several attempts before she was satisfied, then relieved her feelings in a long letter to Lizzy.

Mary languished in her room for two more days until Kitty reminded her that she would not be able to visit Jane if she were considered to be ill.

Mr Montagu had made a second call at Longbourn, bringing a novel and flowers from the park for the invalid. Nervous that she might have to see him and then be in the difficult position of declining an invitation to Cuthbert Park, Mary fell to persuading Kitty to take long walks.

In this scheme Kitty was a willing participant, if the walk were to Meryton. Few entertainments were to be had beyond the haberdashery or milliners in Kitty's reckoning, but she thought Mr Dalrymple might more easily be passing Meryton than Longbourn. In this logic she found herself happily correct on one occasion.

Mr Dalrymple's high-point collar and elegant polished top boots were a distinctive sight among the inhabitants of the town. He made the sisters an elegant bow.

'The Misses Bennet, upon my word, a very great pleasure. I would have called at Longbourn but I have been engaged in sourcing a potion for my aunt.'

'Have you been successful, sir?' enquired Kitty.

'I have, and glad I am of it. The lady is most specific in her requirements and the devil of a time I have had searching. Now I have my reward in meeting you. Tell me, do you frequent the monthly assemblies?'

Mary replied, 'We do, sir, though the nights with a full moon are not always reliable and Papa will not have the coach set out in thick cloud for fear of accidents.'

'Just so. We must contrive other circumstances in the meantime, eh, ladies?' This he accompanied with a hearty wink.

28

Mary nestled as far as she was able into the corner of Mr Bingley's comfortable chaise. She closed her eyes against the open skies and fields that fell away on either side. Her journey had been more exhausting than any before. Mr Bennet had seen her to the halfway point and into the safekeeping of Jane's lady's maid, a woman of mature years and a quiet temperament, suited to Mary's mood.

They had travelled past fields of oats and barley promising a bumper yield. They had plunged through dark forests of trees arching over the road to form a tunnel, only to emerge over rolling hills and back into combinations that seemed to repeat all she had seen afresh.

Mary's thoughts bore similar repetition. She went over and over all that had happened until her nerves were stretched as taut as the coachman's reins.

The road was mercifully free of mud but the ruts had baked hard and caused a good deal of jolting. Again she wondered if her impulse had been sound.

Jane's letter had certainly caused some dissention, even as Papa announced the invitation over breakfast.

'Well, Mary, it appears your sister Jane feels the need of your assistance with my grandchildren. What do you think of that?'

Mary darted a glance at Kitty for reassurance.

'I would be very happy to see dear Jane and the children, Papa. Oh, and Bingley, of course.'

'You have lately been ill; perhaps I should send Kitty in your place.'

Mary's eyes flew open in alarm.

'Oh, no, Papa. I am completely well again and Jane did ask for *me*.'

'Well, I am against the plan; not that I begrudge dear Jane the assistance of her sister. Kitty should go,' Mrs Bennet said before returning to her chocolate and eggs with gusto.

'Mrs Bennet, is there some reason for your naysaying?' enquired Mr Bennet.

His lady fiddled with her napkin looking somewhat flustered.

'I have expectations of a proposal from Mr Montagu,' she countered in defensive tones.

Mary's body froze, though her wide eyes implored Kitty for help. Kitty returned a helpless shrug.

Mr Bennet's tone was deceptively silky.

'What, pray, gave you cause for such hopes, my dear?'

Mrs Bennet's eyes lit up.

'He danced twice with Mary at Clovisford and has enquired after her health since she became ill,' she lowered her voice for emphasis, 'in the most affecting manner.'

'I see.' Mr Bennet put down his napkin and settled back in his chair. 'It is possible that his singling Mary out for a second dance was an error of judgement from one who has been in foreign climes for some time. As for his enquiries about Mary's health, I would do the same if a friend became ill while visiting my home.'

'But he—'

'He confided his sense of responsibility to me as I would expect of a gentleman. I spent an hour with him and he has made no request of me in regard to Mary and no other indication that I can see.'

Mary had turned her face from one end of the table to the other during this conversation. She dared not speak, but feared remaining mute.

'I tell you, he's smitten!' Mrs Bennet raised her voice.

'This is dangerous talk, Mrs Bennet, and I desire you do not repeat it to anyone. That goes for you too, Kitty.'

'Yes, Papa.'

Mrs Bennet's eyes gleamed as bright as her cheeks. She desired a removal to her parlour and left the room with her handkerchief applied to an eye.

Mary breathed out forcibly, unaware until now that she had been holding her breath.

'Well, then, Mary, you must make your preparations, else my next grandchild might arrive before you.' Mr Bennet helped himself to an additional dish of chocolate, apparently pleased with his small joke.

In the privacy of Mary's room, Kitty quizzed her even as they sorted gowns for her trunk. She assured Kitty with alacrity that her plan was sound, but in truth the uncertainty remained.

So engrossed in these recurring thoughts was Mary, that she failed to notice the carriage had entered the long drive to Mr Bingley's estate. The maid's adjustments to her attire caused Mary to look up. In wonder, she exclaimed, 'Oh look, there are deer by the lake. How beautiful they are.'

Excitement that Jane was near and her burdens safe for now transformed her countenance.

The lake formed the base of a natural basin to her right. On the left of the carriage, a steep wooded slope appeared to touch the sky. The drive circled around the arc of the basin before reaching a handsome stone property of no less than three storeys. The imposing height of the facade softened under bowers of yellow climbing roses.

Jane and Bingley stood in the middle of the four columned portico, wreathed in welcoming smiles. Barely grazing the footman's proffered glove as she alighted, Mary flew forward with none of her customary reserve; so glad was she to see them. As Jane embraced her, Mary stilled a sob lest Bingley should be alarmed.

That kind gentleman had lost not a whit of his jollity. His figure bore a little more authority, but his youthful countenance remained as it had been when first he came to Netherfield.

Jane's contentment and delight in her surroundings was evident and motherhood became her. Her former girlish reticence had been replaced by a laughing assurance. She remained as beautiful as ever and her grace, even though her confinement was near, was barely diminished. As they entered the house, Mary finally felt certain that her decision to leave Longbourn had been right.

29

Kitty was cast down in an echo of her youthful pettish moods. Knowing better did not suit her at present. Whilst she could not envy Mary a visit to her sister, having been twice herself, Kitty wished herself in the Bingleys' happy company again.

One had but little society with Papa. His happiness in conversation, beyond a gentle joke, lay in matters of more weight than her education allowed. Mrs Bennet's society could be pleasurable but depended much upon the lady's frequent humours. Kitty was therefore grateful for the release offered by a visit to Longbourn from Lady Lucas, Maria and Georgina. The mothers fell to their ritual habits of conversation, leaving the young ladies to roam the gardens.

Georgina's ardent desire for further diversion after her first taste of society at Clovisford was made clear in her constant praise of the event, which appeared to her the zenith of all possible parties. At first her ingénue excitement was enjoyable.

'How wonderful the musicians played,' she enthused. Then, 'Lady Sandalford has the most exquisite drawing room I have ever beheld.'

On she trilled in this vein until Kitty began to regret

the visit. Even Maria, complacent as always, showed signs of tiring, and speaking in a pointed manner said,

'Georgina, Lady Sandalford's party was indeed all that one might expect in matters of taste and generosity. But truly, you will attend other grand affairs, balls and the like; even perhaps at Clovisford.'

Georgina was not to be quelled.

'Were there not several handsome gentlemen?'

'We have a general lack of unmarried gentleman, but there were perhaps one or two who were not ill-looking.'

'I begin to think Mr Montagu is a *very* fine gentleman.' Georgina cast Kitty a sly look.

Kitty shrugged with apparent boredom.

'He is a happy addition to our society. I allow him to be a man of good character.'

'You believe Mr Dalrymple handsome,' said Georgina with arch accuracy.

Refusing to be drawn, Kitty replied, 'Mr Dalrymple was most kind to Mary.'

'He was not kind to Imogen and me. He refused to dance with us.' Georgina kicked the turf in disgust. 'Were it not for Mr Montagu, we should have had no young men to dance with us at all!'

Kitty smiled. 'Georgina, I have no doubt of both you and Imogen finding a quantity of partners in the future.'

Georgina huffed. 'That is all very well but I have been out for full two months now and there has been just one dance and an assembly. How I long for a ball. To be whirled around the room in a beautiful gown with handsome gentlemen admiring one is the epitome of romance.'

To emphasise her point, Georgina danced through the rose border, snagging her gown. Kitty and Maria gave in to laughter.

'*I* should marry first, Sister. You will have to wait,' said Maria.

Georgina halted. 'Oh no, I wish only for the romance.' She tucked her arm through Kitty's own. 'I do not desire to fare as poor, dear Charlotte. Perhaps it is wrong to say it, but Mr Collins is so prosy and preaching, I should die if I were to be married to any gentleman of his sort.'

Kitty stopped and flicked a playful fan in Georgina's direction. 'You should not say those words to anyone else, but you may safely say it to me. Mr Collins is our cousin but he is everything unnatural in our family. However, your sister has married him and she will have the joy of one day living at Longbourn near her old home.'

Maria was unusually reproving. 'No young lady can continually seek romance, Georgina. To be considered fast is to ruin every chance for marriage and to bring discredit to your family.'

Georgina pouted. 'You sound just like Mama.'

'I am sure Maria doesn't mean to scold.' Kitty contrived to make a hasty peace. 'But a young lady's reputation is her most prized possession. I know you would not ruin Maria's chances for all the world by endangering your own reputation.'

'Is it not an injustice that my brother, Albert, may act as he pleases, Kitty?'

Kitty opened her fan and made a small shrug.

'I never think about it. A gentleman's life is simply different from our own. We may envy him his freedom, but perhaps he may envy ladies the opportunity for quiet leisure. He too, has some restraints upon his conduct.'

They returned to the house, Georgina now quiet and thoughtful, while Kitty mused how similar she had been to Georgina at the same age. Her thoughts were quite different today. She wondered if Lydia had altered. Letters from the colonies were as brief as they were rare. She concluded that Lydia's robust character was unlikely to alter, particularly under the persistent bad influence of Wickham.

'There you are, girls,' beamed Lady Lucas. The two mothers sat side by side on the small sofa. 'We have news to please you all, I fancy.'

'What is it, Mama? Is there to be a ball?' Georgina's eyes were shining.

'No, my dear. Nothing so grand, but you will be diverted, I am sure.'

Between them the mothers related the news overheard in the haberdashery by Lady Lucas. The news was second hand as Mrs Blain had overheard the conversation when Mrs Montagu had been buying her lavender silks.

'For it has been fully a year since Mr Montagu senior's passing,' said Mrs Bennet, reaching for the tea strainer.

Her friend continued. 'Mrs Blain overheard Mrs Montagu say that she would give a dinner party in honour of her old friend, Mrs Fulcross, who comes to stay at Cuthbert Park on her return journey from Bath to the north.'

Mrs Bennet continued the tale. 'There is a daughter I apprehend.'

'I was coming to that,' interrupted Lady Lucas with a cross expression. 'The daughter, Letitia, is her only child and will inherit a considerable fortune, I am told.'

Kitty sighed. Mary had been right. Mrs Montagu was surely pushing eligible females into her son's path. She tried to marshal her features into a pleased expression as Lady Lucas continued.

'Invitations are to be sent out today, I believe.'

Georgina at least was the picture of happiness, almost bouncing in her chair.

'Will Imogen Drummond be in the party?'

Mrs Bennet answered, 'I do not know; but I imagine they will be present.'

Kitty suspected there was little doubt of Lord Drummond's attendance with his daughters. Mrs Montagu would account it an opportunity to once again present the beautiful Sylvia to her son's notice. Poor Mary. How right she had been to remove herself from Meryton.

30

Mary had been at Stonehythe fully three days without revealing the true reason for her visit. There were further puzzles. She kept a good deal to her room. She was seen playing gentle nursery games with the children. Mr Bingley, always at pains to satisfy his guests, had given Mary the freedom of his library. Although receiving this bounty with polite enthusiasm, Mary had shown only cursory interest in visiting that room. She presented an altogether subdued character.

Jane asked her sister no direct questions in regard to her secret. Family life offered few occasions when they might speak in private. At last, on Monday afternoon, Mr Bingley took his children for a drive in the pony trap. The ladies remained in Jane's sitting room sewing tiny clothes for the anticipated arrival. Mary held a chemise up to the light and murmured:

'So tiny, one can scarce imagine a baby would fit into this.'

She dropped the cotton garment into her lap and thought how unutterably sad it was that she would continue to make such items for her sisters, but never for herself.

'Yes, even after two, I am still surprised by how tiny

they are. But as you can see with James and Susannah, they grow at an alarming rate.'

Jane appeared anything but alarmed.

'Indeed, Jane, they are quite energetic.'

'It takes much of my energy to keep up with them. You will see when you have children.'

Mary's words were barely audible in the silent room.

'Then I shall not see, because I shall not have children.'

Jane turned to her in surprise. 'My dear sister, you cannot be sure of that circumstance at all.'

Mary's voice wobbled.

'Oh, but I can, dear Jane. I am very sure now that I shall never be married.'

Jane cast aside her own sewing.

'What is this? How can you be sure of such an eventuality?'

'Because the only gentleman that I could ever love enough to marry will never declare now; if indeed he ever intended to declare.'

A tear fell on the soft linen at Mary's fingertips.

Jane arose awkwardly and removed the garment from her small hands. She held out her own hand.

'Come now to my room, where we can be sure of no disturbance. I think it is time for you to unburden yourself of the whole.'

Mary offered no resistance and trailed behind her sister. When they entered Jane's bright, comfortable room, she finally spoke of all that was in her heart.

'I am sorry, Jane. You have been very patient with me and kind. I should have told you every circumstance days ago. In truth, it has been a comfort to me just to observe your happiness and to try to put some distance from my own problems. But unhappiness follows one.'

Jane nodded. 'That is undeniably so. Time is the greatest cure for unhappiness. Now, pray, Mary, tell me everything.'

They sat on the striped satin sofa by the window, oblivious of the pretty room or the beauty of the scenery in the gardens beyond. Mary left out no detail. Her sister embraced her, causing fresh tears.

'My poor, dear sister. Mrs Montagu's cruel talk was unconscionable. It matters not that she did not know you to overhear her. A lady should not speak of another in such a manner. I am quite shocked by her behaviour. But, dear Mary, why did you listen to such spiteful talk for so long?'

'I was trapped.' Mary hugged herself as though to stem the pain. 'There were two servants in the library behind me, packing the last of the books. I could not have returned there, for my countenance would have betrayed me. The only remaining doors gave onto the salon where Mrs Montagu sat with Lady Sandalford, or to the servants' passage. When I heard Peters come along, I was concerned that he would think I was eavesdropping. There was just enough time to hide behind the screen.' Mary's hands flopped into her lap. 'By then I had heard all that I have told you. I decided that I must risk leaving by the servants' passage, before Peters came to search for me.'

Jane's blue eyes framed her dismay.

'It is quite, quite awful. But what of Mr Montagu in all of this? If his feelings are engaged, then he is bound to reveal himself.'

'I do not know with any surety if his feelings *are* engaged.' Mary stood up and paced over to the bed. She turned to Jane. 'I had begun to think so, but oh, I am so confused. I have no great experience with gentlemen. Why wouldn't he want to marry Sylvia? She is, well, perfection. Even if he cared for me, which must be doubtful, it is clear that I could not live in the same house as his mother.'

'I can see that such a circumstance would be most difficult. But, my dear, sometimes circumstances change. Perhaps there is a reason for Mrs Montagu's behaviour. A misunderstanding, or perhaps a curious lack of judgement may go some way to excusing her role in this. I realise that sounds unlikely and it is equally hard to excuse such vulgar behaviour from a lady. You must not give up hope.'

Mary shook her head.

'But I have given up hope, Jane. Mrs Montagu means to marry her son off to an heiress or a titled young lady and possibly both. How can I hope to compete? I do not possess your beauty or even that to equal my other sisters. My social graces are not easy like your own. I no longer even think myself superior in accomplishment as I once did. Everything I ever thought or felt has been turned on its head.'

Mary threw herself on the coverlet and wept.

Jane sat beside this new incarnation of her sister, stroking her hair as she often did for the children. At length the sobs subsided to gentle hiccups. Jane spoke with decision.

'Mary, dear, you are far from ill-looking and a little observation and application will improve your reception in society. I am sorry to say that our dear Mama is much at fault for making foolish comparisons between us all.'

Mary's muffled voice rose from the sanctuary of the coverlet. 'There can be no doubt that I am plain.'

'I believe there is considerable doubt, Mary. Because you believe yourself to be plain, you do not trouble to prove otherwise. Let us consider: dresses made to suit me were handed down to you, with your different figure and colouring. Such uninspiring beginnings caused you to make a friend of your books and music while ignoring the ribbons and fashion plates. You must confess that your hair has not altered from those two severe braids wrapped above your forehead since you were a child. It is small wonder that you believe yourself plain.'

Mary raised herself on one elbow, her speech tremulous.

'Do you truly think I might be improved?'

Jane smiled her encouragement.

'I am certain that we can affect great improvement.'

Mary cast her tearstained face back down.

'But there is no point. My situation is hopeless.'

Jane's efforts to appear stern were generally unconvincing in one with her gentle temperament. However, she tugged Mary's arm and spoke as though scolding a child.

'Mary, you have travelled far to seek my advice, so please heed it now. Regardless of the circumstances, your feelings about yourself and your hopes have altered. The old Mary was happy as she was but the Mary I see before me is full of recrimination for herself.' Jane stroked away a tear sliding towards the counterpane. 'We can do something about that at least. Should you return to Meryton with your head held higher because you feel a superior creature to the one who left, you will have the happiness of knowing that you are the equal of anyone among your acquaintance in every respect. Is that not an aim worthy of attainment?'

Mary's sober face regarded her sister. She nodded her assent.

'Dear Jane, how kind you are. I confess any form of distraction at present is preferable to the torment of my thoughts. I am in your hands.' She stood and regarded herself in the glass. Her face was mottled from crying. She noticed how faded her old gown had become. The woman looking back at her in the glass would be passed in the street without notice. Mary held her skirts out and dropped them in a hopeless gesture. Lifting her arms in entreaty, she enquired, 'Where shall we begin?'

Jane clapped her hands with delight. 'We shall begin with my wardrobe, though there is much that is unsuitable in colour. We shall have to appeal to Lizzy for that. Her colouring is a better match. But I have one or two items which will suit you far better than I. We shall amuse ourselves so much that I cannot wait to begin.'

Thus commenced a daily ritual for the sisters. Though initially doubtful of success, Mary attended to Jane's every word and tried hard to remember everything she said. Despite the distraction of her growing form, Jane reclined on the satin chaise in front of the window, directing Mary to remove gown after gown from her wardrobe.

'No, blue does not become you so well, nor will the pale pink. Ah, now here is something. The green travelling costume. A great mistake of mine. I am ashamed to say how costly a mistake.' Mary shook out the heavy velvet folds of the gown. 'Do try it on, Mary. I can see that the colour goes perfectly with your eyes.'

Mary obliged. She was encouraged to add the warm pelisse, embellished with frogging and a little raised collar. Stroking the arm of the pelisse, she realised that she had never worn cloth of such quality. Jane crowed her delight.

'I knew it. Why, with some alteration to the sides and hem, the gown is perfect for you.'

'But, Jane, I cannot accept so expensive a gown.'

'Nonsense.' Jane grasped the side of the chaise, struggled to a standing position and walked over to Mary, laying a hand on the soft velvet. 'You are my sister. I cannot think who else might wear it, for I will not.'

Jane's attention was soon called elsewhere, but despite regular interruptions, within a few days Mary was the richer by a trio of gowns infusing her own drab items with colour. In addition to the velvet travelling ensemble, Jane had added two fichus, a pelisse and a reticule. She fondled the soft drape of her new rich brown walking costume with pleasure. A Greek key around the hem and cuffs relieved the plain colour, while a matching layer at the neck guarded against chills. Surprises of a more exacting nature followed.

Jane was adamant that a transformation could only be wrought by a more modish hairstyle. Her lady's maid was summoned and instructed to demonstrate two new styles which Mary might manage by her own hand. After considerable discussion between Jane and her maid, they settled upon a simple style for day, piling the hair at the back in a neat bun secured with mother of pearl pins. Next, tendrils were teased down from the temple to soften the whole. For evening, Mary's hair was pleated high upon her head with a comb or jewelled clasp for ornament. Gentle curls were twisted beside the ears. The effect of both styles amazed all the ladies. Gone was the severity of the crossed plaits. Mary's brow, previously so broad across her face, now created a neat heart shape. Mary stared at her reflection in the glass and believed herself almost pretty.

Jane beamed with pride.

'Why, this is what has been missing.'

Mary raised her hand tentatively to her hair.

'I had not imagined that the style of one's hair could alter one's appearance so.'

Her wonder was put to one side as she was made to practise each style daily until her scalp hurt and the maid was satisfied that she could do each perfectly without aid. Unaccustomed as she was to such work, Mary struggled to achieve the necessary dexterity.

'I say, how becoming you look, my dear sister-in-law,' said Mr Bingley as he joined the ladies in the mirrored anteroom before dinner. Mary flushed with pleasure. 'Was there ever a fairer posy of sisters than the Bennet girls? Darcy and I are the most fortunate of men to marry into such riches.'

He swept the ladies a deep bow.

Jane turned a glowing smile upon her husband.

'You will turn our heads, Bingley my love, and I cannot answer for the consequences.'

The effects of Mr Bingley's compliments assured Mary that she was indeed improved. His words were given generously, true to his nature, and without prompting from Jane.

*

When not closeted with Jane, Mary proved as good as her word by helping with the children. By turns she joined their games with good humour and provided simple instructions to engage their busy little minds. Mary would indulge four-year-old James in a race down the nursery corridor, and help three-year-old Susannah to toss a ball at the skittles, before taking them out to identify butterflies and insects. The children provided a balm to soothe her troubled thoughts.

Jane wrote Elizabeth a new note to confirm an expected visit. In it she wrote that her concern over Mary's stern nature in a previous letter was quite mistaken. Mary was so natural with the children that Jane fervently hoped she would have her chance at marriage and motherhood.

31

Elizabeth and Darcy arrived with little Charles Fitzwilliam in time for morning coffee. The trio made an impact. Darcy bore himself with great assurance and looked every inch a gentleman of means. Lizzy's happiness was evident in her liveliness and unaffected joy in a reunion with her sisters. Her travelling pelisse and gown may have been in the first stare of fashion but the wearer was unconscious of the adornment. Charles looked like Darcy in miniature. Lizzy's bright eyes grew soft as she watched her son scamper off to play with his cousins.

Mary always felt a little disconcerted by Darcy. One could never read his expression. However, his greeting to her was most civil and he made polite conversation. Lizzy greeted her with warmth and Mary found herself returning the embrace with enthusiasm. She realised that she had missed her sisters more than she expected. When they had married and left Longbourn, Mary had known a little relief from the feeling that she never did quite right in their eyes. For a short time it had been enjoyable being the eldest sister at home, until the privilege paled somewhat under her mother's never-ceasing demands.

When the gentleman went off to inspect Mr Bingley's new folly, Jane begged Mary to check that the children did not run wild, and once the door closed, Jane and Lizzy settled to a cosy conference in Jane's comfortable sitting room.

Mary took care to allow her sisters time to talk, knowing that the pair were happiest with their heads together. She wondered if they were discussing her problem, but was soon distracted as she joined the children in a game of make-believe soldiers under Lord Wellington, and found herself laughing at their carefree antics.

Once she had enquired after Jane's health, Elizabeth exclaimed, 'Jane, you have wrought quite the most surprising change upon Mary. I congratulate you.'

'I wanted to talk to you most particularly about Mary, Lizzy. You will find her altered in other respects.'

Lizzy laughed. 'Good heavens, Jane, have you magicked further wonders in so short a time?'

'Not at all. Indeed, this is no laughing matter.'

'Now you alarm me, dear Jane. Tell me the whole.'

Jane hesitated. Finally, she said, 'Perhaps Mary should speak for herself. I will not break her confidence, but I can tell you that she has been very unhappy and as you know, felt the need to remove herself from Meryton.'

'For a young lady to be so unhappy, love is usually the culprit,' Lizzy replied. 'But Mary, I never think of her loving anything more than a good book or a good reprove.' Her lips curved into a mischievous smile.

'Lizzy, how harshly you judge. I think you will be surprised when I tell you the depth of her feeling. I had to comfort her like a small child.'

Elizabeth's smile left her face in an instant, to be replaced with concern.

'Then I am deservedly reproved. But in appearance our sister is much improved, which can only be to your credit, Jane.'

Jane demurred. Her sweet nature eschewed high compliments.

'I confess even I am amazed at the change a new hairstyle and a flattering gown can make,' she confided. 'Mary's gratitude was most affecting. I am quite determined that she must be given her chance for future happiness. Mary should not return to Longbourn a dowdy, unhappy spinster!'

'I rarely see your passion so excited. Rest easy, my love. Such excitement is not advised in your condition.'

Lizzy reached for her sister's hand and gave it a soothing rub.

Jane sighed. 'You are right, of course. But I do so wish to improve Mary's prospects and I will have other preoccupations soon.'

'Why, Jane, are you manipulating me to the shackle, you wily vixen?'

Jane cast her sister a sheepish glance.

'Dear Lizzy, it would be such a help if she could visit you at Pemberley. My condition keeps us quiet here. I feel Mary would benefit from greater society. In addition, you are more direct than I when it comes to advice.'

Elizabeth gave her sister a cheery reply.

'I suppose you would have me turn out my wardrobe as well; for I feel sure that I recognise Mary's morning dress as one I have seen you wear?'

Jane admitted the charge and provided an inventory of her bounty.

'Most of her gowns are quite aged on the whole, Lizzy, and in general unsuitable.'

'You are complete to a hand. All right, I will speak to Darcy and prepare my wardrobe for a clear-out,' Elizabeth laughed. Then in seriousness: 'Perhaps I have been thoughtless in regard to Mary. Her character might have benefited more from our attentions in the past. If she is as unhappy as you say, Darcy and I will do our best to improve matters.'

Jane clasped her sister's hands.

'I knew you would understand and come to our aid, dear Lizzy.'

At that moment the door opened and they were joined by the gentlemen.

'Come, ladies, luncheon awaits and we are famished after our running about.'

Bingley assisted his wife from the chair. Elizabeth sprang from her chair and tucked her arm through Darcy's.

The children's presence made luncheon a gay affair. Afterwards Elizabeth managed a quiet word with Mr Darcy. Before the party set off for Pemberley, an invitation had been proffered for Mary to visit and arrangements made for her conveyance one week hence. Mary felt a little suspicious of the reason for the invitation, but since it was extended in kindness and much endorsed by everyone save James and Susannah, she acquiesced with grace.

32

Mrs Montagu's dinner party could not arrive soon enough for Kitty. Her hopes were firmly harnessed to the appearance of Mr Dalrymple. The day arrived at last. Georgina was delighted in the appearance of her new friend Imogen, who tripped along behind her sister trying her level best to ape Sylvia's graceful manners.

Lady Sandalford was swift to greet the Bennets with bonhomie, then retreated to a corner of the salon where she engaged Lord Drummond in a tête-à-tête.

Mrs Montagu introduced her old friend Mrs Fulcross and her daughter, Letitia, with the triumphant flourish of a conjurer. The former was a round, gossipy sort of woman with an infectious smile. By contrast, her daughter shrank somewhat behind; a difficult task, as she stood a full head taller. Kitty attempted to put Letitia at her ease, but found Mrs Fulcross answered almost all enquiries on behalf of her daughter, for which Letitia appeared grateful.

Kitty wandered nearer the windows, looking towards the lime trees on the drive, the better to see if the Glendinning party would arrive. She was intercepted by Mr Montagu, suddenly appearing to her right.

'Miss Bennet, it is good to see you.'

Kitty noted that although he smiled, Mr Montagu's eyes were searching her face.

'It is a great pleasure to return, sir.'

Kitty favoured him with a reassuring smile.

'I understand that Miss Mary Bennet is visiting her sister. I hope that she is now fully recovered from her indisposition?'

'Yes, indeed. Her letters tell us that she is even managing to keep pace with our small niece and nephew. That is quite a feat, as I recall.'

He removed his fob watch and checked it in a distracted manner.

'Whilst not wishing to deprive your sister of a moment's pleasure, I hope that we may soon see her returned home.'

'Then I fear you must be patient, Mr Montagu. My sister Elizabeth and her husband, Mr Darcy, have invited Mary to stay at their home, Pemberley, which is fewer than thirty miles from the Bingleys'.'

A look of dismay passed across Mr Montagu's face, which he failed to mask fast enough to avoid Kitty's detection.

'Please excuse me, Miss Bennet, for I see that the Glendinning party have arrived. I must greet them.'

He gave a slight bow and walked away, his long legs making rapid progress.

Kitty patted her hair in place and searched the room for someone to engage in conversation. The party was soon seated to dine, causing Kitty great annoyance. She had failed to gain an opportunity to speak with Mr Dalrymple, and now she found herself seated at the opposite end of the long dining table, near his odious cousin. Lady Sarah greeted every conversational gambit with cold disdain. Sir William Lucas, seated on her left, soon lapsed into silence during those removes when he was required to engage her in conversation. Mr Dalrymple, by contrast, amused his neighbours and appeared to almost relieve Mr Montagu of his duties as host. Sylvia was seen to laugh several times and even the timid Letitia Fulcross ventured a smile. Observing all of this through the banks of flowers down the length of the table, while appearing disinterested, tested Kitty's ingenuity to the full.

The day being fine, with good light into the evening, Mr Montagu proposed a short walk in the garden after the early dinner. All of the young people readily consented. Mrs Montagu remained behind to attend Countess Glendinning, Sir William and his lady, who all declined the exercise.

Mr Montagu led the way across the land bridge between the lakes, in conversation with Mr Bennet. Mrs Fulcross and Letitia walked abreast, with the older lady contributing commonplaces throughout. Lady Sarah and Mr Dalrymple followed some steps behind; Lady Sarah stalking along, saying little.

Next came Georgina and Imogen stepping either side of Mrs Bennet, who could be heard extolling the finer points of the gardens at Pemberley and Stonehythe. Kitty prayed Mr Montagu did not hear her mother's comparisons.

Lord Drummond continued his discussion with Lady Sandalford, some way back at the rear, behind Sylvia and Kitty.

Sylvia paused before turning into the rhododendron walk, 'I had hoped to see your sister here today, Miss Bennet.'

'Mary is visiting our elder sisters in Derbyshire.'

'You must miss her.' Sylvia's expression was sympathetic.

'I confess I do.' Kitty realised the truth of her remark. 'Of late we have become better friends.'

'Then I am glad for you. Now that our mother is gone, I find myself becoming closer to Imogen. Though at times I feel more like her mother than her sister.'

Sylvia laughed and Kitty joined in the amusement.

'I feel sure she is a handful. My younger sister, Lydia, and I were positively wild at her age.'

Sylvia flicked her fan at a stray bee.

'How lucky we are to have sisters. Despite our differences, a brother would not have the same understanding at all, I fear.'

'Heaven help us if we marry,' said Kitty, 'our understanding of gentlemen will be very limited.'

'For my part, I do not wish to form an alliance until I know the gentleman in question well enough to establish his kindness and constancy.' Sylvia's tone had turned serious.

'Those are excellent qualities. I would add amiability to the list,' said Kitty.

Mr Dalrymple appeared before them. Ahead, Lady Sarah could be seen hurrying towards Mr Montagu.

'Ladies, may I walk with you?' They assented with a nod and he inserted himself between them. 'How I admire these grand gardens. One day I hope to have something of the like myself.'

Sylvia regarded him with interest. 'Oh?'

'One must have ambition, Miss Drummond, otherwise youth and intelligence are a waste.'

Mr Dalrymple's expression left the two young ladies in no doubt he considered himself to possess all of the aforementioned qualities.

'Indeed, sir.' Sylvia moved back to Kitty's side as they reached a hedge and the party began to turn back.

'Sylvia, Lady Sandalford and I wish to have a word with you. I hope you will pardon us Miss Bennet, Mr Dalrymple.' Lord Drummond led his daughter away.

'The honourable Sylvia Drummond is quite the important young lady,' ventured Mr Dalrymple in a tone that dripped censure.

'I do not find her in any way high in the instep,' replied Kitty, giving Mr Dalrymple a puzzled look.

'Yes, indeed. But young ladies of her cut are aware that they do not need to take humble lawyers seriously. I expect she is above even Montagu's touch.'

Kitty frowned and wondered where this conversation might lead. Was Mr Dalrymple interested in Sylvia? She enquired,

'Does that trouble you, sir?'

'Not at all when I am in your company, Miss Bennet.'

A shy, relieved smile smoothed Kitty's features.

'I am sure you must be aware, sir, of the caution an heiress must exercise. You would doubtless protect your own cousin from folly.'

He lowered his voice. 'My cousin's character defies a gentleman's protective instincts, whereas you, Miss Bennet, inspire one.'

Kitty blushed. 'Thank you for the compliment, sir. I cannot imagine how I came to have such an effect.'

'Then I esteem you all the more for your lack of artifice. Would that more young ladies were so.'

Kitty strayed a glance at his face, which appeared serious. She teased, 'Now I think you are flattering me. If you spent a deal of time in my company I think you would find me quite like most young ladies.'

'In your company, Miss Bennet, a gentleman might find time slipping through his fingers, yet I would willingly allow the loss.' He plucked a stray wallflower from the grassy path and wagged it in her direction.

Alive to Mr Dalrymple's flirtatious tone, Kitty responded in equal measure.

'Sir, my mother would be pleased to welcome you at Longbourn again. It is some weeks since we saw you there.'

'Charming as I would find such a visit, I would far rather see you alone.'

Kitty gasped and looked down at the path. Mr Dalrymple leaned in close until she could feel his breath upon her neck.

'Come, Miss Bennet, I do not suggest anything sinister; but merely to speak more freely than the drawing room allows. Say you will meet me at the derelict mill by the stream.' He gave her arm a short, light press. 'No, do not answer now. I will be waiting at three o'clock on Thursday. It shall be our secret.'

With that, Mr Dalrymple melted away and within moments he was conversing easily with Mrs Bennet and the two youngest ladies. Kitty stared after him in shock. His words burned in her mind, yet she could scarce believe he had uttered such sentiments. She avoided eye contact with him for the remaining short duration of their visit.

Before entering her carriage, Sylvia hurried to Kitty's side.

'Miss Bennet, if I write to you at Longbourn will you furnish me with your sister's address? I am to go away soon and I would not wish to leave without establishing a means of correspondence.'

Kitty nodded, though her thoughts were dominated by Mr Dalrymple's invitation.

33

On the journey from Stonehythe to Pemberley, Mary's misgivings had begun to rise. The comforting company of Jane, Bingley and the children had been balm to her injured soul. Pemberley would be more challenging. Mary retained a lingering nervousness of Darcy. He did seem to be a changed character since his marriage, but she had spent little time in his company. Quick-witted Lizzy, too, had been the most likely of her sisters to engage in a verbal duel. Then there was the added concern that the Darcys might entertain frequently, subjecting her to the scrutiny and curiosity of strangers.

Mary began to chide herself. The invitation had been graciously made. Her nephew, Charles Fitzwilliam, was a sweet little fellow. Pemberley possessed a fine library and an excellent pianoforte. These were all to be anticipated with pleasure. Derbyshire, with her sisters, was infinitely preferable to the pain awaiting her at home in Meryton.

At last the beauteous aspect of Pemberley emerged through the trees. In between the drive and the house were a pair of steep banks leading to a gently flowing river. Bathed in full sunshine, the wide stone expanse of the house appeared to glow as though polished with golden gloves. The carriage paused as if to make a mark of respect, before crossing a rustic stone bridge and taking the short climb to the courtyard entrance.

Elizabeth's welcome was warm and unaffected. Little Charles clung to her skirts, demanding to know when his Aunt Mary would come to play with him, as she had at Stonehythe.

'Charles, your poor aunt has just arrived. We must give her time to rest and unpack.'

He looked disappointed and hung his head. Mary knelt beside him and tipped a gloved finger under his chin.

'We shall have plenty of time for play and other things, Charles.' She gave him a warm smile. 'I should very much like to see your most special toys. Do you think that you might set them out to show me in the nursery? I promise that I will come to see them later.'

The child's eyes gleamed as he ran off to do Mary's bidding. Elizabeth looked at her sister as though for the first time.

'Why, Mary, you were masterful with him. He has been looking forward to your visit, you know. Don't let him wear you out with his games.'

Mary chuckled. 'He cannot be more exhausting than James and Susannah. You are lucky, Lizzy; he is a lovely little fellow.'

Elizabeth smiled. 'I am all good fortune, it is true. Now I have the chance to share a little of it with you. Come, let me show you to your room. You have a wonderful view of the lake and the woodland beyond.' Elizabeth tucked her arm through Mary's and escorted her inside.

Mr Darcy had leisure to observe Mary unseen from the nursery door, fulfilling her earlier promise to Charles. The two dark heads were bowed together, setting exquisite painted toy soldiers in their ranks.

'You do it like this.' Charles spoke with authority in his high-pitched voice.

Mary placed the soldier according to his instructions.

'Should I put the general at the front? Can you tell me his name?'

Charles held up two more soldiers.

'This one is Wellington and that one is the Frenchman, Bonaparte. We call him Boney. I'm usually Wellington, but you can be him if you wish.'

'I detect your aunt is popular with you, Charles.' Darcy strode into the room and hoisted his son into the air. Over the laughing child on his shoulder he said, 'For even I am not allowed to be Wellington. Welcome, Mary. My apologies for not being here to greet you. One of our tenants had a fire and I wanted to assess the damage for myself to expedite matters.'

Mary bowed. 'I am glad to be here, Mr Darcy. Pemberley is in splendid looks.'

'You will find Pemberley is always in splendid looks. Do please call me plain Darcy. It is by far the easier than Mister or Fitzwilliam. I am instructed by your sister to bring you downstairs for some refreshment before this young man takes you prisoner.'

Charles accosted his father.

'I should not take my aunt prisoner, sir. She is a lady, and besides, I like her!'

Darcy roared with laughter. Mary marvelled at the sight of her brother-in-law, so joyful compared to the remote man she had known in Meryton.

Aware of Jane's warning that Mary had taken three days to reveal her story, Elizabeth allowed her sister grace to confide her circumstances at a time of her own choosing. There was little doubt to anyone who knew her that Mary had altered. Although naturally of a quiet nature, Mary was given to waspish observations; tolerated by her family but a cause of unpopularity elsewhere. In this aspect of her character she appeared reformed. Jane had wrought a good deal of improvement in her appearance too. Lizzy had noticed Mary's look of surprise when she saw herself passing a mirror. If Mary did not appear so solemn and wan, Elizabeth might have rejoiced.

Strange, too, was her welcome behaviour towards little Charles. In place of sermonising and strictness, were play and tenderness. The child began to heed Mary's every word. Elizabeth noted to Darcy how cleverly her sister imparted wisdom without her son's noticing a lesson. Darcy replied that he had expected Pemberley's magnificent library to swallow Mary whole, but had not found her there on a single occasion. Whilst she selected a few volumes for her room, it was as though Mary could not bear to enter the library. She could be prevailed upon to play for them in the evening, but with a becoming sense of modesty in contrast to her former eagerness for approbation. Impatience to solve the mystery began to register on Elizabeth's cheerful features.

*

For her part, Mary knew by now that her troubles would follow her. There was no escaping the pain in her heart or the despair when she thought of her future. But Pemberley appeared to make time stand still and she felt like an almost ghostly presence inhabiting the many halls and grand rooms. The vastness of Pemberley had held Mary in awe for a day or two. Despite the pleasingly logical design, set around inner courtyards, she had found herself becoming lost at least once a day.

It was well known that Elizabeth's favoured antidote to most ills involved a reviving walk. Summer dazzled with a full display of natural beauty. Pemberley's lake glittered, ancient trees creaked under the weight of fluttering leaves and birdsong tinkled through the air like tiny bells. Mary was persuaded to join her sister in her daily routine of a morning walk. Elizabeth energetically pointed out the many improvements made by her husband. She had influenced the choice of a magnificent greenhouse, which provided the rooms with exotic blooms throughout the year and offered up rare fruits for the table. Mary gasped at the enormity of the structure and was several times forced to ask the name of an unusual fruit or vegetable.

'One could never imagine such things in our English climate, Lizzy. It is a wonder.'

'It is astonishing how many exotics our gardeners can grow. We are the envy of the county. In winter we heat the rooms with hot water from these vents in the floor. It is all very clever indeed. The produce is particularly useful when visiting a sickbed. I am able to tempt the invalid to eat, which is often a relief to their poor relatives.'

One morning, Elizabeth led the way through one of the many avenues in the park to show Mary a cottage.

'This is the home of our head gardener. It was the first project upon which Darcy and I embarked after our honeymoon.' She sighed, as though lost in happy memory.

'It is very grand for a gardener.'

Elizabeth laughed. 'You are quite right. But the cottage makes a pleasing aspect for a passing carriage and the gardener will not be tempted away!'

'You appear to have undertaken many projects, Lizzy.'

'I enjoy it. The activity and the variety give me satisfaction. Of course, collaborating with Darcy multiplies the enjoyment and binds us more securely.'

'To work together must surely be the ideal in a marriage. How happy you must be.' Mary blinked and looked away quickly.

'But I believe I detect that you are not happy, my dear sister. My ear stands ready to relieve your burden.'

Mary spoke in a low voice.

'I shall tell you what is troubling me, Lizzy, but I beg your patience. To speak of events is painful and I would wish to be mistress of myself before I tell you the whole.'

Elizabeth placed her hand on Mary's arm in a tender gesture.

'Dear Mary, your pride is understandable but perhaps misplaced. One cannot reveal one's emotions in public, but there is no shame in a private display among sisters.'

They walked in a semicircle, with the formal rose gardens presenting a vista of gay colours like a quilt below them. A slight drift of perfume carried on the breeze. Elizabeth darted forward.

'Come, let us select armfuls of these beauties for the bedrooms. Then you must come to my room and we shall see if I can compete with Jane to refurbish your wardrobe.'

Cares were set aside as the sisters filled two trugs to overflowing with roses, then spent a happy hour arranging bowls and urns to their satisfaction.

'I do believe this is a much happier task for two people,' declared Elizabeth. 'It is an altogether sober task completed alone, for one constantly looks with a critical eye and is rarely satisfied.'

Mary nodded her agreement. 'I have always considered arranging flowers to be one of those mindless tasks imposed upon a female, but I now admit there is a simple joy to be had in displaying nature to her greatest advantage.'

34

Elizabeth gave every appearance of delight in sharing her wardrobe. Discussions of the merits of gowns and bonnets had been common currency with Jane at Longbourn, but such simple moments were now rare.

Mary proved a little reticent.

'Truly, Lizzy, your kindness is excessive. I have already taken so much from Jane that my trunk is near full.'

'Excellent,' Lizzy beamed, 'then we shall take those old gowns of yours, which no longer serve, and donate them to the poor. The need is great, you know.' Mary knew when she was outmatched and submitted to the logic of her sister's assertion. 'Now let me see.' Lizzy studied her sister from head to foot. 'I am persuaded that gowns for day and evening are most required, for your new travelling and walking costumes suit you admirably.'

Lizzy's boudoir was vast. She even had two enormous chests of drawers in a suite of furniture made for her husband's late mother by Mr Chippendale. She instructed her maid to bring forth gowns and undergarments at a dizzying rate.

Mary touched the supple silk of a chemise in wonder. 'I have never worn anything so fine. A gown would simply slide over this.'

'Indeed you are right,' her sister agreed. 'Silk feels like you are wearing almost nothing and yet it is warming in winter and cool in summer. Do not look at me so, Mary. You must wear it to do justice to an evening gown. I gave Kitty one just like it, you know!' Lizzy considered her sister with a critical eye. 'I feel sure you would not be happy with a good deal of decoration.'

'Oh, Lizzy, that is so true. I should feel like a chicken in feathers and flounces.'

Lizzy laughed. 'Just so. Your instincts are sound. I often think petite girls look very silly in a cloud of ribbons and bows. They invariably turn out to be empty-headed creatures too, in my experience. One should dress to suit one's character – and propriety, of course. Rigby, let us see the green striped poplin.'

The gown, though bright, was restrained by a plain fit with a simple puff at the shoulder and a matching sash around the high waist. Mary tried it on and Elizabeth nodded.

'A triumph! We have a beginning. How lucky we are similar in size and colouring.'

Mary smiled. A winter gown of pale grey relieved by black lace at the cuff, hem and under the bodice, followed. A pelisse of darker grey with matching lace completed the costume. Rigby was instructed to make slight altertions to the gown to fit Mary's narrow frame and the maid looked pleased as she carried out her beloved mistress's instruction. Mary stood in her underclothes, awkward and grateful for the attentions she received. The next creation, simple and white, gained the approval of all three ladies. The muslin gown had a higher neck than was usual, relieved by a wide scalloped lace band, which was repeated on the short sleeves.

''Tis fresh and demure, madam.'

'I agree, Rigby.' Lizzy nodded approval to her maid. 'Simple and perfect. Mary, you shall be able to wear a straw bonnet or indeed any bonnet trimmed as you wish; it makes no difference, you shall always look a picture.'

Mary made to speak, but her sister and Rigby were now of an accord.

'I have been considering the twill, madam, if I may be so bold.'

'Why, Rigby, of course, the twill would be ideal and you know, it becomes me ill.'

'Madam! That is not so, and well you know it.' Rigby gaped at her mistress.

'Fetch it, Rigby, please.'

The gown, woven with lilac and the muted colours of heather, appealed to Mary at once. She tried it on.

Lizzy shook her head. 'No,' she said, 'too dull.'

Turning to face the looking glass, Mary's face had barely registered her disappointment before Rigby draped a wide embroidered muslin fichu around her neck.

'That is a clever transformation, Rigby.' Lizzy spoke with admiration. Rigby blushed with pride.

'Lizzy, please, I am humbled by your generosity, but no more. I cannot,' said Mary.

Lizzy gave Rigby a complicit look.

'Would you spoil our fun? Mary, has it escaped your attention that we have yet to address evening gowns? We entertain frequently at Pemberley, you know. I cannot allow my sister to look less than her best. We shall have tea and tomorrow we will begin again.'

Lizzy was as good as her word.

The next morning Mary surveyed her bedroom. Outside, the day spoke fair with puffball clouds and deer grazing the lush grass. All around her lay old gowns that she had laid out ready to pass to the needy. Her critical eye wondered if anyone should want them. Certainly they were serviceable. Some were hardly worn. But they represented someone she now knew she must cast off. She had embraced life via books and lived through those wondrous pages, yet had failed to live a life herself. Mary admitted to herself that she had lived in fear of engagement. The dullness of her costume had served this purpose well. She had too easily dissuaded herself from approaching any small criticism with a determination to reform or learn a lesson in life. Mary resolved to learn from Lizzy, her boldest sister, how to proceed. In this spirit she embraced the afternoon's foray into Lizzy's evening gowns. Rigby had already offered a selection to her sister for approval before Mary arrived in the boudoir.

'Mary, what entertainment we shall have this afternoon,' Lizzy exclaimed. 'Now, you are not to spoil my enjoyment by your humble talk.'

Mary gave her sister a mutinous look of old.

'You are far too good to play the bully, Lizzy, so pray dispense with it. For my part I promise to submit and be eternally in your debt. Are we agreed?'

Lizzy hugged her sister.

'Mary, you are back with us again. I thought we had lost you. Rigby, present a gown before my dear sister changes her mind.'

Rigby proffered a gown of deep rose-coloured satin. Diaphanous white panels crossed the bodice and formed small draped sleeves. The effect was altogether charming.

Mary had seen such gowns before in the better homes of the county, but had not imagined ever wearing such a beautiful creation. Very little alteration would be required for a perfect fit.

'You must dress your hair with a rosebud or two, Mary.'

Mary stopped adjusting the panels of the gown.

'I am not sure that I will manage rosebuds. I am already all fingers and thumbs trying to manage my two new hairstyles.'

'No matter, I will send Rigby to assist you.'

Lizzy's next choice was an ivory gown. Gold filigree edged the low neck, puff sleeves and hem. A trail of violet embroidered flowers flowed around the slim hemline, finishing in a raised point at the front.

'A tortoiseshell comb for the hair, I think, and a simple locket,' said Elizabeth as she searched a drawer for the useful articles.

Mary was struck dumb by the beauty of her gowns. Rigby presented the comb.

'Surely, Lizzy, you cannot give up two such beautiful gowns?'

'I have many wonderful gowns, my dear sister. I did tell you that I wished to share my good fortune.' She swept her arms wide in illustration of her huge boudoir. 'We are like to be in London for part of the winter and I shall be able to order anew.'

'Thank you, dear Lizzy and Rigby, for your kindness.'

Rigby beamed. ''Tis my job, and a pleasure, miss.'

'We are not finished,' Lizzy commanded with a wave of her hand. 'The bolt of French silk, please, Rigby.'

Rigby pulled the most exquisite silk in a brilliant turquoise from a drawer.

'I have never seen such a beautiful colour,' Mary exclaimed.

Lizzy stroked the fabric with satisfaction.

'The Parisians are magicians. Let us hope the troubles really are at an end, so one may safely travel there again.' Lizzy draped a fold of the fabric over Mary's shoulder. 'I have a gown from this already and I can see at once that it will bring life and sparkle to your eyes. I propose that we have a ballgown made for you. I cannot promise a ball, but I will wager that you have been wearing the old one for a long time.'

Mary nodded, a little shamefaced.

'I admit that is true. Mama offered a new one last season but I could not see the point. I rarely dance, you know.'

'When you are seen in your new gown with your hair fashionably dressed, I doubt that you will have time to sit down,' Lizzy declared with firm authority.

Mary's eyes became bright with unshed tears and her lips began to crumple. In haste, Lizzy requested Rigby to take away the first two gowns and begin such alterations as were necessary.

'Here, sit by me, Mary.'

She led her sister to a large, damask-covered sofa.

'Oh, Lizzy, you must think me foolish.' Mary drooped.

Her sister stroked her hand. 'Foolish? Good heavens, no. You are our clever sister, Mary.'

Mary crumpled a handkerchief in a dejected fashion.

'I used to think myself clever, but now I know it to be the most false perception.'

'It is not false at all.'

'I have a store of knowledge, Lizzy, but that is not the same as clever. Look how foolish I have been, ignoring all opportunities to present myself in an appealing way. I have thought badly of my own sisters. I am ashamed to say I have judged you all as frivolous in the past.' She turned to Lizzy. 'But it is *you* who are clever; you, Jane and Kitty. In some ways, though it pains me to suggest it, even Lydia is my superior. For all of you have been engaging properly with society, while I have been hiding behind judgements based on little more that the treatises of high-minded books.'

'Do not treat yourself so unkindly.' Lizzy put an arm around her sister's slumped shoulder. 'We are none of us perfect. You have perceived a need for some correction, and how well you have transcended the problem already.'

Mary shook her head. 'I owe any transformation to you and Jane. But the changes are merely physical. My character faults remain, and I beg you, Lizzy, to correct my every error in society and in private.'

Lizzy pulled her arm away as though stung, then, hesitating, she placed a soothing hand in Mary's own.

'What has caused all this self-doubt? You have ever been so certain in your opinions, yet now you describe yourself in such critical terms.'

Mary described her meeting with Mr Montagu and her visits to Cuthbert Park. That her feelings for Mr Montagu were far from neutral could be read clearly on Mary's face.

'But I do not understand,' puzzled Lizzy. 'It appears that you had indeed begun to engage more freely with society. Nor can your face hide from me your feelings for Mr Montagu.'

'That is not the entirety of the story.'

Mary revealed the conversation overheard from the anteroom at Cuthbert Park. A few silent tears slid down from the corners of her eyes as she uttered Mrs Montagu's cruel words. She blinked hard and quickly dried her eyes on the now much-twisted handkerchief.

'Monstrous woman,' choked Lizzy. Her fine eyes blazed. 'Cruel and vicious. Not at all ladylike. How dare she?'

'Her words were cruel and wounding, but with hindsight I realise that many of her words were also truthful,' said Mary.

'I think she has exaggerated beyond all measure. I detect some form of jealousy at play here.'

'Jealousy?' Mary's head jerked up.

'Yes. What other reason could bring forth such violent discourse?' Lizzy stood and paced the room. 'Of course I cannot be certain, but let me think out loud. The lady has only recently had the pleasure of her son's residence and must still be grieving her husband. She wishes to arrange his life to suit her own ends and has detected that you are a rival to her plans. I do not understand her motive, but it must be so!'

'But, Lizzy, why would she be so rude about me?'

Mary leaned forward, the question dying on her lips.

'I believe that she has noticed your tenderness for him and his preference for your company above the young ladies she chose to introduce.' Lizzy, calmer now, came to sit beside her again.

'Mr Montagu has made no representations to me, nor, I believe, to Papa,' said Mary. 'His mother must know he has not.'

Lizzy waved away her objections.

'He may not be in a position to do so at present.'

'He did dance with me twice at Clovisford, but spoke in advance of gossip, so I did not accord any seriousness to his actions. Kitty is convinced he has intentions, but, oh, Lizzy, Mrs Montagu is too strong an impediment to any marriage, even if his affections are serious.'

Lizzy stroked her hand again.

'There is no doubt that the situation fosters a good deal of uncertainty and I do not wish to raise false hopes, Mary. It is a blessing that you had the good sense to come to Derbyshire. A little distance will do no harm and may do a great deal of good.'

Mary clasped her sister's hands and looked into her eyes as she uttered a heartbreaking plea.

'Please continue to guide me as you have been doing. I do so ardently want to return to Meryton a more developed soul than I left it. Jane suggested that I might hold my head up high when I return if I have improved. I know there is wisdom in her words. If I must live within two miles of Cuthbert Park, then my need of self-possession will be great.'

Lizzy's own eyes gleamed with unshed tears in response to Mary's impassioned plea.

'Dear, dear girl. I believe that you are much changed already in your heart and your person, in ways that cannot fail to make your progress in society happier than in the past. I will do everything I can to assist you. But, Mary, do not change entirely to suit the whims of others. You have valuable aspects to your character that are yours alone. Change only those aspects which displease you or make you unhappy.'

35

Kitty pondered Mr Dalrymple's meaning in asking her to meet with him alone. His tone had suggested all innocence of intent but try as she may, Kitty could not dissuade herself of the impropriety of such an event, nor could she believe Mr Dalrymple could be in ignorance of the implication of his words.

Even as she determined not to attend the rendezvous, Kitty found herself seeking excuses to be out walking on Thursday afternoon. She reasoned to herself that no harm could come from *accidentally* meeting Mr Dalrymple as she was passing by. His plea had held an urgency. What if he wanted to declare his feelings for her where he could be sure of privacy? She recalled his words. 'I do not suggest anything sinister, but merely to speak more freely than the drawing room allows.'

With a basket over her arm containing a pie for the invalid Mrs Endicott, she strolled in the direction of the stream and was distressed to find Georgina Lucas advancing on the cross path.

'Georgina.'

Kitty could have cried with annoyance. She tried her best to look purposeful.

'Where are you going?'

'To visit Mrs Endicott.'

'La, but you are good. I have a good mind to join you, for Mama often preaches to me to make responsible visits. It will be much merrier if we go together.'

'Oh, no.' The words escaped Kitty's lips. 'What I mean is – merriment is not the objective, Georgina. Were you not going somewhere else?'

Kitty struggled to hide her impatience.

'Actually, no. I was out walking to avoid the penance of a visit from the colonel, who bellows so. At least Mrs Endicott is a *quiet* invalid.'

'Georgina, I do not feel that you enter into the spirit of this visit at all. Perhaps it would be better if you continued your walk alone.'

Georgina hung her head.

'I am sorry, Kitty. I do let my tongue run away with me. Mama would be so pleased if I visited Mrs Endicott,' she pleaded.

'Well, you may as well join me,' Kitty said in cross tones. She sighed and looked with longing toward the riverbank as they set off.

'Did you enjoy Mrs Montagu's dinner?' Georgina enquired.

'Yes, in general.'

'I saw you with Mr Dalrymple.' Georgina's features took on a sly cast. 'He was paying you particular atten-tion. What were you talking about?'

'It was nothing of importance.' Kitty shrugged.

'Then why were you whispering?' Georgina demanded.

'I did not whisper.'

Georgina huffed. 'If you do not desire to tell me your secret, then say so plainly.'

Kitty hesitated. Georgina was not an ideal confidante, but she longed to discuss the matter with somebody.

'I do not have a *secret* exactly.'

'I knew there was something afoot!' Georgina exclaimed.

'Georgina, if you wish me to tell you, you must listen sensibly and promise me faithfully that you will not divulge a word, not even to Maria.'

'I promise on my mother's life.'

Kitty could not help laughing.

'Would it not be fairer to promise on your own life? No matter, just keep your promise.'

'I will. Oh do, please, tell me.'

'Mr Dalrymple has asked me meet him by the old mill. It is wrong of him, of course.'

'I knew it! He intends to propose! Oh, I am the first to know!'

'Nothing of the sort, Georgina. If he intended to propose, he would come to Longbourn and pay his addresses correctly before speaking to Papa.'

Even as the words left her lips, their truth rang clarion in Kitty's head. Georgina whirled around and whooped.

'How romantic. Oh, this is beyond everything exciting. When are you to meet him?'

Kitty stood uncomfortably still.

'Oh no, is it now? Are you on your way to meet him now? I am in transports! I shall be your confidante. Give me the basket. I will take it to Mrs Endicott then meet you later to hear everything!' Kitty regarded Georgina with alarm as she continued in rhapsody. 'You must arrange another assignation while you are there and we will contrive to say that you are meeting me for a walk.'

Kitty continued to regard Georgina as one who had seen a ghost. Indeed, she had seen the ghost of Lydia. Poor, foolish Lydia, whose love of intrigue and excitement had led her into the path of Wickham and a life abroad, far removed from her family. Lydia's elopement had very nearly led her sisters to a ruinous future. If she attended this rendezvous, her own reputation could suffer and any chance Mary might have to marry would suffer by relation. As she observed Georgina's shining eyes, Kitty made her decision.

'No, Georgina, I am going to visit Mrs Endicott. You are most welcome to join me.'

It was Georgina's turn to look alarmed.

'Surely, Kitty, you jest?'

'I do not.' Kitty's voice cracked. 'Mr Dalrymple's request is in every way improper. I see it clearly now. No good can come of such a rendezvous. I have been giving in to romantic dreams. Only think, Georgina, his motives could be base and I would have no defence.'

'I do not believe that a gentleman would behave so,' Georgina returned scornfully.

'Perhaps not. But a true gentleman should not suggest such a meeting and would think poorly of the lady who was foolish enough to attend. My decision is made.'

'I would not care about such dull convention.'

Georgina crossed her arms and stood firm her face set with a stubborn look.

'If you were observed, you would come to care very much,' Kitty said in a barely audible voice. 'Your reputation would be in tatters and then no gentleman would ever marry you. I wouldn't wish such a fate on either of us, Georgina.'

36

My dear Mary,

Your sister Catherine kindly provided me with your direction. I write to you with the presumption of friendship, which I so earnestly hope meets with your own sentiments. Frankness is to be preferred among friends, so do not be shocked when I tell you that finding someone like myself, with a strong regard for books, knowledge and intelligent conversation, is heaven-sent. Though my acquaintance is not very wide, I have nonetheless met a great many vapid females with no thought in their heads, other than bonnets and beaux.

I tell you all of the above for two important reasons. First, I hope to achieve a lasting connection with you, wherever fate decrees we must go. Secondly, because you are in Derbyshire and I am to go to Bath at Michaelmas in readiness to make my bow before the Prince in October. I do not know if you shall return before I am gone.

Lady Sandalford convinced Papa that I must be launched into society before the London season. I am then to go to London when Parliament sits, chaperoned by Lady Sandalford. She has shown great kindness and attention on my behalf, though I confess that as yet I feel no yearning for a husband.

The London theatre is a great attraction, however, and I admit to considerable curiosity about the many diversions of the capital and the inhabitants therein.

I have seen Mr Montagu but once since your departure. He was in good health but appeared a little distracted and asked if we had corresponded.

Mrs Montagu has her old friend Mrs Fulcross, with her daughter, Letitia, to visit. Of the former we all heard much, but the latter proved as quiet as a mouse.

That concludes any news of moderate interest I have to impart. I do hope that you are enjoying your sojourn with your sisters and that we may meet again soon, if not in person, then through correspondence.

Your friend in waiting,
Sylvia Drummond

The letter was sealed with the Drummond crest. Mary read the letter again. Her heart had stood still at the mention of Mr Montagu. He had enquired after her. Also, Sylvia had seen him only once and was going away. Sylvia said she did not wish to be married at present. Did that mean Mr Montagu had asked her and been refused? She frowned at the news of Mrs Montagu inviting yet another heiress to meet him and felt some small comfort in not being present to witness the event. But the receipt of the letter made her smile with pleasure. She had never before had a proper confidante beyond early childhood. A thorn between pairs of roses among her sisters, Mary had cleaved to herself and rarely confided in anyone. Now she felt blessed with an embarrassment of riches. No less than three of her sisters had taken her to their bosoms and now she had a bona fide friend.

With customary reserve, she withheld her impulse to respond with verve and slept with the letter beneath her pillow and a smile upon her face.

37

Lizzy and Mary took their morning walk through a heavily wooded area of the park. The heat elsewhere was oppressive and quite difficult to escape, even on the north wing of the house. Yesterday the sisters had resorted to reading in the sculpture gallery in the hope that the cool marbles would have a restorative effect.

In the woods, ancient trees created a welcome canopy overhead, while the soft woodland floor smothered the sound of footfall. Beyond an occasional feeble birdcall, the sisters could hear nothing save the gentle swish of their skirts. Lizzy paused to take a seat on a fallen elm. 'We have a visitor arriving today – Lord Applefrith. You will like him, Mary. He is a genial sort of fellow and likes to come to Pemberley for the shooting.'

'Is he a particular friend of Mr Darcy?'

Mary felt apprehension rise in her throat. She had begun to feel settled at Pemberley, and to take her lead from Lizzy with visitors. But a houseguest was a more permanent concern.

'Darcy enjoys his company, but he is more a friend of his cousin, Colonel Fitzwilliam. They served together. Henry, Lord Applefrith, is a second son, but he lost his older brother the winter before last.'

'How dreadful it must be to lose a sibling.' Mary breathed in the peaty forest air.

'Too awful to contemplate. Henry was happy in the regiment. I imagine running an estate is quite a change for him.'

Mary considered how onerous Mr Montagu had found his challenge and murmured her agreement. She began to feel compassion for their impending arrival.

They returned to find a carriage approaching. A well-built young gentleman leapt out, ignoring the footman and heading toward Lizzy with a beaming countenance.

'Mrs Darcy, how lucky to meet you at the entrance.'

Mary had leisure to observe their guest as her sister stepped forward to greet him. There was a hint of laughter in his brown eyes, which were darker than his hair. His height was moderate and there was something military in his bearing. He bowed with self-mocking exaggeration and took Lizzy's hand briefly into his own.

'We expected you later, sir. Allow me to present my younger sister, Miss Mary Bennet.'

'Splendid, how d'ye do, Miss Bennet. I took a chance on arriving early. Woke early, you know, with the infernal heat, and thought, well, why am I languishing here when I could be there? So I rustled up the ostler and away I came as soon as I had breakfasted.'

'Well, Darcy will be delighted to see you. Do come in and take a glass of cool cordial.'

Elizabeth offered Lord Applefrith her arm.

The next time Mary saw Lord Applefrith was at dinner. His lively nature invigorated the languid air carried over from the heat of the day. He escorted Mary into the dining room behind the Darcys. 'Have you been in Derbyshire long, Miss Bennet?'

'A short time, sir. I have had the good fortune to visit both my sisters.'

'Ah yes, your other sister being the elegant Mrs Bingley. How do they go on?'

'Very well. They are shortly expecting to welcome a new family member.'

Footmen standing behind the gilded chairs began the process of seating the party.

'That is good news,' he said, 'the Bingleys are excellent people. So many of my friends appear to be happy and settled. My mother tells me it is high time I joined the fray.'

Mary was unsure how to respond to so direct a statement from a stranger and sought to change the subject with haste.

'Elizabeth tells me you are here for the shooting.'

'Darcy has wonderful game drives.' He flapped his napkin in an excited fashion. 'I am monstrous fond of pheasant and grouse shooting, but you will find no complaint from me about a bustard or a partridge.'

Mary decided his ebullience required very little conversational effort on her part, save a show of interest.

'Then we must look forward to the spoils.'

'I shall do my very best, ma'am. I often think ladies miss out while we enjoy a fine day's sport. What with the sewing and whatnot.'

Mary laughed. Lord Applefrith was nothing if not diverting, with his plain manner of speech and high good humour.

'In truth, sir, we do not pine for long. We have much to keep us amused. Elizabeth enjoys nothing more than fresh air and a long walk. We have music and books, among other pastimes.'

'Well, you make it sound quite jolly. Which is your favourite pastime, Miss Bennet?'

Mary drew in a breath and hoped he would not find her answer dull.

'I am very fond of music, but books allow one a glimpse of the world, so they must be my preference.'

'Upon my soul. A female devoted to books. That is a rare occurrence. We must compare notes, Miss Bennet. I am a man of action but even I am fond of a good poet.'

'I hope we may prevail upon you for a reading, sir. Darcy's library has every text you might desire.'

Mary surprised herself by talking in so natural and emboldened a manner with a stranger. She realised that this owed as much to her modish looks as to Lord Applefrith's informal manners. She became aware that he regarded her with a frank interest she had only previously seen in Mr Montagu. She felt a trifle lightheaded from the attention and spoke up as never before, questioning Lord Applefrith about his friendship with Colonel Fitzwilliam.

'Capital fellow, Fitzwilliam. I'm sure you know.'

'I know him but little, though Darcy is very fond of his cousin and that must recommend him.'

'Quite right, quite right. Both capital fellows. Fitz is a fine shot, you know.'

'I suspect a fine shot is enough to recommend him to you without his other qualities,' Mary teased.

'Ha, you've rumbled me, Miss Bennet. It's true. A day's sport with a fair catch for the larder makes me happy. Give me a good dinner and a book of poetry by the fire and I would not swap my lot even for my army days.'

'How admirable you make the commonplace appear by your enjoyment. You give me a lesson in being satisfied with my own circumstances.'

Lord Applefrith appraised Mary with a look that she could not mistake for anything other than admiration.

'I have looked forward to my visit to Pemberley, Miss Bennet, but finding you to be one of the party makes the visit all the more happy.'

38

Lord Applefrith proved as genial as Lizzy's recommendation. He put one in mind of Mr Bingley with
his constant good spirits. His enjoyment of hunting
frequently peppered the conversation, but he did not lack
for manners. Mary imagined that he would have made an
excellent brother. Lizzy was wont to treat him as such,
while Darcy evidently enjoyed the masculine company.

Little Charles Fitzwilliam accorded Lord Applefrith the
highest status for his intricate knowledge of soldiering.
So endearing was the child's interest in the world that
both Mary and Lord Applefrith took to visiting him in
the nursery before dinner. The visits afforded her both
amusement and a curious sense of satisfaction. Mary had
the distinct impression that they had the same effect on
his Lordship. When playing with his soldiers, Charles
was commanding beyond his years.

'Lord Applefr . . .' The child struggled with the name.

'Call me Lord Apple,' his subject suggested with
kindness.

'Lord Apple is a proper officer; aren't you, sir?'

'Oh very proper,' replied his Lordship.

'So he must play the Duke of Wellington.' Charles
directed a look of concern at Mary. 'I hope you don't

mind, Aunt Mary. You can play him again when Lord Apple leaves us.'

Mary's eyes were alive with delight but she played her part with a sober face.

'I think your plan is only fitting and proper. Will you play Boney, Charles? You know a good deal more about him than I.'

The child was on his hands and knees in an instant, arranging his soldiers.

'Well, that is because you are a girl, Aunt. But you can be a general if you like.'

Mary's voice wobbled as she agreed. She met Lord Applefrith's eyes over her nephew's dark, wavy locks and each threatened to give way to laughter. They turned away in mutual accord and gave themselves over to the battle. All three sat on the nursery floor. Mary wrapped her sprig muslin gown around her ankles to avoid knocking the toy soldiers. She had never given much thought to battle tactics – rather the fighting and charges her father read aloud from news sheets. She watched as Lord Applefrith taught Charles some simple plans. The child was all rapt attention. His Lordship must have fought in many battles. He would no doubt appreciate having his own son to teach one day. As though hearing her thoughts, Lord Applefrith looked up and said,

'I have a fine pupil here, Miss Bennet. Perhaps one day I shall have my own officers.'

'You will have a great deal to teach them.'

'What will you teach your own girls, if that is not an impertinent question?'

She could not answer without revelation, but had no wish to be other than friendly with his Lordship, so tried to enter the spirit of the enquiry.

'I imagine I should have to call on my sisters to teach any daughter or niece of mine the usual arts. You have not met Catherine – Kitty to the family – but her skill with the needle is much admired. Lizzy sings quite well, though she rarely practises. Jane is our gentle moral guide. None of us paint. I shall rely on my knowledge of the pianoforte and of course, teach what I know from books.'

Charles looked up from one adult to another. He lowered his head and emitted a disgusted, 'Pah! Needlework and music. What a waste of time when one might play at soldiers.'

This time, his seniors were unable to contain their mirth.

Looking in one afternoon, Elizabeth and Darcy noted the domestic scene and treated one another to significant glances. In her boudoir later that evening, Darcy said to Elizabeth,

'Henry gives every appearance of a man considering a domestic future.'

Lizzy removed her topaz necklace.

'I believe his mother has encouraged him in that direction. With the loss of her first son, she must desire to see her second settled and the line secure. Lady Applefrith is in indifferent health, I understand.'

'That is all to the purpose. Henry is a sound fellow. He is not one for the petticoat line, but he does seem enamoured of your sister.'

Elizabeth sighed. 'Henry would make an excellent husband for many a young lady, yet I know Mary's heart to be engaged elsewhere.'

Darcy raised an eyebrow.

'Oh? Well perhaps we should let matters rest for now. Our friend's intentions are not yet clear, I suspect even to himself.'

Elizabeth rested a hand on her husband's shoulder, stroking the fine linen of his shirt. 'Your thinking is sound, my love. Of all people, we know that where the heart is concerned, matters will take their own course.'

Mr Darcy took his wife into his arms and leaned down to kiss her.

'I should wish all my friends as happy as we are, yet I do not believe it is possible.'

39

Breakfast at Pemberley was a late and relaxed affair. The numerous tall windows of the breakfast room caught any sun to be had most of the year, with the happy effect of enhancing the moods of its inhabitants. It was customary to linger in the sunshine with any personal post after breakfast. Darcy opened one such letter and read aloud;

My dear son-in-law,

You may be surprised that I write to you instead of Elizabeth, but there is no cause for alarm.

I have a notion to make a brief journey into Derbyshire to meet my newest grandchild when he, or she, appears. Mrs Bennet is disinclined to travel, as the movement of the carriage causes her frailties to bloom in magnificent style. Kitty is determined to accompany me and I see no reason to withhold my consent.

The foregoing is of little consequence to you, but I mention it for general illumination. I do, however, have an application for your consideration:

My young neighbour, Mr Montagu of Cuthbert Park, is recently returned to manage his estates after the passing of my friend, his late father.

Mr Darcy broke off as Mary's knife clattered to her plate.
'Are you acquainted with the young man, Mary?'
Her face white, Mary replied,
'He is well known to us since his return.'
Lizzy accorded Darcy a speaking glance, so he pursued
the matter no further other than to raise a questioning
eyebrow and read on;

*Mr Montagu is an excellent young man and has
sought my advice on the matter of introducing something new to his estate; an instance that will communicate to you the paucity of good advice at his
disposal. The land has mixed arable and livestock.
Mr Montagu has decided that he should invest in a
premium herd. I told him he could do no better than
your Herefords, of which there are few, and no finer
in these sceptred isles.*

*On his behalf, may I prevail upon you to share
some of your knowledge with him? Mr Montagu is
prepared to travel with us to Derbyshire and return
home alone. I shall not travel until we hear from you.*

*Mrs Bennet, Kitty and I send our loving wishes to
you, Elizabeth, Mary and little Charles.*

Etc.

Mary sat frozen with shock. Lord Applefrith, uncon-
cerned with family matters, continued to make a good
breakfast from the array of silver dishes at his disposal.
Darcy turned to Lizzy.
'Well, my dear, what do you make of that? Shall
we hold ourselves up to be Hereford cattle experts and
entertain Mr Montagu?'

Lizzy made a cautious glance to Mary, who, lost in her thoughts, gave no hint as to her preference.

'I think it would be kind to assist a young friend of the family if we are able. Should we invite them all to stay here? I fear Jane and Bingley will be too much troubled by guests, albeit family, at a time when their attentions are much preoccupied.'

'It is you, my dear, who must bear the greater burden, so if you are willing, I will write to invite the whole party to make themselves comfortable at Pemberley. Your father will doubtless disappear into my library and barely be seen above mealtimes. Mr Montagu may join us in a little hunting during his research.'

At the mention of hunting, Lord Applefrith raised his head and said, 'Good show!'

Mary excused herself as soon as possible from the table and hurried away, her thoughts in turmoil. What did the proposed visit signify? Papa's letter had mentioned Mr Montagu's determination to create a new herd. She had suggested something of the like herself. Did Mr Montagu welcome the prospect of a visit or did he feel perhaps obliged to come after her father's advice? Then again, Sylvia's letter had alluded to Mr Montagu's being distracted.

Mary tried to set her thoughts to one side until her morning walk with Lizzy. They had not ventured far into the shrubbery before Mary sought her sister's opinion.

'I would willingly give it, Mary, but I do not know the gentleman. To surmise might be to give you a false impression.'

Mary stopped and folded her hands in front of her, not moving at all. Her frown showed that she could not be satisfied with such an answer.

'But let us consider the facts as we know them,' Lizzy continued. 'Mr Montagu has applied to Papa for advice. Papa is aware that Darcy has a high quality cattle stud and hence, recommends Mr Montagu to pursue his researches here.'

'Lizzy, I do not know what to think. Will he wish to see me? Can I face him with composure? It is all so difficult.'

Mary twisted her bonnet strings in knots as she spoke, without noticing her actions.

'Poor Mary. Life is not a beribboned parcel, all neatness and joyful expectation. Let the facts be your guide. Mr Montagu is at the very least your friend, is he not?' Mary nodded. 'Then you owe him the civility of friendship. Your conduct towards him must not alter from that which he knows, unless you are given just cause.'

With that, Mary had to be content. Lizzy's advice would be her guide, though the mere thought of the visit bought a warm colour to her cheeks and caused her heart to beat faster.

In the privacy of their own rooms, Lizzy allowed Darcy a simple account of Mary's flight to Derbyshire. He dropped into a chair, quite astonished.

'I own your sister is much altered in appearance and I have noticed such changes in her character that I had put down to increasing maturity, but I never suspected her to be of a sensitive nature.'

Lizzy turned from her seat at the looking glass to face him.

'I believe that she has matured and with a degree of rapidity. Mary is at last engaging with society. She has learned to doubt herself. Indeed, she now doubts herself too much. Her sensitivity has been hidden from us all.'

'Your sister gives me cause for concern. If this Montagu story is correct, then I do not see a happy way forward.'

'Much depends upon Mr Montagu, my dear. When we make his acquaintance I feel we shall be in a better position to form a judgement and thus to see if we can be of assistance.'

Darcy's concerned frown relaxed. 'My very wise wife.'

40

The journey was interminable in the poorly sprung old coach. The heat and road dust added to the discomfort. Kitty had forgotten how desultory conversation became when one spent hour after hour hostage to the same company. She wished she had thought to bring something to read with her as Papa and Mr Montagu had done. Mary would not have contemplated such a journey without reading.

At least Mr Montagu proved to be a better companion than Mama, who had always plagued everyone on long journeys with her ailments and odd humours. Kitty had tried to draw out Mr Montagu in regard to Sylvia and Mary but politeness demanded she was circumspect in her probing and Mr Montagu's natural reticence meant that she was not satisfied with her efforts. In other respects she began to see why Mary liked him. When he was engaged in some lofty conversation with Papa, he became quite boyish in his enthusiasm, but was otherwise measured and thoughtful. Such a quiet gentleman would suit Mary very well. Kitty's own taste was for someone more inclined to amusement. Her thoughts turned to Mr Dalrymple, the very incarnation of amiability, though she now knew his character to be of a low order.

'Pardon, Miss Bennet?' Mr Montagu enquired.

'Oh, was I speaking my thoughts aloud? It was nothing at all.'

They relapsed into silence against the hard backs of their seats. Mr Bennet dozed in his favoured corner seat; head rocking gently with the sway of the coach. Kitty resumed her brooding over Mr Dalrymple.

She had wondered day and night what he might have thought when she failed to meet him. He had not called at Longbourn, much to her mother's chagrin.

'Depend upon it, dear, he is thinking about you. No doubt his aunt and cousin demand much of him. We must contrive to bring him to Longbourn or meet him at an assembly at the very least. One cannot allow such an eligible gentleman loose upon society for too long.'

Kitty had kept Mr Dalrymple's wicked suggestion a secret from her parents. While there remained the smallest possibility that he might be in earnest, she would not fail him. She had caught sight of him with Lady Sarah once in Meryton. He, handsome and well-dressed as ever, capturing his cousin's attention with his conversation. Their eyes had met across the street and his held a question. The presence of Lady Sarah forbade any answer. Kitty knew her own features had registered confusion, making her feel as gauche as a girl of Georgina's age. Her errands that day had taken her to the haberdashery for some tatting thread. With an elaborate effort to appear casual, she had asked Mrs Blain if Lady Sarah was a customer.

'Not in general, Miss Bennet, no. Her sort buy in London and have their dressmaker do all the work. I doubt she even does her own fancy work.'

Mrs Blain compressed her lips and shook her head with disapproval. Kitty was about to turn away when Mrs Blain added,

'She called in today, though. Buying her cousin some new cravats – finest linen, mind. Said to him as he was leaving soon she wanted to see him off in style.'

Kitty had flinched at this remark and was lucky that Mrs Blain had turned to tidy a stack of damasks, so did not notice. Still talking, the lady added,

'He's a fine young buck, the cousin. Very much your London man. He was charming to his cousin but not to me – if you take my meaning.'

Kitty had nodded her understanding. *He was leaving. When?*

A week later she told her mother what she had learned from Mrs Blain. Mrs Bennet cast several aspersions upon the heads of fickle young gentlemen and had attempted to comfort Kitty with the words that Mr Montagu was not married at least and that efforts must be redoubled in that quarter. When she learned that Mr Montagu would be travelling with Mr Bennet to Derbyshire, her impassioned support of Kitty's plan to join the party ran so far as to the supply of a new grosgrain travel bonnet and a summer pelisse.

41

Events moved at a pace. Darcy had scarce written his invitation to his father-in-law to visit Pemberley when a messenger arrived from Stonehythe. The house party were playing whist in the blue damask withdrawing room after dinner when the butler called Mr Darcy away. He returned with a scrawled note from Bingley, apparently written in haste.

My dear Darcy, Elizabeth and Mary,

You may be the first to felicitate Jane and me on the safe arrival of our son, George Adolphus John Bingley. Jane is fatigued but elated and our boy is a lusty little fellow by first impressions. More anon.

Your faithful servant,
Bingley

Lizzy clapped her hands with joy, then embraced her husband and Mary. Lord Applefrith pumped Darcy's hand and bowed to the ladies.

'Mrs Darcy, Miss Bennet, my congratulations on the new addition to your family. Growing up among such excellent relations, he cannot help but become a capital fellow. Why, I could wish to be one of you myself!'

The family broke into happy laughter. Lord Applefrith's exuberance of expression could not be other than appreciated for his well-intentioned sentiments.

News of their Meryton guests' imminent arrival came two days before Mr Bennet's coach appeared at Pemberley.

The household hastened to greet the arrivals. Mary hung back behind Lizzy, wishing that Charles were present so that she could hold his small hand for comfort. So many questions assailed her. Her common sense told her that Mr Montagu's expression could not answer them all, but sensibility wished for such a result. Mr Bennet stepped down from the carriage before offering Kitty his hand. Of Mr Montagu there was no sign.

'My dear Lizzy, how well you look, or are my old eyes fading?' Mr Bennet teased. 'And, Mary, your visit agrees with you prodigiously. You show fair to eclipsing your sisters.'

Mary flushed pink with pleasure despite her nervousness about meeting Mr Montagu again. She went smiling into her father's embrace, while Kitty greeted Lizzy and Mr Darcy.

As Mr Bennet stepped away to greet his son-in-law, Mary was left standing in front of the carriage. Mr Montagu stooped and emerged through the narrow door, with the sun lighting his golden hair from behind. Lizzy looked on, approving Mr Montagu's delicacy in allowing the family time to greet one another. He stood before Mary, eyes directed to hers. Mary appeared to be struck dumb.

Lizzy stepped forward with her hand outstretched and a cheerful tone,

'Mary, will you not introduce me to your friend?'

Mary jumped. 'Oh, I beg your pardon. Mr Montagu, allow me to present my second sister, Mrs Elizabeth Darcy.' As Lizzy went smiling to shake his hand, Mary looked away. *I am supposed to be acquiring polish, yet one look at him and I cannot manage even a simple introduction.* She bit her lip.

Mr Montagu gave no signal that he had noticed any awkwardness.

'Mrs Darcy, I do believe that we may have met as children, though I hope you do not recognise me from the ungracious little urchin of yesteryear.'

Lizzy laughed. 'Mr Montagu, we were none of us prepossessing in those days, excepting perhaps my elder sister, Mrs Bingley. Welcome to Pemberley. Do come and allow me to present my husband, Mr Darcy.

With introductions made, Lizzy conducted her guest to his room, leaving Mary to take her father and Kitty to rooms they knew well. Mary was grateful for the interlude. She had tried telling herself that she would feel differently when she saw Mr Montagu, but his emergence from the carriage had given lie to her thoughts in an instant. She had felt breathless. The joy of seeing him seemed overshadowed by the tumble of questions she could not ask him.

As she made him familiar with his rooms, Lizzy said to Mr Montagu,

'I shall not torment you with a tour of Pemberley at present, but when you are more settled, Mary will be delighted to conduct you. She is quite knowledgeable.'

Mr Montagu favoured his hostess with a wide smile.

'I should expect nothing less of Miss Bennet.'

Taken at the fashionable hour of 6 o'clock, dinner was a quiet affair for the increased party. The travellers had determined upon early starts and long days in order to minimise their time on the dusty summer roads. The ageing carriage had often felt oppressive to each of the occupants, though politeness dictated such inconveniences were overlooked, and caused them all to feel all the more weary for their restraint.

Lord Applefrith offered Mary his arm to be escorted into dinner, leaving Mr Montagu trailing behind Mr Bennet and Kitty. A footman seated him next to Lizzy, at the opposite end of the table to Mary. Lizzy accorded her guest a good deal of attention and applied her charm to put him at his ease. In turn Mr Montagu complimented her on the fine aspect to be had from the house and the beauty of his surroundings. Lizzy kept him entertained with a combination of intelligence and wit through the removes of soup and fish. The French chef displayed his expertise with the grouse to perfection. Mr Montagu voiced his appreciation to Mr Darcy.

'We are indeed lucky to have found such a wonderful chef,' Darcy conceded. 'These Frenchmen are so fashionable that the competition is fierce. But for the grouse, you must convey your thanks to Lord Applefrith, for the majority of the bag is his.'

Lord Applefrith demurred.

'Well, sir, we are nevertheless indebted to you and the excellent chef,' said Mr Montagu.

''Tis a pleasure and no trouble at all, I vow. Darcy has fine shooting and an even finer chef. I enjoy the eating in equal measure.'

Lord Applefrith beamed around the table. Each of the weary travellers were pleased with their new acquaintance's refreshingly open manners. He did not stand on ceremony, nor did he adopt any airs. He wore his title as the lightest of cloaks.

As the gentleman took their port, Mr Darcy invited his guests to hunt the following day. It was a surprise to him that his father-in-law agreed. While not unknown to the field, it was Mr Bennet's delight to begin a visit to Pemberley discovering any new volumes in the well-stocked library. Mr Montagu readily agreed to join the hunting party.

Mr Bennet, claiming the toll of his years from the journey, announced his desire to be excused and abed at an early hour this evening, but he took Lizzy aside to announce his intention to learn more of Lord Applefrith at first hand before his sojourn came to an end. The young man had paid Mary considerable attention and appeared to amuse her. Mr Bennet suggested that these were novel occurrences in his experience.

42

After breakfasting on a selection of French breads, preserves, plum cake and toast, with liberal cups of coffee and chocolate, the gentleman departed to the gunroom.

The ladies lingered in the morning room. Lizzy read aloud from a brief new note in Mr Bingley's hand.

My dear Elizabeth,

I write principally to you, to save my darling Jane exertion. Do not be alarmed, for she is very well, though young George is very demanding for such a little fellow, and Jane insists on undertaking those small tasks for him which might be taken on by a nursery-maid. James and Susannah are unsure what to make of their little brother, but are coming around to the conclusion that he must stay. Mr Bennet must be anxious to meet his new grandchild, as indeed you ladies must be to meet your new nephew. We would be very happy to receive you as soon as you wish to come. My compliments to Darcy, Mr Bennet and your sisters.

Your servant,
Bingley

The three sisters enjoyed a half hour's discussion and conjecture over Bingley's letter, before the customary morning walk. Kitty broke the companionable silence.

'How lovely it is for us all to be walking together again. How many times did we walk into Meryton?' Since the question was deemed rhetorical, neither sister responded. 'All we need now are dear Jane and Lydia.'

The picture in her mind of those former occasions seemed a very long time ago to Mary.

'I truly wonder if we will ever see Lydia in England again.' She noted Kitty's dismay with chagrin. 'But then of course, we cannot know the future. Who would have imagined any of the events among us in recent years?'

Lizzy replied. 'Not I, nor indeed Jane.' She knelt to gather blue columbines growing wild among the grasses. 'Fortune has smiled upon us both and I am forever grateful.'

'For myself, I should be content with a good deal less,' said Kitty. 'And you, Mary?'

'I think I could wish for nothing more or less than a companion who would be my partner in all things.' The image of a blond head thrown back in laughter sprang unbidden into her thoughts. 'In as much as I am asking too much, I believe I must be content with a roof over my head, a piano and a good book.'

She bent down to pluck a fern and handed it to Lizzy for her small bouquet as her sisters laughed.

'I do not think you ask too much,' began Lizzy. 'Such happiness should be the lot of all women, though perhaps remains the joy of the few.'

'Well, I do think that you may achieve your heart's desire, looking as you do now, Mary. Though for myself,

I should prefer a husband who takes the lead. A partnership sounds quite frightening, if not fatiguing.'

Kitty set her sisters again to laughing.

In the distance they could hear gunshot carrying on the breeze. A flock of alarmed birds raced over their heads and they paused to watch them in flight.

'Lord Applefrith will be enjoying himself,' Lizzy opined.

'He appears a very amiable gentleman,' said Kitty, as she retied her bootlace on a convenient mound of turf.

'Oh, most amiable,' Mary agreed, though her thoughts again strayed to another, more reserved young gentleman.

Kitty shot her a sly look.

'Amiable enough to marry?'

Mary frowned. 'Good heavens, Kitty. Not every young man is hanging out for a wife.'

Kitty's response was fast and sure.

'Not every young man sets out to entertain one at a dinner as Lord Applefrith applied his conversation to *you*, Mary.'

Mary dropped the woodland larkspur she had been sniffing, her expression wide-eyed and stricken.

'Do you think it's so? I should not wish to give Lord Applefrith a false impression for the world. He's all amiability, and I feel as comfortable with him as a brother.'

Lizzy's soothing tones intervened.

'Lord Applefrith does show a partiality for you, Mary, but he has made no formal declarations. I would, however, advise you to be clear and blameless in your behaviour towards him.'

'What of Mr Montagu?' demanded Kitty.

'There is no alteration in my regard for Mr Montagu.' Mary's shoulders sank and her voice took on a wistful quality. 'Nor can there be any hope for the future, as you both know. But I am resolved to turn myself to good account and that must be my goal.'

Kitty gave her a mutinous look and appeared to be about to argue the point; but after a repressive glance from Lizzy, she lapsed into silence.

Two miles across the estate, Mr Bennet was benefitting from his hunting expedition. The younger gentlemen afforded him every assistance. Mr Darcy settled him in the most advantageous positions. Lord Applefrith was free with his hunting tips and Mr Montagu insisted on carrying his shot. He appeared to quite forget any plan to interrogate Lord Applefrith in the excitement of shooting a brace of pheasant.

In the lulls created between drives, Mr Montagu and Lord Applefrith discovered that they shared common ground in recently inheriting an estate to manage. Lord Applefrith displayed more than a nodding acquaintance with modern methodology and farm culture, whilst Mr Montagu's grasp of financial management became the subject of much interest from his Lordship. As Mr Montagu gave himself up to the day's sport and acquitted himself well, the pair began to form the basis of a friendship. All four gentleman could boast of a good day's work when they met the ladies in the drawing room before dinner. Taking full advantage of his title's precedence, Lord Applefrith once again escorted Mary into dinner.

For a day the fine weather halted and a veil of rain hung softly over the Derbyshire hills.

Delighted to have the undivided attention of so many, young Charles spent an excitable morning playing games with the adults. He soon outran all but Mr Montagu's long legs with his tireless energy.

In the afternoon Mr Darcy and Mr Montagu retired to the estate office to discuss Hereford cattle. Mr Montagu proved eager in his questions. The cattle were hardy, adaptable and produced fine quality beef. Mr Darcy's agent, a meticulous man, had recorded each animal from the beginning of the stud. After considerable discussion, Darcy stated his willingness to part with enough speci-mens to start a new stud, though his handsome features were set in stern formality as he said,

'I make no bones about it, Mr Montagu.'

'Sebastian, please.'

'Sebastian. I do not part with livestock as a rule, for there are those who are lax and downright cruel in their treatment of animals. I judge you to be a different sort of gentleman.'

Mr Montagu sat across the giant partner's desk and levelled a direct look at Darcy.

'I believe that I am, sir. I would turn off any man in my employ who showed cruelty to man or beast.'

Mr Darcy held out his hand.

'Darcy or Fitzwilliam, please.'

'Darcy.' Sebastian returned the firm grasp and smiled. 'You will be welcome at Cuthbert Park any time you are visiting Meryton. You will see how the cattle go on. Besides which, we can offer you tolerable hunting.'

Darcy closed the cattle register with a thud.

'Then I shall look forward to both.' His lips turned up at the corners and a faint twinkle came to his eyes.

'I dislike troubling my mother-in-law's hospitality day and night during a visit.'

Having stood patiently through a fitting for her ball-gown, Mary had been rewarded with a fine paisley shawl by Lizzy. Kitty received another in rosy hues, which delighted her. Afterwards, slipping along the long gallery, Mary almost bumped into Mr Montagu as he entered.

The room suddenly seemed powerfully large and she felt very small.

'Miss Bennet.'

He broke into a wide smile and stepped up toward her.

'Mr Montagu.'

Her delight in the encounter was marred by concerns as to the direction their conversation might take if they were alone together.

'Mrs Darcy tells me you are quite the expert on Pemberley's treasures. Will you afford me a tour?'

'Did my sister really tell you I am an expert?' He nodded. Mary saw that she must acquiesce with grace. 'I fear she is mistaken but if you will forgive my omissions, I shall endeavour to do my best.'

'Your best is always good enough for me.'

One of his direct, serious looks again. Mary wished she could read his thoughts. As she warmed to her task, Mary forgot her self-consciousness. Though she was aware that Mr Montagu looked at her as often, and more attentively, than he did the paintings and fine examples of furniture, she delighted in showing the house's treasures. He was perforce to pay more attention to the fine china and sculptures as Mary was wont to catch his eye to point out a detail here and there. They moved from room to room, each seemingly larger and more grand than the last.

'You seem quite at home among all these riches.'

His aside was casual, but there was gravity in his tone.

'Only in as much as I have visited before and they are now part of my nephew's future heritage. I think the Honourable Sylvia Drummond would be more suited to such surroundings than I. We live a more simple existence at Longbourn.'

He turned to her with a broad smile.

'Then you have no great desire for riches?'

His eyes held hers. Mary considered.

'I admit to a desire for comfort. To wish for more would be to give in to the temptation of greed. Since I already enjoy a measure of comfort, then I shall only wish to maintain my good fortune.'

He nodded, as if to himself.

'Such modesty does you credit. However, a lady who appreciates history and beauty deserves such surroundings as will satisfy her senses.'

Mary blushed. Mr Montagu stepped toward her. She stepped back in confusion. There was something in the determined cast of his expression which foretold a dangerous turn in the conversation.

'Please excuse me. I – I have promised Kitty that I will loan her something before dinner.'

With that, Mary rushed out of the room.

43

It was but the work of a few days to arrange a visit to Stonehythe. Lord Applefrith and Mr Montagu were included in the invitation. The former had met with the Bingleys on a previous visit and Jane would not hear of the latter being left out of the party. So that the party could make a return to Pemberley within the day, saving Jane a surfeit of hostess duties, luncheon would be deemed to be the significant meal of the day. A generous supper would be served on their return to Pemberley.

Accordingly, the party set off in Mr Darcy's chaise and four and Lord Applefrith's coach. Mary and her father entered the coach with young Charles, while Kitty and Mr Montagu were to pair with the Darcys. The two gentlemen spent some of the journey in discussion of the Herefords. Mr Montagu apologised to Lizzy and Kitty for discussing such matters in their presence and was assured that they were not bothered a whit, if the gentlemen would only forbear with their talk of fashion plates and old acquaintance.

Lord Applefrith began a lively conjecture in his carriage as to the likely features of baby George. In this game Mr Bennet enjoyed giving full allowance to his humour. Charles was much diverted by their foolish face-pulling and falsetto voices, and forgot to enquire about the duration of the journey at all. Mary found the game faintly silly and gave some of the journey over to admiring the fine Derbyshire countryside.

Mr Bingley met the party with his customary bonhomie, greeting one and all with delight and ushering them indoors, where they came upon Jane, looking like an angel, and holding baby George in her arms. A nurse-maid hovered nearby, ready to whisk George away, but Lizzy quickly claimed him. As soon as she was able, Jane welcomed Mr Montagu.

'I have long wished to make your acquaintance again, sir.' Mr Montagu looked puzzled. 'My memory of you when we were young children is quite hazy, but Mary has spoken of you in such glowing terms as piqued my curiosity.'

Surprise and something quite like hope registered on his face.

'Miss Bennet is most generous in all things. I doubt that I can live up to her words.'

Jane issued him with the warm smile that won her many friends.

'Your modesty does you credit, but my sister is usually certain in her judgements and not prone to exaggeration.'

'There I must agree with you. Miss Mary Bennet's good sense and sound advice have been invaluable in the months since I have returned to assume my father's place at Cuthbert Park.' His voice rang with sincerity.

'You must sit by me at luncheon and tell me all about your plans. We have so little time on this short visit to become reacquainted.'

Just then, there was a general 'ah', which could only allude to baby George. Jane turned to see her son in Mary's arms.

Lord Applefrith exclaimed, 'He smiled at Miss Bennet, I declare.'

Mary, pink and smiling herself, looked up directly into the eyes of Mr Montagu. For a moment they remained locked in a gaze, then Mary dragged her eyes back to the infant nestled in her arms.

Kitty demanded her turn with the baby, but was thwarted by the announcement of luncheon.

Following a considerable feast, Mr Bennet and his younger daughters sought to supervise a game of hoops with the children. The gentlemen all joined in the exercise amid a great deal of laughter. Jane and Lizzy repaired to the former's sitting room.

'Well, Jane, have I met with your expectations for Mary?'

'I believe so, Lizzy dear. Her raiment is all that is pleasing, and I see that Rigby has taught her another new arrangement for her hair.'

'She was, as you predicted, humbly grateful for assistance. I began to feel we would never see our Mary of old again.' Lizzy chuckled. 'I missed her strident opinions in the most curious way.' She crossed to Jane and tucked another cushion behind her. 'I believe she has regained a little of her old confidence.'

'Thank you, Lizzy, that is more comfortable.' She picked up her embroidery. 'Mary's reserve with Mr Montagu is writ plain and, from my observation, worries him.'

'Naturally, he's confused by her behaviour, as well he might. The longer he remains with us, the more I see that he is truly attached to Mary, and the more I like him.'

'I saw it for myself today. He is all eagerness where she is concerned and so full of plans for the future that I can only imagine him to be contemplating a settled life. What is to be done, Lizzy?' Jane gave her sister a quizzical look. 'They clearly care for each other and they appear to be suited.'

'What indeed? I cannot think of a way forward. Then there is Henry.'

'Lord Applefrith?' Jane paused in the act of threading her needle. 'What has he to say to anything?'

Lizzy carried on sorting silk threads, but a knowing smile crossed her face.

'Did you not notice his partiality for Mary? He is fascinated by her intelligence, but I do not consider them a suitable match. He, though, does begin to talk about the notion of marriage and his mother encourages the idea.'

'Lord Applefrith and Mary.' Jane shook her head. 'The picture becomes complicated, Lizzy. I agree with you; their characters do not quite signify a match.' She put down her work. 'But what does Darcy say?'

'He sees things as I do, but feels it is not our place to interfere.'

Unable to resolve the matter, the sisters moved to those daily issues within their power to solve.

When the party disbanded, Mr Montagu found himself happily seated opposite Mary in the Darcy's chaise. He wasted no time in praising his hosts and the delightful prospect of Stonehythe. He ended his comments by saying,

'Mr Bingley is such a happy gentleman.' This latter statement was addressed principally to the sisters. 'But that is no surprise, as Mrs Bingley could not be more kind or pleasant in nature.'

Darcy said, 'Beyond ourselves, I believe there to be no happier couple in England.'

Delighted by an opportunity to tease her husband, Lizzy asked, 'Have your enquiries been extensive, my dear?'

'You know they have not, Elizabeth, yet you must allow my opinion to be possible.'

Lizzy's eyes danced. 'Ah, but we must look to our laurels, for what of the future? What if Mary or Kitty or Mr Montagu, for example, were to excel in matrimony. What then, my love?'

'One cannot make claims upon the future.' Darcy leaned forward and kissed his wife's hand. 'But mark you do look to your laurels, Mrs Darcy.'

Mr Montagu entered into the light-hearted spirit of the conversation. 'Can one excel in matrimony?' His eyes drifted towards Mary. 'I had rather hoped that it was a state of comfortable intimacy between two people whose thoughts and feelings each lent countenance to the other.'

Darcy clapped a hand to his knee. 'Well, Sebastian, I do believe that you have just succeeded in describing the exact conditions for excelling in matrimony.'

Lord Applefrith's coach had not travelled far along the Derbyshire roads before Mr Bennet succumbed to the steady rhythm. His head drooped against the padded corner of his seat and he was soon sound asleep. Charles Fitzwilliam also fell prey to the after-effects of excited exertions with his cousins and before long was nestled against Lord Applefrith, with his lips curved sweetly in his sleep. Kitty smiled indulgently at her nephew.

'You are most clearly a favourite with my nephew, sir. For all he is sociable, he does not place his trust in everyone.'

Lord Applefrith looked down at the sleeping boy and whispered, 'He is a wonderful little chap, Miss Bennet. I suspect my popularity with him rests with a good knowledge of soldiering.'

'A soldier.' She spoke out loud and then dropped her voice as Charles stirred. 'I should have suspected it from your bearing. But do I collect that you are no longer with the regiment?'

Kitty sat forward, all interest.

'Correct, and a little sorry for it.' His face clouded for a moment. 'I enjoyed military life more than my poor late brother enjoyed the life of a country squire.'

Kitty's face fell. 'I am sorry for your loss.'

'Thank you.' He shrugged. 'But that is in the past now. My brother is with his beloved maker, for he was fierce pious. I am making a fist of reviving our estates. 'Tis only my mother who struggles to make peace with circumstances. My brother, Dominic, was a great favourite with her, you know.'

This latter was uttered without a trace of bitterness.

'Poor Lady Applefrith. The unnatural loss of a child must be very great indeed. But you must be a comfort to her.'

'I do my best, but I fear I am ill-suited to the task.' He frowned. 'Too much the bluff soldier, I'm afraid.'

'Perhaps ladies are more naturally suited to tending wounds, to flesh and feeling.'

Kitty lifted Charles' dangling foot onto the seat. His cherubic face smiled in his sleep.

Lord Applefrith looked down on the sleeping child.

'You have it exactly, Miss Bennet.' He made a mock wipe of his brow. 'I must say you Bennet sisters are all of a piece with cleverness.'

'Oh, sir, you are quite wrong. My older sisters are all quite clever. I had never thought books and such mattered, but I see now when I watch you all talking that I am very wrong. I am determined upon a course of self-improvement.'

Lord Applefrith frowned. 'Upon my word, I do not think it necessary.'

'Oh dear, I was rather hoping for a little advice from you.' Kitty pouted and sank back in her seat.

'From me? My dear Miss Bennet, your exalted father, Mr Darcy, and your neighbour, Mr Montagu, are all most excellent men when one wishes for a scholar.'

She nodded with vigour.

'Exactly so. That is the problem. They are so truly immersed in their scholarship that one fears to ask where to begin, lest something beyond one is proposed.'

'I do see your problem.' He sat in pensive silence for a minute or two. 'I shall not be at Pemberley many more days, but it will be my foremost thought to recommend a light course of reading for you.'

Kitty clasped her hands together.

'You will? Oh, Lord Applefrith, I am all gratitude. But you must allow me to return the favour in some fashion.'

'There is no need, Miss Bennet.'

'But I must repay the debt.' She leaned forward again, eyes alight. 'You say you are at some loss to comfort your mother?'

'I am, indeed. But I fail to see how anyone can help. Perhaps in time . . .' Lord Applefrith trailed off, shrugged and looked out of the window.

Kitty persisted. 'Time, sir, can be of great assistance, I am sure. But tell me, does her Ladyship have a good deal of time on her hands?'

He sighed. 'She does. While, of course, I have the opposite. It has been very time-consuming trying to retrieve those areas of estate management so foreign to my poor brother's clerical sensibilities. Pemberley is the first occasion I have had to leave home for leisure in more than a year.'

Kitty folded her arms.

'Well, my Lord, forgive my forwardness, but I believe that your mother wants occupation.'

'I suspect you are right. No doubt that is why she encourages me to marry, so that she might have grandchildren.'

He uttered the words in all seriousness, but Kitty blushed at his candour.

'Perhaps.' Kitty placed a cool hand to her cheek. 'But the need is now. Is there not something which will occupy her time and thoughts? A ball, perhaps? A ball requires a lady to occupy herself with prodigious preparations, and there is a great deal of uplifting enjoyment to reward her efforts on the evening of the ball.'

He shifted in his seat as well as he was able under the weight of Charles, and frowned. 'Your plan is splendid in many ways, but I fear she is in no mood for celebration.'

'Hmm.' They sat in silence for a few minutes.

'But of course!' Kitty said.

Charles stirred, then settled. Lord Applefrith regarded her in some surprise.

'Consider, sir, if you told your mama that a ball would be the perfect means by which to meet marriageable young ladies. Would she not agree?'

A broad smile spread across his features, restoring his usual cheerful looks.

'Why, Miss Bennet, that is a stroke of genius. I do not see why you say you are not clever.'

'Balls and dancing are not clever, but I do know a good deal about them.'

'I shall suggest it.' He fell back against the padded seat at ease. 'Nay, I shall insist upon a ball the moment I return. You suggest a most excellent strategy. Wellington himself would be impressed. Miss Bennet, you and your sister must be the first among our friends to be invited. You will come, will you not?'

'I'm sure Mary and I will be honoured, sir. We shall need to secure a chaperone, but I believe that we may be counted upon.'

Lord Applefrith returned to his customary high spirits for the remainder of the journey, asking Kitty's advice over numerous details in the polite art of hosting a ball. Kitty, in her element, was most happy to oblige.

44

M r Montagu and Lord Applefrith each approached the end of their stay at Pemberley with regret at the loss of leisure and genial company. Mr Montagu had gladly accepted a seat in his Lordship's coach. He could collect his own mount at the coaching inn where they must break the journey for their respective estates, some thirty miles apart.

Before leaving, each gentleman had business to attend. Lord Applefrith kept his promise to Kitty. With Darcy's permission, he scoured Pemberley's library for reading materials suitable for a young lady unused to scholarship. With military precision, he spent an hour on two days in succession guiding her in the merits and pitfalls of the volumes she would read. The intimidating size of the library was considered too onerous a venue for discussion, so, with the door left open, the pair repaired to the ante library, which offered greater light through its new window.

'I beg of you, Miss Bennet, do not commit too much time each day to your endeavours. You have other talents which bring pleasure to your family and friends.'

Kitty assured him that she was unlikely to take her reading to excess. She removed a slim volume of poetry from the small pile of books he had selected for her.

'I fear my mind is too easily distracted to admit a good deal of information.'

'Miss Catherine, pray take my advice and take the medicine slow.' They sat as near as propriety would allow in order to share the texts. Lord Applefrith answered Kitty's questions with patience and simplicity. 'When you come to my ball, we shall see how you have progressed and amend any efforts of mine such as have been a failure.'

Kitty favoured him with a warm smile.

'Sir, there can be no failure where there is such kind intent. I hope only to make a worthy pupil for your patronage.'

His Lordship appeared much affected by this sentiment. He stood up and bowed.

'What is your favourite dance, Miss Bennet?'

'Oh, I am fond of them all. Perhaps the cotillion.'

'I am quite rusty after a year of seclusion at Gediston Park. Would you trace the steps with me so I might acquit myself with credit at the ball?'

Kitty dimpled. 'We have no music or partners to make up a quad, but let's try.'

Lord Applefrith had great difficulty imagining the missing dancers and led off on the wrong foot three times, to Kitty's great amusement. At last he managed a credible pass and flopped into a chair flourishing a handkerchief in dramatic fashion. Kitty's peals of laughter drew her brother-in-law into the room. Lord Applefrith's accounts of his travails earned him a clap on the shoulder from Darcy and an amused request to pull himself together for the sake of mankind's reputation.

*

Any hopes Mr Montagu may have entertained to find some time alone with Mary were dashed. In the mornings she walked with her sisters and was at times engaged with them in the afternoons. If not, she was like as not helping Charles with his letters. The evenings after dinner were spent with guests or the house party at cards, principally Quadrille or Whist. Music was popular even when there were no extra invited guests. Mrs Darcy would, on occasion, produce a light air in a sweet voice. She was usually accompanied by Mary, who played very well. Once or twice Mary had been persuaded to play a longer piece. She gave way to the music with passion. As the supper table was laid out one evening, Mr Montagu remarked upon her skill.

'You play with great accomplishment, Miss Bennet. Are we not to have the pleasure of your singing?'

Mary considered for a moment before giving a little shrug with a smile.

'I cannot be other than honest with you, sir. My conscience will not allow it, though my vanity fights with me. So I must burden you with a confession. It is something that I have only recently admitted to myself. My voice is of the most modest quality, though my pride has long refused to admit the fault.' She met his eyes with a rueful smile. 'All my life I have worked hard for accomplishment; eager to win my share of any praise which may be offered. It is hard to stand out among five sisters, and indeed, I did not. In the attainment of knowledge and skill at the pianoforte, such work was almost all pleasure. I have expected others to bear the fruits of those modest talents too often. In truth many other young ladies have greater claims to fame. In future, I am resolved to be more appreciative of the talents of others and a little less so of my own.'

Mr Montagu's piercing gaze was full of wonder. He cleared his throat.

'You always surprise me, Miss Bennet. Of your many virtues and talents, I have long been aware. Yet now you add humility, which quite overwhelms me.'

He made her an elegant bow.

The gentlemen's final evening at Pemberley approached and with it, any opportunity for Mr Montagu to converse alone with Mary. To make matters worse, the Darcys had kindly invited neighbours to make up a small party to say farewell to their guests.

The evening was warm for so late in the summer. Candlelight from huge sconces glowed around the principal rooms. The air was redolent with the scent of roses. The company, all dressed in their best for a visit to the grandest house in the county, sparkled like the gemstones many of the ladies wore in abundance. The effect was magical, but Mr Montagu appeared preoccupied on several occasions throughout dinner, and again when the gentlemen convened over port.

A late supper was served to fortify the guests before their departure. Mary slipped out onto the cool space of the long terrace. Plucking a yellow rose from a vase, Mr Montagu followed her. Soft pools of light filtered between the shadows on the terrace. Mary stood, a slight figure in her white gown, beside the stone balcony, silhouetted against the night sky. She sensed his approach before he spoke, but felt a lassitude creep over her instead of the desire for flight.

He spoke quietly, though the sound carried. 'The evening is very warm.'

'Indeed it is.'

'I have stolen a rose from your sister's arrangement.' He retained a cautious distance as he handed it to her. 'Do you remember the day you came to the picnic?'

'I shall never forget it.' Mary's words were laced with sincerity.

'I said that I should plant roses to remind me of the ladies' colourful gowns, commencing with the yellow and red worn by you and your sister.'

'You were most gallant, Mr Montagu.'

As though to underline his thoughts, the musky smell of a climbing rose drifted up to the terrace on the night air.

'I planted a rose garden, Miss Bennet. But I could not bring myself to plant any colour other than the yellow of your gown.'

Her sharp intake of breath was the only sound. She could see the outline of his tall figure and fair hair, but the detail of his face eluded her. *If only matters were different. How magical this moment would be for me.*

'Miss Bennet . . . Mary, I must speak. You must hear me, I beg of you.'

'Mr Montagu, I should . . .' Her words trailed away. In that moment, she needed to hear him speak and the consequences faded into the background.

'Please hear me.' He, too, took a deep breath. 'From the moment you first stumbled at my feet these many months since, you have slowly but surely stolen my heart. *Yours* is the face I see in my waking hours and my sleep. *Yours* is the sweet, sensible voice I hear speaking to me when I am thinking. You may wonder why I did not speak sooner.'

'No!' She jolted to her senses. He must not continue these sweet words when her answer could only cause pain.

His voice deepened and he spoke with urgency, disregarding her objection.

'I wanted to wait until I had a measure of control over my estate, so that we might forge the perfect start together. I want to offer you the partnership in marriage that you desire and deserve.' He sank on one knee and possessed himself of her hand. 'Miss Bennet, I love you and you will make me the happiest I have ever been if you will consent to marry me.'

There ensued a long silence. Two sets of audible breathing the only sound on the empty terrace. Joy fought with logic until Mary's thoughts tumbled from her lips.

'But what of Sylvia? Did you speak such words to her?'

'Sylvia? Why would I propose to her? It is you I love.' She stepped back; an instinct based in uncertainty.

'But I thought . . . is it possible?' Mary's voice quivered. 'Oh, Mr Montagu, you cannot know the feelings that your words have unleashed. You honour me beyond anything I could have hoped or wished for in my life. It would be the greatest dishonesty if I did not tell you that your feelings are returned.'

'My love.' He reached for her other hand and kissed it.

In a small voice, Mary replied. 'But I cannot marry you. It is not possible.'

She detached her hand with reluctance.

'What is this? What possible impediment can there be?'

She could see the flash of his amused smile through the darkness and her heart broke. 'I know not how to say this. To injure you in any way is to feel injury myself. We could never be happy. Your mother, sir, finds me detestable.'

'My mother! Good heavens, surely we moved past that small difficulty many months ago?'

'I had thought so, too. But I was wrong.' She exhaled with force and gripped the stone balustrade for support as she sensed him standing upright. 'Sebastian, your mother dislikes me with intensity and has great plans for your future. It pains me deeply but you must see that there could be no lasting happiness for us, living with your mother between us.'

'I do not see it! Do you make light of my feelings, Mary?' His voice was harsh.

'Never. I do not, sir!'

'Is this some excuse?' he rushed on with hot, angry words. 'You are much altered here in these grand surroundings. I see Applefrith dangling after you. A man of simple fortune cannot compete with *his* title.'

Mary gave a short, bitter laugh, which ended in a sob.

'You mistake the matter most surely, sir. *I* am not impressed by fortune or title. I have not changed in any internal way. You have my greatest regard, but I cannot give you my hand. I bid you goodnight.'

She gathered her skirts and ran from the terrace. Inside, she walked as fast as she dared, past the windows and out of the supper room, before hurrying to the sanctuary of her own room.

Mr Montagu remained pacing the terrace in turmoil. After some time he mastered his emotions and took himself off to bid his hosts goodnight.

If he had hoped to gain further illumination or to end the quarrel of the previous evening before his departure, Mr Montagu was to be disappointed. Mary lingered behind her relations, eyes fixed demurely to the ground, save one pained glance and the merest press of her fingers as a goodbye.

45

Mr and Mrs Darcy were in good spirits due to the reduction in their duties as hosts. The young ladies of the family were less enthusiastic. Kitty immediately felt the lack of company, while Mary had barely uttered a syllable throughout breakfast. Mr Bennet looked forward to a morning's leisure in the library. As the family prepared to go about their day, Mr Bennet was surprised to find a letter delivered to him at the breakfast table.

'Well, girls, it appears that your dear mother has stirred herself to write to us. I wonder what treasures lie within these pages?' He paused as the family resumed their seats. '*My dear Mr Bennet and my darling girls, not forgetting Mr Darcy and dear little Charles, of course.*' Mr Bennet said in an aside, 'I see your mother has lost none of her address.' He continued reading: '*How I wish I could be in the bosom of my family, but my delicate health will not permit it, even to welcome a new grandchild. Just imagine, there are now four, which is superior to the Lucas effort, as I pointed out to Lady Lucas this very week. Charlotte may have produced first, but we are now in the ascendancy.*'

The sisters exchanged appalled glances. Mr Darcy gave his wife a resigned look and disappeared behind his newspaper. Mr Bennet read further:

'But that is all as nothing, for you will never guess the news. There has been such uproar as the county has not seen in several years. All Meryton is occupied with the details and I dread to think what is said in Countess Glendinning's own village. But I am carried away with excitement, for I have yet to tell you the news!

'My dears, Lady Sarah Glendinning has eloped to Gretna Green with her cousin, Mr Dalrymple! I was never so taken in. That young man made a nuisance of himself here at Longbourn. It is well Kitty did not heed his advances. As to Lady Sarah, we must all be taken in by such rash behaviour from a cold fish like her.

'I hear Countess Glendinning is prostrate. She expected her daughter to marry into the ton. We can only hope that she rallies, as it is said that the newlyweds are making their way back from the border to make amends. How I wish you were all here to share the excitement. I send you all my fondest sentiments, etc.'

Mr Bennet placed the letter on the table. 'Any doubts I had about that young man are proven wrong. He far exceeds my expectations for his enterprise. He shall go all the way in politics, likely to 10 Downing Street, I shouldn't wonder.'

Mary looked carefully across the table. Kitty's face had drained of all colour. She quietly excused herself from the table. As soon as she was able, Mary made her way to knock at Kitty's door. A muffled 'enter' sounded through the thick panels.

Kitty sat before her window gazing out over the beautiful vista of deer grazing by the river. Bright clusters of late wild-flowers popped up along the bank. Mary stood behind her sister for a moment appreciating the silence and the view.

'Kitty, I hope you are not too distressed by the news of Mr Dalrymple and Lady Sarah Glendinning.'

'You are kind to think of me when Mr Montagu has scarce departed. Would you be surprised to know that I feel some relief?'

Kitty turned to her sister and saw that she was indeed taken aback.

'I confess I am surprised.' Mary relaxed and smiled. 'But also very pleased to hear that you were not hurt by the news. When I was at Longbourn you were quite delighted by him.'

'How right you were to be reserved in your judgement of him, Mary. I censure myself for my impulsive reactions to Mr Dalrymple, without waiting to know his true character.'

'You did nothing wrong, Kitty.'

'But I so very nearly did. Mr Dalrymple tried to persuade me to meet him alone. I knew it to be wrong, yet I almost yielded to temptation. If it wasn't for Georgina Lucas I might have ruined my reputation.'

'Georgina Lucas.' Mary frowned and shook her head. 'What has she to do with this unsavoury plan?'

'It was the strangest moment. I was on my way to see Mrs Endicott, but in truth I knew that this was the path towards Mr Dalrymple. Then Georgina Lucas came along. She questioned me and quickly divined the story.'

'That is unfortunate.'

'No, it is quite the opposite.' Kitty began to re-enact the scene. 'Georgina was thrilled by the plan. She stood there full of excitement and plans for deceptions, and oh, Mary, all I could think of was Lydia. Poor, foolish Lydia, always so full of romantic notions and me her older, but willing, companion. Georgina rendered me speechless at my stupidity. Mr Dalrymple's intent could only be base or ungentlemanly and I knew it in my heart. Georgina, though unwittingly, made me realise. I continued on to visit Mrs Endicott and you will laugh, but I felt older and wiser.'

Mary sat down heavily. 'How near you came to . . . to possible ruin.'

Kitty shuddered. 'Now you see why I am relieved. I might have ruined my reputation and put yours in danger. Even now the village will gossip about him visiting Longbourn. Can you forgive me, Mary? After everything Lydia bought upon us, I very nearly made such a dreadful error of judgement.'

'There is nothing to forgive.'

Mary placed her hand in her sister's.

'But I—'

'There is nothing to forgive because nothing occurred.' She gave Kitty's hand a squeeze. 'Your head always knew the right course of action. Even without Georgina's intervention, I believe you would have come to your senses. It is Lady Sarah who must live with the true consequences of rash behaviour.'

Kitty's brow knitted in a puzzled frown.

'I cannot but wonder why Mr Dalrymple showed me such attention.'

'As you have been telling me, his character is deficient.' Mary opened the sash window, allowing the scent of mown hay to enter the room. 'Might he have used you to make his haughty cousin jealous? I do not mean to upset you, dearest, for I also have no doubt he genuinely liked you from the first, which is no surprise.'

'But, of course.' Kitty plopped onto a chair. 'Lady Sarah did indeed give me peculiar looks.' Her voice softened. 'She must have cared for him a great deal to perceive me as her rival. Dalrymple is a base fortune hunter. He would never have married me. I am the luckiest girl in England to have escaped him.'

Mary said with a grimace, 'I should have detested to call him brother. Are you sure you harbour no feelings for him?'

Kitty grasped Mary's hand and could not contain a choking laugh.

'I know you will think me flighty, but he is replaced in my affections by one far more worthy. Someone amiable, kind and protective. Lord Applefrith, in fact.' She added, 'This time I am certain.'

Despite her low mood, Mary could not help but smile.

'Dear Kitty, I think he would be perfect for you. He is everything you say.' She sat beside her sister. 'You have developed the most positive nature. I hope in future I may learn to be more like you.'

It was Kitty's turn to laugh.

'It is I who am bent on a course to be more like you. I had not placed any prize upon books and learning, but now I see you and Lizzy conversing so easily with the gentlemen in all manner of subjects. I see their admiration and I feel my loss.'

Mary regarded her sister with amazement and her lips twitched.

'What an odd pair we are. You wishing to be more like me and all the while I have been trying to learn feminine arts to be more like you.'

'Then we must continue to assist one another,' Kitty cried. 'I do like the way we have grown to become better friends.'

'I too.'

They embraced and stood with linked arms drinking in the view as the sun glittered rainbow colours through the dew in the park, before realising that they were late for the morning walk with Lizzy. Pelisses were hastily fetched and they descended the grand staircase with something less than decorum, causing a raised eyebrow from the butler.

With the days becoming inexorably shorter, the sun had not long risen above the trees. The sisters decided to walk in the open on a dry road.

Lizzy bent to pluck a stalk of pelargonium on the verge.

'I shall miss having an excuse to arrange quite so many flowers now that the gentleman have departed.'

'No doubt you will soon have more guests to indulge.' Mary shook droplets of dew from her hem.

Lizzy buried her nose in the bloom and sighed.

'True, we do entertain with regularity. Though it is never so pleasant as when family come to visit.'

Kitty flung a careless arm over her sister's shoulder. 'You flatter us, Lizzy. We are very glad to be here and for a little while longer.'

'I selfishly wish sometimes that I could keep you both near me. But you will go off and before long have families of your own.' Lizzy's words were met with a chorus of dissent. 'Why, Kitty, you are barely above twenty. There is plenty of time.'

'But a lack of suitors,' came Kitty's hot retort.

'Mary, you must be encouraged. Lord Applefrith might have been emboldened if you had encouraged him, and there remains the issue of Mr Montagu . . .'

Lizzy broke off as Mary stopped in her tracks.

'You might as well both know that Mr Montagu proposed and I rejected him.'

Her sisters also halted on the track, one blue pelisse, one brown, staring at her in utter dismay. Kitty burst forth with vehemence.

'But you love him, Mary, I know you do.'

Mary threw her arms wide in frustration.

'Kitty, we have discussed this. Indeed we have all discussed my dilemma, but no solution has been found. I do not deny that I find my distress all the greater now that I know that my feelings were reciprocated.'

Lizzy demanded, 'What was Mr Montagu's response to your reasons?'

Mary's eyes drooped and the very air appeared to leave her body. 'He did not understand. I cannot blame him – it was impossible to tell him the details. I do not think he believed me at first, but I assured him of my deep regard. He was very upset and we quarrelled. The next day he left with Lord Applefrith.'

'Oh, my poor, dear Mary. You did not speak of it.'

Lizzy regarded her sister with respect before enfolding her in a comforting embrace.

'It is hard to speak of painful matters, but now you both know. There is nothing to be done. He has gone away and his mother will probably marry him off to Letitia Fulcross if she cannot dig up a titled young lady.'

'Well, I think it all very, very wrong!' said Kitty, stamping her foot.

They concluded their walk in silence, all lost in their own thoughts.

46

Lizzy consulted with Darcy about Mr Montagu's proposal. He sat in a deep wing chair, with one leg crossed and listening in silence, before giving the benefit of his thoughts.

'My dear, I do not see how we may intervene. I agree it is a highly undesirable state of affairs and they both have my sympathy. But I feel that unless good sense can prevail here, principally from Mrs Montagu, then the cause may be lost. Sadly, I do not know the lady.'

Lizzy gave the study's servants' bell a savage tug. 'I know her but little. The late Mr Montagu was a great friend of Papa's and his wife took her part among the society of ladies near Meryton. I recollect nothing more than the commonplace about her.'

'Sebastian Montagu is an excellent fellow. He is just what one might wish for Mary. If he is sincerely attached to her, and I don't doubt that he is, Lizzy –' he looked upon his wife with affection '– he will find a way through I am sure. For now, I can see that you have made excellent progress with Mary, so let us continue, while she is here, to show her some society.'

*

Lizzy had to exert herself very little to take up her husband's advice. Many of the local gentry had met Kitty during her previous visit and several had now been introduced to Mary. Among other diversions, the sisters accepted an invitation for a late summer ball before the long journey home.

Kitty looked a vision in demure cream trimmed with rose velvet ribbon, and her new rose shawl. Mary wore Nottingham lace over a green chemise. Rigby had harried her into learning a new hairstyle with a high-coiled plait studded with pearl pins.

The evening was a great success. Mary and Kitty were sought after as dancing partners to the most flattering degree, though Lizzy restrained herself to just a few partners.

The grand house, while not as large as Pemberley, possessed the largest ballroom in Derbyshire. The intricate pattern of the inlaid marble floors were visible despite the numbers thronging the room. Their hosts were known for providing sumptuous suppers. White soup, chicken, ham, turkey, cheese and fruit were interspersed with sweetmeats and jellies, flummery and even ice cream. Any number of young men vied for the opportunity to escort the sisters to supper.

During a quiet moment Kitty considered how much Mary had altered of late. The greatest change had taken place in her demeanour. Despite the suffering Kitty knew her sister to be feeling, Mary danced and conversed as one without a care. While their supper escorts were exchanging a few words, Kitty gave her an encouraging smile and said,

'How pretty you look, Mary. I am glad we were able to manage at least one ball during this visit.'

'True. We must enjoy it to the full. I haven't forgotten my pledge to be more like you, Kitty.'

Mary nibbled delicately as she surveyed the room. How easy it was to be among strangers without the encumbrance of knowing their history, nor they knowing her own.

As they swept up Pemberley's grand staircase to bed, Kitty felt Lizzy's detaining hand on her arm. Mary bid them goodnight and Lizzy signalled for Kitty to follow her to own apartments.

Kitty draped her shawl over the curved back of a chair and watched as Lizzy began to let down her tresses. Lizzy's amber silk gown shimmered in the candlelight.

'Kitty, there is little we can do when you leave us. Longbourn is so far away. Jane and I look to you to promote any possibility of Mary and Mr Montagu making amends. We need hardly remind you that Mary is in love with him and is unlikely to give her heart again. It is not in her character.'

'As you say, Lizzy, you need hardly remind me,' Kitty pouted.

Lizzy turned to face her. 'I know you will do what you are able. It is just that Jane and I are worried about Mary. She is a singular person and it is clear that but for the impediment of Mrs Montagu, Mary and Sebastian Montagu would be very happy together.'

Kitty's good-humoured expression returned.

'I do not doubt it, but I am at a loss to know how to help them.'

Lizzy's tone was reassuring. 'If the slightest opportunity arises, you will know how to proceed because you have Mary's best interests at heart.'

Kitty looked doubtful. Lizzy touched her hand.

'Trust your instincts. Persuade Mary otherwise if she shies away from a chance, and above all, do not breathe a word to our mother!'

47

Mrs Blain leaned her chubby arms across the counter, assuming a conspiratorial air with her customer, a thin-faced woman, whose turban sat like a pumpkin on a candle.

'Oh yes, there's not much what misses Blain and I.'

She spoke in full voice as the haberdashery was empty save her eager-faced customer. Mr Blain wrestled with his monthly accounts in their private quarters, much to his wife's satisfaction. Taking charge in Mr Blain's absence was one of Mrs Blain's chief pleasures, offering as it did the twin powers of authority and no critical eye.

'It's me what notices which young lady is secretly putting together bride clothes,' she cackled. 'Blain and I often wonder if the intended knows he is the intended.'

Her customer shared in the joke, which encouraged Mrs Blain to expand her role.

'I'm the one who sees a changing shape in the way of a baby, if you take my meaning.'

'I must call more often,' the turbaned lady replied.

'You'll always hear the news here first, I say. For instance, we were the first to hear about that scoundrel Dalrymple eloping with the hoity-toity daughter of Countess Glendinning. What a to-do! I feel sorry for the Countess, I really do.'

The customer, sensing something new in the air, leaned forward, her thin lips moving at an excited rate.

'Indeed their behaviour was shocking. We were all convinced he would offer for Catherine Bennet.'

'As well you might. But what is the pretty daughter of a gentleman compared to a plain heiress, eh?' Mrs Blain tapped her pudgy finger to the side of her nose. 'We shall soon know all about that tale, for I hear that the Bennets' carriage returned to Longbourn yesterday.'

As she spoke, she jerked her head up to see who had opened shop door and was aghast to see Mary and Kitty Bennet on the threshold.

'Oh, my, the Misses Bennet. Welcome back, dear young ladies. I trust your journey was pleasant and your lovely sisters well?'

Mary stepped in front of Kitty, whose countenance had drained of colour as she overheard the gossip. She spoke in cool, measured tones.

'We thank you, Mrs Blain. Our visit was full of pleasure and our sisters thrive in the *good-mannered* society of Derbyshire. But do not allow us to detain you or your customer. Our errand is small, so we will return at leisure.'

Mary turned on her heel, forcing Kitty to do the same if she were to avoid a collision. They made a dignified exit.

Mrs Blain's mouth opened and closed like a lake pike on a fishing line.

'I never meant . . . they could not have heard . . . oh Lord save us.'

The customer, having the grace to look shamefaced for listening to gossip, slunk towards the door and betook herself off to the milliner, where she was persuaded by increments to tell the whole in return for a sympathetic ear.

48

Out on the street Mary took charge.

'Do not droop so, Kitty. You will only feed the foolishness of women like Mrs Blain.'

Kitty shook her shoulders back.

'It is most vexing. I had hoped there would be something new to occupy the gossips by now.'

Mary adjusted her straw bonnet.

'It is a certainty that something new will busy them soon. Our best course now is unconcern. We are better off talking far and wide of the delights of our visit to Derbyshire.'

'How glad I am that we are in town together, Mary. I should have lost all countenance alone.'

Mindful of harmful tattle, the sisters made sure to call upon several neighbours over the following days, cheerfully dispensing tales of the north and their sisters' families. If anyone were ill-bred enough to mention Mr Dalrymple's escapade, they agreed that they would meet the occasion with the words 'quite shocking' and quickly move on to another tale.

They could not have judged just how successful their plan would become. Hunger for news from the wider world had Meryton's inhabitants vying to invite the Bennets to dine. Any news of the two older Bennet sisters who had married exceedingly well from their closeted environment was seized upon.

However, it was Mary who captured attention. Hosts marvelled at the change wrought in the person of Mary Bennet. It was as though, by frequent invitation, she might suddenly return to the dull, retiring young woman of memory. This new, confident and cheerful Mary, who matched any of her sisters for beauty, won over the harshest critics. One or two mothers resorted to searching for relatives in Derbyshire, convinced that their uninspiring offspring might return transformed from a visit to the north.

Only one household withheld an invitation. Mrs Montagu heard tales of the Bennet sisters and Mary's transformation from several sources. When it pleased her, she pleaded an indisposition to avoid those small soirées where they must inevitably meet.

A young woman of lower intellect than Mary would easily have noticed the difference in her reception by old friends. Mary had privately been nervous of the reaction from people she had known all her life. The conversation overheard in Blain's haberdashery banished her nerves and galvanised her into action to spare Kitty from harmful gossip. She appreciated the irony that the more she acted the part of a cheerful, lively young woman, the more natural the behaviour became to her. Kitty was happy following her sister's strong lead.

Unlike her daughters, Mrs Bennet rarely troubled herself with misgivings. Mary could not recall such approbation from her mother, whose excitement at her improved appearance and wardrobe she did not trouble to contain. 'My dear, dear girl, how becoming you look. My clever, generous Jane and Lizzy. Oh, how I miss them. Derbyshire is fortunate to have them. We must visit all of our friends. How they shall envy me having five daughters who all favour their mother. Thank goodness the autumn assembly season comes soon, girls. We must renew our efforts among the young gentlemen.'

News travelled beyond Meryton, far enough to reach the ears of Lady Sandalford.

Intrigued, the lady set out to visit her nephew and sister-in-law. It took but a moment with each of them to divine that something was amiss.

Sebastian joined the ladies briefly for morning coffee, but proved uncharacteristically terse. His appearance lacked colour and he seemed a little thinner. Mrs Montagu held forth with her usual inconsequential chatter, but there was an edge to her conversation. Lady Sandalford diverted herself with the challenge of understanding the game at play.

'Tell me about your visit to Derbyshire, Sebastian. Were you successful?'

Sebastian brightened a little, but his speech was cautious. 'I can give you only the briefest details, Aunt, as I have business to attend. But, yes, I met with some success. The Darcys were excellent hosts and I persuaded Mr Darcy to part with some of his prized Hereford cattle to begin my own herd. He and his agent were very generous with their knowledge.'

Lady Sandalford nodded.

'I have heard nothing but good of the Darcys. I met him in London a few times as a younger man and found him rather stiff and formal. It seems Mrs Darcy has softened him to his betterment.'

Sebastian smiled at his aunt; his voice teasing,

'I cannot comment as I know only the present Mr Darcy. If you will excuse me.'

'Of course, dear. I shall ask you another time if you saw Mrs Darcy's sister during your visit.'

'Just so.' He made his aunt a curt bow and threw his mother a glance. 'Mother, do not expect me for tea. I will return for dinner.'

He strode from the salon.

'My nephew appears very businesslike this morning.' Lady Sandalford drained her cup and set it down on the painted table. Mrs Montagu grimaced.

'Sebastian has committed himself to a heavy workload since his return. I barely see him these days.'

'Perhaps he is working too hard, Prunella. He looks a trifle gaunt to me.'

'My son will rise to the occasion, Arabella.' Mrs Montagu failed to disguise her irritation. 'He has your brother's blood in his veins. I see no occasion to worry.'

'Has he discussed his sojourn in any detail with you?'

Mrs Montagu appeared momentarily frozen.

'I have heard this and that. Nothing of notable interest.' She busied herself with the coffeepot.

Lady Sandalford shrewd eyes narrowed a little.

'I hear that Mr Bennet and his daughters are lately returned from Derbyshire.'

Mrs Montagu relaxed into the comfort of her sofa and the dissemination of news. 'Yes, Mr Bennet travelled to see his new grandson. I believe Mrs Bingley is mother to three now. I imagine she has a talent for it. She was a great beauty and possesses a most gentle nature. One had but to meet her to be won over.'

Lady Sandalford helped herself to a dainty finger of cake.

'I recall the two older girls, but they were barely out of the schoolroom at the time. Certainly the elder was an incomparable and there was a liveliness about the younger. She must have possessed significant qualities as well as looks to attract Fitzwilliam Darcy.'

Mrs Montagu gave a vigorous nod.

'Oh, yes, Miss Elizabeth Bennet was also a beauty and said to be quite a wit. I imagine her good sense proved the added attraction for Mr Darcy. Though, to hear Mrs Bennet crow, you would imagine she had engineered both marriages.'

Lady Sandalford looked her sister-in-law forcibly in the eye and enquired archly, 'Have you met with the Bennets since their return, Prunella?'

Mrs Montagu looked away.

'I have been rather occupied of late.'

'Yet I hear society is consumed with the daughters.'

'I do not listen to gossip, Arabella.'

Mrs Montagu huffed with indignation. Lady Sandalford repressed a laugh.

'Indeed, gossip is odious in any event. Yet Miss Mary Bennet is surely deserving of an invitation after her labours on behalf of Cuthbert Park?'

Mrs Montagu failed to keep the irritability from her voice.

'I do not understand this line of questioning, Arabella. The Bennets are old friends and shall be guests here in the fullness of time. Mrs Bennet came to morning coffee quite recently.'

Lady Sandalford allowed the matter to drop for the moment. Taking her leave earlier than usual, she directed her coachman to drive through the village to Longbourn. She sat back against the plush velvet of her seat with a smile of quiet satisfaction.

49

Her Ladyship swept into the Bennet's drawing room with an elegance born of commanding many a London soirée. She extended her hand to Mr Bennet, while smiling simultaneously to the remaining occupants of the room. She waved Mrs Bennet, Mary and Kitty back to their ease with a flick of her gloved wrist.

'How good of you to call on us, your Ladyship.'

'It is my pleasure, Mr Bennet. We have not met in an age.'

Mrs Bennet rang for tea even as she enquired if her Ladyship would care to partake of refreshment. Her Ladyship divested herself of her gloves.

'I should be delighted, Mrs Bennet. The journey home is not long, but long enough, especially with the recent rain slowing the coach.'

'Have you been to visit the Montagus?' enquired Mrs Bennet.

'I have indeed, though it was dull work today. My nephew is working too hard and could spare little time.'

As she spoke, Lady Sandalford turned her head a fraction in Mary's direction.

Mary's features displayed concern as she spoke. 'I do hope Mr Montagu is not unwell.'

'I suspect his malaise is more of the mind, though I do not know the cause.' Lady Sandalford paused to give Mary a long look. Mary's colour rose. 'One can only trust he deals with his problems, for he begins to look gaunt.'

There was an exchange of glances between the sisters.

'The mist begins to clear,' Lady Sandalford muttered under her breath.

Kitty breached the short silence.

'The Honourable Sylvia Drummond tells us she will shortly join you in London for the season, your Ladyship. Will you travel after Christmas?'

'London will be bereft of company until Parliament commences in mid January.' Her ladyship examined the pattern on a tapestry coaster. 'Christmas and the New Year are much more enjoyable in the country. There is such hurly-burly during the festive season in London.'

'But how alive one would feel,' rejoined Kitty, making Lady Sandalford laugh.

'You are quite right, of course. I felt the same way at your age, Miss Bennet. I hope you meet with the opportunity.'

'I shall wish for it, too,' claimed Mrs Bennet.

Mr Bennet passed a hand across his brow and declared that any such jaunt would never include him.

'Miss Mary Bennet, what is your opinion?' Lady Sandalford turned in her chair.

'I think perhaps the idea has greater attraction than the reality.' Mary's lips curved into a lazy smile. 'After a short time I imagine that I would be happier beside a log fire at home.'

'Well said,' commented her Ladyship 'We are all susceptible to a dazzling perception.'

The conversation was interrupted by the arrival of a maid with a laden tea tray. Lady Sandalford seemed more inclined to easy chatter than imbibing.

'I recall my late brother told me you have many special volumes in your library, Mr Bennet.'

He returned his cup to his saucer.

'My old friend flattered me. His was the greater collection.'

'False modesty, Mr Bennet,' Lady Sandalford admonished. 'My brother was not given to exaggeration and I have seen that your daughter knows a good deal about the value and quality of books, which can only come from you, sir.'

'Mary has inherited my passion for books, which I suspect is deplorable in a female. Of course, anything society deplores is cause for entertainment.'

His guest delivered her winning smile to the company.

'Then we must be deplorable together, Miss Bennet. There is strength in numbers. Mr and Mrs Bennet, if Mary is willing, would you allow her a sojourn at Clovisford? I admit that it is time to organise my own library and I cannot face the task alone.'

Mrs Bennet gave an excited start.

'Why, it is kind of your Ladyship to take an interest in Mary.'

'The kindness would all be on Miss Bennet's side.'

Her Ladyship gave Mary an enquiring look.

Much as she expected she would enjoy Clovisford and Lady Sandalford's company, Mary was concerned that she might meet with Sebastian or his mother. However, other than the party at Clovisford, she was unaware of any visits by the Montagus, so perhaps she would be further away from a chance meeting than in Meryton. Mary looked up at her father.

Mr Bennet removed his pince-nez.

'Does the notion appeal to you, Mary?'

'Yes, Papa.'

'Then we must accept your delightful offer, Lady Sandalford.'

'Wonderful. Autumn will not now feel so dull.'

Mary agreed, 'I shall look forward to it, Lady Sandalford.'

Her mind was yet conflicted.

50

Within a few days another visitor graced Longbourn. Lord Applefrith called. Mrs Bennet was moved to invite him to dine with them, which the good-natured gentleman accepted with alacrity. While her daughters walked out with the gentleman to show him the quickest route to Cuthbert Park, she remarked to her husband:

'I am very pleased with you, Mr Bennet, though you ought to have written to me about his Lordship.'

'I am delighted to have pleased you, my dear, and would be more delighted if I knew why.'

'Do not tease me, Mr Bennet. A Lord!' Mrs Bennet's face wore a beatific expression. 'Why, even if he is impoverished, there is still a title! A very likeable young gentleman he is too. There is something of the soldier about him. He would look well in regimentals. Has he any fortune, dare I hope?'

'Now that I cannot say, my love, for I did not ask him,' her husband replied in a bored tone.

'Mr Bennet, have you no notion of sense?'

'I see that I have displeased you already, my dear. My time in the sun was but short. Perhaps I can redeem myself by telling you that he was indeed in a regiment and he does have an estate some thirty miles away.'

'Oh, Mr Bennet, to think of one of our girls with a title!'

'My dear wife, Lord Applefrith has consented to dine. I do not think he should be forced to marry one of our daughters for the price of a meal.'

'Mr Bennet!'

The subject of their conversation returned to the room with Mary and Kitty. Lord Applefrith confessed his call to Longbourn was made with the intention of keeping his promise to invite the Bennets to a ball at his family home, Gediston Place.

'I am indebted to Miss Catherine Bennet for the suggestion,' he explained to her mother. He turned to address Kitty. 'You perceived my mother's malaise correctly, Miss Bennet. I have not seen her so animated for a twelvemonth.'

Lord Applefrith turned back to Mrs Bennet with a serious expression.

'How proud you must be, madam, to have a daughter with such good common sense. Nay, several such daughters.'

Mrs Bennet bestowed him with a benign smile.

'Indeed, sir, Mr Bennet and I are truly blessed with the finest daughters in nature.'

Kitty, bemused by the only compliment to her common sense she could ever recall, thanked his Lordship prettily and added, 'I hope my idea has caused Lady Applefrith no undue exertion.'

Lord Applefrith clapped his thigh.

'Not a bit of it! I have not witnessed such happy employment in her Ladyship since my late brother and I were boys.'

'Then I am much rewarded, sir,' Kitty rejoined with warmth.

His Lordship continued. 'Now it is a good many miles from Gediston Park, so my mother begs that you will all stay the night.'

'You are very good, sir,' cried Mrs Bennet. 'We are accustomed to superior society, but there is so little to be had of late,' she confided.

Lord Applefrith rubbed his hands together before the fire and beamed around the room. 'I shall demand early dances of you young ladies. My consequence shall grow unchallenged with you both as partners.'

'I think the dancing slipper shall be on the other foot, sir, for it is you who shall lend us consequence,' Mary said smiling.

As they dined, the sisters did their best to divert Lord Applefrith's attention from the overt attentions of their mother, who alternately offered coy statements with disproportionate levels of respectfulness. Better acquainted as he was with Mr Bennet and his daughters, his Lordship gave no evidence of noticing Mrs Bennet's excesses. He appeared to be at great ease and rose to leave his three former Derbyshire friends with a show of reluctance.

51

Clovisford offered up a splendid autumn display for Mary's delectation. Trees formed clouds of colour from soft green to yellow ochre and on through the spectrum of oranges, tans and browns: all set against a rare bright blue sky. Layers of multi-coloured leaves scattered beneath trees, while here and there a single leaf cartwheeled across the park in the light breeze. Mary caught several and marvelled at their infinite variety of shape and intricate design. Despite the level parkland, she was reminded of her walks at Pemberley with Elizabeth. There was something of the same feeling of being open to the vast sky, where no building or man intruded. A small lone figure dressed in grey, she scooped up an armful of golden leaves under a spreading lime and threw them into the air, laughing as they rained down all over her gown.

Lady Sandalford's many charming qualities extended to her style as a hostess. She neither monopolised one nor left one at a loose end. Mary felt like a valued guest and blossomed in response. Her sisters having done everything possible to make her welcome and revive her prospects did so for familial love. Here, Mary knew she was wanted for herself, and her gratitude was boundless.

'Do make yourself at home for a few days, Mary. Wander around and get to know Clovisford. I promise not to harry you with thoughts of my library for a little while yet.'

With these kind words Lady Sandalford had encouraged Mary to explore. Mary had followed her instruction to the letter and, exploring the house and park, she found much to delight. The estate had a dairy, orangery, ice house and a carpenter's workshop. All was as neat as Kitty's perfect stitchery. In addition to elegance, Lady Sandalford had a taste for modernity, which was well within her means to indulge. Paintings by Mr Turner and Mr Constable glowed fresh and alive as others receded on the walls. She even had amusing drawings by Mr Cruikshank hidden away from the principal rooms. The pianoforte was magnificent and polished to such a sheen one could see everything nearby reflected. A mahogany music cupboard contained a wealth of scores including the most recent popular London works. Mary delighted in daily practise and played most evenings. When there was no company in attendance, Mary had leisure to ask her hostess about the paintings and objets d'art in the house and found her ladyship to be an enthusiastic and knowledgeable guide.

'How I do like a keen mind,' Lady Sandalford exclaimed. 'So many of my guests occupy their conversation with the commonplace. They have no regard for the toils of the artist or the author. Instead they busy themselves with the smallness of their own lives.'

Mary replied with candour. 'Perhaps, ma'am, your guests are so used to being cocooned among treasures that they cease to appreciate their surroundings.'

'I daresay you are right, my dear. Yet there are a few, like you and my dear nephew, Sebastian, who break free of such constraints and give one hope for the future of England.'

At the mention of Sebastian's name, Mary flushed.

'Mr Montagu has the benefit of a superior mind mixed with the blessing of seeing something of the world.'

Lady Sandalford raised her lorgnette.

'You express the matter exactly, my dear. I find in you a model of economical expression. Most young ladies have much to say about nothing. It is small wonder that you and Sebastian are friends. Your minds are of a piece.'

'You flatter me, madam. Mr Montagu would perhaps not be in agreement. His knowledge and experience exceed my own efforts.'

'I have heard my nephew speak of you in similar terms, Mary. He is not one to dispense idle praise. Sebastian is a clever young man and has no time for simpering young misses. I'll wager he will not marry for anything less than a meeting of minds.'

Mary looked down at her stitching, not realising that her Ladyship was observing her, or that her needle lay idle and her arms were hunched tightly by her sides.

52

In her sister's absence, Kitty found her time divided principally between amusing her mama and trying to read the few texts prescribed for her by Lord Applefrith. She felt determined to report good progress to him by the time of the ball at Gediston Place.

A letter arrived for Mary bearing Lord Drummond's seal. Kitty undertook to package it with a letter of her own. Dallying in Meryton, she presently saw Mr Montagu's bay horse riding towards her.

'Miss Bennet, good afternoon.'

Mr Montagu slid from his mount and bowed.

'Mr Montagu, how good to see you. We have not met these many weeks since Derbyshire.'

He looked a little sheepish.

'My pardon. I have been quite occupied of late. I must pay my respects to your father very soon.'

'He will like that. With Mary gone, Longbourn is rather empty.'

'Gone?' His voice rose in alarm.

'Yes, did you not know? Mary is visiting your aunt, Lady Sandalford.'

'I did not know.'

Mr Montagu turned away with an abrupt movement. He led his mount around to his right side.

'She has been gone almost a week. Indeed, I am on my way to the mail with letters for her.'

'I see.' He brushed his hand over his chin. 'Miss Bennet, may I prevail upon you to entrust me with your commission? I have been neglecting my aunt of late and am overdue a visit. Your letters would be safely delivered tomorrow.'

Kitty dimpled up at the earnest face framed in its shock of fair hair.

'Then that is the very thing, sir.'

She fished the small packet from her reticule and pressed it into his large palm.

'I wish you a very pleasant visit.' She made a small bow. 'Please send my compliments to your aunt.'

Kitty set off down the street with a jaunty walk, her face lit by a wide smile, which caused several persons passing to look back and wonder at the cause.

The following afternoon Mr Montagu arrived at Clovisford. His aunt bade Sebastian a warm welcome and ushered him indoors.

'Mary, look who comes to visit us!'

Mary looked up from the letter she was composing. She was seated at a little table set before the window, which placed her as though in a frame.

Mr Montagu exclaimed, 'That is how you should be painted; set before the window at your desk.'

His aunt gave an amused titter. Mary was aware that she blushed a fiery red. She lowered her eyes demurely and gave Mr Montagu quiet thanks for his compliment.

He started forward.

'I must not forget, your sister has charged me with delivering these letters to you. I saw her in Meryton yesterday. She is very well. Oh, and delivers compliments to you, Aunt.'

'Very pretty,' said her Ladyship.

Mary took the letters, tucking them into the pocket of her twill gown. Her worked lace collar began to feel uncomfortably hot all of a sudden.

'It was kind of you to bring the letters, Mr Montagu.'

He looked into her eyes.

'I can think of no good reason why you should wait for them, when I intended to visit my aunt.'

'Of course.'

An awkward pause ensued, brought to a swift close by her Ladyship.

'Mary, kindly pull the bell for refreshments. Now, Sebastian, while we're waiting, tell us all the news of Cuthbert Park.'

Prompted to recall his overt reason for visiting, Mr Montagu told them of his pleasure at the arrival of Mr Darcy's Herefords, who were in prime condition despite the journey. He had been busy instructing his stockmen as to their care and welfare. He turned to Mary.

'As in so many things you were right, Miss Bennet. By introducing something new, I command the attention of my men and they already begin to think my opinion counts in other matters.'

Mary clapped her hands and her face glowed.

'Bravo. I am sure you will go on famously.'

Sebastian's eyes lingered on her face.

'If I do, it is thanks to you. I shall not forget.'

Tea arrived. Lady Sandalford steered the conversation while Mary busied herself with the accoutrements of the tray, laying out dishes, strainer and spoons. Sebastian was consulted by his aunt for his opinion on various matters about the park. Somewhat de trop in this conversation, Mary could not resist watching him. His aunt had been right; he did appear to have lost weight and there was a strained tightness about his features. As tea drew to a close, her Ladyship mentioned the orangery.

'My dear Sebastian, you must take your mother the last of the plums. Can you hold the basket for him, Mary? I feel too fatigued to be walking about the garden this afternoon.'

Mary looked at her with dismay. Her Ladyship was most decidedly not fatigued. Indeed, she appeared to be in high spirits. What was she about? Mary tarried as long as she dared before they set out across the lawn in silence; Mary hugging the basket in her arms.

At length Mr Montagu said, 'I must apologise for our parting on discordant terms in Derbyshire, Miss Bennet. That was not at all my intention and an opportunity to make amends before my departure was lost to me.'

'Pray do not speak of it, sir. Let us pretend that it did not happen.'

Mary quickened her pace and entered the steamy warmth of the orangery.

'Miss Bennet, I cannot pretend.' He followed, ducking his head to enter. 'I am at a loss. You spoke of my mother's objections to you, but I cannot discover any serious malice in this. Surely this is a difficulty that can be overcome with some effort on our part?'

Mary sat down on the window ledge. 'Mr Montagu – Sebastian – I had hoped we should not return to this fruitless subject. There can only be misery in it. I have no wish to come between you and your mother. In fact, I will not. It would be wrong of me to describe to you the circumstances of the knowledge I bear, but I beg you will believe that I am certain of the strength of your mother's feelings. I could never contemplate a union where a family would be splintered by my arrival.' Her eyes searched his face, beseeching him to understand. 'Our lives would be intolerable. Do you not see that the situation is hopeless?'

Mr Montagu had been idly plucking the remaining few fruits as he attended her words. He knelt to deliver them into the basket, putting his face directly opposite Mary's own.

'Forgive me, I can see that you are in earnest, but I do not pretend to understand.'

Mary sighed. There was a dullness in her tone.

'Your first duty must be to your mother, sir. She is your closest family and means to do well by you.'

'Miss Bennet – Mary – it is only because I have the greatest respect for your opinion that I refrain from losing my temper. It seems to me that my first duty is to look to the future of the family. That two people should be firmly attached and have no significant impediment to marriage would seem to me to be the perfect circumstance. Shall I tell you something? My books arrived from Portugal before I left for Derbyshire. How I rejoiced at the thought of us arranging them in the library together. They remain in their crates, Miss Bennet, for I have not the heart to open them without you.'

With that, Mr Montagu scooped up the basket and strode out of the orangery.

53

Much later, in the privacy of her room, Mary drew her chair to the fire and read by the comforting glow. Kitty's letter spoke of the commonplace events at home, which this evening Mary felt sorely desirous of hearing. A visit by Mrs Philips, the mysterious disappearance of a jar of potted Michaelmas goose, and Kitty's progress with her studies were all balm to Mary's pained soul.

Sylvia's letter, on fine paper and sealed with her father's crest, remained. Mary opened it with happy anticipation.

My dear Mary,

So much has happened since I received your kind response to my last letter.

Our journey to Bath proved uneventful and it was exciting to see Weston and the town beyond unfolding below us as we entered. I could only wonder at the rush of the River Avon below the Pulteney Bridge. So much is newly built here, but in such elegant proportions as to remind one to be refined of conduct.

Our lodgings are delightful, with just a handful of rooms. It is quite something not to have to order arrangements in a large house. At first, I scarce thought I would find enough occupation.

We have the good fortune to enjoy a small acquaintance in this bustling place. The widow of the late Lord Calbraith, who was a friend of my father, has kindly agreed to act as my chaperone: for you know my dear Papa dislikes to dance since Mama died and has become devoted to the card room. Lady Calbraith is here with her younger brother, Colonel Wisgrove, who sustained a bad injury to his leg in the Peninsula War and takes the waters daily to rebuild his strength. They have been a great source of courage to me in the crush of the Assembly Rooms.

I am shocked by the number of people who throng the twice-weekly balls. One is pressed back against the walls to allow room for the dancers. Some of the attendees appear quite coarse. In truth, as much as I enjoy the dance, I am as like to sit quietly and converse with the colonel, who has a great store of adventurous tales and is happy to answer my foolish questions.

I have seen the Prince at a distance, cloaked as he is by his large and noisy retinue. Were it not for Mr Brummell, I fear the assembly might turn to riot. Soon I shall make the Prince Regent my bow, though I have no notion of what one should say to him. Perhaps it is wrong in me to say so, but he appears to be corpulent, dandified and so very tired of life.

Though she can be a sad romp, I miss Imogen. She, however, is much taken with Georgina and is enjoying her stay with the Lucas family.

I have received the oddest letter from Mrs Montagu, full of kind sentiments and warning me not to admit the beaux of Bath to my close

*acquaintance. She cannot believe Mr Montagu and I
to be more than friends, though it is difficult to
perceive any other meaning. Your opinion on the
matter would be valuable to me. I imagine that you
will have visited Cuthbert Park by now and should
be able to gauge Mrs Montagu's thoughts. It would
be awkward to return from Bath to a mistaken
perception on her part.*

*I must hurry to dress now. Colonel Wisgrove has
agreed to escort me to the pump room and I shall
endeavour to post this letter as we go along.*

Do write all your news soon,
Yours,
Sylvia.

Mary sat back in her chair, lost in thought until the
fire guttered. Her smile while reading Sylvia's letter had
faded with the intelligence of Mrs Montagu's letter.
Deciding to make a reply in the morning, Mary nevertheless tossed and turned as she mentally composed a
suitable missive.

While Lady Sandalford instructed her household after
breakfast, Mary procured paper and ink, then retired to
the small desk by the window where Mr Montagu had
met her the previous day.

My dear Sylvia,
*You find me not at Longbourn, but enjoying a
visit with Lady Sandalford at Clovisford. She is all
civility and I can only hope to be of some small
service to her.*

There can be few prettier places than Clovisford,
which abounds with every modern amenity. I have
the comfort of a wool mattress and might use a
pump bath if I wish, though the water is too cold at
this time of year. From my window, the trees are the
colours of jewels in the sunlight.

I have seen Imogen twice since our return from
Derbyshire and am in happy agreement that she
flourishes among the Lucas family.

Your concern over Mrs Montagu's letter gave me
some pause for thought, but I hope I might set your
mind at rest. I believe that Mr Montagu's feelings are
engaged elsewhere and that he has not given his
mother cause to hope of your connexion.

However, she is a proud mama with high hopes
for her son's future and is perhaps wishful of your
making an attachment in future. If you feel sure that
there is no possibility of an attachment between you
and Mr Montagu, a gentle hint regarding your
father's wishes for your future might depress further
thoughts of an alliance.

Bath must be second only to London for a good
deal of society. I hope that one day I shall visit, but
not when the Prince is in town, for his own visit
must cause commotion wherever he travels. I shall
imagine you making your graceful bow to him with
your proud father near your side. Lady Calbraith
and her brother must be a great support to you amid
the excesses and strangeness of society, so far
removed from our quiet little county.

When you go to London for the season, you will
feel the benefit of no longer being the ingénue. I hope

that we are able to meet before then and indeed
before the elderberry wine matures for Christmas.
My family are invited to Lord Applefrith's ball at
the full moon. Life beyond that, I imagine, will
return to a quiet routine.
    Fond salutations,
    Mary

The afternoon proving unseasonably fine, Lady Sandalford proposed a walk.

'For,' she said, 'this sunshine cannot remain. I refuse to dragoon you into the library while we may enjoy these last beautiful days.'

'Your Ladyship, I should be very happy to assist you at any time. You have shown me every kindness.'

'Nonsense. I am grateful for the company. Society is a good deal smaller here than in London. There are friends, of course, and my relatives but fifteen miles away, but one is alone some of the time.'

'Dear Lady Sandalford, I do hope you are not lonely.'

'Do not think of it, child. That is a rare event for me. Though I do not in general recommend life alone for a woman. My rank and fortune, as much as my disposition, make the case to my advantage. In general, I recommend marriage for a younger woman.'

Mary lowered her eyes and trifled with the dry leaves around her small foot.

'Your Ladyship makes marriage sound like a choice one can simply make by deciding to take part.'

Lady Sandalford laughed. 'How different the world would be if that were so. But I fear there are young women who choose not to marry for reasons of devotion to family or some perceived imperfection in an unexceptionable suitor. I would hope you would not be the type, Mary.'

'No, I do not think either apply to me, though I would not marry a man I could not respect.'

'Just so. That is wise. The aforementioned young women end their existence lonely and bitter for a single error of judgement. You would not, I am persuaded, reject an eligible gentleman without reason.'

Her Ladyship halted in her tracks as she spoke, requiring Mary to do the same, and to look at her for the cause. Mary tussled with the reply but finally uttered, 'No.'

'Tell me, my dear, have you ever disappointed a gentleman in his proposal?'

Mary dropped her gaze and muttered, 'Yes.' She was surprised to hear her Ladyship say:

'I thought you may have.'

Mary looked up, holding her breath.

'Let us sit awhile on the bench over here and enjoy the sun.' Lady Sandalford turned, saying over her shoulder, 'You can tell me the whole.'

Too late, Mary perceived the trap. Her feet dragged towards the fated bench, where she spent some time in the uneasy adjustment of her skirts.

'Now, tell me about this unfortunate gentleman,' her Ladyship was attentive, 'does he lack the proper means to support a wife?'

'Oh, no. I am quite sure his situation is most comfortable.'

'But his character is lacking, which cannot earn your respect?'

'Indeed, your Ladyship, I respect him beyond all other gentlemen of my acquaintance, save my father.

He is of a thoughtful disposition and has both reserve and sensibility.'

Mary was unaware that her voice broke impassioned from her lips.

'Ah, then his sad characteristic is some form of physical repulsion. One cannot easily overcome such a circumstance.'

'I cannot allow you to think it of him, even though you are not in possession of his name.'

Lady Sandalford turned towards her guest.

'You leave me at a loss, Mary, for I cannot discover the fault. The gentleman sounds like a paragon of virtue, and if I may observe, you give every appearance of a young woman most sincerely attached.'

Mary looked away towards Clovisford in the distance, inviting her to sanctuary.

'Your Ladyship, I cannot deny either charge. But there is an impediment to our union, which I believe to be insurmountable.'

'My dear, this is most distressing news. Two young people should not be thus unhappy.'

Mary had been plucking at her skirt in a distracted manner. Her Ladyship stilled Mary's hand.

'I mean you no harm in prying, but please divulge the problem. Age brings many inconveniences, but I flatter myself that it has also purchased me a little wisdom, which may be of service to you.'

Mary looked up into the intelligent blue eyes and the compassionate face. 'You are all kindness, but I do not know that it can serve. My older sisters were unable to advise a course of action other than the employment of time.'

Lady Sandalford nodded, 'Time can be wondrous useful, but experience tells me that young people are not patient. I pronounce myself at your service.'

Mary sighed. Not to tell Lady Sandalford would appear to be rude in the face of kindness. Besides, she felt too weary to play cat and mouse.

'The impediment is the gentleman's mother. The lady dislikes me with an intensity which can only cause unhappiness in any marriage. I would not come between a man and his family. His first duty must be to his mother.'

Her Ladyship blinked her astonishment.

'You are more generous than most young women in dispensing with your own happiness. How can you be sure of this lady's feelings? No lady would be so ill-bred as to make such sentiments public.'

'Mrs . . . the lady is not ill-bred. She was not aware . . . that is, I had the misfortune to overhear her strong expressions. I would not have listened, but I was not in a position to walk away. There can be no doubt that she finds me to be repugnant in person and in character.'

Her Ladyship stood. 'It grows cooler. Let us walk back for a drink of chocolate and some warmth.'

They walked back for some minutes in silence, eventually broken by lady Sandalford.

'Have you seen this lady recently? You must know that you have returned from Derbyshire with such improvements about your person that can only bring you credit.'

'Your Ladyship is most kind to say so. I have not had occasion to see the lady and own that I am reluctant to encounter her, though I must eventually. In the lady's defence, many of her criticisms were justified, if cruelly made. But I believe her mind to be fixed and you must know that my lack of fortune will weigh with her. She has great ambition for her son.'

Lady Sandalford locked her arm through Mary's own.

'I am going to say something that will shock you. Do not be angry with me, for I have your best interests at heart, and you may count on me to be the soul of discretion.'

Mary regarded her hostess with mild alarm, which amplified into a wide-eyed gasp with her next statement.

'I believe that the gentleman we have discussed is my nephew, Sebastian, and the lady in question is my sister-in-law, Mrs Montagu!'

'Oh, I should not have divulged my tale to you. I beg you will not speak of it.'

'As to that, I make no promises other than to employ my discretion for the benefit of all. Do not despair, Mary. I have long suspected my nephew of falling in love with you and, indeed, of you with him. Have no fear, I approve of the match. You are very well-suited. As to my sister-in-law, well, there is much I could say on that head, but I shall keep my peace. I intend to give the matter my earnest thought and in return, I wish to extract a promise from you that you will do nothing rash.'

'I am not given to rash impulses.'

'I imagine not. Though I suspect your visit to Derbyshire happened in haste. No matter, that decision proved wise. Do you promise?'

'I promise,' Mary replied in a small, exhausted voice.

'Then promise me something further. Do not give yourself over to worry.'

54

The breezy days of sunshine and cotton clouds gave way to rain. The leaves that had blown so merrily about the park hunched into sodden piles, while steady drips fell on every window ledge. Mary drooped in concert with the weather.

Lady Sandalford dealt with the change with the same briskness she applied to all her affairs.

'We have the perfect weather for burying ourselves in the library. There will be a dearth of callers in this drizzle.'

Mary permitted herself a smile.

'Your spirits often put me in mind of my sister Elizabeth. She is positive and active in all weathers. I am persuaded you would deal well together.'

Her Ladyship regretfully took up the last forkful from her dish of eggs.

'You are speaking of Mrs Darcy. I look forward to the pleasure of meeting her again as a grown woman. I met Mr Darcy as a younger man. He was a little stiff in his collar in those days, but I hear your sister has caused him to mellow.'

'She has, and I think you would like him now. He and Mr Bingley are the best of brothers-in-law.' Mary set down her own cutlery. 'Come, lead me to your books, Lady Sandalford.

A fire danced in the grate. Two lamps set on tables helped to cast the room in a cosy glow. Smaller than the library at Cuthbert Park and shaped like a hexagon, Lady Sandalford's library showed the refinement and taste of one who read for pleasure in surroundings of great harmony. Long silk drapes swept either side of the windows. Sculpture and objet interspersed some of the shelving, suggesting airiness. Lady Sandalford paused before each bookcase explaining what she knew of the contents before moving on to the next. It was clear she knew many of the volumes as old friends. They sat before the fire discussing some of their favourite novels.

'So, Miss Bennet, what do you think of my library?'

'It is very fine, your Ladyship. Your influence shows in the decoration.'

'I see you mean to flatter me, but I will keep the compliment.'

'Not at all. I have no talent for artifice and I do like your library very much.' Mary opened her arms wide to the room. 'Who among persons who read could fail to enjoy such surroundings?'

Lady Sandalford looked pleased.

'Now, if you please, Mary, tell me how I may improve the order.'

Mary considered. 'In general, the order appears well. But I wonder, do you read the late Lord Sandalford's volumes on farming, for instance, or his novels?'

'But few. One or two novels and occasionally a reference to natural science or Mr Shakespeare.'

'Yet the works enjoying the most comfortable and light-filled positions are gentlemen's subjects. Could they not remove to the high shelves or behind the door?'

'The very thing. How clearly one sees with fresh eyes. Go on, Mary, what else?'

All the awkwardness of the previous day was set aside as Mary warmed to her subject. The ladies were surprised by a soft knock at the door and the arrival of the refreshments. As with every aspect of her Ladyship's world, meals were always generous in measure.

A visit from Major and Mrs Luckington en route to visit their daughter's family provided the sole disturbance at Clovisford for a few days. When they were gone, the two ladies, the elder tall and fair, the younger petite and dark, returned to their work – side-by-side and aided by a footman – to rearrange the room. Several long intervals punctuated the work as books were discovered or rediscovered and discussed. At last they sat back in easy chairs, delighting in their accomplishment.

'That is a relief. I knew something in here must be altered but could not decide or face the assault alone. Thank you, Mary, you are quite the whirlwind when you bend to a task.'

Mary smiled. 'A shared task such as this one is a joy. My father is a great exponent of healthy pursuits for the mind and the body. My sisters and I are rarely idle.'

'Your father shows great good sense. Idle ways lead one to introspection and ill health. I am never idle and therefore never ill.'

Lady Sandalford plucked a walnut from the ornate dish on the small Pembroke table beside her.

'I'm used to thinking of Papa's dictums as just his way, but you show me the proof of it and now I shall take ownership of the result.'

'Mary Bennet, you have quite a natural charm if you but knew it. I should have been proud to have had a daughter like you, if God had decreed it.'

Mary's eyes misted. 'You pay me the dearest of compliments, Lady Sandalford. God must have been forgetful in missing such a fine lady for the purpose.'

In turn, Lady Sandalford's eyes gleamed over-bright. She cleared her throat.

'Well, this is very fine talk, but we must make haste for we have earned our dinner.' With that, the lady hurried away.

55

As the ball approached, Mary was restored to her family. Lady Sandalford's compliments gratified Mr Bennet and thrilled Mrs Bennet. The lady strained to store every word, the better to regale her friends with the intimacy between the two houses.

Kitty was delighted to have a sister to relieve the dullness of recent days. By the afternoon they had left Mrs Bennet complaining of desertion and escaped to visit the Lucas household.

The Lucas girls and Imogen continued to delight in one another's company; their thoughts and expressions in constant, comic accord. As the group gathered in the music room of Lucas House, away from the younger Lucas children and the ears of their elders, Imogen stated herself to be very much at home.

'For you must know,' she declared with solemnity, 'Sylvia is forever scolding me in the most un-sisterly way.'

The Bennet girls exchanged speaking glances and their lips twitched.

'Older sisters are prone to scold, but they mean well and are usually correct,' Kitty rejoined with sympathy.

Maria Lucas broke in, 'I am sure Sylvia has your

best interests at heart. I now value much of the advice Charlotte gave me in the past.'

'Well, it is an impertinence now that I am out of the schoolroom,' declared Imogen with considerable warmth. Georgina was not to be outdone by her friend.

'And as for Charlotte, lucky for you, Imogen, that you don't know her!' She frowned at her sister. 'Maria may think her a saint but she was always scolding me. I was almost glad she married prosy old Mr Collins and moved to Kent.'

'You do not mean that, Georgina.' Mary seated herself at the pianoforte and struck an idle note. 'You miss Charlotte a great deal. We all do.'

Georgina pouted. 'Yes, well, I suppose it is true, though I would as lief stay at home as visit them and be forever lectured by Mr Collins and have to visit Lady Catherine de Burgh at Rosings.'

Maria, who like Georgina was a fine mimic, imitated her brother-in-law.

'Dear Lady Catherine de Burgh is all civility to my dear Charlotte. She misses no opportunity to advise her in the correct way to raise a child.'

Georgina broke in, speaking as Lady Catherine.

'Listen to me, Mrs Collins. Your husband may be a humble clergyman, but I take it as my Christian duty to spare no effort in telling you how to live your life.'

Laughter erupted around the room, for the fame of Mr Collins and Lady Catherine de Burgh was legend in the Lucas and Bennet households.

The five young ladies walked into Meryton, parting at the baker's bow window, where Georgina and Imogen were tempted by gingerbread and Maria by a fancy cake. The Bennet sisters meandered on to the milliner and the haberdashery, where Kitty supplemented her embroidery silks and Mary deliberated over velvet ribbons to trim a new bonnet. Mrs Blain was all attention. Her sharp eyes swept over Mary with calculating boldness.

'How well you look, Miss Bennet. I expect your visits to Derbyshire and to Lady Sandalford were most agreeable.'

'Indeed they were, Mrs Blain. Thank you.'

'Ah,' said the shopkeeper, 'it is a pleasure, as I always say to Blain, when good fortune smiles on one of our customers. Such news you must have to share.'

Mary's repressed smile gave away none of her inner thoughts.

'Should I ever be the beneficiary of more good fortune than my family and health provide, Mrs Blain, I am certain that you will be among the first to know . . . by one means or another.'

Mrs Blain gaped as Mary turned her attention back to the velvet ribbons, filtering an emerald green between her slim fingers.

Kitty had set aside three new embroidery silks and still her eyes were drawn to the enticing display. As she bent over the rainbow of colours in a glass case, Kitty observed a figure approaching the shop from the corner of her eye.

She hissed: 'Mary, do not look up. Mrs Montagu is about to enter the shop.'

Mary fixed her eyes on the ribbon and uttered a tiny groan. She whispered to Kitty, 'What shall I do? It has been months, but I do not know how to address her.'

Kitty replied in a low voice.

'The fault is Mrs Montagu's. Remember what our sisters advised and how much you have altered. You are equal to addressing anyone and may hold your head high.'

'Oh, Kitty, I am so glad you are here. I could not have faced her alone.'

Mary gave herself a little shake. Kitty whispered that Mr Blain was attempting to serve Mrs Montagu at the far end of the shop.

Mary raised her head and spoke in a commanding manner, 'Mrs Blain, I have made a selection.'

Mrs Blain bustled over as the sound of Mary's voice caused Mrs Montagu to jerk her head in search of the familiar tones. Kitty stood behind Mary's back, blocking her from view, then walked forward to greet Mrs Montagu. She amused herself by striking small alterations of movement to intercept the craning of Mrs Montagu's neck. Mary completed her purchase, straightened her back and turned.

'Mrs Montagu, how very nice to see you. It must be several months since we met. I trust you are in good health?'

Mary extended her hand and fixed an assured smile upon her victim, who looked quite bewildered.

'I . . . Miss Bennet. I am well, thank you. You . . . you are in good looks.'

Mary offered up a self-deprecating tinkle of laughter and looked down at her gown.

'Thank you. They do say clothes maketh the man, but it seems to me they are of even greater importance to ladies. Don't you agree?'

Mrs Montagu nodded dumbly.

'Well, we must not detain you, Mrs Montagu. Indeed, we are expected at home ourselves. Good day.'

Kitty echoed the sentiment and they passed into the street. Beyond the corner, they slowed.

'That was very well done, Mary.'

Mary's face was a little rosy and her smile betrayed a tremulous pride.

'I did not know that I could carry off such a performance, but your reminder of Jane and Lizzy made me determined to do them credit.'

'Well, you certainly have. Did you see Mrs Montagu's face?' Kitty tugged Mary's arm and began pulling foolish faces. 'She did not know whether to take in your costume or heed your words, and seemed incapable of both. I fancy she was on the verge of an apoplexy.'

Kitty whooped with laughter. At length she infected Mary, who nearly collapsed as her rigid form disintegrated with relief.

56

As he closed the shop, Mr Blain cracked to his lady: 'What do you suppose was the matter with Mrs Montagu this afternoon? Looked like she'd swallered an egg whole, she did.'

Mrs Blain placed her hands on her rounded hips and sent forth a hearty laugh. Her husband's turn of phrase never failed to please her.

'So I noticed. 'Tis not certain, but I've heard tell that she's been boasting of netting her son a very big fish. Happen she planned to lord it in grand society. But it's all come to nowt. Don't know what the Bennet girls have to say to the matter, unless . . .'

'Mrs Blain, what do you know, you wicked woman?'

'I am not wicked and I don't know owt. But this I will say. Mary Bennet spent a lot of time up at Cuthbert Park before she went away, but now that she's back she is never there. What's more, she is a changed young lady. Some of her gowns must have cost a king's ransom. She keeps a close lip, that one, but what if someone's died and dropped her a bundle and Mrs Montagu has let her heiress slip from right under her nose, eh? What then?'

'Just you be careful, Mrs Blain. We got to trade here. Happen you may be right, but we got no proof.'

Mrs Blain's lips pressed together in a thin line.

'That's as may be, but I'll wager I'm up to the mark. The ironmonger's wife is no fool; she'll know the way of it.'

57

The Bennets set out early for the ball at Lord Applefrith's particular request.

'You must have time to settle and my mother most especially desires to meet you all before the other guests arrive.'

'It is certain they are people of quality to show such civility,' opined Mrs Bennet.

Nobody felt the need to respond, so she ventured, 'A Baron, you say, Mr Bennet? One can tell by the classic handsomeness of his figure.'

'A mere Baronet, I'm afraid, my dear. We must hope that does not let down his address.'

Mrs Bennet gave a satisfied pat to the brooch clasping her travelling cloak.

'No matter, he must be superior to the gentlemen of our acquaintance. That is how it is with the aristocracy.'

'As to that, Mrs Bennet, I have not observed a significant difference. But he strikes me as a gentleman of good character and he has served his king, so we may take comfort in such a friendship.'

'I should take great comfort if I knew him to have at least three thousand a year.' Mrs Bennet winked at her daughters.

On approaching Gediston place, Mrs Bennet decided that the figure must be nearer four thousand at least, causing her husband to call a halt to such vulgar deliberation.

The house, built of late Tudor timbers, with many mullioned windows, had endured few of the alterations conferred on other houses by subsequent generations. It sat well in mature formal gardens festooned with topiary. The drive through the park seemed near a mile, with a number of ancient trees lining the road. Lord Applefrith hastened to the circular carriageway to greet them, taking exaggerated care to assist the ladies from their carriage. The family was spared conversation as Mrs Bennet gave vent to her excitement in a series of compliments. Lady Applefrith came forth to meet them in her small sitting room.

'Please forgive my meeting you here, but this room is cosier when we are small in number and the household is busy with preparations.'

'But it is charming of you to invite us into your inner sanctum, your Ladyship.' Mrs Bennet succumbed to simpering.

Mr Bennet bowed as Lord Applefrith made introductions. As their elders spoke, the young ladies had leisure to observe their hostess. The loss of her firstborn had clearly taken a toll on the lady's features. Not long out of mourning dress, Lady Applefrith's lavenders seemed almost to blend with her pale, bird-like frame. A warm smile revived the tired eyes and hinted at hidden promise. As Kitty made her bow, Lady Applefrith stepped forward proffering both hands.

'I apprehend that it is you that I have to thank for the notion of a ball. My son has shown such enthusiasm for the idea that I have found myself quite caught up in the excitement.'

'Then I am more amply rewarded than I deserve, Lady Applefrith. For dancing, you know, must be reward enough for me at any time.'

Lord Applefrith intervened.

'I hope you will reserve me the second dance, as the first must go to the lady of highest rank.' He looked across at Mary. 'If I can persuade Miss Mary Bennet to the third dance, then my evening must be a success.'

The sisters demurely acquiesced before his mother insisted they all remove their travel apparel and join her for refreshment.

Later, as the sisters assisted each other with their toilette, Kitty declared her sympathy for their hostess.

'Yes, the blow must have been severe. Could you imagine our sisters or their husbands if one of our nephews or our niece were to be lost?'

'It would be unbearable for us all, Mary.' Kitty placed a tidy pin in Mary's hair. 'I shall make an extra special effort to engage Lady Applefrith in conversation. She is deserving of a little gaiety.'

The house party was to gather in the hall before dinner. The sisters linked arms to descend the wide central staircase, unaware of the charming affect they had on the party below, who were reduced to momentary silence. Lady Applefrith overheard, 'By Jupiter,' slip from under her son's breath, causing a smile of complaisance to spread across her own countenance.

Mary wore her new turquoise gown, which shimmered about her as she moved. Kitty had helped arrange her hair into a high plaited coronet with soft curls about her heart-shaped face. Long French gloves and a matching fan completed the costume. She felt that she had never looked so well and could at last hold her place with any young lady whom they should encounter in the ballroom.

Kitty wore the cream, rose-velvet trimmed gown that had been such a success in Derbyshire. She had made herself new matching shoe roses. Mary had been schooled to arrange her hair in smooth curls, loosely threaded with a bandeau to match her gown. The effect was simple and artless, giving Kitty the innocence of a fresh carnation.

Mrs Bennet nodded her quantity of ostrich feathers in vigorous approval. As she later whispered to Mr Bennet as though he were going deaf, 'It did no harm at all for our girls to garner all the attention before any rival young ladies arrived.'

As general conversation ensued, nobody noticed two newcomers descending the stairs. Mary was startled to see Sebastian and his mother appear. Mrs Bennet was all delight at the appearance of her friend. The Bennet family triumph would now have a witness.

'My dear Mrs Montagu, how very delightful to see you here,' she trilled.

Mr Bennet bowed. Lord Applefrith marched toward his new friend. The two young men made a handsome duo in their satin knee breeches, buckled pumps and dark, moulded, superfine wool jackets.

'Montagu, the penalty for your arriving last is fixed. I have secured Miss Kitty Bennet for the second dance and Miss Mary Bennet for the third.'

Sebastian gave him a rueful smile.

'These evening cravats are devilish difficult to arrange. I have already had to apologise to Mama for keeping her waiting; now I must beg your pardon, Lady Applefrith.'

'It is nothing at all, Mr Montagu. We await two of Henry's friends to join us.' She glanced towards the entrance, 'Ah, here they are now.'

A round of introductions to Mr Thomas and Lieutenant Skipton preceded the party in to dinner. As they took their seats, Mary heard Mr Montagu passing behind her speak *sotto voce*. 'I beg you will save me the first dance, Miss Bennet.'

By the time she looked up he was already at the other end of the table, but his eyes were fixed upon her. She accorded him a brief, cool nod and turned her attention to Mr Thomas.

The two young gentlemen were lively companions. They had known Lord Applefrith for many years and told tales of their joint escapades to general merriment. Acutely aware of the Montagus at the other end of the table, Mary concentrated on conversing with Mr Thomas and her father. Mr Thomas lost no time in pressing his claim to dance. Such was the competitive nature of their two new acquaintances that by the time they arose from dinner Mary found herself to be engaged for the first four dances and Kitty for the first three.

As guests began to file in for the ball the old house seemed to come alive. The soft glow of gems in the candlelight and a hubbub of excited voices seeped through the low-beamed rooms. When it seemed they were fit to burst at the seams, a final flurry of guests arrived. Mary, who had been fetching her mother a glass of ratafia, was taken aback to see Mr and Lady Sarah

Dalrymple arrive with Countess Glendinning. She deposited the glass without pause in her mother's hand and hurried in search of Kitty. She found her in conversation with Lord Applefrith and Mr Thomas. Even as she attempted to draw Kitty aside, Mr Thomas exclaimed, 'Good God, is that Dalrymple over there?'

Kitty's startled eyes followed Mr Thomas's direction. Mary laid a warning hand on her sister's arm. Lord Applefrith answered his friend.

'Yes, I was obliged to invite him as his aunt is an old connexion of the family, but I shall avoid the fellow beyond a civil greeting, which I had better manage now.'

With that he marched off. Mary turned to Mr Thomas.

'We met the countess with her daughter and Mr Dalrymple during the summer. How are you acquainted with him, sir?'

'I know him but barely. We were at university at the same time.' His frown was severe. 'I do not consider him a friend, Miss Bennet.'

Mary met his eyes with an open expression.

'Then we are at one in our opinions, Mr Thomas.'

Mr Thomas unbent and seemed to relax.

'I'm glad to hear you say so. For all his sophisticated veneer, I do not account him to be quite the thing.'

By now people were drifting into the ballroom. As the sisters joined the throng, Kitty spoke in an undertone.

'I wonder what Mr Thomas is *not* saying about Mr Dalrymple? He so obviously takes him in dislike.'

'Apparently you acted wisely, Kitty, for it is also clear that Lord Applefrith disapproves.'

Kitty shivered. 'I shall remember that afternoon always.'

'Let us do as his Lordship has and go together to speak to the Glendinning party. Then we may enjoy ourselves for the rest of the evening having done our duty.'

Kitty gave her sister a doubtful look.

'I am dreading it, but I suppose we must.'

Mary linked arms. 'Come along. I am beside you and there is nothing they can say to hurt you. Remember, we have the advantage over him because we know his true character.'

They crossed the ballroom and bowed to the countess, who was as good-natured and complaisant as ever. They turned next to her haughty daughter.

Mary spoke first. 'Good evening, I believe it is Lady Sarah Dalrymple, now?'

Lady Sarah uttered a mirthless laugh.

'Thank you, Miss Bennet. My husband and I have lately returned from honeymoon, so we are behind with news. I take it that I have no need to offer you or your sister any felicitations?' She raised an eyebrow as she spoke and gave them each a pointed stare.

Incensed on Kitty's behalf, Mary rejoined, 'No, indeed, Lady Sarah. My sister and I intend to be most careful in the character of any gentleman we may choose to marry.'

Mr Dalrymple, who had turned and caught most of the exchange, winced. Kitty looked him boldly in the eye before saying, 'Hurry, sister, the musicians are beginning and we must find our partners.'

Out of earshot, Mary gave way to her anger.

'Odious creature!'

'Yes,' replied Kitty thoughtfully, 'but did you see, Mary, she looks as miserable as ever. Marriage to Mr Dalrymple does not seem to make her happy.'

Lieutenant Skipton claimed Kitty for the first dance. Before she could move a step, Mr Montagu appeared at Mary's side to lead her away. Her heart beat in a dizzying rhythm, quite at odds with the harmony played by the musicians.

'You are quiet, Miss Bennet. Did your dinner companions exhaust your conversation?'

Mary could not but smile, nervous though she felt.

'No indeed, sir, though they may have exhausted themselves.'

He threw back his head and laughed in the way she had come to enjoy. They joined their next partners in the set and when they came back together he said, in a voice for her ears only, 'Did you wonder that I asked you for the first dance?'

'I was a little surprised,' she murmured.

He leaned in more than the movement of the dance required.

'I mean to demonstrate to you that my mother's opinion carries no weight with me. It is your good opinion that matters.'

They moved off again, but neither offered their next partners their due attention. As Mr Montagu once again claimed her hand Mary frowned slightly.

'My good opinion of you remains constant,' she said, a little breathless, though not from exertion. 'I once told you that I am not in the habit of changing my mind. But the good opinion of Mrs Montagu does indeed matter.'

His eyes became dull and his mouth set in a grim line. The dance came to an end. He escorted her from the floor without a word. Mary looked up at him. He made to speak, but at that moment Mr Thomas claimed her for the next set.

As the gay country dance progressed, Mary noted Kitty dancing with Lord Applefrith as though they were partners of long standing, so natural was their synchronised movement. The four remained talking on the dance floor at the end of the set as they were to swap partners for the next country dance. His Lordship was in high spirits, at one with the pace of the dance, and Mary felt herself infected with his mood. Lieutenant Skipton in the next dance also proved himself to be a nimble partner.

Kitty repaired to her room to retrieve her forgotten fan after her dance with Mr Thomas. As she returned to the hall, Mr Dalrymple appeared out of the gloom behind the stairs.

'You startled me, sir.'

'Forgive me, Miss Bennet, I feel that I owe you some explanation of my conduct.'

'Pray, do not trouble yourself.' Kitty snapped her fan. He advanced towards her and she instinctively stepped back.

'But I cannot allow you to think ill of me.'

He cut a fine figure, but his wheedling tone was ugly.

Kitty stiffened. 'My thoughts, sir, I claim to own for myself.'

He spoke in a rush now. 'You must know, Miss Bennet, when I asked you to meet me, my feelings for you . . .'

She held out her fan at arm's length as a warning against any advance.

'Pray desist, Mr Dalrymple. There is no profit in this conversation. Your wife—'

'Ah, my proud wife,' he spat out with bitterness. 'She has everything I need in life, but for a warm heart. When I saw you tonight I knew it most surely.'

He darted forward and she slipped behind a large circular table, preventing him from reaching her. Panic began to rise in her throat.

'Dalrymple! Your wife is looking for you.'

Mr Dalrymple coloured at the rough edge of Lord Applefrith's tongue. Mr Thomas, beside Lord Applefrith, issued a baleful stare. Kitty's eyes prickled with tears.

'There, my dear, do not take upset.'

Lord Applefrith held out his handkerchief.

Mr Thomas turned and followed Mr Dalrymple back to the ballroom, while Lord Applefrith went to Kitty's side and led her away from view.

'You must think me foolish.' Kitty dabbed her eyes. 'But he stepped out of the shadows and insisted on speaking to me in the most unwelcome manner. I'm so glad that you and Mr Thomas came in.'

'He will not bother you again, we shall see to it. I overheard enough to know that his attentions were unwelcome,' he thundered. 'By God, he is only just married.'

His Lordship's anger, so foreign to his usual genial self, caused Kitty to fear for his next action.

'Before he eloped with Lady Sarah, Mr Dalrymple had given rise to some expectations among our acquaintance. I realised that his character was flawed and was glad of the opportunity to escape to Derbyshire.' She returned his Lordship's handkerchief and gave him as calm a look as she could muster. 'Tonight was the first time we have met since. I believe he wished to convince me of his innocence, but his demeanour was crude and he spoke so cruelly of Lady Sarah.'

Lord Applefrith's tone remained harsh.

'Well, she has made her sorry bed. Now, are you sure those pretty eyes are dry? Let us go and speak to Mama before supper.'

Kitty gave herself a little shake, smiled and spread her fan.

'Of course, we must not be missed. I have been wanting to congratulate dear Lady Applefrith on her triumph.'

In the ballroom Lady Applefrith had been ensuring she spoke to all of her guests, and was presently seated between Mrs Montagu and Mrs Bennet.

'I understand that you are both situated near Meryton?'

'Yes, indeed, we have known one another these many years,' explained Mrs Bennet.

'My late husband was a great scholar and friend of Mr Bennet,' added Mrs Montagu.

Since the opportunity to boast of one's children is the object of every mother's heart and Lady Applefrith was a good hostess, she enquired, 'Is your son, Sebastian, also a scholar? I should be delighted if Henry has made a more cerebral friend.'

Mrs Montagu shook her head with vigour, almost dislodging a gemstone in her silk turban.

'Sebastian has inherited his father's passion for books. I own that I do not see the attraction.'

'Mr Bennet would be quite lost without his library,' Mrs Bennet interjected. 'I think it is a proper pastime for a gentleman. Though I declare that I am happier now that Mary has developed interests beyond the library.'

She fluttered her fan, causing an alarming ripple of swaying ostrich feathers on her head. Her Ladyship nodded.

'Henry praises your elder daughter. He wrote to me from Derbyshire much impressed by her knowledge and good sense.'

This news caused Mrs Montagu to think so hard that a frown pinched two vertical lines above her aquiline nose.

'Lord Applefrith is a favourite with both my younger daughters and that is as it should be,' said Mrs Bennet, 'not enough young men today have his pleasing and open manners. Mr Bennet is quite taken with his hunting skills.'

The object of their conversation arrived with Kitty and invited Mrs Bennet to dance. Mrs Montagu leaned to her left to hear the lady beside her speak.

Kitty availed herself of her mother's vacated seat to speak to Lady Applefrith. She had wondered a good deal about her Ladyship from the first time Lord Applefrith had mentioned her in Derbyshire. Now the lady was made flesh, Kitty was intrigued to form a proper impression.

'Your Ladyship's ball is a great triumph.'

'Thank you, my dear. It is too long since we entertained at Gediston Place.'

Kitty fluttered her fan. 'Such a romantic house is made for enjoyment.'

Her Ladyship laughed. 'You are generous, Miss Bennet. I fear Gediston is made for draughts and leaks more than enjoyment, but we love it despite the inconvenience.'

Undeterred, Kitty replied, 'My nephews would think it a wonderful place for their hide and seek.'

'Are you fond of children, Miss Bennet?' Her Ladyship's eye glinted.

'Oh, yes. My niece and nephews are delightful. I am only sorry that they are all in Derbyshire.'

Her Ladyship sighed. 'It feels like only yesterday that my own two dear boys were playing their games about the house. They were very different, you know. Dear Dominic always so serious and Lucas rushing about playing at soldiers. How I miss the sound of childish voices.'

Kitty's tears, so recently extinguished, rose to her eyes again.

'Dear Lady Applefrith. You have endured a great deal. Surely God will grant your wish and Gediston Place will again be blessed with children.'

Her Ladyship patted Kitty's hand.

'Your sensibility does you credit, my dear. You must not listen to any more of my foolishness. Why, here is Mr Montagu.'

Mr Montagu bowed. 'I have failed to secure a place on your card, Miss Bennet. Have I missed my chance of dancing with you?'

Kitty returned him an impish smile.

'You are saving my reputation, Mr Montagu, for I only know three other gentlemen and I have danced with them all.'

'Then may I lead you into the set before supper, and then to supper?'

'With pleasure.'

Both sisters had the happiness of participating in almost every dance under the approving eye of their mother. It was generally agreed by the assembled company that the Bennet girls quite eclipsed the other young ladies in the ballroom.

Seated beside Mrs Montagu at supper, while her son bespoke drinks for the party, Kitty enquired of their journey to Gediston Place.

'Oh, it was all of a piece. We shall break overnight on the return at Clovisford to visit my sister-in-law.' The lady lapsed into silence. Then, she turned. 'Tell me, Miss Bennet, your sister is in very good looks. Did Derbyshire agree with her excessively?'

Kitty felt disinclined to discuss Mary with her tormentor. While wondering about Mrs Montagu's purpose, she could do no more than praise her sister.

'Mary is not a creature of excess, Mrs Montagu. But she did indeed enjoy herself in Derbyshire. Our sisters and their husbands showed her every attention. She overcame her reserve and blossomed in local society.'

'You met Lord Applefrith there, of course.'

'Yes, that was a particular pleasure of our visit. He is a favourite with Darcy and Elizabeth and his nature is such that we all soon shared their good opinion. We are delighted to have renewed our acquaintance now that we are come home.'

Mrs Montagu glanced across the room to see Lord Applefrith bringing Mary a dish of jelly. She frowned again.

58

Kitty arrived early in the breakfast room, hoping to fulfil a promise to Lord Applefrith by reporting her study progress. She found he had the same idea.

'I was determined to approach every text you recommended to me before the ball.'

'And how did you find them? Not too dull, I hope?' he said with concern, as he helped himself from a silver platter.

Kitty admitted, 'I did need to apply to Mary once or twice for aid, but I managed. I fear that it may take years to make up for my lamentable lack of knowledge.'

She lowered her eyelashes, embarrassed.

'Miss Bennet, t'would be a dull thing if every lady were to be bookish. Why, where would we find our mothers?' He gave her a rallying smile. 'Who would sew or paint the pretty baubles in the home?'

'I admit that I am more suited to those things.' Kitty cheered a little. 'But a lady should be accomplished.'

'An half hour every day spent in the acquisition of knowledge is my prescription. Think how much you shall learn in a year. Indeed, now you have read all the texts I suggested, you are well begun.'

He offered her a saffron roll from a large salver.

Kitty thought he was kinder and more thoughtful than any other officer she had met. She wondered that her opinions had been so easily swayed by the handsome appearance of a uniform or the sophistry of Mr Dalrymple. Lord Applefrith sat before her with a smile and the good manners to avoid mentioning last night's distressing moments. Indeed, he was a superior gentleman to the others altogether.

'Sir, before the others join us, I must thank you for your kindness and protection last night.'

His face became stern.

'Upon my honour, Miss Bennet, Dalrymple had better not step into my path again.'

Mr Montagu joined them, asking, 'What has Mr Dalrymple done to cause such ire?'

Kitty blushed but Lord Applefrith came to her aid.

'He's the worst kind of fellow. Last night Thomas and I caught him upsetting Miss Bennet here, but Thomas was on his guard early. They were at Cambridge together. There is an unsavoury tale about Dalrymple engaging another penniless student to write his essays and then refusing to pay the fellow.' He paused a moment. 'There are other tales too, but not fit to tell in the presence of a lady. He's a scoundrel.'

Kitty gasped. Mr Montagu addressed her in his gentle way.

'I am sorry he should have distressed you, Miss Bennet. His elopement aside, I have always found it difficult to like the fellow and felt the guilt of it. I see now that my instincts were sound. It is good news for us all that I overheard him say that they will remove to London for the season.'

Kitty let out a little sigh of relief. The further away the Dalrymples went, the happier she would feel.

'I'm glad to be rid of him. Let us agree to forget him.' Lord Applefrith rubbed his hands in anticipation as a servant appeared with another dish and the aroma of mushrooms filtered into the breakfast parlour.

Mr Bennet arrived in jovial mood, teasing his three juniors in turn about their many partners and the likelihood of sore limbs.

'Not a bit of it, sir,' Mr Montagu assured him.

'I should say no,' declared Lord Applefrith.

Mr Bennet wagged a finger.

'Then I shall test you both out with a short walk in the garden after breakfast, before the indolence of coach journeys dampens the day.'

As the gentlemen prepared to depart, Mary and Lady Applefrith entered the room. Mary smiled into Mr Montagu's eyes, but his 'good morning' came with a perfunctory nod and he did not pause. Her eager anticipation of breakfast melted away. *Was this how they would fare in future when they met?*

Kitty removed to the window seat with the morning sun glowing all around her.

'My, how fresh you greet the morning Miss Bennet,' declared Lady Applefrith.

Her son turned to look over his shoulder. He halted momentarily, a strange look stealing across his face, before joining the others.

With the arrival of Mrs Bennet and Mrs Montagu, the ladies made a light breakfast. Mrs Bennet was voluminous in her compliments to Lady Applefrith while Mrs Montagu turned her attention to the sisters.

'Did you enjoy the festivities?' she demanded of neither in particular. Mary responded.

'Yes, ma'am. The ball was the equal of any one could hope to attend. Lady Applefrith spared no effort for the enjoyment of all.'

Mrs Montagu coughed. 'Prettily said. And you, miss?' She arched an eyebrow towards Kitty.

'I fear there is little I can add to my sister's description. It was a wonderful evening. Are we not all fortunate to enjoy such hospitality?'

'Quite.' Mrs Montagu turned to her hostess. 'The young ladies voice my own opinion well, Lady Applefrith. We are all of an accord as to the perfection of your arrangements.'

Lady Applefrith appeared to suffer under the weight of praise. She turned her attention to politely questioning her two older guests. The two friends' reactions were oddly different. Mrs Bennet, though fulsome in her enthusiasm, proved positively demure in her descriptions of hearth and home. Mrs Montagu, by contrast, displayed such pride, one may have supposed her to be a marchioness at least. Her Ladyship later told her lady's maid she rejoiced that Mrs Montagu did not possess an attractive daughter.

59

The Montagus' coach covered the fifteen miles to Clovisford and bowled along the carriageway at a smart pace. Lady Sandalford strode out onto the chilly portico. The atmosphere between her sister-in-law and nephew was cooler than the weather. She greeted mother and son with her characteristic warmth and showed them into the drawing room, where a large log blazed below an intricately carved lintel.

'I have had a light repast prepared for you, in case you may be hungry.'

Mrs Montagu shuddered.

'Your thoughtfulness is appreciated, Arabella, but I cannot face the thought of food. Sebastian may oblige you. He is not sensitive in the least.'

Sebastian did not respond to this challenge but merely seated himself in a tall wing chair near the fire. Lady Sandalford looked from one to the other with a slight frown. Mrs Montagu became absorbed in checking her travelling costume for misadventure. Sebastian regarded his fingernails.

'Well, you must tell me all about the ball,' declared her Ladyship.

Her sister-in-law developed a look of deep distaste.

'I beg you will excuse me, Arabella. I have the headache; it is not to be other than expected after that draughty old house and the jolting of the road in our ancient coach.'

'Our coach is not yet ten years old, Mother.'

Mrs Montagu snapped, 'It is very well for you. You are young.' Her eyes appealed to her sister-in-law for agreement. 'But that is the young. They care for nobody beyond themselves!'

Lady Sandalford ushered her sister-in-law out of the room, speaking soothing words as they went.

'Come, Prunella, you will feel better for a lie down. I shall send your maid up with a lavender water cloth and a dish of Chinese tea. A soft bed and quiet are what you need.'

Mrs Montagu allowed herself to be led away. When her Ladyship returned to the sitting room, she carefully closed the heavy door behind her. A tray bearing a steaming teapot reposed untouched at Sebastian's side.

'Now, Sebastian, what manner of upset has caused your mother to take to her bed and you to be so grave?'

He stood up and gestured to his aunt to sit while he poured the tea.

'Gracious, am I in need of a restorative?' His aunt's voice was teasing, but her eyes betrayed her concern.

'Perhaps.' Sebastian's serious face relaxed into a wry smile. 'Though I have never known any female less in need of cosseting. Your refusal to dissemble and your vigour are just two of the reasons I love you, Aunt.'

'Dear boy, I love you like a son. It is clear to me that you are unhappy. I do not doubt that unhappiness has everything to do with your being in love with Mary Bennet.' He almost dropped his cup. She waved him to sit. 'No, do not deny it – I am not a fool.'

He brought his cup half way to his lips, then sighed deeply and set it back down again as he sank in his chair to face his aunt.

'No, you are not a fool and I cannot deny it. But Mary has refused me.'

'She has refused to you despite the considerable advantages of the match and the fact that she is in love with you.'

Mr Montagu balanced his elbows on his knees and held his face in his hands.

'Does she love me? She says as much. Yet there is nothing I can do. She is not a lady in the habit of changing her mind.'

'That is usually a virtue, but in your case an encumbrance.'

Eyes still fixed firmly on the floor, he removed his head briefly from his hands to nod agreement.

'I begin to think you would have greater luck if you had fallen in love with the Honorable Sylvia Drummond.'

He barked a short laugh.

'She is nothing to compare! Though I am pleased to call her a friend.'

His aunt raised an eyebrow at the vehemence of his words.

'I am glad to hear you are friends at least. In truth, she is the most eligible young woman and shall have her pick in the ballrooms of London.'

'That is very likely and the correct place for her, Aunt.' Sebastian's features were sober. 'Sylvia is a born hostess. But Mary suits my every notion of a wife. The quiet life is her metier and my own. She makes me think about things in new ways. Her advice is sound in every particular. She makes me laugh and to feel protective.' His hand betrayed a slight tremor as he reached for his tea. 'That is the nub of it; she makes me *feel*!' He sighed. 'So I have made a decision.'

Lady Sandalford leaned forward in her chair, a study in concentration. He turned to give her a firm look, his face quite haggard.

'I cannot bear to remain in Meryton, where I will see her often and know that another man may win her hand. I have decided to find a manager for Cuthbert Park so that I may return to the vineyards in Portugal. That is why my mother is so angry with me.'

'For once I agree with her. How can you give up so easily, Sebastian?' his aunt cried.

His shoulders dropped. 'I see no other choice. I have tried to speak to Mary; to persuade her, but she is resolute to, and I own I still do not fully understand the strength of her cause.'

'You may not, but I do!' His aunt paced in front of the fire. 'This will not serve. You may depend upon it that Mary is both mature and just in her actions. Indeed, she puts you above herself.'

Sebastian's eyes grew wide. He started and gripped the arms of the chair hard.

'How can you know all of this, Aunt?'

Lady Sandalford drifted over to the fire.

'Because I tricked her into revealing herself.' She turned to him. 'Your mother must be brought to heel. However unwitting, she has done you both great harm.'

'Then it is all true about my mother being the cause of Mary's refusing me?' His expression mixed hope and confusion. 'Can you really know what she has said? My mother can be capricious but I have never thought her truly unkind.'

'No, she is not truly unkind, Sebastian, but she vents her thoughts unguarded and the very worst of them were overheard by Mary. Luckily, perhaps, those thoughts were addressed to me; otherwise they would be all over Meryton and beyond. Your Mary has endured much, while still protecting your mother's reputation and displaying true moral character.' She walked towards Sebastian and steepled her hands together as though in prayer. 'Your mother is proud and ambitious for you, and indeed for herself, to the point of foolishness. In so doing, she has made both you and Mary her victims.'

Sebastian stood and threw his arms in the air.

'I am at a loss; cannot begin to think clearly. Dash it! Why is there no logic in love?'

His aunt patted his shoulder and issued a soft chuckle.

'Logic has nothing to do with love. One is of the head and the other the heart, dear boy. Without both, we are not whole.'

He grasped her hand.

'It is good to speak of it at last. There are times I have felt that I had lost my reason.' His voice cracked. Lady Sandalford stood beside him for a while. Her hand rested on his shoulder, clamped beneath his own large fingers. Finally she said in a low voice, 'Sebastian, will you do me the honour of delaying your plans for Portugal, at least until Christmas has passed?'

He turned with a half-smile,

'For you, certainly.'

'However, I do not see any necessity to confuse your mother further. Let her believe that your plan is advancing.'

'Aunt Sandalford, what are you plotting?' A smile reached his sad eyes.

'Plotting is such an unfortunate term. I do not know exactly how I may influence events, but depend upon it, I shall make a valiant effort.'

He kissed her forehead.

'I know you will. There is no one else in the world other than you who could give me hope at this moment.'

Mrs Montagu appeared but briefly at dinner where she made a hearty meal in spite of her malaise. Lady Sandalford and Sebastian endeavoured to make polite conversation, but Mrs Montagu determined upon a course as peevish as it was querulous. She made her apologies after the meal and retired to her room, which satisfied everybody but her lady's maid.

By the breakfast hour Mrs Montagu's spirits had revived. Lady Sandalford suggested that Sebastian make himself scarce by investigating the rearrangement of her library or indeed any activity he pleased, which divided him from his parent for an hour or two. As good as his promise he made an early breakfast and vanished from sight. The ladies breakfasted at leisure and then had their coffee served in the quiet of the morning room.

'I am glad to find some time alone with you, Arabella.' Mrs Montagu stopped short as though uncertain of her next words, 'I am in need of your counsel.'

'Why, Prunella, that must be the most flattering thing you have ever said to me,' said her Ladyship with a gently raised eyebrow.

'Do not be superior with me, I beg you,' Mrs Montagu snapped. She continued in more conciliatory tones.

'Has Sebastian told you that he intends to return to Portugal?'

'He has.'

'How could he? He is my only child. I have longed for his return. I did not agree with his father sending him there, you know, barely a month out of university. I had such plans for him, for the future.' She searched about her lace cuffs for a handkerchief. 'Now I shall be left to moulder away at Cuthbert Park. I may never see him again. He might marry a godless foreigner and I shall never lay eyes on my own grandchildren. What shall I do?'

With that she began to sob in a manner quite unseemly. Lady Sandalford appeared distressed at the sight of someone so discomposed and at a loss as to how to comfort her sister-in-law. After a little pointless fluttering, she waited until the storm abated. At length she rang the bell to request strong coffee and sugar biscuits. Then she sat back on her eau de nil sofa and awaited the various dabbings and flutterings required for her sister-in-law to compose herself.

As she poured the coffee, Lady Sandalford coaxed her guest to imbibe a little sugar for her shock.

'Now, Prunella, we are going to have a serious discussion. Sebastian is very dear to me. My late husband's relations are all very well in their way, but it is my brother's child who touches my heart. You have a fine son, Prunella, but you must allow him to be a man and to make his own choices.'

'But he has a free hand in running the estates both here and in Portugal,' Mrs Montagu protested.

'Come, Prunella, let us not fence. You take my meaning, I am sure. He must be in charge of the *whole* of his life without interference. We have made our choices; now the young must make their decisions.' She set her face in a stern look. 'I truly believe that his decision to leave can be reversed if you will only make reparation.'

'I do not know what you mean, Arabella. What crime have I committed in your eyes?'

'It is not a matter of my good opinion, my dear. You desired my advice.' Her features relaxed to a kinder expression. 'Sebastian has borne your pushing unsuitable young ladies in his direction with admirable forbearance. But you know in your mother's heart that he is in love with Mary Bennet.'

Mrs Montagu snapped in peevish tones, 'Mary Bennet, indeed. The Bennet women are as scheming a bunch of bluebells as ever I have seen. Barely a portion to be had between them, or so I have heard.'

Lady Sandalford turned away to repress a smile. In a voice that was not altogether steady she replied,

'I recollect your opinion of Mary Bennet as quite different; the very opposite of a scheming temptress. As to her older sisters, both were acknowledged beauties and made, I believe, very happy marriages.'

Mrs Montagu huffed.

'Mrs Bennet makes no bones about her ambition to marry off her daughters.'

'And who can blame her? Five daughters are a heavy burden. But you cannot visit the sins of the mother on the child. Both unmarried Bennet girls are as natural and unaffected as any mother-in-law could wish. Come now, we avoid the facts. Sebastian loves Mary Bennet and she returns his feelings.'

Mrs Montagu threw down her fan in an attitude of disgust.

'Then let him pursue her. Much good it may do him.' She issued a bitter little laugh. 'She has returned from Derbyshire in all her finery and has Lord Applefrith dangling in her wake.'

'Oh, Prunella, I fear your prejudice will make Sebastian lost to you forever. You must see that they are attached and so very well-suited.'

'What have I to say to the matter? If he wishes to make her an offer, it is within his power.'

Mrs Montagu banged down her delicate china cup, causing her sister-in-law to wince.

'I think we shall have another cup and another biscuit.' Lady Sandalford began to look as though she were in need of a palliative herself as she reached for the bell pull. 'This is difficult . . . can it be that you do not know he has offered and been refused?'

Mrs Montagu registered shock. She drew herself up in great affront.

'How can this be? Why did he not tell me? How is it that you know this?' She began to fan herself furiously. Lady Sandalford spoke with alarm.

'Please, calm yourself, Prunella. I will answer all of your questions. First, I know because I suspected the possibility and set about inveigling the truth. I am not proud of my methods on that head. As to why Sebastian has not confided in you, I cannot say with surety. He must be aware of your disapproval and perhaps felt there was no need to reveal his rejection.'

Mrs Montagu stormed,

'He has been distant since his return from Derbyshire. How dare she refuse him! This is the cause of his returning to Portugal. *She* is to blame!'

Mrs Montagu began to pace about the room in a fury. 'Stop, Prunella! I will not countenance this.'

Lady Sandalford blocked her path. Mrs Montagu did as she was bid. In frozen accents she demanded of Lady Sandalford, 'Pray, reveal yourself. What can you mean by such behaviour?'

Lady Sandalford straightened her back, folded her hands in her lap and turned a bold eye upon her sister-in-law.

'You are the reason he was refused, Prunella. Yes, I am serious, it was *you*.'

She paused a moment as Mrs Montagu to digested the shock of this statement.

'*Me?*' Mrs Montagu's foot began to tap on the plush pile of the rug. 'Outrageous!'

'No, dear, not outrageous at all.' Her Ladyship gestured toward the sofa. 'Please sit down. Mary Bennet had the sense and indeed the sensibility to realise that there can be no happiness in a union where the sole member of her suitor's family disapproves of the bride. I salute her superior understanding that two women cannot live together in the same house, when the incumbent and senior feels as you do.'

Mrs Montagu flopped into a Louis XV1 chair, which rocked under such rough treatment.

'This is too much. I am much maligned. I own you are enjoying your superiority over me, Arabella.'

Lady Sandalford demurred.

'Do not deny it,' her sister-in-law snapped. 'Your family did not scorn my fortune, but the fact that it was based on the port trade; *that* you did not like. No, do not interrupt me. I have known it all these years. Then of course, off you go marrying Lord Sandalford, gaining both wealth and position at a stroke.'

Mrs Montagu raised a handkerchief to her eyes, which now overflowed. Lady Sandalford regarded her with morbid fascination. At length she spoke in a quiet voice.

'You reveal so much, Prunella. Perhaps we would not have found ourselves in our current situation if we had shown a greater spirit of openness in the past. If I have ever given you the impression that you are in some way inferior, please accept my apology.' Lady Sandalford leaned forward in her chair, her eyes sharp and bright. 'But surely you cannot think that my late brother and I took the attitude of our parents? You are my sister-in-law; the mother of my adored nephew and a member of our small family. As such, you are ever valued.'

'Then you have my apology, for it seemed so to me, Arabella; though you cannot doubt my suffering all these years,' sniffed the wounded mother.

'Indeed, and I am sorry to be the unwitting cause of it. But I am determined that between us we will reach some resolution for the young people. They are the future after all. You quite naturally want Sebastian to live here in England, and of course you can wish nothing but his happiness; for he wants for nothing in life except happiness.'

Mrs Montagu gave her Ladyship a beseeching look.

'I do not see, Arabella, how *I* can make Mary Bennet change her mind. She appears to have some general idea that I dislike her, despite my being civil to her on every occasion.'

'Ah, now we arrive at the crux of our problem.' Lady Sandalford took a deep breath. 'What I am about to say is extremely distressing and reflects quite badly on both of us for differing reasons. You will think me interfering but my motives are pure. It was my conviction, as I said before, that Sebastian and Mary were attached but unhappy.' Her Ladyship rearranged her skirt, conveying as she did so, a rare look of uncertainty. 'I invited Mary to Clovisford and during the course of her stay, tricked her into revealing the truth. She revealed no names and was therefore mortified when I supplied the names.'

Mrs Montagu could not resist a smug interruption.

'That was very badly done of you, Arabella. Mary Bennet was your guest.'

Lady Sandalford pressed her lips together and her eyes grew hard.

'Indeed she was, but as I said, my motives were pure. Mary was most upset and begged me not to reveal what I had learned. I told her that I could not make that promise but would use my discretion.'

Mrs Montagu shifted in her seat, a growing discomfort reflected in her mannerisms.

'In what manner does this sordid story relate to me?'

Her Ladyship levelled her a direct gaze.

'Do you recall a conversation we had at Cuthbert Park about Mary Bennet? At the time we were discussing the young ladies you continued to invite to the house. You were rather angry and spoke out against Mary in the very strongest of terms.'

'Yes, I recall our disagreement and I admit I spoke in anger. But what of it? Our conversation was private.'

This statement was met with a shaking head across the room.

'Except it was not. Mary was on her way into the salon when she overheard a raised voice. Not wishing to cause embarrassment, she halted for a moment and then became privy to your opinion of her.' Lady Sandalford sighed. 'She was trapped in the anteroom, unable to return to the library for fear of revealing her distress to the servants and unable to enter the salon. She hid behind the screen when she heard Peters coming and ran the gauntlet of the servants' passage to make her exit.'

Mrs Montagu's hands rose to her face in horror.

'She heard everything?'

Lady Sandalford nodded.

'The only saving grace is that no other person in Meryton knows, with the likely exception of her younger sister. She has protected your reputation by her silence. More important to current events, she did not reveal the truth to Sebastian out of delicacy.'

Mrs Montagu's mortification gave way to fresh tears.

'I have never been so distressed,' she uttered between sobs. 'This is quite insupportable.'

'Quite,' snapped Lady Sandalford. 'Imagine poor Miss Bennet's distress. But the remedy lies with you, Prunella. Do not, I beg of you, fail to act.'

Mrs Montagu sniffed and dabbed at her tears. Lady Sandalford, unused to such emotional conversations, sank back in her chair. Her usually upright carriage and firm voice were overcome by weariness.

'You are overwrought and we have given one another much to digest. Let us have no more serious discussion today.'

Mrs Montagu returned to her room for some quiet repose. After some time, Lady Sandalford heaved herself from her chair and went in search of her nephew. She found him in the library with a volume of poetry on his knees.

He looked up and smiled when he saw it was his aunt.

'I can see Mary's hand in your new arrangement.'

His aunt returned his smile. 'I am most grateful for her practical eye.'

'Have you been talking to Mama?' he asked in a sudden change of attitude.

She nodded. 'I have. I confess it was not a task to which I am well-suited'

Lady Sandalford gave him a brief recount of the important details of the conversation with his mother. She withheld any detail of Mary's overheard conversation and dispensed with the use of emotional language in describing some of the wilder outbursts, ending with the words,

'I have asked your mother to act. The remedy lies with her.'

60

Mary and Kitty returned to the warmth of Longbourn's cheerful parlour after a bracing walk to deliver apricot marmalade and raspberry vinegar to Mrs Endicott. That poor lady's gratitude made them happy to have ventured out over the frosty ground. They hung their pelisses and bonnets on pegs and hastened from the hall to the fireside.

Mrs Bennet called out to them. 'You are back at last.'

Mary rubbed her chilled hands before the flames.

'Mrs Endicott sends her compliments, Mama. She looks a little better.'

'As well she might, my loves, with such treats and a visit from you both.'

Kitty took up the shawl she was embroidering. Mary wandered to the window and shivered at the sight of sugar frosting throughout the garden. All was quiet and frozen, as though under a spell. *My heart may freeze over again like this,* she feared. *How happy I was in that short time of sunshine in my life.*

Her mother broke into her thoughts.

'Your Aunt Philips has been to visit.'

Mary turned in surprise. 'It is unlike her to venture out in such weather.'

'Aha, but she has such news! You will never guess.'

Mrs Bennet became pink of cheek in her eagerness to play the news game. Kitty dropped her embroidery into her lap. She was fond of such pastimes.

'Has Mrs Smythe been safely delivered?'

'No, there is no news of the Smythes. There has been talk of Mary, however.'

'Me?'

Mary stepped back to the fireside. Kitty regarded her sister with interest.

'What can there be to say about Mary?'

Their mother looked from one daughter to the other with glee.

'Ha ha, it is quite the joke. There is talk in Meryton that Mary has been left a large inheritance and is being courted by several gentlemen of means.'

The sisters joined in with their mother's laughter. Mary took a seat, shaking her head and smiling.

'Well, thank goodness you were able to tell Aunt Philips that her journey was wasted and I am still a spinster of few means.'

'Not at all, my dear child.'

Mary's eyes grew wide.

'You cannot mean it, Mama. There is no truth in the rumour; not a shred.'

'But I do mean it, and you two girls should make it your business to neither deny nor confirm.'

Kitty frowned. 'I do not understand you, Mama. There is no sense in falsehood.'

'Nor honour,' her sister added.

'There will be no need for telling falsehoods.' Mrs Bennet's smile vanished. 'You simply say that it is not your business to discuss such matters.'

'But why should we not deny it?' Mary demanded.

Her mother spoke as though to a person of slow wit.

'Because it can do no harm for people to think you have come up in the world. You will be surprised how your stock shall rise.'

'I do not like it, Mama.' Mary looked to Kitty in appeal, but was returned a helpless shrug. 'We have no need of the sort of people who toady to those they consider can bring them gain. I will not countenance subterfuge.'

'Mary, Mary, quite contrary. What do you suppose would happen if you make a strong denial to those who may enquire, hmm?' Mrs Bennet did not wait for a response. 'They will think that you have reason to hide your good fortune and will multiply the amount in their head. That is what.'

Mary stared at her aghast. 'This is unconscionable. Papa will forbid it.'

Mrs Bennet snapped back, 'Your father will not know because you will not trouble him with the tale, miss. Now ring the bell for Hill, please.'

The sisters, who were now in the regular habit of assisting one another with their toilette, talked the matter over in Kitty's larger bedroom. 'I know you are angry with Mama,' said Kitty, looking thoughtful as she styled Mary's hair, 'but some of her words made sense. People will contrarily believe that which is firmly denied.'

'But it is a lie, Kitty. One cannot profit by such behaviour.' Mary appealed to her sister through the mirror.

'I suppose so.' Kitty sighed. Then she brightened. 'Though I must admit I would enjoy being feted a little.'

Mary changed places and as she began to brush Kitty's hair, snorted.

'You would not enjoy being cut by polite society when the truth was discovered or, indeed, seeing their affections being made over to the latest person of fashion in town.'

She tugged at the brush.

'Ow! The trouble with you, Mary, is that you are so practical in your thinking. Daydreams can be such a comfort to one.'

'I allowed myself to daydream once and the results were not happy.'

'Only once?' Kitty retorted. 'That is hardly showing any enterprise at all. Why, I daydream all the time.'

'Really?' Mary concentrated on threading a ribbon through Kitty's hair. 'What is your present daydream?'

'Oh, that is easy. I imagine Lord Applefrith festooning the floor with roses before I enter the room. Then he drops to one knee and declares that he cannot live without me!'

Mary could not help but laugh.

'Poor Lord Applefrith, crippled by love as he kneels among the thorns.'

61

My dear Mary,

I am escaping the flurry of packing activity to write to you. We begin our journey home tomorrow. Papa insisted on remaining for Sunday services.

Soon, I hope, we shall be able to meet. You can tell me all about Derbyshire and the ball at Gediston Place and I shall regale you with tales of the Prince Regent and Bath.

I am not sorry to leave Bath society, but I shall miss the company of Lady Calbraith and Colonel Wisgrove. The Colonel continues to make a good recovery and one can scarce notice his limp. He intends to winter at his home in Westerham, Kent, before joining the many inhabitants from Bath who spend summer at the spa in Tunbridge Wells.

Following your sensible advice, I have written a letter in the past few days to Mrs Montagu. It is true that Papa does not wish me to form any decided attachment before I have passed the season in London. I am in confiding in you, Mary (and no other), that I do not think any gentleman will please me half so well as Colonel Wisgrove. For now that must remain in confidence.

*Do let us meet as soon as we may arrange the
practicalities.*

*My salutations to your family and good wishes to
you,*
    Sylvia.

Mary reread the letter. It was now Thursday and
Sylvia would be at home. How glad she would be to see
her again. For once, Mary had a journey of her own to
discuss, and she looked forward to Sylvia's news. Mary
sat at the small desk in her room and began to write.

The day offering up a watery low sunshine, Mary and
Kitty ventured into Meryton to mail Mary's letter and
undertake small commissions for their mother. Splinters
of ice and muddy water nipped at the hems of their
costumes and a chill wind whipped the ribbons of their
bonnets. Mary was glad of the warm clothing donated
by her sisters. She buried her hands deeper into her fur
muff. Kitty continued along, smiling frequently. Mary
glanced at her.

'Are you daydreaming, Kitty?'

Her reverie broken, Kitty dimpled. 'Yes.'

'Is it your favourite daydream?'

'Yes.'

'If it makes you forget this chill, then I may have to
revise my methods.'

Kitty laughed. 'I shall convert you yet.'

The mail assigned, the sisters stopped at the ironmon-
gers for fresh candles. The ironmonger's wife stopped
in the middle of her conversation, as her sharp eyes
followed Mary around the shop. At the apothecary the

sisters had the uncomfortable sensation of several pairs of eyes following them. The contents of their purchases attracted undue scrutiny. Exiting the shop, Mary seethed.

'This is all Mama's fault!'

Kitty attempted to soothe her. 'It is likely that many would have believed such news simply because they thrive on rumour and gossip.'

'Then they have too little occupation,' Mary snapped.

Kitty consoled her sister and decided that a visit to Blain's haberdashery would be best left to another day. Before they could return home it was necessary to place an order for flour.

'You do it, Kitty. I cannot bear any more foolish wealth speculation.'

Mary stood outside the shop stamping her feet against the cold as she waited for her sister. Why was Kitty taking so long? Mary's compressed lips parted as she saw the stricken look on Kitty's face as she rejoined her in the street.

'You were an age, Kitty. What is the matter?'

Kitty caught up Mary's arm in her own as they began to make their way home.

'There was more gossip at the counter, Mary, but this time it wasn't about you.'

'Who are they burying with their tittle-tattle now?'

'I don't think it was uninformed gossip.' Kitty squeezed her sister's arm. 'I checked. Mr Montagu is leaving Cuthbert Park for Portugal. He is seeking a more qualified agent for his estate here and nobody knows when he plans to return.'

Mary stopped and closed her eyes, breathing in deep. Speaking barely above a whisper, she said,

'Is it really true?'

Kitty squeezed her arm again.

'Oh, Mary, I am so sorry, but yes, I think it is true and I wish with all my heart it were not.'

'Then he is lost to me. I knew he would be at some time.' She exhaled a misty breath. 'How bleak the winter is. A forever winter.'

They walked home in silence until nearing Longbourn, when Mary said,

'Please tell Mama when I am in my room, Kitty.'

Mrs Bennet was not disposed to believe her younger daughter's news.

'But I am quite sure of it, Mama.'

'You may be sure it is gossip, Kitty.'

'No, Mama. Mr Montagu is looking for a permanent agent to manage the park.'

'What can he be about?' Mrs Bennet was so exercised as to stand and pace the room. 'I did not read him for a fickle young gentleman. What is the world coming to?' She turned, flapping her arms like leaden wings. Before Kitty could reply she continued. 'He dances with Mary twice and then does not make an offer. What more could he want than one of my two daughters?'

'Perhaps . . .'

'Why, even Maria Lucas is pretty and well-born enough for him. Portugal, indeed. I am vexed, Kitty. After all I have done; to be so ill-used. My nerves cannot support it. Bring me some lavender water. I must lie down.'

62

The letter Mrs Montagu had been reading with some eagerness a few moments earlier fluttered onto the sofa beside her as she reached for her handkerchief. She made her way unsteadily to her room, though the hour had barely advanced from noon.

Her lady's maid was interrupted as she placed linen in a heavy Portuguese chest. Her mistress started as she closed the lid with a thud.

'Are you unwell, madam?'

'I have the headache and feel the need of some rest. You may bring me a little lavender water.'

Mrs Montagu staggered to the sanctuary of her bed. The maid hurried away. As she fetched the lavender water she grumbled to Betty, the still-room maid.

'Mrs Montagu has been acting strange of late. She has been in decline ever since her visit to Clovisford. Pleading headaches, taking to her bed, tears without warning. It's all extra work for me. I wonder if the mistress is giving way to madness.'

In truth Mrs Montagu's sufferings were prodigious. She had returned to Cuthbert Park from Clovisford in near silence, but undoubtedly oppressed by all she had learned from Lady Sandalford. Since then, Sebastian had been in her presence very little and when he did sit to dine, seemed preoccupied with his own thoughts. Neither mother nor son spoke of any subject beyond the commonplace, though the discerning observer might have detected a wish to do so from both parties on occasion.

Within a day of the Montagus' return to Cuthbert Park, Sylvia Drummond's letter appeared. Any hopes Mrs Montagu may have continued to cherish regarding Sylvia were certainly dashed by the contents. Sylvia was lost to Cuthbert Park; there could be no doubt. All the while her mortification grew as Lady Sandalford's words pressed upon her. Mary Bennet had overheard vile words and falsehoods from her own lips. The girl had not revealed the story of her terrible behaviour to Sebastian or their acquaintance, and finally: 'The remedy lies with you, Prunella . . . do not fail to act.'

The latest blow, though not in truth severe, only served to lay Mrs Montagu's spirits lower. This afternoon she had been pleased with the distraction of a letter from her old friend, Mrs Fulcross. She began to read with a small smile, then frowned and finally her distress returned in force as Mrs Fulcross shared her enthusiasm for the recent engagement of her only daughter, Letitia, to a wealthy brewer from Manchester.

Her eyes closed beneath the compress of lavender water on her brow, Mrs Montagu spent a considerable time telling herself she had been misunderstood and ill-used. Having exhausted every injury upon her good intentions and generous nature, the small voices burrowed once again into her conscience and she was perforce to admit to herself that her conduct had been both imprudent and unworthy of a lady. An uncomfortable hour later her thoughts strayed so far as to admit that her victim had behaved with considerable propriety. By the time her maid arrived to prepare her dress for dinner, Mrs Montagu's chagrin was so complete that she was minded to make handsome amends to Mary Bennet. Her new purpose brought some relief to her suffering.

The maid, seeing her mistress roused, sought to enhance the cheering mood by the delivery of some local gossip.

'Mrs Blain came personally this afternoon to deliver your new shawl, madam. She had a deal of news.'

'I do not care for tittle-tattle, as you know, but since it pleases you to reveal it, I am all complaisance.'

The maid had been in Mrs Montagu's employ too long to be taken in by this artful speech.

'Just so, madam, but it is wise to be informed of the local news.'

'You have a point.' Mrs Montagu held out her arm to be assisted from the bed. 'Pray reveal your information.'

'Well, according to Mrs Blain, who notwithstanding is not always correct in her news, there is an heiress among us.'

Mrs Montagu produced a weary sigh. The maid looked disheartened.

'Well, spill it out. Who is this heiress?'

The maid presented a gown for approval.

'You will be surprised, madam, as the lady has been a frequent guest in this house. I admit I cannot credit it but—'

Mrs Montagu passed a hand across her brow.

'Good heavens, do you wish my headache to become worse? Who is this paragon?'

'Why, Miss Mary Bennet, madam.'

'Miss Bennet? Impossible.'

The maid pursed her lips and attended her lady's hair. Her ramrod straight back betrayed her annoyance.

'Yes, madam.'

Her mistress wheeled around in her chair and demanded, 'Where would Miss Bennet acquire a fortune, pray?'

'That I cannot say, madam, but according to Mrs Blain, it is believed that she befriended an old lady in Derbyshire who has left her fortune to Miss Bennet. Though it is thought that there are conditions attached.'

'Conditions?'

'Yes, though nobody seems to know them, but it was suggested Miss Bennet would marry the lady's near relation.'

Mrs Montagu produced her fan and employed it at great speed, despite the ice being already settled in the butts outside the house. The maid began to look frightened and tried to wrap her mistress in a shawl, which was flung away with impatience.

'Mrs Blain is a dangerous gossip.' Mrs Montagu fixed her maid with a severe look. 'I doubt that there is any substance to her news. Please report any other intelligence you hear of this story to me. Miss Bennet is the daughter of friends and we must be careful to protect her reputation.'

'Yes, Madam.'

After the servants' dinner Mrs Montagu's lady's maid lingered in the servant's hall to talk to Betty, who was her own age. Betty scrubbed the long pine dining table.

'You would not believe it, Betty. I don't know how I kept a straight face. The mistress has spoken ill of Miss Bennet several times. I'm sure she forgets I'm there. She's losing her reason beyond doubt.' The pair pushed the bench stools under the table. 'There is nothing for it; I must write this very night to my cousin Betsy, who is lady's maid to Lady Adcock, asking for a recommendation to a new mistress.'

Mrs Montagu progressed to dinner slowly and in deep thought. So earnest were her efforts to engage her son in conversation that Sebastian became confused and begged to be excused soon after dinner, whereupon he retreated to the sanctuary of his library. Mrs Montagu spent the evening in solitary reflection by the fire in the vast, empty salon.

63

With the weeks to Christmas fast descending, the Longbourn ladies were kept too busy to assign any significant time to considerations of Mary's newfound fame. Mary sought to quietly depress any notion of her reputed wealth when the family dined with neighbours. The sisters privately discussed hopes and fears with no great conclusions, but their days were filled with ample tasks.

Of prime importance was the great quantity of food to be organised. Pigs had been slaughtered and the cheeks set into brawn with aspic. Even with the assistance of two housemaids, the cook's duties were onerous at this time of year, so over the years each of the sisters had done her duty in stirring a plum pudding or a fruitcake for twelfth night. There seemed to be a continual need to walk into Meryton for fresh ingredients; salted anchovies for stuffing the mutton or nutmeg for the oyster gravy. Quantities of mince pies were consumed by Mrs Bennet's visitors, though as Kitty said to Mary, 'I have eaten but one mince pie, yet we have mixed dozens. Whenever they are served, Mama sends me off on some errand or other and they are all gone when I return.'

Mary concurred. 'I feel quite guilty sometimes as we distribute orange wine and apricot cakes to our less fortunate neighbours, for I quite crave them myself.'

Any spare hours were filled with making gifts. A new tapestry spectacle case for Papa, a reticule for Mama, soft toys for the children. The list seemed inexhaustible, peppered as it was with visitors and small assemblies. Yet all the activity brought liveliness and cheer, though neither Mr Montagu nor his mother were present at any of these merry events. Mary deprecated the long winter days to come. In the past she had looked forward to solitary hours with her books when the icy roads slowed the number of excursions and visits. Now she felt gloomy at the very thought. In just such a doleful frame of mind she was aroused by the maid announcing Lady Sandalford. Giving her hair a quick tidy, she hurried to meet her friend, with Kitty following behind.

Mrs Bennet presented the picture of happy complaisance as she sat by the fire holding court with her Ladyship.

'Oh, yes, Catherine and Mary were most popular at the Gediston Place ball. Why, they had not left the dinner table before Mary was engaged for the first four dances and Catherine the first three.'

Her ladyship nodded and smiled with all the appearance of attention.

'Lady Sandalford, how kind of you to visit us at Longbourn.' Mary made her bow.

'Nonsense, my dear, the pleasure is all mine. I wished to see how you go on.'

'Very well, thank you. The season keeps my sister and I from all thoughts of idleness.'

Mary took up a seat near her friend, while Kitty nodded her agreement with Mary's words.

'Well, the industry becomes you both.' Lady Sandalford's look took in both sisters. 'Your mother has just been telling me of your successes at the Gediston ball.'

Mary glanced at her parent.

'Mother is indeed our champion, Lady Sandalford, though the real success belongs to Lady Applefrith. Her many thoughtful attentions assured all her guests a memorable evening.'

'So my nephew told me.'

Mary blushed. Mrs Bennet spoke with a hint of bitter censure.

'I am told your nephew intends to return to Portugal. That is a great pity for all the young ladies. A young gentleman of property should be settling himself with a wife.'

Lady Sandalford looked directly at Mary as she spoke.

'Indeed it is the greatest pity and a loss to us all. I still hope that he can be persuaded to remain at Cuthbert Park.'

Mary crossed to the window in an effort to compose her countenance. Kitty created a diversion by asking her Ladyship about her arrangements for London.

'I remember, Miss Catherine, you are keen on the metropolis. 'Tis true that there is but a short time until our departure in January. I have but a little organisation to attend. On that head, I rather hope that I might find Mr Bennet at home.' Lady Sandalford raised an enquiring eyebrow. 'There is a small matter of business that I should like to discuss with him.'

Kitty offered to check the library. It was an established though unwritten rule at Longbourn that even if Mr Bennet was known to be at home, it was wise to warn him of any visitor who wished to see him. Most intrigued, he returned with her to escort Lady Sandalford to his haven.

. Mrs Bennet watched their departure with interest.

'I wonder what her Ladyship can want to know from your father, girls.' She lowered her tone. 'She is known to have a hundred thousand pounds at least and they say she is as astute as any gentleman in the management of her fortune.'

With no answer forthcoming, Mrs Bennet returned to her laments at the folly of Mr Montagu's plans and his likely fall into ruin abroad.

64

Once the servants had removed the covers from the dining table, no amount of questioning could elucidate details of Lady Sandalford's business with Mr Bennet. For all her improvement in the feminine art of responding to the signals of others, Mary knew she had no talent for subtle manoeuvre and in her usual manner she addressed her father with simple directness.

'Did you have an agreeable discussion with Lady Sandalford, Papa?'

Mr Bennet gave her an appraising look.

'Indeed, Mary, I did. She is a lady of considerable force and persuasion.'

Mary recalled how easily she had been coerced into revealing herself to Lady Sandalford.

'That is undoubted, Papa, but her intent is, I think, always to good purpose.'

Mr Bennet smiled at his daughter.

'Just so, child. One is lucky to call her Ladyship a friend.'

Mrs Bennet broke in.

'Come, Mr Bennet, you must not keep us in suspense. We all like to know the news from our friends. What was her Ladyship's business?'

Mr Bennet took care to apply his napkin to his lips and then folded it with aching slowness.

'There I must disappoint you, my dear. Lady Sandalford does not wish the details of our discussion to be broadcast, and I must honour her wishes.'

Mrs Bennet's eyes popped. Her voice rose a tone.

'This is most vexing, Mr Bennet. Her Ladyship cannot mean you to keep the news from your family.'

Mr Bennet's regarded her with a benign smile.

'Yes, that does seem provoking, does it not?'

The ladies retreated and silence reigned over the matter until the supper tray arrived many hours later. Kitty resumed with a sly attack as she delivered a teacup to her father.

'Is it true that Lady Sandalford conducts business like a gentleman, Papa?'

Her father's response was rueful.

'I suspect she is a good deal more clever than most gentleman, Puss, though I hold your uncle Gardiner and two of my clever sons-in-law in high esteem.'

Kitty drew up a footstool near his slippered feet and perched upon it.

'I admire her prodigiously. It is a wondrous thing for a lady to manage her own fortune. What methods does she employ?'

'There is hope for you yet, Kitty.' He looked down at her with a twinkling eye. 'If you would manage your own affairs. Though I fear your portion is only equal in scale to your intellect and thus profit from such small capital is unlikely in the event.' Kitty pouted and he patted her hand. 'There now, do not be offended, for you are as pretty as a picture when you do not frown and some young gentleman will doubtless wish to relieve you of such burdens.'

'Must we always be at the behest of gentlemen?' Mary enquired in cross tones of nobody in particular.

Mrs Bennet was moved to rejoin.

'My dear girl, how else should we go on?'

Mr Bennet fixed Mary with a kindly eye.

'You may benefit from instruction, my dear, but I am not the man to give it. Such little that I hold in entail for Mr Collins I manage quite ill, which affords me some solace in the matter.'

'Mr Collins indeed! A pretty mess he shall make of Longbourn and the home farm, I shouldn't wonder, and all of us thrown upon the mercy of our neighbours.' Mrs Bennet applied her lace handkerchief to the corner of her eye.

Mr Bennet held his hands up to his ears.

'Enough, I beg of you, Mrs Bennet. Your feelings are well known to us all. I commend you to the pursuance of warm relations with Darcy and Bingley, both of whom have kindness and wealth in abundance. In the event of my untimely demise, you may throw yourself upon their mercy.'

'Oh, my dear, I could not possibly go on without you.'

With that Mrs Bennet dabbed her eyes in a most affecting manner.

65

A visit from Lady Lucas and her daughters brought a temporary halt to seasonal preparations.

'We have news.' Georgina's eyes danced.

'Be quiet, Georgina. *I* shall tell the news when we have enquired after our friends,' her mother admonished.

Mrs Bennet beamed at her friend.

'But there is no need for ceremony among good friends. You see how we are all in spirits, my dear. It is one's duty in this season, is it not?' She smoothed her expensive shawl; a gift from Jane. 'I do all I can to set aside my poor headaches. Do, please tell us your news.'

Lady Lucas accepted Mary's offer of a seat by the fire in the deepest and most comfortable chair. She waved her daughters to sit elsewhere. Maria and Georgina perched either side of Mary on the morning room chaise while Kitty sat at a small table fiddling with her netting work and lending an ear to Lady Lucas.

'Well, we had no sooner said goodbye to Imogen Drummond than we received a letter from Mr Collins.' She gave her daughters a sideways look. 'It is well that Charlotte wrote across it or we should not know what to think.'

Mrs Bennet leaned forward with such eagerness that her lace cap slipped.

'What does Charlotte have to say?'

'Oh, it is so interesting,' began Maria.

She received a quelling look from her mama.

'Charlotte and Mr Collins wish us to accommodate a distant relation of his, who is also a member of the clergy.'

'A relative of Mr Collins,' echoed Mrs Bennet with distaste.

Lady Lucas nodded. 'But Charlotte was at pains to stress that the young gentleman is of quite a different character.'

'Charlotte underlined that part,' said Georgina.

'Yes, he is not well known to Mr Collins, being younger. He will be travelling here to discuss a very good living, which means he would become a near neighbour.'

'How old is he?' Mary enquired.

'Just a little older than myself.' Maria looked down at her hands, which were folded in her lap. 'Charlotte thinks I might like him very well,' she added.

Kitty turned her attention back to her netting, thinking, *I hope he does suit Maria.* The threads fell slack in her hands as she realised that she hadn't the slightest interest in any new gentleman's acquaintance. Instead, Lord Applefrith leapt to mind. What would he be doing now – hunting? Was it too cold to hunt? Would he call upon them or had the contretemps with Mr Dalrymple made him doubt her character? The thought made her feel miserable. The sound of her mother's excited voice made her set aside her concerns.

'We shall look forward to meeting him.'

'In the fullness of time,' replied Lady Lucas, inspecting the latticed cuff of her woollen gown. 'There are so many of us at home that we don't want to confuse the poor young gentleman with a quantity of neighbours.'

Letting go of her sleeve, she favoured Mrs Bennet with an arch look. 'We shall ask Mr Montagu to dine. He is such a nice, quiet gentleman. As for ladies, Maria and Georgina will be ample company. Perhaps later on . . .'

The words hung over the crackle of the fire. Mrs Bennet's uncertain smile was a piteous thing.

'Yes, you must think only of yourselves. Indeed, we will be glad to be at home, as there is some likelihood of Lord Applefrith paying us a call.

She tossed her head, which had the unhappy result of dislodging her lace cap altogether. Mary hastened to retrieve the offending item and helped her mother to rearrange her dignity. Kitty's slight shake of her head went unnoticed. Maria and Georgina showed rare tact in changing the subject to Christmas fare until the visit ended on a cordial note.

Mary unpinned her hair and was pleased that her new skills were now so ingrained that the practice took little time. Shivering, she swaddled a shawl around her shoulders and another over the lower part of her nightgown as she sat on the floor close to her small bedroom fire. Barely two pages of her novel were read before she put it aside. Wrapping her arms across her knees, she bent her head onto them, allowing her hair to cocoon her brooding face.

Beyond that final terse, 'Good morning,' Mr Montagu's final words to her had been that it was her good opinion that mattered most to him. Was she foolish as Kitty had said to set store by his mother's opinion of her? Both Jane and Lizzy had hinted that she might overcome the obstacle. Mary bumped her head against her folded arms a few times. It was impossible. She could not live as though familial discord did not matter. Had she not lived for many years with the knowledge of feeling apart from her sisters? Yet she loved him. She had pushed him away and hurt him too much for Mr Montagu to continue to love her. Somehow, that hurt all the more. How could she go on? Living with Mama would be a penance beyond endurance.

66

Kitty peered through the parlour window, still laced with morning frost. 'There's a carriage approaching. Wait . . . yes, I think it is Lord Applefrith, Mama.'

'Oh, my goodness. Make haste.' Mrs Bennet leapt from her chair as though scalded. 'Kitty, Mary, run upstairs and change your gowns. Quickly, girls, quickly! And be sure to tidy your hair, both of you.'

Mrs Bennet tugged the servant's bell, then quickly adjusted her costume before tugging the bell again with some might. 'Servants! Why are they never about?' she asked the empty room.

Within a few minutes a red-faced Lord Applefrith was ushered before her.

Mrs Bennet advanced to greet him, all smiles.

'Come in, sir. Sit by the fire, for it is severely cold out. Though I am sure your carriage is well appointed. But I do go on. Will you take a dish of tea or perhaps some warming chocolate with us?'

'You are all kindness, ma'am. Some chocolate would be welcome.' Lord Applefrith made for the cheerful fire with hands outstretched.

Mrs Bennet applied to the embroidered bell sash again. 'My daughters will be with us in a few moments.'

'Is Mr Bennet also at home?'

Mrs Bennet beamed. 'Indeed he is, sir.'

Lord Applefrith was spared any further enquiry by the arrival of Mary and Kitty. He greeted both as old friends. Mrs Bennet's beady eyes searched for their guest's reaction to each of her daughters. His eyes alighted on Kitty and he offered up his seat to her. Kitty blushed and was unusually retiring in her manner. Mary made polite enquiries as to the health of Lady Applefrith.

'My mother does very well and sends you all her compliments. The ball was quite the tonic she needed. The company of so many old friends together restored her spirits.' His gaze swept the room. 'She was delighted to make the acquaintance of my new friends from Meryton.'

'Well, we are equally delighted to see you visit us here at Longbourn, sir.' Mrs Bennet said with grace. 'I hope you will come often. Now, where is that tray? I shall chase it myself. Mary, come out to find your father.'

Mary and Kitty both wilted under their mother's obvious stratagem. Mary patted her sister's shoulder unobserved as she departed. In the hallway, Mrs Bennet hissed, 'I am sure he is come to propose.' Her eyes narrowed. 'I am right. It is Kitty he favours?' Mary frowned but nodded agreement. 'Go and tell Hill the footman not to hurry with the chocolate. Oh, and we must have the best china and cake.'

'But I am to fetch Father,' Mary said in some confusion.

'No, no, leave him. I shall attend to that task when I judge the moment right. They must be left alone together.'

Mrs Bennet waved Mary away. After speaking to Hill she had no choice but to go to her room and imagine what might be happening in the drawing room. If

Lord Applefrith proposed, Mary had no doubt of his being accepted. Kitty had altered since her encounter with Mr Dalrymple. The giddy girl had been replaced by someone softer and more thoughtful. Her romantic thoughts about Lord Applefrith were grounded in amiable respect, which could only augur well for the future.

A movement in the drive distracted her from her reverie. Another carriage. She couldn't supress a smile. Her mother would be furious if visitors arrived now. Polite discourse with another visitor must hinder developments. Mary hurried down the stairs to divert the visitors to the drawing room, and at that moment the maid appeared with a note.

'It is for you, miss.'

Mary unfolded the note, surprised to see it was indeed addressed to her.

My dear Miss Bennet,

Please forgive my writing to you and not attending in person. I am unequal to the task of journeying out at present. It would give me comfort if you could visit me at Cuthbert Park, though I have no right to ask it. I have directed my chaise to wait for you and you shall have it to convey you home as soon as you may choose.

My compliments to your parents,
Prunella Montagu.

Mary read the note again. She shook her head, unable to divine the meaning behind the request. At length she sighed and went in search of her mother.

Mrs Bennet was in such a state of agitated anticipation that she paid little heed to the note.

'Of course, the very thing. Off you go. It will be a nervous headache. Mrs Montagu is a fellow sufferer, though my sensibilities are the more fragile. Be sure to take some raspberry vinegar with you. It is good for the headache, as I well know.'

Mary hurried to find the warm brown pelisse given to her by Jane. It was suitable for the weather and she knew it looked well over her green stripe, but her real reason for wearing the pelisse was the courage imbued by feeling her sisters close at hand as she stroked the velvet cloth.

67

Kitty sat in silent embarrassment, aware that her cheeks were flushed by more than the heat from the fire, and praying for divine guidance as to how she should behave. In normal circumstances, discourse with his Lordship would come about in a natural and unaffected way. In her own home she was acutely aware that she should play the hostess.

'How are your . . .'

'How goes your . . .' They spoke in awkward unison, which served to break the tension with smiles on both sides.

'Ladies first, Miss Bennet.'

Kitty's eyes lit with inspiration.

'How are your good friends, Mr Thomas and Lieutenant Skipton?'

He returned the look with warmth.

'They are in hearty form, full of mischief as always. They charge me with conveying their admiring compliments to you and your sister.'

'Thank you.' Kitty inclined her head. 'They are returned our very good wishes.'

Lord Applefrith leaned in a nonchalant manner against the mantelpiece.

'Now if I may ask a question, how does your course of improvement progress?'

Kitty dropped her eyes, suddenly demure.

'I am ashamed to tell you that my successes have been quite inconsequential since the ball. One is constantly requested to visit or besieged by visitors as Christmas approaches.' Kitty looked up at him, eyes wide with alarm. Her hand flew to her lips. 'Oh, I beg your pardon. I do not, of course, refer to you, sir. Your visit is most especially welcome.'

Lord Applefrith seemed to search those startled eyes and a smile twitched at the corner of his full lips.

'I am relieved that I am most especially welcome, for it makes the thirty mile journey to see you as a mere trifle.'

Kitty was unsure how to respond. Her pulse raced and she made to rise from her chair to cover her confusion. He stepped forward.

'No, don't get up just yet.'

She sank back down.

'I cannot imagine what has happened to the chocolate,' she said in a tremulous voice. 'You are in need of warming refreshment after your cold journey.'

'There is but one thing I crave after my journey, Miss Bennet.'

Kitty swallowed and whispered, 'What might that be, sir?'

'Miss Catherine, when we met in Derbyshire, I found you and your sister to be such interesting young ladies in quite different ways. I marvelled that I could live so near to Meryton as thirty miles and not know of you both.' He paused a moment and gave her an uncertain smile. 'At first I thought that I had a brotherly regard for you and now I am glad of it because I know that my feelings are grounded on the firm foundations of friendship.'

Lord Applefrith sat on the footstool by her chair and reached for the neat hand resting in her lap. Kitty offered no resistance but followed the course of his hand with her eyes, before allowing her gaze to rest on his face. Her heart beat so hard she felt breathless.

'Dear Catherine, you quite saved my mother with your notion of the ball and she loves you already. I believed myself to admire you by the time we first danced, but I was wrong.' Kitty blinked. 'When I saw you sitting in the sunlight of the breakfast room the following morning, I realised that my feelings were much stronger.' He gave her a searching look. 'In short, I was in love with you. You looked as though you should ever be sitting there on the window seat and I shall carry that image in my heart for ever. So, dearest Catherine, will you allow me to see you every morning in the breakfast room by doing me the honour of becoming my wife?'

A tear trembled on the edge of Kitty's eyelashes before sliding down her pink cheek.

Outside the drawing-room door, Mrs Bennet verily bit into her handkerchief in frustration as she could detect no response from Kitty despite having her ear stuck fast to the door jamb.

'Catherine, Kitty, I beg of you, please do not cry. Perhaps I was wrong . . . I should have—'

Kitty held up the palm of her hand and spoke with a strong hint of a tremor in her voice.

'Stay, sir. Pray, do not misunderstand my emotion. I am a trifle overcome by the elegance of your address and by my own regard for you.'

He examined her hand in wonder.

'You return my affections?'

'Most sincerely, Lord Applefrith. Henry,' she added in a timid voice. 'At first I thought you quite attached to my sister, Mary, and in so doing, felt quite at ease to make friends without the usual speculation which must arise between a single lady and gentleman.' She blinked her tear-stained lashes and looked at him through misty eyes. 'My disposition, sir, is romantic, but I have not always been mature in my thoughts. As time passed my regard for your kindness and good nature began to grow and I realised that my affections had become most sincerely attached.'

The sentiments which followed this speech went unheard by Mrs Bennet who, rushing away, threw open the library door and staggered over the threshold.

'Mr Bennet, Mr Bennet! You must come. You will never guess. I am overcome!'

Mr Bennet glanced over the top of his glasses and, noting that his lady wife was unusually pale, went to her aid.

'Now, my dear, sit down. You are correct; I shall never guess, for in these many years you have always confounded me. Calm yourself that you may tell me the news.'

'There is no time!' the lady cried. 'Lord Applefrith is in the drawing room proposing to Kitty.'

Drawing upon a higher strength, Mrs Bennet grasped her husband's hand and pulling him across the hall, bundled him through the doorway.

Thus, the bemused, happy couple observed the near collision of a tray of hot chocolate, an effervescent Mrs Bennet and a gentleman not quite delivered in mind from the peace of his contemplations just a few moments prior.

68

As the Montagu's chaise glided along the drive to Cuthbert Park, Mary looked upon the dirty slush of spent snow with unseeing eyes. Her thoughts ran hither and thither from curiosity to curiosity. Was Mrs Montagu very ill and why did she need a visit from someone she confessed to abhor? Would Mr Montagu be present or even at home? Despite her warm rug, Mary shivered, feeling the fear of meeting her accuser and a little desperate at being from home while events unknown took place. How fervently she hoped Lord Applefrith had come to propose to Kitty. Having no great confidence in her father keeping a strong check upon her mother's extremes of behaviour, she agonised on Kitty's behalf.

The carriage jolted and she realised with some alarm that she had arrived. Waiting to be let down the steps, Mary gave herself a stern admonition to retain her dignity and comport herself with the poise that would make her sisters proud.

Mrs Montagu's lady's maid awaited her and indicated that Mary should follow. Never having ascended the upper levels at Cuthbert Park, she could not but notice the fine balustrade carving as she progressed. A large Flemish tapestry commanded the head of the staircase.

Mrs Montagu's apartments took up a sizeable space to the left. Mary stilled a small tremble as they entered.

'Miss Mary Bennet, madam.'

'Thank you, Annie, you may go now.' Mrs Montagu sat upon a chaise longue by the fire but rose to greet her guest. Mary observed she looked surprisingly well, though a little tired around the eyes. The ladies made their bow. 'Miss Bennet, it was good of you to come with so little forewarning. I trust you are not inconvenienced?'

The question was rhetorical, but Mary decided to establish some measure of equal footing. Her irritation grew with the knowledge that her hostess appeared both well and dismissive of Mary's own inconvenience.

'We had not long welcomed an important visitor when your note arrived, Mrs Montagu; but I deemed that your need must be important and that perhaps you were unwell. My mother sends her compliments and some raspberry vinegar in case of the headache.'

Mrs Montagu retreated a step with a shamefaced look.

'Please, Miss Bennet, take a seat by the fire. My maid will bring some tea, or perhaps you would prefer another refreshment.'

'Tea is perfectly acceptable, thank you.' Mary paused to emphasise her next words. 'My preferences have not changed.'

'Quite. Though one might be forgiven for imagining so, as there has been a transformation in you.'

The lady directed Mary an arch look. Mary returned a level look and spoke in a cool voice.

'I assure you, Mrs Montagu, that I am the same person, unchanged in character or principles. The world refines a great deal upon one's outward appearance.' She paused.

'It would seem that a few alterations are cause for such approbation in society as one could wish were accorded for the refinement of conduct.'

Mrs Montagu shrank back a little.

'Indeed, Miss Bennet, your sentiments do you credit.'

The tea arrived. Mrs Montagu busied herself with fussing over crockery. Mary sat erect in awkward silence, mystified as to the reason for her summons. She longed to ask after Mr Montagu but pride forbade her giving in to the notion. She was glad to accept the tea dish for want of occupation. Mrs Montagu resumed her seat on the chaise longue.

'Miss Bennet, I apologise for calling you from Longbourn, particularly when you have an important visitor.'

She left a pause, which Mary recognised as an invitation to divulge the visitor's name. Growing annoyance made her decide that she would not. Mrs Montagu gave a little shrug.

'I have brought you here by employing some subterfuge. I am not ill. At least not in the physical sense. But I hope you will forgive me when I explain my reasons.'

'Madam?'

Mrs Montagu flushed. 'May I speak to you with complete candour?'

'I should welcome it.' Mary's voice was cold. 'For I own I am quite confused by the circumstances of your request and in my ability to be of assistance to you now that I am here.' She frowned as her perplexity and anger grew. Mrs Montagu gave a deep sigh.

'I find myself at a loss to make a sensible beginning. I have much of importance to impart to you, my dear, and I confess a dread of declaring myself with incompetence, such as to destroy my intention.'

361

Mary noted that Mrs Montagu had commenced to wring her hands and felt some compassion descend over her tension.

'Mrs Montagu, pray let us put an end to this mystery and your evident distress. As a lady and the daughter of your good friends, you have my word that I will respect your confidence.'

The lady began to weep.

'You are too good.' She hiccupped, 'I am a wicked, wicked woman.' She began a frantic search on the chaise for her handkerchief.

Mary produced her own and crossed to hand Mrs Montagu the lace edged square of linen.

'Come now, Mrs Montagu, your nerves are overset. Let me pour you some more tea and we shall speak of other things. Would you like me to call for your maid or Mr Montagu?'

'No!' Mrs Montagu appeared both alarmed and frightened. 'Please, Miss Bennet, I must speak with you. I shall take the tea and compose myself.'

Mary sipped her refreshed tea with slow delicacy, eyes downcast to spare Mrs Montagu's feelings. Her anger and distrust of the older lady dissipated with each passing moment that Mrs Montagu struggled and sighed over her tea. At length the lady exhaled deeply and addressed her.

'It would seem, Miss Bennet, that I have another cause to apologise to you.'

Mary raised her eyebrows. 'Another?'

'Yes. My intemperate display just now is but the smallest of my misdemeanours.'

Mary waved away the assertion.

'Oh, but it is true, my dear. I have wronged you

grievously, and in turn my own dear son.' Mary fell back against the crewel work cushions in surprise. 'You agreed I might speak candidly, Miss Bennet, and I must. You overheard me speaking to Lady Sandalford about you in a cruel and unkind fashion. I spoke in a manner vastly unbecoming of a lady and my words were all falsehood. There, it is said.'

Mrs Montagu dropped her shoulders, relieved of her confession.

Mary's lips parted in a small 'oh'. Mrs Montagu permitted herself a grim smile.

'You may wonder why I should behave in such an odious manner. In your shoes I would be both puzzled and very offended. I shall not sully myself with unworthy excuses. My behaviour owed everything to my foolish pride and a distasteful spirit of competition with Lady Sandalford.'

'But—' Mary started forward.

'You may question me anon, Miss Bennet, but allow me to continue now, before my courage betrays me.' Mrs Montagu closed her eyes for a moment.

Mary gave a faint nod. Her hostess spoke in a rush, 'I spoke of you in so reckless a manner because I detected that Sebastian had developed a tendre for you and that you returned his sentiments. I was filled with vexation because such developments thwarted my plans to have Sebastian married into a family of either rank or fortune.' The lady looked away with embarrassment as she spoke. 'In my disgrace I also told Lady Sandalford a falsehood, pretending that Sebastian and the Honourable Sylvia Drummond were likely to marry.' Mary held her breath. 'This foolish desire fuelled my need to draw accolades and consequence to myself.

I spoke those falsehoods in my anger to spite Lady Sandalford. I was perhaps all the more of a viper because I knew that she took Sebastian's part in liking you.' Mrs Montagu's eyes held Mary's with a plea. 'That you might overhear did not occur to me then or subsequently. Your suffering is unimaginable. I now realise that your visit to Derbyshire is connected to a desire to escape any possibility of being near Cuthbert Park.' Mrs Montagu hiccupped again. 'Miss Bennet, please know that I am most truly and humbly sorry for the injury I have done you. I do not ask your forgiveness, for I shall never forgive myself.'

Mrs Montagu's tired eyes filled with fresh tears. She hastily applied Mary's handkerchief. Mary remained pinned against the cushions; her breath curiously absent and a swirling feeling dizzying her mind. She frowned as she tried to piece Mrs Montagu's words clearly in her mind. The sound of gentle weeping brought her back to the present.

Once again, Mary crossed to the chaise and knelt beside Mrs Montagu, looking up at her tormentor with some wonder.

'Please distress yourself no further on my behalf, Mrs Montagu. I find myself drained of anger. Indeed, if forgiveness is required, then I am a well of such thoughts.'

Mrs Montagu paused with something of Mary's own look of wonder about her features. She sought Mary's hand.

'Dear Miss Bennet, Mary, I can scarce believe your words. Can you really find it in your heart to forgive me?'

Mary nodded. A small smile hovered about her lips. 'I may even have cause to thank you.'

'Thank me! Please, Miss Bennet, do not make sport of me.'

Mary gave a little shake of her head.

'I had not fully acknowledged the thought until the words left my lips just a few moments ago.' She spoke these last words as though to herself, then looked up at Mrs Montagu. 'You are correct in your supposition that I ran away to Derbyshire to remove myself from the painful possibility of seeing either you or Mr Montagu. You see, I felt the truth of your words in addition to so many other feelings.'

'Oh, no, please do not think it!'

'But I do – did – think it.' Tears stung Mary's eyes as the pain flooded back. 'I could not deny to myself the veracity underlying those sentiments. The truth played upon my mind alongside all my other injured feelings. Up to that moment my vanity had me believe myself to be admired for my intelligence and accomplishments. That alone gave me a false feeling of superiority. I saw in an instant that others perceived me in a very different light.' Her eyes were full of frank openness as she continued, 'I was arrogant and judgemental. It is shaming to acknowledge that such excessive pride led me to censure others, including my own family.'

'Oh, how you must have suffered.'

Mrs Montagu twisted the handkerchief.

Mary's eyes dulled. 'I own that I did suffer acute pain such as I pray never to encounter again. But the blame rests with me for refusing to look at the world outside my books and music.' She settled herself on a footstool. 'You mentioned my transformation, which I wholly owe to my sisters. I threw myself upon their mercy. Each of them has unselfishly given herself to helping me. My older sisters both applied themselves to the refurbishment of my neglected costumes and encouraged me in acquiring greater social polish. But it was their love and generosity of spirit which has been my happiest gain and greatest lesson.' Mary paused a moment and smiled. 'Catherine and I have become better friends these past months, which affords us both a felicity we have never known. So you see, those unhappy moments many months ago have produced some good.'

Mrs Montagu smiled through her tears.

'Mary Bennet, what a foolish old woman I have been. Lady Sandalford tried to make me see that you were the perfect wife for my son, but I refused to acknowledge the truth. From your own lips you prove her right. You are not only generous of spirit, but you have been both brave and resourceful; traits Sebastian will ever admire.' She sighed. 'I should have liked an heiress.'

'Rumours of my inherited fortune are without substance,' Mary admitted.

'One could not doubt it. But I love my son, Miss Bennet, despite my foolish behaviour, and I cannot but love the woman who makes him happy. That is a different kind of fortune. I realise that now.'

Mary said miserably.

'I have heard that Mr Montagu is returning to Portugal.'

'That is my doing. I have almost driven him away with my foolishness. After he returned from Derbyshire still singing your praises, I told him plain that he should look higher for a wife.' Mrs Montagu gave Mary a shamefaced glance. 'Our relations have become increasing strained.

Since he announced a return to Portugal we have spoken little above the commonplace.' Mrs Montagu reached toward Mary. 'But you could change his mind, my dear, if you wish it.'

Mary dipped her eyes to her skirts.

'I love him with all my heart. It is strange to hear myself say those words, for I never imagined that such sentiments would be mine.'

Mrs Montagu clasped her hands to her breast as though offering up a silent prayer of thanks.

'You give my feelings the greatest relief.'

Mary smile was sad. 'How happy I should be to do so. But I fear it is too late to change his mind. He will not want to hear from me now.'

'What possible reason can there be?' Mrs Montagu's voice rang with alarm.

Mary blushed. 'Mr Montagu has proposed to me and been refused. I have twice obstructed his attempts to persuade me since.'

'Refused, more than once?' The lady dropped her handkerchief and blinked her surprise.

Mary's words were gentle. 'I could not in all conscience accept in the circumstances. To marry a man while believing myself repugnant to his closest family would lead to unhappiness for all. His first duty must be to family and I would not break that bond.'

Mrs Montagu grasped Mary's hand again.

'You astonish me more than any young lady I have ever met. You are most certainly not your mother's daughter! You are his match beyond question.' She struggled to her feet and spoke with new boldness. 'You must leave Sebastian to me. He shall be in no doubt that my opprobrium is of the highest magnitude. In this I shall not fail!' She clasped Mary's shoulders. 'I have no doubt I shall call you daughter before the twelfth night fruitcake is cut!'

69

Mrs Montagu expressed a number of motherly sentiments and tender assurances. She was quite exhausted in her relief. Mary arose to take leave, adjuring her hostess to take some repose.

'I shall ask Peters to call for the chaise.'

'Thank you, my dear. I own that I do feel vastly fatigued. But rely upon it, I shall speak to Sebastian directly when he returns from hunting.'

Mary descended the stairs in such dazed preoccupation that she was surprised to find herself in the hall addressing Peters.

'I shall see to it immediately, miss.' He opened the salon door. 'There is a fire in the salon where your wait will be more comfortable.'

Mary found herself too agitated to sit. She drifted aimlessly about the room and was presently seized by the notion of taking a peep in the library. Many months had passed since her work had been completed. A frisson of expectation stole over her as her hand turned the doorknob. Her eyes were immediately drawn to three crates of books on the floor opposite. A small squeak of surprise escaped her lips as she recalled Mr Montagu telling her that the books would remain unpacked without her assistance. In a trice Mary crossed the room and sank to her knees beside a crate. Her fingers caressed the uppermost covers, examining the titles. She lifted out a slim volume of poems, examining the cover.

'I believe you would enjoy that book.' Mary swung around, startled. Sebastian continued with apparent serenity. 'It has long been my companion by a lonely hearth.'

'But you are hunting.' The words tumbled out.

'Evidently,' he replied drily.

He stood by the large desk near the door.

'Forgive me. I had no conception that you were here.'

'Again, evidently.'

She rose with haste; her colour also rising.

'I shall not disturb you further. The carriage will be drawn up imminently.'

He stepped in front of the door in one smooth stride of his long legs.

'Not so fast, Miss Bennet.' His eyes burned. 'What is your purpose here?'

'Sir, I must go. I am needed at home.'

Mary grew agitated and made to pass him. He remained impassive.

'It will wait while you oblige me with an answer.'

She grimaced with annoyance, trapped by the hundreds of beloved books and his imposing presence.

'I have been visiting Mrs Montagu. I . . . I came into the library while awaiting the carriage and then I saw the books . . .' Her voice trailed away.

'Ah, yes, the books. I told you I would not unpack them without you. Now it seems that decision was to good purpose, as they will travel with me.'

Mary's eyes searched his in dismay. She saw only piercing coldness and dropped her gaze.

'Why were you visiting my mother?'

'She requested it.' She pressed her lips together.

'Yet you insist my mother dislikes you, nay, detests you. Why would you visit her?'

Mary drew herself up, indignant.

'Pray allow me to pass, Mr Montagu. These questions serve no useful purpose.'

Unmoved, he folded his arms across his chest.

'Your pardon, Miss Bennet, but they serve to assuage my curiosity. Since you so decidedly rejected my proposal on the grounds of my mother's feelings, I confess I find myself nonplussed as to why she would invite you to Cuthbert Park.' His tone became bitter and mocking, at odds with the gentleman she knew and loved. 'But rumours of your newfound fortune abound. Perhaps you have come to announce your engagement to some fine gentleman?'

Mary blazed. 'Ask her yourself!'

He regarded her through narrowed eyes.

'Oh, I shall. Though like you, Miss Bennet, my mother shows an alarming talent for speaking in riddles.'

'This is intolerable.'

Mary pushed past him and rushed towards the hall.

'Miss Bennet, wait!'

'I cannot delay. I am wanted at home.'

Her words were flung behind her as she stepped with surprising speed through the hall to the waiting carriage. Mr Montagu was left to stare in amazement at the sight of his own carriage disappearing along the drive. He mounted the stairs two at a time on the short walk to his mother's room.

70

Mary arrived at Longbourn to a joyous reception. The incumbents had exhausted themselves in congratulations and descended upon her to unburden themselves to fresh ears. At the sight of Kitty's sparkling eyes and rosy face, Mary forgot her temper and embraced her sister, before offering her sincere congratulations to Lord Applefrith.

'You must call me Henry now, for you are to be my sister.' His lordship's easy smile seemed like to stay on his countenance through Christmas. 'I hope you will be our first visitor when we are married and stay often.'

'I should be honoured. It will be a real pleasure to have a brother who does not reside in Derbyshire.'

His beaming features flushed with pleasure.

'I had not thought so far as having sisters, but now that I do, it is a very fine thing.'

The whole family laughed.

'That is because you have never had a sister,' chimed Kitty. 'I must warn you that we are a formidable group. Our brothers in Derbyshire take care never to be alone when we are in numbers.'

Mrs Bennet stepped amongst them.

'Such nonsense, Kitty. Do not heed my daughter, Lord Applefrith. She is delirious with joy.'

'I should say you are well warned, sir,' Mr Bennet chuckled.

'I shall write to Darcy for advice,' Henry said in jovial tones. 'If he can survive the campaign, so shall I. Now I must take my leave, for there is much to arrange and I must take my mother the happy news.

'Dine with us on your return, come Friday. My table is the envy of our neighbours, but you must acquaint me with all of your favourite dishes.'

Mrs Bennet faltered between a bow and a curtsy. Lord Applefrith displayed the sweetness of his nature by sweeping her a generous bow and saying,

'Madam, I should be delighted with any dish you may put before me. I am already acquainted with the excellence of your arrangements and the company threatens to surpass.'

Having dispatched of the happy bridegroom, Mr Bennet professed himself satisfied. 'You were born under a lucky star, Kitty. Not only is your young man happily circumstanced in life, but he is a fine shot so you will never go hungry. You may count on more visits from your dear mother than any of your sisters and, if you are especially unlucky, I shall join her.'

Having gained his family's laughter with his small jest, Mr Bennet announced he would repair to his library for some quiet reflection. Mrs Bennet hurried away to dress. She expressed an urgent desire to visit Mrs Philips. The sisters sat together while Kitty related every particular of the events during Mary's absence.

'Mary, do you mind very much that I am to marry?'

'Of course not. I always felt sure that you would be married. You seem made to suit the institution. Besides, Henry is your heart's desire and you are very well-suited.'

Mary was determined to show happiness for her sister in spite of her own turmoil.

'But you are the elder and should be first,' Kitty acknowledged.

'I think Lydia rather threw that tradition to the four winds, Kitty.' Mary sighed. 'Besides, we must take the chance at love when we may.'

'That reminds me.' Kitty regarded her sister with curiosity. 'You have been to Cuthbert Park.'

'Yes, one way or another it has been the most extraordinary day.'

Mary related much of her conversation with Mrs Montagu.

'But that is wonderful, Mary.' Kitty hugged her sister with joy. 'There can be no cause for distress between you and Mr Montagu now.'

Mary gave her sister with a shamefaced look.

'I fear that matters are quite dark indeed. He discovered my visit and treated me with suspicion as a result of my continually rebuffing him. I'm afraid I became vexed and we quarrelled.'

'Oh, no. Matters must mend. They simply must.'

Mary began pacing the room. She clasped her face in her hands and turned to Kitty. 'My thoughts are quite addled. I think perhaps that events have taken us too far from rapprochement.'

'Surely that is not so?' Kitty frowned.

Mary made no reply, but merely looked into the dancing flames in the grate as though to seek an answer. Several minutes later both sisters were disturbed from their reveries by the thud of the doorknocker.

A tall shadow loomed behind the servant as she

announced Mr Montagu. Kitty rose in a swift movement to greet the visitor.

'Mr Montagu, welcome. You come on such a happy day.'

He bowed to each lady and enquired,

'Then I am fortunate. What is the happy occasion?'

'There is an engagement in the house.' Kitty dimpled. His startled gaze moved from Mary to Kitty and back again. Kitty laughed. 'You may wish me happy. I am to marry Lord Applefrith.'

His delight was manifest in his light laugh and bright eyes. He bowed to Kitty again.

'That is famous. I do, wish you happy that is. Henry is a capital fellow, and now he is also a lucky fellow.'

Kitty stretched out an arm to her sister, as though to draw her into the conversation.

'I have just been relating the whole to Mary.'

Mary remained where she stood. Seeing her heart's desire so near brought a complex mixture of feelings to the surface, and she knew not what to say. Mr Montagu's face became grave.

'I see now why you were in a hurry to return home, Miss Bennet.'

Mary inclined her head. With great presence of mind, Kitty knocked a water glass, splashing her gown. The glass rolled at her feet. 'Oh, how clumsy of me.'

Mr Montagu dropped to one knee to retrieve the glass. He held it to the light. 'No harm done, I think.'

'Thank goodness, but I must change my gown.' Kitty placed the glass on the table with care. 'I shall return directly.'

As she exited the room, Kitty's smile would have matched that of the naughtiest schoolboy. She meandered forth to make a leisurely choice of replacement gown. If Mrs Bennet had been present, she would have been overcome with pride in her fourth daughter.

Mr Montagu quipped, 'I seem to spend an inordinate amount of time on my knees before you, Miss Bennet.'

Mary returned a nervous smile.

'I am unused to the advantage of level height. One feels more equal.'

Mary knew not from where her speech issued, for her mind felt as fluffy as new shorn fleece. He did not move a muscle and his voice remained sober.

'You are my equal, Miss Bennet. If not in height, then in mind.'

'You are very kind.'

Really, Mary, she reproached herself, *is that all you can say? He will leave and any chance of making amends will be lost.*

'I was not kind to you this morning, for which I humbly apologise.' His direct gaze, as ever, did not waver.

'Oh, no, the fault is mine. I intruded and allowed my agitation the advantage over me.'

'You had just cause.'

He stood up and the sensation of his height so near caused her vision to swim as he spoke.

'I have had the most enlightening conversation with my mother. She has thrown my travel plans into some confusion.'

'Have you decided to postpone your journey?' She asked, breathless.

'That rather depends, Miss Bennet.' His eyes held hers. 'Do you think I should?'

Seconds passed like weeks. At last she uttered,

'It is not for me to say.'

'Venture an opinion. You always have one.'

Mary hesitated. 'I do not think you should go.'

'Why?'

His eyes remained fixed upon her face. The single word felt like the most important question she would ever answer. Her courage failed and she spoke in a rush.

'Because you would be terribly missed at home and because you have worked hard to gain control of your estate.'

He was not to be stalled.

'Terribly missed by whom?'

'Your mother. Your aunt . . . Everyone.'

The words sounded hollow to her own ears.

'You, Mary?'

The words fell soft from his lips.

Mary blushed. 'Decidedly.'

His sombre face gave no clue as to his thinking.

'My mother tells me that you have forgiven her unpardonable conduct with exceeding generosity. She related the entire abhorrent tale and is truly contrite. It grieves me that you were subjected to such conduct in my home and from my own mother.' He hesitated. 'Please, sit here on the sofa.' She did so without a word and he sat quite near; his words spoken in gentle tones. 'I hope that I am now correct in my understanding of your previous reticence? You once told me that you returned my feelings. Do I dare still hope that your feelings remain constant?'

She turned to him, a strange mixture of boldness, happiness and wonder causing her heart to beat fast.

'My feelings have not changed. They could not change.'

'Please tell me that you now believe we are free to marry. I do not think I can bear a final rebuttal.'

His very being pleaded with her. She proffered her hand. 'We are as free as the birds in the sky.'

71

Mrs Bennet arrived back at Longbourn breathless in her haste to convey the success of her visit to Meryton. She had found Mrs Philips entertaining several friends and had revelled in imparting her news to an admiring audience. Due to the lateness of the hour, the pleasure of a visit to Lady Lucas would have to wait until the morning. News of her triumph trembling on her lips, Mrs Bennet burst into the hallway and was momentarily taken aback to see Mr Montagu exiting Mr Bennet's library.

'Ah, Mr Montagu, have you come to take your leave of us so early? Surely we will see you over the festivities?'

He bowed and with some measure of gravity replied,

'I do believe that you will indeed see me at Christmas, ma'am.'

'Well, it is very nice of you to visit Mr Bennet.' Mrs Bennet removed her bonnet and patted at her curls. 'He misses your dear departed father. Have you enjoyed your discussion?'

'We have indeed.' Sebastian's lips twitched. 'I cannot recall a more edifying occasion.'

Mrs Bennet raised an eyebrow at this remark, but recalling her news, assumed her most winning smile.

'And you come on such an auspicious day. No doubt you already know that this very day our precious Kitty has become engaged to Lord Applefrith. The wife of a baronet. We are blessed.' She preened a little. 'You must tell your dear mother, though I will call upon her as soon as my engagements permit.'

'My heartfelt congratulations to you, Mrs Bennet. Lord Applefrith is an excellent gentleman. I am sure he will make Catherine very happy.'

Mrs Bennet tapped him lightly on the shoulder with her fan.

'You must not leave it too late yourself, Mr Montagu. We may have few young ladies in Meryton, but I do not imagine you will find better on foreign shores.'

Mr Montagu was betrayed into a wide smile.

'Rest assured I have already taken the lesson to heart, ma'am. Forgive me, I must bid the young ladies good day.'

Mrs Bennet puzzled over this speech as she knocked on the library door. Mr Montagu departed to the sitting room. A few minutes later the newly engaged couple, who were sharing the happy detail of their news with Kitty, heard a scream.

The sisters rose from their seats in haste. Sebastian bid them to stay seated.

'Do not disturb yourselves. I met your mother in the hallway a few minutes ago. I imagine that your father has just imparted the news.'

To their great amusement, he commenced to entertain his fiancée and Kitty with a light-hearted account of his conversation with Mrs Bennet. A short time later, a dishevelled Mr Bennet appeared in the doorway.

'Girls, where might one locate your mother's smelling salts?'

'Oh, dear.'

'She fainted.'

'Good heavens, we must go to her.'

'Oh, she is quite well. The swoon quickly passed. But now she is intent on savouring the moment.'

Kitty laughed. 'Then I shall take pity and find the smelling salts. Mr Montagu, pardon, *Sebastian*, your penance is to remain to suffer the consequences.'

Sebastian clasped Mary's hand heroically to his chest.

'I'm going nowhere and declare myself equal to the test.'

In truth, his test was far from severe. Mrs Bennet's interview was short in length and long on approval. At first she was of the opinion that everyone had colluded to hoodwink her and chided the misuse of her poor frayed nerves. Sebastian drew Mary to stand beside him and assured her of the utmost sincerity of his proposal.

'Can it be true?' Mrs Bennet looked from one to the other with incredulity. 'You are to be married?'

'We are,' they replied in unison.

'When you saw me in the hallway, ma'am, I had just left Mr Bennet and gained his approval. The engagement is settled.'

'And you did not tell me but allowed me to encourage you to seek a bride. Well, that is a very good joke even though it is against me.' Mrs Bennet's good humour could be summoned at will and she did not disappoint in her hour of triumph. 'Imagine, Mr Bennet, two daughters affianced in a single day to singular gentlemen! Are we not the happiest parents in England?'

'Logic contends that we cannot know it, my dear. But logic is a stranger to you and I cannot deny you this moment. We are blessed with both happiness and good fortune.' He contemplated the smiling young people. 'How quiet the house will be with no daughters in attendance.'

Mrs Bennet's eyes chanced upon Mary, whose own eyes were locked in an intent gaze with her fiancé.

'Mary, you have been very quiet. How comes it that you have not confided in your loving mother?' Mary sought around her for support. 'Ah, but then you are like me in that. I, too, was demure and shy. You must learn to speak up, my love.' Mary smiled with relief as her mother continued unheeding.

'I shall call upon your mother tomorrow morning, Mr Montagu. Oh, my shawls, two weddings to arrange. It will test my poor nerves to the limit. But do not fear, where my girls are concerned, I am selfless to the last.'

72

Sylvia perched demurely on Mrs Bennet's best chair and cast an appreciative look around the morning room.

'Why, this is quite the prettiest room! Our own morning room has become quite shabby, but I cannot bring myself to make alterations. I fear dear Papa and Imogen would dislike any change from the familiar comfort of Mama's arrangements.'

'My dear Miss Drummond, you are too kind,' said Mrs Bennet. 'Our humble abode cannot hope to emulate your own superior family home. As for the alterations, I am sure that Lord Drummond will one day feel able to look more to the future. In the present, you have the adventure of a London season for amusement.' Mrs Bennet glared across the room at her daughters. 'Mary, you were quite remiss in failing to inform me of Miss Drummond's intended visit.' She turned back to their guest. 'I am engaged to go out and must make my excuses. As though we were not busy enough with two weddings in preparation, the good citizens of Meryton will pester me with invitations, so eager are they to hear our news. Goodbye, Miss Drummond, and my dear girls.' Mrs Bennet sallied forth to meet her public, wreathed in smiles and purposeful of carriage.

When the door had fully closed, Sylvia ventured,
'Did you really forget to mention my visit?'

Mary and Kitty both lowered their eyes.

'I may have omitted to mention it,' Mary said, a smile hovering on her lips.

Kitty chimed in, 'And then it was too late to alter Mama's plans.'

Sylvia began to laugh, which proved infectious.

'Oh, dear, poor Mama,' Mary choked. 'But I did so wish to share my news with you first-hand and to hear your own, Sylvia.'

The three young ladies fell to a long and joyful discussion of their months apart. There was so much to say that refreshment became a necessity rather than a polite interlude. Imogen had regretfully declined the invitation in favour of a visit to her friends the Lucas girls.

On hearing Kitty's tale of her courtship, Sylvia was all rapt attention.

'How I look forward to meeting Lord Applefrith. He sounds all that is amiable and has obviously made you so very content, Catherine.'

Kitty blushed. 'I am so happy. You will see why when you meet him. He is so kind and has even arranged for us to visit London during our honeymoon. I am the luckiest girl.'

In telling her own tale, Mary chose not to mention the many obstacles to her betrothal that had been so recently overcome, but sufficed her friend's curiosity with every appearance of delight and no small gratitude for her good fortune.

'I wonder that you did not see how well you were suited, Mary.' Sylvia's fair face was kind. 'Or perhaps you did see but Mr Montagu was the slowcoach. Gentlemen do not always appear quick to see that which is under their own nose. For myself, I always felt that you would make a match of it.'

'Then you were more perceptive than I,' said Mary. 'Mr Montagu . . . Sebastian – I shall have to become used to saying the name – was much preoccupied in creating order in his new life at Cuthbert Park,' She paused and her manner became serious. 'But it is perhaps well that we took time to honour our true feelings. One cannot be too careful in thinking about a lifetime's commitment.'

'No, indeed,' Sylvia replied with sober intent. 'My thoughts follow the same direction and I am a little glad that I have the season to make a clear decision about my future.'

'Oh.' Kitty regarded Sylvia with interest. 'Did you meet a particular gentleman in Bath?'

'I see you have not revealed my secret.' Sylvia glanced at Mary.

'It was not for me to reveal.'

Sylvia gave Kitty an appraising glance and then nodded.

'I have rather revealed myself, so I shall also tell you, Catherine, but I entreat you not to speak of it other than to myself or Mary.' Kitty agreed. Sylvia continued. 'The brother of my chaperone in Bath is Colonel Wisgrove, who received an injury in the Peninsula War. I found his company preferable to that of anyone we met in Bath.' Sylvia looked from one sister to the other. 'Indeed, I did not feel quite at home in Bath society. I think that Papa suspects my feelings for the colonel and has borne upon me the importance of taking up Lady Sandalford's kind offer to chaperone me for a London season.'

'My goodness,' breathed Kitty.

'Colonel Wisgrove is thirty-seven, but I do not feel that the difference in our ages signifies. It is my intention to petition Papa at the end of the season. He will find it more difficult to refuse me then, as the colonel pointed out to me.' Mary frowned. 'Oh, do not think him scheming,' Sylvia exclaimed. 'He is the most honourable of men and agrees that we must wait. His fortune is not large, but he is quite comfortable, I believe. His house in Westerham sounds quite commodious and I long to see it. At least the time apart will give his leg injury time to completely heal.'

Mary could not successfully eliminate her worried frown, but responded, as she felt sure a good friend must, with a cheerful smile.

'We must look forward to the occasion when we can make the colonel's acquaintance.'

'I feel sure you will all like him.' Sylvia was in gay spirits. 'Now, I know that all your news is very recent, but you must both tell me if you have begun to make firm wedding plans.'

73

With a spirit of reconciliation evinced by the intended bride's fine example, Mrs Montagu hosted a small party for intimate family and friends. Cuthbert Park had never looked so beautiful. A yule log burned in the grate and the rooms were redolent of the scent of the pine which decorated every surface, along with branches of holly and dried fruits. Lord Applefrith and his mother were invited to stay so that both happy couples might be toasted by those who loved them. The Drummonds were also in attendance. Mrs Bennet's exuberance, unchecked by her husband, lost a little power in an attitude of deference to Lady Applefrith and her son.

After receiving more congratulations than they could count, the two young couples hovered together, looking happier than any of them might have previously expected.

'On a fine day I daresay a curricle would cover the thirty miles between us in a trice,' declared Lord Applefrith.

Mr Montagu considered. 'The ladies may have something to say to that. Curricles do sway a bit and it makes women nervous.'

Lord Applefrith appeared quite struck by the notion.

'Lord, you are right. I am not used to consulting females. Catherine, you'll have your work cut out training me, my dear.'

Kitty dimpled. 'Then I shall begin by asking you to fetch me another ratafia.'

'Well, it looks as though I am under the command of a new general.'

Mary nodded to her fiancé to signal her desire for refreshment. Already their communication promised to rival that of a long-married couple. The gentlemen strolled off to complete their task while the sisters returned to their current favourite subject. Neither sister could yet quite believe her good fortune.

'I feel that I have done little to merit the life of comfort and happiness ahead of me,' Mary asserted.

'Merit is not the manner of fortune, Mary. But knowing you, there will be no lack of conscientious application towards the less fortunate.'

Mary sighed. 'I hope that I may ever feel the injustice for young ladies without fortune. A gentleman may study or use his wits to improve his prospects. But ladies are unable to make a living by any means other than those poorly recompensed and considered suitable. A governess or companion is always at the behest of their so-called betters. The misery of some quite casts my spirits down.'

Kitty touched a finger to her lips.

'Hush, Mary. We cannot change the world but merely do our best for those we encounter.' She linked arms with her sister. 'Now is the time to enjoy your new freedom and look to becoming a good wife. Take care your serious side does not overwhelm you.'

'Dear Kitty, you are right. How glad I am that you are to live nearby. You will be able to remind me of my foolishness.'

'The brides together.' Lady Sandalford approached them waving her fan. 'We should have you painted thus in such a charming attitude.'

Her clever eyes twinkled as the sisters flushed with pleasure.

'Your Ladyship flatters us,' Kitty rejoined with enthusiasm.

'Not at all. I think it interesting to look back on the likeness of one on the threshold of life's big adventure. To look back on two should double the fun.'

Lord Applefrith returned to claim his fiancée. Mary levelled her gaze at Lady Sandalford.

'I am glad to have a moment to say something serious to you.'

'If it is serious, then we should repair to the fireside in the library. We shall not be missed for a few minutes. There is something particular I should like to share with you.'

Mary raised an eyebrow, but moved toward the anteroom door, scene of her former humiliation. She could not suppress a shudder as she passed through the door.

'You should alter this room.'

Lady Sandalford swept the anteroom with her eyes as she made her way to the library door.

'So much has happened since that dreadful day.' Mary's lips drew a line. 'But it is impossible to forget those moments in this room.'

'Then do not try.' Lady Sandalford swished her fan in an arc. 'Make the room your own by giving it a purpose suited to you.'

They moved on and sat before the gentle glow of the library fire.

'Perhaps I could change the anteroom.' Mary spoke up. 'For those wise words and so many interventions and kindnesses you have made on my behalf, I must thank you with all my heart. That is what I wished to say to you, though the words feel inadequate.'

'It is me who is in your debt, Mary.'

Mary's gasp of amazement appeared to amuse her Ladyship.

'Do not be so surprised. I feared greatly for my nephew's future until I saw how it was between you. He would not have been happy with some vapid female, though he did not know it until he met you.'

'I should not be thanked for the accident of introduction,' Mary demurred.

'But, moreover, you have provided me with some purpose. By spending time with you, I remembered the young woman I used to be.' Lady Sandalford leaned forward and spoke in confiding tones. 'Like you, my brother and I had no wealth. We simply had a broken estate and our wits. It was luck that we each met with good fortune.' She sank back and sighed. 'His late Lordship and I were not blessed with children. His estate will pass to his cousins upon my demise. But he left me a wealthy woman. Much of that wealth will pass to Sebastian, but of course he's not in great need. Cuthbert Park is comfortably situated and the port estates are highly profitable. I should like at least some of my wealth to speak for those who do not have my advantages. So I have chosen you as the voice.'

'I do not understand.' Mary frowned.

'Then allow me to explain. I am providing you with a dowry of £20,000 to remain within your control.'

Mary gasped. 'But—'

Lady Sandalford held up her hand to stay further speech.

'£20,000 properly invested should bring you a private competence of a not inconsiderable sum.'

'But why?'

'Why?' Her ladyship gave her a wide smile. 'Because you have intellect and deserve the means by which to exercise it. You have youthful energy and time on your side in which to achieve something lasting if you should wish it. There can be no doubt you shall be well provided for in this house, which means the income may be used as you see fit. What is more, I have stipulated that any residual is to remain in the female line at your discretion and that of the daughter or other lady you choose to inherit.'

Mary's face was a picture of bewilderment. Lady Sandalford continued.

'You may think my behaviour irregular and perhaps it is. But I intend to use my money as I wish, and where better than ensuring the future of the women in our family and community? In you, Mary, I have found the ideal person to carry the proposal forward.'

Mary exhaled with force, thunderstruck. She leaned towards Lady Sandalford.

'This is your earnest wish?'

'It is my wish, and it is already arranged.'

Mary frowned. 'Does Sebastian know of this?'

'He does not, though I expect approval from him. Only your father knows.'

'Father. Surely he refused so generous and unsolicited an offer?'

'Indeed he tried, but I'm very persuasive.'

'It is like a dream. I cannot quite believe it.' Mary sat back in silent contemplation for a minute. 'I believe I once said that if I were wealthy I should choose never to marry.'

With admirable calmness Lady Sandalford replied,

'And what do you think now?'

'I think that the old Mary was rather a poor creature. True wealth is surely happiness and a life well-lived.' Mary sprang forward in her chair, eyes shining in the firelight. 'There is so much I could do to change the situation of others.' She halted a moment. 'That is, if you are sure, your Ladyship.'

Lady Sandalford clapped her hands with delight. 'There, you see; there speaks the voice I alluded to earlier. And you must soon call me Aunt.'

Her Ladyship's shrewd eyes twinkled. She stood and offered Mary her arm.

'Come, we must return to your fiancé. Tomorrow we shall tell my sister-in-law. I cannot wait to see her swoon when she learns she has netted an heiress after all!'